Love in Sight

Holly Gilliatt

Turquoise Morning, LLC
P.O. Box 43958
Louisville, KY 40253-0958

LOVE IN SIGHT
Copyright © 2014, Holly Gilliatt
Trade Paperback ISBN: 978-1-62237-276-8

Cover Art Design by Calliope-Designs.com
Editor, Judy Alter

Digital Release, June, January 2014
Trade Paperback Release, February 2014

For Jay. I wasn't really me until I had you. You are my love, forever.

LOVE IN SIGHT

Looking for love is easier if you can see where you're going.

Like most people, Jason's looking for that elusive happily-ever-after. But although he's good-looking, athletic, funny and charming, he's starting to realize that his white cane isn't exactly a chick magnet. When he meets Heather, he can't believe such a sweet, smart, beautiful woman is falling for him. Best of all, she doesn't seem bothered by his occasional run-in with a low-hanging tree branch or inability to color coordinate. They soon become inseparable. But as they begin to negotiate their life together, they encounter obstacles even his white cane can't navigate.

While Jason's dreams seem to be slipping from his grasp, he's forced to face his insecurities and accept who he is…and maybe see things more clearly than ever before.

Love in Sight is a novel about coming to terms with what you can live with and what you can't live without.

Prologue

If someone had told Jason a year earlier that he would be babysitting a three-month-old, he'd have clearly thought they were brain damaged. Yet here he was, rummaging through a dresser drawer, his fingers searching piles of tiny clothes with snaps and ruffles and bows to change the baby. A blind man, coordinating an outfit.

Poor kid.

"Let's hope these aren't mismatching plaids or something," he said as he pulled a clean shirt over her head. She started to fuss. "Hey—what are you complaining about? It's your fault. If you hadn't spit up half your breakfast, you wouldn't be faced with the agony of having a blind guy as your stylist." He pulled on her pants and kissed her on the cheek, her powdery scent wafting all around him, inevitably causing him to smile. "Is that better than those stinky wet clothes? Let's go back in the living room."

When they reached the blanket spread out on the living room floor, he put her down for some "tummy time" like Mommy said to. Rubbing her back, Jason's mind wandered. He marveled at the unlikely course a year could take. So much had changed. So many highs, but also more tragedy than he ever imagined, drowning him with tremendous pain and guilt.

But he couldn't think about that. It was getting easier, day-by-day. *Stay positive*, he told himself. *Look ahead.*

Well, figuratively, anyway.

The baby made some gurgling noises, pulling Jason out of his head.

"Let's play, huh? What should we play? Well…you're no good yet at shooting hoops, so we'll pass on that. And I don't think you'd want to play catch with me. So how about…" His hands searched the blanket and found—what? Some kind of stuffed toy. He couldn't tell what it was. An animal? It was an odd shape his fingers couldn't distinguish. "How about this?" He shook it in front of her and she giggled. "Yeah, isn't this a great…squishy thing? I have no idea what this is, but it's making you laugh so I'll keep shaking it." He tapped her on the nose with it and more giggles erupted. "Well, I'm pretty sure you don't know what this is either, so we'll just call it Frank. Isn't this the best Frank ever?"

He never knew how much a baby could light up your world, even for someone who was always in the dark. But she sure had. And at a time when they needed it most, she gave them all a reason to push forward. A reason to smile.

But a year earlier she wasn't even a fetus yet in her mommy's womb, and Jason could not have predicted the journey he was about to take.

Chapter One

"You shoot first," Shawn said, placing the basketball in Jason's gut.

Jason grinned. "Scared to take the first shot, eh?" He dribbled the ball, heading toward the backboard. "He shoots!" He launched the ball toward the hoop. *Swish!* The distinct sound of ball sinking through net was like music to his ears.

"He scores!" shouted Shawn. "Nice one, Jason. My turn." He grabbed the ball and dribbled back from the net while Jason followed the sound of the ball hitting the ground and Shawn's footwork. "I'm gonna go for it from the line."

Jason jumped up high, his arms outstretched in an attempt to block the ball. He heard a *swoosh* and knew that Shawn got all net. "Way to go, Mathes!" Jason cheered.

"Why do you try to block me? I've got six inches on you and you can't even see me."

Jason knew Shawn had a point. But he'd never let a little thing like blindness get in the way of having fun, so he played as many different sports as he could. While they played basketball, a box on the backboard emitted a loud beeping sound so he knew where to throw the ball.

Both high school teachers, Shawn and Jason were frequent fixtures in the gym after school, using it for their own fun when it was unoccupied. Jason always figured they must make an odd-looking, even comical, pair. Jason's average-sized, muscular frame and light brown hair must have appeared in stark contrast to Shawn's fiery red mop and gangly six feet five inches.

"Why do I try to block you?" Jason repeated as Shawn put the ball in his stomach. "Because there have been two or three times that it's worked. And you're an asshole."

"Mr. Scharp," he heard a bellowing voice say from the doorway of the gym. He recognized it as the principal.

"Yes, Mr. Johnston?"

"I don't mind if you two use the gym to play ball, but I do expect you to behave like teachers as long as you're on school property."

"Yes sir."

"Yelling obscenities at a fellow teacher is not professional conduct."

"Yes sir." Jason looked down. "I'm sorry. I didn't know the door was open."

There was a slight pause and then, "Well, conduct yourself as if the door is always open."

Jason waited a few seconds and then asked Shawn, "Is he gone?"

"Yeah. You got busted!" Shawn laughed. "And I can't believe you pulled the blind card—'I didn't know the door was open,'" he mimicked in a whiny voice.

"Well, it was worth a shot to get me off the hook," Jason said with a sheepish grin. Quietly he added, "And you're still an asshole."

"Could be. But you've only blocked me a handful of times over the course of five years or so. Just give it up, my sightless friend."

"Never. I'm relentless. And you giving me shit just makes me more determined." He started dribbling the ball in place, relishing the familiar echo in the gym when the ball smacked the slick wood floor. He walked forward a few feet before attempting another shot. He heard it bounce off the backboard.

"You never do give up, do you?" Shawn said with admiration. "Too bad for you I'm so good."

"You're not that great, you're just some freak giant that's closer to the net."

"At least I have working eyes, Scharp," he joked, taking another shot. Jason listened to it hit the backboard and go in. "Did you see that?"

"Wasn't worth looking at." Jason laughed, grateful

Shawn didn't treat him like he was some delicate china doll or do the awkward you're-different-so-I-don't-know-how-to-act-around-you routine. It was refreshing to be treated like just one of the guys. Jason knew being taunted was as much a pastime of men playing sports as the sports themselves.

"Oh, but it was beautiful," Shawn said.

Jason felt the ball being placed in his hands. He went for the shot and heard backboard again. No swish.

Shawn's loud size fourteen shoes echoed through the gym while he chased the ball. "When are they going to invent a beeping basketball so you can go after your own ball?" he asked.

"I read online that someone did, but it's not mass-marketed yet. I would love to have one. Trust me—I'd rather do it myself." Jason wasn't a fan of needing people to do things for him. In fact, it drove him crazy. So he made damn sure he relied on others only when it was an absolute necessity. He used audible clues to follow Shawn again and did his best to block him. He heard the ball hit something. "Did that bounce off the rim?"

"Yeah. And you know what? You almost got a piece of it that time. You were within an inch or less of tipping it."

"See, I told you it works sometimes." Jason smiled smugly.

"Hey, do you want to head to the bar and grab a couple of beers when we're done?"

"I would, but I've got class tonight. Working on my masters, you know."

"Yes I know, you overachiever. But I thought we could pick up some girls tonight. How long's it been since you went on a date?"

"I don't know," Jason lied.

"Well, it's been at least six months." Shawn touched Jason's hand with the ball.

Jason grabbed it, knowing full well it had been ten months since his last date. Not that he hadn't tried.

"We need to get you laid, Scharp, and bar whores put

out."

In a matter-of-fact tone, Jason said, "Not to blind guys they don't."

****

Click click...click click...click click. Jason's mind wandered from the lecture in his night class and focused on someone to his right, absently clicking a pen. The guy in the row behind him chimed in with the pen, breathing loudly through his mouth when he wasn't busy blowing his nose. Jason finally settled his attention across the aisle—to the woman near him with the most delicious scent.

Getting his Master of Arts in Education seemed like a good idea, but it didn't mean he enjoyed it. It was merely a means to increase his pay as a high school history teacher and give him more ammo for all his detractors who thought a blind guy had no business teaching in the first place. Jason thought he always had to work twice as hard as everyone else to prove himself.

But although he was never one to mind a challenge, on nights like this, he wished he was anywhere but stuck in that classroom. The professor did not have the most exciting teaching style and used lots of charts, graphs, and PowerPoint presentations in his classroom. Visual aids. Just what Jason needed.

As a teacher himself, he didn't rely too heavily on visual stimuli for his students. Mindful that different students learn in different ways, he showed movies or photos to add more depth to the lessons, but for the most part, he didn't want to use too many tools that he couldn't even see. So he used his personality and excitement about history to relay the lessons to his students and tried to make his classes as interactive with the kids as possible. But tonight he wondered if he bored his students as much as this professor bored him.

And there he found himself again, back to focusing on the lovely scent of the classmate next to him. Unlike the professor, she held his interest.

After three weeks of the course, he'd been keeping

tabs on her. She participated in the class discussions quite a bit and impressed Jason with her inquisitive mind. It was obvious she was bright, and she had a great voice. A little lower than most women, but melodic and smooth. He wondered what she looked like. Blonde or brunette? Thin frame? She sounded young, maybe in her twenties like him? All he really knew was that she smelled fantastic. Not only could he smell her perfume, he smelled the hair products and soap she used as well, which blended to make a very clean yet musky aroma. He liked it. A lot.

Jason didn't know her name or, obviously, what she looked like. But after weeks of trying to summon the courage to take a stab at meeting her, he figured that tonight was the night. She had taken the seat next to him, so this was probably as good a chance as any to strike up a conversation.

"Well, that just about wraps it up," the professor said, and Jason heard the rustle of students gathering their things. "I'll see you all on Thursday."

Jason stopped the recorder he used during the lectures so he could listen to them later. They were his notes, so to speak. He heard the object of his olfactory affection close her book. After putting on his coat, he took a deep breath and reached his hand across the aisle to her.

"Excuse me," he said, touching her arm. It felt slender underneath a lightweight ribbed sweater.

"Yes?"

"I've noticed you usually leave from here and go to the coffee shop on campus. Would you mind if I join you tonight?" He added with a grin, "I promise I'm not a stalker."

"Oh…uh, sure. Why not?" She sounded surprised but pleased. He could hear her smile.

"Great!" Jason stood up and pulled his folded cane out of his bag. He flicked open the white stick. "Are you ready?"

"I'm just putting on my coat and then we can go." He heard a zipper and what sounded like the thump of a stuffed bag landing on her shoulder and against her body. "Okay, I'm ready."

"Let's go," Jason said, walking forward. He found his way down the aisle and then could sense her next to him when they walked to the doorway. The hallway filled with the noisy sound of students, so he waited to talk until they got outside.

The cold air struck them like a whip as they stepped out the door. Another bitter, cold February in St. Louis. But Jason was relieved it was much quieter outside where all the noise could travel.

"So I'm Jason, by the way," he said as they walked together down the sidewalk toward the coffee shop. His cane created a rhythmic beat while he tapped it back and forth on the concrete.

"Nice to meet you, Jason. I'm Heather." Her voice wavered as she shivered in the bitter wind.

"Cold, eh?" He laughed. "You're shivering."

"Yeah, I'm sick of this—I just can't wait until spring." Their feet fell into rhythm together. "So I have to ask, how do you know I always go to the coffee shop?"

"Oh, well, I go this way to the bus stop and you always veer off for coffee." Walking side by side, he figured her to be just a few inches shorter than him, probably about five feet, seven inches.

"Can you see a little bit?" Heather asked, sounding confused.

"No, nothing at all."

"Then how do you know it's me?"

"I'm like a dog, Heather. I can smell you from quite a distance."

"What?" Her laugh was hearty, and he thought to himself that even her laugh was intriguing. "Like I stink or something?"

"Oh, no no no. You smell quite fantastic. But distinct. And once I smell you, I can hone in on your footsteps, which are also specific to you."

"So how long have you been stalking me in this

14

manner?" she teased.

"Oh, at least a couple of weeks now." He grinned broadly. "You had no idea, did you? I'm very discreet."

"You could be in covert operations or something," she said, stopping. "This is our turn."

"May I take your arm?" Jason asked, holding out his left hand. It completely irritated him that he had to ask her for help. Half his life spent blind, and he still couldn't stomach asking for help from some people. Regardless of how charming or funny or good-looking he was, he figured hanging onto your date to avoid running into a wall was never impressive.

"Of course." Heather placed his hand on her arm. They continued down the path and Jason just held his cane in front of him, no longer tapping back and forth. Once inside the warmth of the café, the nearly overwhelming aroma of coffee enveloped them as soft music played in the background. A loud hum of conversation filled the room; Jason figured the place must be packed.

"I see an open table in the corner," Heather said. She carefully guided Jason around the chairs and legs and feet of the other patrons. "Here we are. There's a chair right in front of you."

"Thank you." He found the seat, sat down and shoved his folded cane into his messenger bag.

"Oh my God, it feels wonderful in here, doesn't it?" Heather said as she took off her coat.

"Yes, I'm finally starting to get the feeling back in my fingers."

She giggled at his joke. "I'm going to head up to the counter to order—do you want to go with me, or would you like me to get something for you?"

"Well, if you don't mind, I'll stay here and avoid the maze there and back."

"What would you like?"

"Just a large coffee, black. I'm easy."

"Yeah, you are. That's the easiest coffee order I've ever taken."

"I'll treat." He held out a ten-dollar bill.

"Well thank you." Heather gently took the money. "I'll be right back." Jason listened to her sure, strong footsteps as they drowned in the noise of the coffee shop. He wondered how he looked—did his hair look okay? He kept it short so it didn't take much care, but with the wind outside, he hoped it still looked all right.

He'd managed to calm his nerves when he heard Heather's heels on the tile floor approaching their table, and his anxiety raged again. He stood up when she returned.

"Here you go, one large black coffee," she said with a smile, placing it in his hand.

"Thank you very much." He sat down and decided to keep his hand on the cup at all times, to avoid his less-than-cool act of using his fingers to scour the tabletop looking for it.

Heather took a large gulp of coffee. "Oh, that hits the spot. I just love this song—do you?" An old R.E.M. song, *The One I Love*, played in the background.

"Yep, it's a classic," he said after taking a sip of coffee. "It's obvious you have great musical taste."

"I like to think so. And since we're both in the same class, you must be a teacher too. What do you teach?"

"Now that's presumptuous. Maybe I'm taking Conceptualization of Education for the fun of it."

"Possible, but highly unlikely," she said, chuckling.

"Okay, you're right. I'm a high school history teacher. You?"

"High school English."

"So we're both navigating the often scary yet uniquely rewarding halls of high school. We have a lot in common."

"We do." She leaned into Jason, her alluring fragrance growing stronger. He swallowed, noticing his palms were sweaty. Of course his right hand was warm from clinging to his coffee cup so he wouldn't lose track of it, but his left hand was sweaty now too. He wiped his palm on his pants leg and Heather took a drink—he could hear the clinking sound of what he figured were bracelets cascading down her arm.

Jason cleared his throat. "You know, Heather, you have an unfair advantage here—you can see me, so you have an idea of my age. If you don't mind my asking, how old are you?"

"Oh, I would love to lie to you, but I won't. I'm twenty-seven. Pushing thirty. Wow, pushing thirty…that sounds terrifying when I say it out loud."

"I'm twenty-eight…thirty's nothing, doesn't bother me at all. But forty…not looking forward to that one. So are you very far along with getting your masters?"

"About halfway through. Just trying to climb up that pay scale. Same for you?"

"Yep, just one more semester to go." Jason fiddled with the lid of his coffee cup to fill a short, somewhat awkward silence. "So, is there a Mister Heather?"

"No," she said, grinning. "Just me, Heather Cook. And you?"

"No, there's no mister for me." A smile crept onto his face.

She giggled. "Very funny. So is there a Missus…what's your last name?"

"Scharp. And no, no missus either," Jason said with a chuckle, relaxing a bit at the knowledge she was available. "So, do you normally study when you come here?"

"Sometimes. Sometimes I just people watch and chill out for a little bit before I head home. It's just nice to hang around adults after working in a classroom with teenagers all day."

"I can definitely relate." Jason nodded.

They talked about teaching and students and grading papers. It felt like a conversation between old friends—the kind that's comfortable and full of laughs.

Jason loved listening to her voice…it was warm, rich and throaty. He wanted her to keep talking so he could lose himself in its gentle timbre. After both polished off their coffees, they agreed it was getting late for a couple of teachers on a school night, although he really didn't want to leave her presence at all. Jason released the death grip on his cup, setting it on the table, and they pulled on their coats, preparing for the onslaught of frigid temperatures when they stepped outside.

"You know," Heather said, leading him to the door, "I'm glad you asked to join me tonight. This was fun."

"Yes—thanks for letting me tag along." He heard the old wooden door creak open. "It's gonna be cold out there."

"I know. I'm dreading it."

They stepped out into the quiet and serene stillness of the winter night. Heather's arm tugged his hand as he heard her fumbling with her scarf.

"Heather, could we do this again sometime?"

She patted his hand, and he noticed the silkiness of her smooth skin. "I would really like that." When they approached the main sidewalk, Heather slowed down. "So are you still going to make the bus?"

"Yeah, there's another coming soon."

"Well, it's too cold to stand outside for long."

"I'll be fine."

"Are you sure? I could maybe—"

"I'll be fine," he said. "I'm used to it. I do it all the time."

"Okay then." She came to a stop. "We're here at the main sidewalk, so you're good from here, right?"

"Yes, thanks again for the great conversation." He let go of her arm.

"Thank you for the coffee. I'll buy next time."

"Deal." He didn't resist the large grin he felt spreading across his face. "See you Thursday."

"Good night," she said.

He turned right to head down the hill to the bus stop. He could hear her footsteps on the concrete as she headed to the parking lot.

****

Heather turned to watch him walking, cane swinging.

She shook her head and smiled. When she climbed into her car, she pulled out her phone and dialed her best friend, Katie.

"Hey girl," answered Katie's friendly voice.

"Hey. How are you?" Heather backed her car out of the parking spot and pulled onto the street. She headed toward the bus stop.

"I'm good, just tired. Getting ready for bed actually."

"I don't know why you're tired just because you're growing a human in your belly," Heather teased. As her car approached the bus stop, she could see Jason sitting on the bench, rubbing his hands together.

"Yeah, that might have something to do with it," Katie retorted. "So what are you doing?"

"Hang on one sec," Heather said, hitting the mute button on her phone. There were no cars behind her, so she stopped in front of the bus stop, rolled down the passenger window and shouted, "You look awful cold sitting there!"

"You think?" Jason hollered back with a smile. Heather thought he looked cute sitting on the bench. His cheeks were turning red like frostbitten cherries, bringing out the boyishness of his features. He looked at least a couple of years younger than his age. His large eyes, although a beautiful blue-gray color, tended to settle with his eyelids slightly closed, giving him a somewhat perpetually sleepy appearance. But they opened more when he smiled, and his full lips produced a broad and contagious grin.

"Last chance for a ride," she said. "Take it or leave it."

"I'm fine, but thanks, Heather."

"Okay. Good night again!"

"Good night." He waved in her direction.

She caught herself waving back and chuckled, realizing he couldn't see it anyway. And he couldn't see her playing with her dark brown hair at the table that night, something she tended to do when she flirted. He couldn't see a seductive look, either.

"Katie?" she asked, taking the phone off mute.

"Yeah, I'm here. So what are you doing?"

"I'm just leaving campus. You'll never guess what I did."

"Okay, then just tell me."

"I had coffee with a guy from class."

"Wow, kind of like a mini-date?" Katie's voice filled with excitement.

"No, not a date, just coffee."

"Well this is exciting. Isn't this your first date since Richard?"

"It wasn't a date."

"Whatever. So did he ask you, or what?"

"Yeah, he asked if he could join me. I almost said no, but decided, what the hell?"

"Good for you. You need to get back out there. So, give me the deets!"

"It was nice. His name is Jason, and he's a teacher too. Teaches history. He's twenty-eight."

"Is he good looking?"

"He's cute, yeah. Not Brad Pitt or anything, but definitely cute. Great smile. It's just…well, it shouldn't matter, but it kind of does."

"What?"

"He's blind," she said, her voice quiet. There. She'd said it out loud. Never said that about a date before. But it wasn't a date—just coffee.

After a pause: "Blind? Like white cane, tap, tap, tap blind?"

"Exactly. Standard issue white cane included."

"Oh, Heather…you never go the easy route, do you?"

"Well, it's not like he can help it. And should that really matter?" Heather wasn't sure if she was asking Katie or herself.

"Of course it shouldn't, but it does. In the real world, maybe not your Pollyanna version of what the world should be, but in the real world—it does make a difference. It would require more work than a typical relationship."

"Well I don't know about that. Rich was a lot of work."

"That's because he was a bastard."

"Well, so far I don't think Jason is. I'd rather be with a blind guy than a bastard any day."

"I know. Heather, just be careful. That's a lot to take on."

"You don't know that." Heather wondered if Katie could be right.

"Well you don't know yet, either."

"We just had coffee. I'll take it slow—for once."

"I don't mean to sound harsh. I just don't want you to get involved in something that may be more than you're willing to handle. You deserve a good relationship. You're due."

"I agree. But whether or not he can see shouldn't be a factor. Besides, it was only *coffee*." She sighed. "It's weird, though. I'm ashamed to admit I never really paid any attention to him. I just thought of him as the blind guy in my class."

"Don't be ashamed. You're human. So you'll see him again on Thursday?"

"Yeah."

"Are you going to go out for coffee after?"

"If he asks me, sure. We had fun. And he likes R.E.M."

"Oh, well then by all means, go for it. He appreciates your precious Michael Stipe. Did you tell him you used to have pictures of him plastered all over your bedroom walls in high school?"

"I'll save that for another time."

"I'm going to bed. If I don't talk to you before, call me Thursday night and let me know how it goes."

"I will. Get some rest for that baby." Heather hung up the phone as she rounded the final turn of her commute. She wondered if Jason made it onto a warm bus yet. She hoped so.

Chapter Two

On Thursday evening, while Heather got ready to head out of her condo for class, she found herself actually excited. Not because of the class—because of Jason. She sensed a real connection between the two of them.

She looked in the mirror. She knew most people would say she was attractive. She didn't feel all that beautiful but knew she turned heads from time to time. Although today she noticed some circles under her eyes—the result of a tiring and stressful day.

"Well, it's not like he can see them," she said out loud. Nonetheless, she grabbed some concealer and covered the circles as best as she could. Just because he couldn't see her didn't mean she didn't want to look pretty anyway. She brushed through her long dark hair, relatively pleased with her reflection.

As she walked out to her car, the biting cold air seemed to penetrate through to her bones. While her car warmed up, Heather thought about Jason sitting at a cold bus stop somewhere. Within a few minutes, she reached campus and walked toward the building that housed their classroom.

She spotted Jason up ahead walking to the door, easy to find with his cane tapping in front of him. She thought about running up to meet him but decided to play it cool. Although there was an undeniable chemistry between them, Katie might be right. She should probably take it slow, see how things go. In her experience, men were enough work…was she really up to the added pressure of dating a man who couldn't even see her?

****

Jason walked into the classroom, slowing down to take in the sounds around him. He headed toward the desks, wondering if Heather would call out to him if she was there. Walking down the middle aisle where he normally sat, he figured she hadn't arrived yet. He couldn't detect her familiar fragrance nearby. The institutional smell of whatever floor cleaner the university used served as the main aroma. So he tapped at a desk in the middle of the row, finding it empty, and took a seat. He slipped off his bag and coat, and thought he heard Heather walk in the door. Her familiar footsteps headed in his direction and then he caught a whiff of her perfume.

Although he could feel his heart start beating faster, Jason tried not to appear too interested. He was aware that he didn't exactly top everyone's Most Eligible Bachelor list. He'd gone out with lots of girls over the years who seemed okay on their first date, but once they went home, they apparently had second thoughts about dating a blind guy. It hurt, but he was used to it. Never made it any easier, though, when they failed to return phone calls or were cold with him on their next encounter. He knew a whole slew of women who wanted to be "just friends."

Jason hoped maybe Heather would be different. He sensed a kindred spirit and some chemistry between them.

He sat up straighter in his chair; his mother badgered him his whole life about slouching. He purposely wore a sweater and button down shirt that his brother Mark once said he looked good in. Mark was more apt to make fun of him than compliment him, so if he mentioned it, it really must look good.

Her steps stopped right next to Jason.

He turned in her direction. "I thought that was you."

"Hi, Jason," Heather said, sounding friendly enough, "is this seat taken?"

"If there's no one sitting there, it's all yours."

"Nice sweater." She sat down.

"Thanks."

Leaning toward him, she lowered her voice and asked with a grin, "So are you ready for another exciting lecture?"

"On pins and needles." He smiled warmly at her,

relieved she still seemed friendly with him.

"So, how was your day?"

He heard the firm stride and click of a man's dress shoes walk in and figured it was the professor.

"Oh, it was good. I've got a pretty good group of kids this semester and in a couple of my classes we're working on the Civil War. That's one of my favorite eras in American history, so I enjoy it. How was your day?"

"Kind of stressful—"

"Okay, class," the instructor interrupted in his monotone voice. "Let's pick up where we left off."

Leaning over to Heather, Jason whispered, "Do you want to grab coffee again and you can tell me about it?"

"I thought you'd never ask," she whispered back in a flirtatious tone.

He tried not to grin too big. Her hair brushed against his cheek and he could feel its long, smooth silkiness.

Jason found it almost impossible to pay attention to the lesson, and he noticed that Heather didn't participate in the class discussion as much as normal. Maybe she struggled to concentrate too. He hoped so.

****

During class, Heather became aware they only had conversation to connect with. Once class started and they couldn't talk to each other, their communication ended. She couldn't catch his eye, or flash a flirtatious smile. It saddened her a bit. But she caught herself staring at him more than once, at the grin that played on his lips when the professor attempted a joke, and at his handsome profile. He was a cute guy.

After class, they resumed their previous banter in the coffee shop. They both jabbered away, laughing and learning about each other.

"So that does sound like a pretty bad day," Jason said after Heather recounted her run-in with a student's parents.

He'd given her some great ideas about how to deal with the uncooperative parents—Heather was impressed. She had no doubt that he was a good teacher, and he was a good listener too.

"Comes with the territory, I guess." Almost done with her coffee, she took another sip and looked at him. For the past two days, her mind had been filled with questions about him. She wanted to ask them, but hoped he wouldn't be offended. She decided to test the waters. "So…have you always been blind?"

Jason shifted in his seat. His usual easy smile drifted into a strained expression. "I wasn't born blind. I could see fairly well until around age nine, and then my eyesight started to gradually deteriorate. I had some complications and lost the last of it by fourteen."

"Oh," Heather said, her voice quiet as she looked into his eyes, which gave no expression, no insight. Just empty pools of blue, the color of the sky on a slightly overcast day. "What caused it?"

"I have what's called retinoschisis." His tone was matter-of-fact; this was clearly not his first time answering these questions. "Most people that have it don't go completely blind. But I never do anything half-assed, so I threw in a couple of detached retinas for good measure, and…bye-bye eyesight."

Looking at him, she felt an ache in her heart for the loss he'd suffered and the difficulties he must have faced. Probably still faced. "That must have been hard, especially as a teenager. But I'm glad to know that you could see for years…so you have an idea of what things look like."

"True. I can't imagine never seeing anything…it would be much harder to create a mental picture. I'm certainly not happy about being blind, but I guess I'm lucky I had some sight for those fourteen years."

"That's an optimistic way to look at it." She took another drink. "You seem to not let it bother you much."

"Oh, I'm used to it now." He leaned back in his chair. "It was hard at first. But I've lived as a blind man longer than I did as a fully sighted person, so now it's just a nuisance, really. There are times it bothers me more than others. But I try to avoid the whole self-pity thing because it doesn't do any good, and who the hell wants to hang around with a whiny blind guy?"

She laughed. It was obvious that he wouldn't take well to someone feeling sorry for him.

"And I have to laugh about it. There's a blind writer, Ryan Knighton, who says blindness is a constant state of slapstick. He's absolutely right. And my students find fun ways to take advantage of that from time to time."

"What do they do?"

"Well, I know my classroom inside and out, so I don't use my cane in there. But one day, a couple of the senior boys decided it would be funny to move my desk when I stepped out of the room for a minute." Jason grinned. "It was pretty funny, in retrospect. I walked back in, went to where it should be...and I have to say, that felt odd. Reaching for something you are just certain is there, and isn't."

"Well that's pretty cruel, if you ask me."

"Oh, they're just kids." He shrugged. "To them it was just a prank, and all teachers get pranked on occasion—I'd feel like an outcast if I wasn't included. They've also done things like tried tiptoeing out of the room, one by one. After about the fifth kid, I heard something and figured it out. Now I keep the door shut all the time, so they have to open the door and make noise to try to skip out on my class."

"Wow, they're pretty brutal."

"Not really. Ninety-nine percent of the time, they're terrific. One of the things I like about teaching kids is they learn a little about acceptance from me. The first couple of weeks of school, I can tell my new students are uncomfortable around me. But once they get used to having a blind teacher, most of them don't think much of it. I'm just another teacher and they seem to enjoy my class."

"So you're teaching them more than just history."

"I'd like to think so, yeah."

She could see the tension on his face, in the straight

line of his normally curling mouth. "I'm sorry if I made you uncomfortable, asking about it."

"Not at all—I'm glad you asked. Now that the big blind elephant is out of the room, we can forget about it, right?" He broke into a big smile.

"Sure." She smiled back, feeling at ease with him. "Well, it's almost nine o'clock now. I should really get going."

Jason checked the hands on his Braille watch. "Wow, the time flew by."

"It always does when we get to talking. Here, I'll take your empty cup," Heather said, grabbing it off the table along with hers. "I'll be right back."

****

Jason heard her walking back to the table and stood up to slide on his coat. "So, Heather, do you want to do this again Tuesday night? We've got that test, so we might need to decompress afterward."

"Sounds like a plan to me," she said. "Maybe the temperature will have raised a degree or two by then." She rested her hand on his arm; Jason was acutely aware of her touch.

He swallowed. "Actually, I think I heard we might have a storm system coming in this weekend. So maybe we'll have snow."

"Are you serious? I am so sick of this winter. I'm ready for swimsuit weather!"

Jason's mind wandered to thoughts of what her body might look like in a swimsuit. He could tell she was thin from her arms, but beyond that he didn't know. So he let his imagination run wild.

"Are you ready to go?" she asked, pulling him out of his bikini-laden daydream.

"Yep." He whipped open his cane and took her arm. They walked through the shop and Jason found himself desperately wishing he could see what she looked like. If her looks even halfway compared to her velvety, musical voice and gentle giggle, then she would be beautiful. They

27

stepped outside, and he was glad to find that the wind had stilled.

"Hey, Heather, can I ask you something?"

"Sure—what?"

"I was just wondering...what do you look like?"

"Oh, well...."

Her voice trailed off with uncertainty and her pace slowed. He wished he hadn't asked. Doing his best to sound casual, he said, "I mean it's just nice to get a mental picture. What color is your hair?"

"Dark brown. It's long."

"Yeah, I knew it was long."

"How did you know that?"

"Well, it brushed against my cheek once and I could tell. And it rustles against your collar when you move your head around."

"Pretty clever. But what color are my eyes?"

"Okay, obviously I'm going to guess here...brown?"

"Ding ding ding—and he wins the prize!"

Jason loved the deep, throaty tone to her laughter, as if it came from deep inside her soul.

"So, long dark brown hair, brown eyes...anything else you can give me?"

"This is hard, Jason, I don't know." She stopped when they reached the walkway where they would go their separate ways. "I mean, I don't know how to rate myself for you or anything. But I'm not hideous."

"Well, I'm sure you're not. I didn't mean to embarrass you...."

"No, you're not." She touched his hand. "I just feel bad because I can't figure out how to describe myself to you. Wait—did you ever see Susan Sarandon? The actress?"

"Yeah, from *Bull Durham*. That movie's a classic."

"Do you remember what she looks like?"

"Yeah, kind of."

"Well, I don't know if I agree or not, but some people say I look like a young Susan Sarandon."

"Really?" Jason grinned. "Now that helps me out. I'm

standing next to the doppelganger of one of the most esteemed actresses of our time."

"Oh, stop it." Heather slugged him with a playful punch in the arm. Her laughter warmed him despite the cold temperature.

"And now she's beating on me. Great, I meet a beautiful woman, and she uses me as a punching bag."

"I never said I was beautiful."

"Well Susan, I mean Heather, you must be if you look even the least little bit like Ms. Sarandon."

"Oh, I should have never said anything! You're awful."

Jason could hear the smile in her voice, and couldn't help but smile himself. "I'm sorry, I'm just giving you trouble. And honestly, thank you. Now I've got an image of you in my mind."

"Well, okay then. Glad I could help." They both stood there in silence, neither one making a move to leave. Finally Heather spoke, "I guess we really better go now. My fingers are turning into icicles."

Jason smiled. "Good night."

"Good night. Are you sure you don't want a ride—?"

"I'm fine." He started walking toward the bus stop. Heather's footsteps had almost completely faded away in the parking lot when he yelled, "See you Tuesday, Susan!"

"Oh, shut up!" she retorted. His hearty laugh rang out in the night.

****

Friday nights for Jason meant dinner at his parents' house. They'd established that ritual when he and his brother Mark got busy in their high school days. On Friday nights, unless they had something really important going on, they had to come home to eat dinner together as a family. Sometimes it got to be a hassle, but for the most part, Jason enjoyed it. Not that he would admit that to his mother.

"Hello?" Jason ventured as he walked through the front door of his parents' home. A barking, furry ball came running toward him. "Hey, Peanut." Jason squatted down and the little Shih Tzu greeted him with licks and panting.

"Hello, my sweet boy," said his mother, Eve, coming into the room.

Jason stood. "Hi, Mom." He rested his cane in the corner by the door, since he knew his childhood home better than just about anywhere. He was familiar with every stick of furniture, every wall, every knob on every door. Suddenly his mother's arms embraced him.

"Jason, I wish you would let me pick you up from work when it's this cold outside."

"It's just a short walk from the bus stop. No big deal." He pulled off his coat, and his mother took it from him. He had always been close to his mom, but since he lost his sight, she tended to be a bit overprotective. Jason always wondered how different their relationship would be if he could still see.

"I'll go put this on my bed." She left the room and Jason headed to the kitchen. He reached in the fridge and grabbed a Coke off the door, where he knew she always put them.

He heard her footsteps approach the kitchen as she asked, "So how are you?"

"Good, Mom, I'm good." He patted her arm. "And how are you?"

"Oh, just fine. I started taking a yoga class and had lunch with your aunt yesterday."

"Yoga? Getting all New Age on me, huh? So what's that I smell for dinner—mostaccioli?"

"Close. Lasagna."

"What can I do to help?" An enthusiastic and skilled chef, Jason loved to cook. He knew sometimes he cooked a little slower than most, but no one disputed that his meals were delicious.

"I'm working on some garlic cheese bread…why don't you throw together a salad?"

"Okay…grab the ingredients and I'll whip it up." It smelled great in the kitchen and Jason's stomach growled. He heard his mother pulling stuff out of the fridge. "So where are Dad and Mark?"

"They should be here any minute. Mark said Angie can't make it though—she won't get back from a business trip until late tonight." She took his hand and put it on each item as she named it. "Here's lettuce, cheddar cheese, carrots, three boiled eggs and a box of croutons."

"Is that big bowl still on top of the fridge?"

"Yes—rinse it out first, in case it's a little dusty."

Jason's fingers groped until he found it, then he stuck it under the faucet. He grabbed the drying towel that always hung under the sink, on the door. After he dried the bowl, he walked across the kitchen to where he knew the cutting boards rested in the corner with the butcher block. His hands searched for the cutting boards.

"What are you looking for, sweetie?"

"A cutting board."

"Oh, I'm sorry. I started putting them under the counter so it wouldn't look as cluttered. Here's one."

"Thanks," he said, feeling it in the palm of his hand.

"Hello hello!" Mark hollered from the front of the house. He walked into the kitchen and as usual, his personality was so enormous that Jason could feel his presence in the room. He often wondered what Mark ended up looking like. The last time he could see his brother they resembled each other, but Mark had always been taller and stockier, and Jason could tell he still was. But the visual images in Jason's mind of family and friends were fading faster than he liked to admit to himself.

"She's putting you to work again?" Mark asked, squeezing Jason on the shoulders.

"I don't mind. You know I like to cook. That means you have to set the table."

"Hi, Mom," Mark said, hugging her. "Table's already set, little bro. Guess I showed up at the right time, eh?"

Jason considered his brother his best friend. Ever since they were little kids, they never tired of playing with each other. Jason always thought Mark was braver, louder, funnier and better at nearly everything. He was the guy all the other guys wanted to hang out with and the girls wanted to date. Mark was a loyal friend, especially to Jason.

His mind wandered to a memory of another instance when Mark had good timing. Jason would never forget one particular day when he was twelve and walking home from school. He had just started using a cane after too many stumbles, falls and accidents forced it. Completely blind in his left eye, he retained some central vision in his right eye, although it was extremely poor and rendered him legally blind. Add to that absolutely no peripheral vision and the cane become a necessity.

As he made his way down the sidewalk of their street from the bus stop, two of the neighborhood bullies jumped in front of him, blocking his path. They taunted him, calling him names and making fun of him.

"I'd rather be blind than stupid," Jason retorted. "Get out of my way." One of the boys, he couldn't see who, snatched his cane.

"Now who's stupid? Let's see you walk home now."

Jason tried to grab it as they swung it back and forth. It traveled in and out of his blurry field of vision.

"You guys, give it back!" Jason started to panic.

"If you want it, come get it." They both laughed.

Jason's anxiety grew. He wasn't sure he could make it home without the cane.

"I'll get it, you shitheads!" Mark's booming voice rang out, and Jason could make out part of him when he grabbed the biggest boy by the arm. Mark yanked the cane out of the bully's hand and held it out for Jason. "Here, Jace, take it."

"Where?" Jason couldn't find the thin white cane in the narrow fogginess of his sight.

Mark tapped Jason's arm with it and he grabbed hold. "Go home, Jace."

Turning his head, Jason could see that Mark was holding onto both the boys. At fifteen, Mark was a big defensive lineman on the high school team and had no trouble taking charge of the situation. Jason took off, as fast as his cane would allow.

Mark snarled, "Don't you ever, ever mess with my brother again." He heard the sound of punches being thrown. "I swear to God I'll kill you little pieces of shit next time if you so much as say one ignorant word to him."

"Okay, okay, please stop," one of the boys cried out.

"Do you understand me?"

"Yes, we're sorry!"

"What the hell is wrong with you, picking on somebody that can't see?"

Jason was almost home when he heard the pounding of the boys' tennis shoes on the pavement as they ran off.

That day, that moment, stayed with him. At the time, he was simultaneously ashamed of himself yet proud and grateful to his brother. He knew from that moment on Mark would always look out for him.

His mind came back to the salad, and Jason dropped the chopped eggs into the bowl. "You always do have impeccable timing," he said to Mark. "Showing up just in time to get out of the work—well played."

"I thought so." Mark started crunching on a carrot.

"Hey, lay off, I need those for the salad. Mom—do you have any red onion?"

"Oh, that would taste good in there, wouldn't it?" she responded. "Let me check. Here's one." Eve handed it to Jason.

Jason heard a car pull in the garage. "Dad's home too."

"Mark, why don't you pour drinks?" Eve asked.

"But I'm eating a carrot," he said in protest.

"Is that like trying to walk and chew gum for you?" Jason asked.

"Just trying to get out of helping."

Soon they were all seated at the table, digging in.

"So what's new with my boys?" John, Jason's dad, asked.

"Angie and I went to see a fertility specialist," Mark said. "They're going to test both of us and see if they can figure out the problem."

Jason knew how devastated Mark and Angie were after unsuccessfully spending the last two years trying to get pregnant. Mark tried to brush it off, like it was nothing. But even though Jason couldn't see the look on his brother's face when they discussed it, he could hear his disappointment.

"When will they know something?" Eve asked.

"We're doing some more tests next week. I get to provide a sample for them—that should be fun," he said with a chuckle. They all laughed.

"Well, you've got plenty of experience doing that," Jason ribbed his older brother. "Thank God we never had to share a bedroom."

"Very funny. Hey, they also talked about genetic testing and things like that. When they asked our family medical histories, you came up, Jason. Angie freaked out a little when I mentioned that your blindness was genetic. She was afraid our kids might get it."

"You told her they couldn't, right? That it only passes down through females to their sons?"

"Yeah, we got it settled. But she's just worried our baby will have every genetic disorder in the book."

"Well, I don't blame her—look at who the father is."

"Okay, smart-ass, because of your little genetic mutation, you haven't actually looked at me in years."

"Yeah, and I consider that to be one of the few advantages of being blind—I don't have to see your ugly mug anymore."

"I'll have you know I grew into one very good-looking guy." Mark kicked Jason under the table. They both laughed. "So I have to provide a sperm sample…what's new with you?"

"Me?" Jason asked, a smile creeping onto his face. "I met someone."

"A girl?"

"Yeah, a woman. Her name's Heather."

"Where did you meet her?" Eve sounded less than enthusiastic.

"She's in my graduate class."

"Is she some young girl wanting to rescue you for the week?"

"What's that supposed to mean, Mom?"

"Well, you know some of the girls you dated in the past seemed to view you as a project of sorts, and then the novelty wore off and they wanted a sighted boyfriend. You know that as well as I."

"Yeah, I know." Jason sighed. "But that doesn't mean they're all like that. I think she's different."

"Well I hope so, little bro," Mark said. "It's about time we got you a lady."

"You don't have to tell me that. I mean, I love my job and my friends are great. But something's missing. I want to find someone to spend my life with. I want a family. You know, the whole happily-ever-after thing like you all have. But the pool of women wanting to introduce the blind guy as their boyfriend is pretty small."

"I wish it wasn't," Mark said, his voice quiet.

"I mean, I might not be able to see, but if only they knew how good I am with my hands."

"Jason!" Eve scolded.

He grinned, shrugging his shoulders.

"So, how did you meet?" John asked.

"Well, I noticed that every night after class when I headed to the bus stop, she stopped at the coffee shop along the way. So Tuesday night, I asked if I could join her."

"You've got the Scharp moves." John's voice was pumped up with pride.

"Yeah, I was pretty slick. It went well. We did it again Thursday night too. And we decided to make it a regular thing."

"What do you know about her?" Eve asked, sounding wary.

"She's a high school English teacher, so we've got teaching in common. She's also working on her masters. No significant other. Oh, and she supposedly looks like a young Susan Sarandon."

"Did she tell you that?" Eve's tone was skeptical.

"Yes. Begrudgingly, though. She said a lot of people have told her that, but she doesn't know if she agrees. She just tried to tell me what she looked like."

"Well, she can tell you anything she wants."

"Why would she lie about that? And why are you so pessimistic?"

"Yeah, Mom," Mark chimed in. "I think it's great he's met someone. And if she's a hottie, that's a bonus."

"Not that it matters to me," Jason admitted. "But it would be nice to have some arm candy."

"I just don't want you to get hurt again." Eve touched Jason's arm. "Girls have not always been so kind to you."

"Mom, I'm not fourteen years old anymore. I'm a big boy. I can take care of myself." She was right, though. He wanted so badly to find "the one" but struggled to find anyone willing to see past the obvious. In his professional life, he worked twice as hard as everyone else to prove himself. But there was no way to prove himself to a woman if he couldn't get one to stick around past a first or second date.

"I know you can take care of yourself." She pulled her hand away. "But can't a mother worry?"

"You worry too much. If it doesn't work out, I'm no worse off. But I really think we've got a connection. And so far, she doesn't seem too bothered that my eyeballs are for decorative purposes only. On Tuesday night I might ask her if she wants to go out next weekend."

"Go for it, Jace," Mark urged.

"Now that's the enthusiasm I was looking for." Jason motioned to his mom. "A little encouragement is nice."

"When it comes to women, the Scharp men do just fine," John said.

"Well, I hope so," Eve said quietly, and Jason could picture his mom shaking her head.

Chapter Three

The forecasters got it right when they predicted a winter storm system would come through over the weekend. Jason hated that snow made it much more difficult for him to get around. It muffled sounds, making it harder to hear his surroundings, and the snow on the sidewalks posed a real hazard for him, since it made things slick and limited the usefulness of his cane. As a kid he'd loved the snow; he wished he could enjoy it more now. But that would most likely require alcohol and an Alaskan malamute for a guide dog.

On Monday they canceled school, which meant he wasn't going anywhere. It gave him more time to study for his exam on Tuesday night. And more time to find his thoughts drifting toward Heather. He tried to turn away from the memory of the creamy caress of her fingertips on his hand or the intoxicating fragrance that permeated even his dreams. While he caught up on his laundry and did some reading, the sound of her laughter ran through his mind, bringing with it a hope and desire that scared him.

His head told him not to get too ahead of himself. They hadn't even gone on a real date yet. Besides, she probably just considered him a friend. Plenty of women considered him a friend. But they didn't consider him partner material. *Yeah, Scharp, maybe the connection you sense is one-sided. Maybe you're blowing this way out of proportion.*

But he didn't think so. He might not have been able to see the expression on her face, but he was pretty sure there was a flirtation in her voice…a pat on the arm that lingered a little too long or a giggle that erupted at one of his less than stellar stabs at humor. His gut told him she felt something too.

At least he hoped so.

It was nighttime and the evening news playing on the TV in front of him went unheard while his mind once again wandered to Heather and the lilting cadence of her warm, husky voice. His thoughts were interrupted by the ringing of his phone.

"Hey little brother," Mark said when Jason answered.

"Hey," Jason replied, muting the TV. "What's up?"

"Not much. Just wanted to see if you have to work tomorrow or if school is cancelled again."

"We've got school, no extra day off for me."

"Well, most of the sidewalks are still pretty ugly, so why don't I drive you to work tomorrow instead of you taking the bus?"

"No, you don't have to do that—"

"I know I don't have to, but I want to. There's no sense in you falling on your ass if I'm not there to laugh at you," he added with a chuckle.

"Spoken with true brotherly love. Thanks for the offer, but I can make it on my own."

"Jace..." Mark sighed. "Stop being ridiculous and just let me pick you up, okay?"

"I don't like being a burden—"

"Damn it, Jason, you're not a burden. You're my brother. Why can't I just help out every now and then without you always getting defensive? It's dangerous for someone with working eyes to walk on the sidewalks right now. Take away vision, and it's an accident waiting to happen."

Jason hesitated before he spoke. "I don't mean to be ungrateful, Mark, I just hate relying on other people. It's emasculating."

"And falling down and getting hurt won't be? What if you break your arm or leg or something? Then you would be a burden."

"Okay, you make some good points," Jason admitted, as much as he hated to. "It would be great if you could pick me up. I was actually dreading walking to the bus stop. Snow scares the shit out of me."

"Now see, was that so hard? I can't believe I had to twist your arm, when you admit it's scary for you to trudge through the snow. Why are you always so stubborn?"

"Because I'm too proud for my own good sometimes." *And I hate that I need help from other people,* Jason's inner voice screamed. *Fucking* hate *it.*

"Well, you have to stop being stubborn and ask for help when you need it. There's nothing wrong with asking for help, Jace. I mean, holy shit, you're blind. I can't believe all the stuff you do on your own. The big man upstairs gave the right Scharp boy the bad gene, because he knew I would have been worthless."

"You'd have been fine, just like me."

"And you'd have insisted on helping me if things were reversed, wouldn't you?"

After a pause: "Probably. So can you be here at six-fifteen?"

"See you then."

****

Promptly at six-fifteen in the morning, Jason heard his doorbell ring.

On the short drive to school, he and Mark enjoyed their usual rowdy banter. Faster than Jason expected, the car came to a stop and Mark said, "We're here—the sidewalks are cleared."

"Where did you pull up?"

"You're right in front of the main entrance. Doors are straight ahead."

"Okay, thanks Mark."

"Do you need me to pick you up?"

"No, I'm going straight to my night class."

"How are you getting there?"

"The bus."

"I'm telling you, you can't do that. It's too snow-packed and icy on the sidewalks. Why don't I take you?"

"Mark, I don't want you to be my chauffeur—"

"Then will you please take a cab?"

Jason shook his head. "Mark—"

"I will be here tonight, waiting to drive you, if you do not swear to me that you are going to take a cab." His tone was dead serious.

"Fine," Jason conceded. "I will take a cab. But you are a pain in the ass."

"No, I'm just trying to keep you from falling on yours."

"All right then," Jason said, laughing. He opened the car door. "Thanks for the ride."

"You're welcome. And you better take a cab—"

"I will, I will." He slammed the door shut and waved to Mark, smiling as he pondered, *do people wave back at me?*

****

Heather stood just inside the doors of the education building on campus, waiting for Jason. She kept telling herself to take it slow, but it wasn't working. She was anxious to see him.

There was just something about him—his wit, his confidence, that toothpaste-commercial smile. They shared a connection, that intangible chemistry that everyone looks for. She had been thinking about him a lot and as clichéd as she knew it sounded, she felt like she had known him forever. He just felt...right.

So there she stood, like a schoolgirl, waiting for the boy she had a crush on to come up the walkway. The thought of seeing him again made her nervous but excited too. It had been a long time since someone made her feel this way. Richard was so careless with her affection that, by the end, she lost most of her feelings for him. Except for anger.

A taxi pulled up and she saw Jason climbing out. He snapped open his cane and started walking toward the building. He looked handsome with a red stocking cap, black pea coat, jeans, hiking boots and his messenger bag slung across his body. Her heart started beating faster.

He walked at a steady, methodical pace...perhaps because he was concentrating on the information his cane sent to him. Jason was about halfway to the building when he faltered on an icy patch, slipped, and dove head first into a bench.

"Oh no!" Heather shouted as she ran out the doors to help him. "Jason, are you all right?" she yelled as she raced to him, mindful of the ice herself.

He faced her direction when she called his name, his face flushed red with embarrassment. Picking himself up, he grabbed onto the bench.

"It's Heather." She helped him sit down on the bench. "Are you okay?"

"Yeah, yeah," he said, sounding unconvincing. "I dropped my cane...."

"Here, I've got it." She pulled it out from under the bench and handed it to him.

Brusquely, he grabbed it.

"You're bleeding, Jason."

"I'm okay. Did you...did you see me fall?"

"Yes, I was waiting inside the door for you."

Jason's head dropped. "Great. Now you know just how smooth I am."

"Well, they should clear these sidewalks better. That's ridiculous. Anyone could have slipped on that ice." Anger was apparent in her tone.

"But not just anyone did. I did." Jason sighed, shaking his head.

"Don't be so hard on yourself." She patted his leg. "I need to get you cleaned up."

"No, I'm okay."

"You're not, you're bleeding, and I need to wash off the blood and see how big that gash is by your temple. Let's get out of this cold and go inside."

"I can take care of it myself." He abruptly stood up.

"I'm sure you can," Heather said cautiously as she stood up next to him, "but sometimes a woman just wants to feel like she's taking care of someone."

"Well," he said, softening, "if you want to play nurse, I guess that's not such a bad game." Jason smiled and then winced.

"Does it hurt to smile?"

"Yes, if I smile too big it does. See what happens when you want to play nurse?"

She chuckled. "Come on, let's head inside. Why don't you hold onto my arm and I'll steer you away from the ice?"

He grabbed onto her arm and they made their way carefully along the sidewalk. "So, you were waiting for me?"

"Yes," she said with a smile. "Is that okay?"

"Sure it is. Except that means you saw me slip like a jackass."

"Oh, stop," Heather said as they walked inside. "You didn't slip like a jackass...it was more graceful than that. Sort of like a swan dive."

"Oh really?" He smiled, wincing again. "Felt more like a belly flop. And until my head smacked it, I didn't even know that bench existed."

"That had to hurt. There are two benches on each side of that walkway, about twenty-five feet apart."

"Good to know."

"Why don't you have a seat here and I'll go grab some wet paper towels?"

"Okay," he said, sitting on a bench just a few feet inside the building.

****

Jason listened to Heather walk away and reached his hand up to his right temple. Yep, blood. And splitting pain.

He sat there for a couple of minutes, listening to students shuffling by in their heavy boots, wondering how awful he looked. And he felt really embarrassed and irritated with himself for slipping like that. The last thing he wanted Heather to see was his limitations. He wanted her to see all that he was capable of, not the stereotypical helpless blind act.

"Okay, Mr. Scharp, Nurse Heather at your service," she said, approaching him.

"Or is that Nurse Susan?" He grinned, a devilish taunt in his tone.

42

"Oh, I regret ever saying that to you." She knelt down in front of him. "Turn your head to the left please." The patient complied. "Oh, Jason, this looks pretty bad."

Pain shot through him when she started wiping it. "Ow!"

"I'm sorry. I'm trying to be gentle. Actually, the cut isn't too bad—you don't need stitches. I guess it's just bleeding so much because of where it is. But there's a big knot on the side of your eye, and it's starting to bruise already."

Jason reached up to feel the bump and their hands touched. It felt like a jolt of electricity to him, and he could tell she felt something too. He put his hand over top of hers and pulled it away from his face. He held onto her hand, enjoying the soft, warm pressure of her skin against his. "Would you like to join me for a date this weekend?"

"I'd love to," she responded, and Jason could hear the smile in her voice. "I thought you'd never ask."

****

The way Jason had to take the test was different from the other students. His tests were transcribed into Braille by the university's Disabilities Services Department, so he could read the questions. Then Jason used his laptop to type his answers, wearing headphones so he could hear the text-to-speech software on his computer. The software read the text on his computer to him; he used the same software at home and for work too—whether he had to type something or browse the Internet. When he finished typing his answers, he would email them to the professor.

Getting Jason to take a simple written test involved a lot, but he considered himself lucky to live in an era where he could do those things on his own. Dogs may have been man's best friend, but to Jason, technology was a blind man's best friend.

When Heather got up to turn her test in, she leaned over to Jason and tapped him on the arm. Somewhat startled, he pulled out his headphones and faced her.

"I'm done now," she whispered. "I'll wait for you in

43

the hall."

"Okay, thanks," he whispered back. About fifteen minutes later, he was the last one to finish, since it took him a little longer to go between reading Braille and typing up his answers. While he put his laptop in the bag and closed it, he heard Heather's footsteps walking in the room.

"So did you ace it?" she asked, getting closer to him. He stood up and put on his coat.

"I don't know if I aced it, but it wasn't too bad." His head was throbbing as he opened up his cane.

"Hey, I think maybe we should skip the coffee house tonight. We probably need to get you home to take some painkillers and put some ice on that. How are you feeling?"

"Well, I do have a pretty nasty headache, but I can still do coffee," Jason said, desperate to spend more time with Heather.

"Why don't I drive you home so you can get home sooner?"

"I can make it home on my own." He didn't bother to hide his irritation.

"I know you can—you do it all the time. I just figured you must be getting sore and should get home to ice that up. And if you ride with me I have an excuse to spend a little more time with you."

"Well, when you put it like that, it sounds like a pretty inviting offer. I accept."

Within a few minutes they reached her car, with Jason holding onto her elbow to avoid wiping out on another patch of ice. He gave her directions to his place and they were on their way.

"So did you have a good weekend?" he asked, holding the right side of his head where it ached. He was in such close proximity to her in the car that it was difficult to carry on a conversation. Her presence distracted him but in a tantalizing way. He enjoyed listening to the musical cadence of her low voice while she rattled on about shopping with her friend Katie. It was hard for him to pay a lot of attention to what she was saying since his mind kept wandering, wondering if he could muster the courage to kiss her. He was experienced at flirting, that never scared him, but his desire to kiss the lips that her sexy voice was spilling out from was enough to drive him crazy. Maybe when they stopped at his house.

"So, Jason, what did you do over the weekend?" Her direct question brought him back to reality.

"Not a lot, but it was kind of nice. Friday nights I always have dinner at my parents'—that's a Friday night ritual."

"Oh, that's neat. Is it just you and your parents?"

"No, my brother too and usually his wife. We've done this since my high school days. Just so we can stay connected and see each other at least once a week."

"That's a great idea. What else did you do?"

"Saturday I worked out, then met a buddy for lunch. Sunday I got pretty much snowed in so I just did like you— graded papers, checked out some TV, cleaned my house." *Thought all day about you.*

"I like weekends where I'm not too booked up. It's nice to have some time to catch your breath."

"Yeah, I know what you mean. So what kind of car is this?"

"An Infiniti I4. It's my baby."

"It smells new." He ran his fingers along the supple leather upholstery.

"It's about six months old."

"It rides really smooth. What color is it?"

"Black with beige interior. It's peppy too, that's one thing I love about it. I tend to have a bit of a lead foot."

"So it's a good thing I'm buckled up?"

"Well, of course you should buckle up. But I didn't say I was a bad driver. I just drive a little on the fast side. So I guess you've never driven a car?"

"Actually, I have. My grandparents have some land out in the country and when I could still see a little bit…I was twelve or so…they let me drive Grandpa's old pickup on their property."

"Well that's cool," she said, smiling.

"And then when I got older, about seventeen or eighteen, my brother used to let me drive his car around in empty parking lots at night."

"Are you serious? Wasn't your eyesight gone by then?" The shock in her voice made him smile.

"Yeah, but we were a little crazy. He just talked me around light poles and dumpsters and things like that. It seemed harmless at the time, but I could have easily wrecked his ride. I have kind of a lead foot too."

"I knew we had more in common than just teaching." She laughed. "I can't believe he let you drive his car."

"Yeah, I can guarantee you he wouldn't let me do that with his BMW now. Back then he drove an old beat up Toyota Corolla. So, do you have any brothers or sisters?"

"I've got an older brother—he's three years older than me."

"Then we're both the babies of the family."

"Well, I did have a younger sister, but she died of cancer when I was twelve. She was only ten."

"Oh, wow, I'm so sorry," Jason said softly. He was so close to Mark, he couldn't imagine what it must have been like for Heather to lose her sister.

"Thanks. It was so long ago, but it still hurts. And I don't think my parents ever really got over it. They divorced a couple of years after that, and I believe that's why. They just couldn't cope with her death, and their marriage fell apart."

"That's too bad. What was your sister's name?"

"Anna. She was a beautiful girl, but so frail and ravaged by the end. I wish I could get those images out of my mind."

Both were silent for a moment. Jason wasn't sure what to say but finally offered, "There are some things I'm glad I can't see. I wish you hadn't seen that."

"Thank you. That's sweet to say." He could tell that she turned to look at him, and she sounded touched. He heard her swallow before she said, "Okay, we're turning on

46

your street now. Which house is yours?"

"1943, on the right hand side. It's got a white mailbox and the house is white with green shutters and door."

"Okay…here it is. It's a nice looking house."

"Well it's nothing fancy, but I like it. I bought it two years ago." A good-sized ranch style house, it had a two-car garage and rather large lot.

"I would like a house someday. Right now I just own a small condo." She parked the car. "Would you like some help in?"

"No, I'll be fine."

"Make sure you put ice on that. You've got a really big knot there and it's turning lovely shades of black and blue. And take ibuprofen for the pain if you've got some."

"Yes, nurse."

"That's right. Be sure and follow my orders. So I'll see you Thursday night?"

"Yes, and I'll try to see if I can actually make it to class without falling on my ass," he said with a grin.

"You get only one free first-aid visit. Next time it will cost you." The way she said it sounded fairly suggestive and made Jason want to kiss her more than he already did.

He yearned to feel her lips on his, to taste her and breathe in her delicious scent even closer. His libido was telling him to go for it, but his brain worried he would lean in and she would pull away, but he wouldn't be able to see it. Or he would do something madcap like miscalculate and kiss her nose. A bundle of nerves, he didn't want to screw up their first kiss. It would have to wait—he didn't have the confidence yet.

He wiped his hands on his pants. "I'll bear that in mind. But then again, I may trip and fall on purpose, just to get treated by you again. You have incredibly soft, gentle hands."

"I do?" She sounded surprised. "Well thank you."

She put her hand on his and squeezed. Jason forgot how good a woman's touch could feel. It had been too long. He cleared his throat. "I guess I should let you go home. Thanks for everything tonight."

"You're welcome," she said. He started to open the car door. "Hey wait!"

"What?" he asked, turning back to face her.

"Do you want to exchange phone numbers?"

"Sure." Jason pulled his phone out of his bag.

"You've got a Smartphone?" She sounded surprised.

"Yeah, I love it."

"How do you use it? It's all touch screen and you—"

"I know, I can't see it. But it has a screen reader that reads everything out loud, so it's actually incredibly user-friendly for me. Watch." He moved his finger around the screen and the phone responded by reading out loud each key he touched: "Contacts, Email, Text Messages, Settings."

"That's amazing," Heather said in awe. "I had no idea."

"Yeah, it's pretty cool. So I can check my email or texts and it reads them back to me. That's how I use my computer too, by using software that reads the text to me. That or a Braille display that I can read with my fingers as it transcribes the words on the computer into Braille."

"Wow, you're high-tech."

"Takes a lot of technology to replace two little eyeballs."

They put each other's numbers into their phones and Heather said, "Okay, well now that we've swapped numbers, I'll let you go. Until Thursday." She surprised Jason with a kiss on the cheek.

"Until then." He felt a slight flush on his cheeks as the kiss stirred his pent-up sexuality. It had been too long since he'd been with a woman.

He climbed out of the car, relieved when his cane told him the neighbor boy he paid to shovel the driveway and walkways had visited. When he got to the front door, he could still hear her car in the driveway, so after unlocking the door he waved in her direction before heading inside.

"Oh, my head is killing me," he said out loud, putting

his cane in the corner and his bag on the floor next to it. Despite the pain, he couldn't help but grin. "But she likes me. She really likes me."

Chapter Four

The next morning at school, Jason figured his bruised face looked pretty bad because it was the topic of a great deal of conversation and excitement. Then again, Jason knew teenagers could blow just about anything out of proportion.

"Mr. Scharp, it's Ethan—did you get in a fight?" he asked after the first period bell rang.

"If by fight you mean with a park bench, then yes, I got in a fight."

"Wow, Mr. Scharp, it looks like it must hurt real bad," said a girl he recognized as Amber. Or maybe Tina. He couldn't always distinguish the high-pitched voices of some of the girls. The classroom filled with murmurs from other students.

"Does it really look that awful?" He touched the knot on his temple.

"Oh, it's bad," Amber/Tina said. The other kids chattered in agreement.

"Did I mention that I won the fight with the bench?" His students erupted with laughter. "That bench will *not* mess with me again. Okay, let's get to work"

After school, Shawn Mathes walked into Jason's classroom, erupting in a low whistle. "Whoa, Scharp! Who or what happened to you?" Jason heard a scraping sound and figured Shawn must have pulled up a chair and sat down.

"Would you believe it if I told you this is the evidence of a serious brawl I won with six gang members in an alley?"

"Uh...no."

Grinning, Jason said, "Okay, then—it was a bench."

"*That* I believe. Shit, Jason, you look like hell." So

maybe it wasn't just the overblown reactions of teenagers.

"Thank you, Shawn, you're always a comfort. So what exactly does it look like?"

"Well, you've got a big lump there and it's dark purple right around the knot, and then it gets a little lighter in color when it spreads out. It's discolored all the way around here." Shawn traced it with his finger on Jason's face. It went above his eyebrow, up and over by his hairline and then back down beneath his cheekbone.

"Wow, that does sound gruesome. Oh well. Comes with the territory."

"It's always fun to see what bruises or wounds you've added to your collection. So, considering you've got that ugly knot on your face—are you feeling up to shooting some hoops now?"

"Sure," Jason responded with enthusiasm.

"Hey, do you want to hang out on Saturday night?"

"I would, but I've got a date."

"A date?" Shawn sounded surprised. "With who?"

"Heather Cook." Jason tried not to grin at the mere sound of her name.

"You dog, spill it."

Jason gave up the fight and let a smile spread across his face. "I met her in my graduate class. She's kind of amazing."

"Is this your first date?"

"We've had coffee after class a few times, and she's coming to my place for dinner on Saturday."

"Way to go, Scharp! So what's she like?"

"Oh, she's great," Jason gushed. "She's got a great sense of humor, she's bright, smells fantastic, and she's a high school teacher."

"Which means she's underpaid and likes adolescent boys."

Jason laughed. "Underpaid yes, adolescent boys—hopefully not."

Just then, James Brown's voice came blaring from Jason's phone singing *I Feel Good/I Got You*. Heather's ringtone.

Jason snatched his phone from his pocket. "Hello, Heather."

"Speak of the devil," Shawn whispered with a chuckle.

"Hi, Jason," Heather said. Jason always thought his name was rather mundane, but the way she said it, it killed him. It sounded musical, new to his ears. "Did I catch you at an okay time?"

"You're fine. Just about to go shoot some hoops with my buddy Shawn."

She paused. "You play basketball?"

"Yeah, I know, sounds crazy. But I play lots of sports. I'll tell you all about it later. So, how are you?"

"I'm great, thanks." She chuckled. "You are a constant source of surprise."

"I'll take that as a compliment."

"It is. Definitely. So anyway, Jason, I thought maybe we could ride together to class tomorrow night. There's no reason for you to take the bus when we could carpool."

"So you drive one night, I drive the next?"

"How about I drive all the time? I'm without a doubt a better driver."

"You haven't even seen me drive. I'm hurt."

Heather giggled, reminding Jason just how much he loved the sound of her laugh. "Should I pick you up at home?"

"Actually, I usually just come straight from work."

"That's fine, I can pick you up at work. What time should I get you? Five-thirty?"

"Works for me. I'll be waiting out front."

"Great!" Heather sounded enthusiastic. "See you then."

Jason hung up with a goofy grin on his face.

"Oh my God," Shawn said with a moan. "You are being way too sweet with that girl. You should play hard to get."

"Why the hell would I do that? She is totally into me—I don't need to play hard to get." Jason put his laptop in his bag. "Hey, put that chair back so the blind guy that works here doesn't find it with his shins."

The metal feet of the chair scraped across the tile floor as Shawn put it in place. "Women like the chase."

"Oh, that's bullshit. Spoken like a serial womanizer."

"Hey, you're the one looking for a girlfriend, not me. I just like to keep it casual and have fun."

"How do you get all these women to go out with you, anyway? Are you that good looking?"

"Hell no, I'm average at best. But I have really big feet. And you know what they say about the correlation between a man's shoe size and his—"

"Yes." Jason laughed. "I know."

****

Jason checked his watch again: five-fifty on date night. His nerves and excitement grew in anticipation, and his hopes were high for the night. Jason just wanted to enjoy Heather's company and show her how capable he could be in his own home, where he felt comfortable and self-assured.

He heard a car pull onto his driveway. Show time.

The doorbell rang. "Scharp, don't fuck this up," he said out loud as he headed to the door. He opened it.

"I'm sorry I'm a few minutes early," Heather said.

"That's fine. Come in, come in." He couldn't contain his smile. She stepped inside, delighting Jason as her scent wafted into the room. "Do you have a coat on I can take for you?"

"Yes, thank you." She took it off and handed it to him. "Your place is really nice. It's starting to get a little dark though…can we turn on some lights?"

"Oh shit, I'm sorry," he said, embarrassed as he flicked on a switch. "Is that better?"

"Much, thanks." She smiled.

"I thought it would be easier to take advantage of you if I kept you in the dark. Then I'd have the upper hand."

"I should have known it was part of your sinister plan."

"Can I just say that you always smell terrific? What perfume do you wear, anyway?"

"Oh, thank you. It's nothing fancy…it's from Bath and Body Works. Black Amethyst."

"Well it smells great. And fancy doesn't mean it smells better, it's just more expensive. That fragrance, combined with whatever you use on your hair, and just you…makes a wonderful combination."

"Well, I usually only wear this in the winter. It seems a little heavy for spring and summer. So I'll be switching it up on you in a couple of months."

"Then I probably won't know who you are," he said with a smile.

"It will just make me more mysterious."

"That's kinda hot." Jason grinned. He extended his hand. "Let me show you around."

Heather took his hand and Jason noticed how it seemed to fit just right inside his. So much of her seemed to fit.

"You look really nice tonight, Jason."

"Well, thanks. I guess I clean up okay."

"Should I take my shoes off?"

"No, no. I'm just usually barefoot all the time at home."

"Well these are really uncomfortable high heels, so if you don't mind, I'll join you. Should I set them by the door?" she asked, slipping them off.

"That's fine. Oh, and I hate to bother you with this, but I have to give you a little Blind Guy 101. I assume I'm your first blind suitor?"

"Yes."

"Well, you never know, you could have a fetish for the sightless." He grinned, leading her into the living room. "Please just make sure if you pull a chair out that you push it back in all the way. And the same with the doors—I leave the doors open all the way, against the wall. So please put them back like that after you're done in the bathroom or wherever. I never use my cane in the house, but since I don't, if there's a chair out or a door partially open or something on the floor...well then I'll have another bruise to match this one." He pointed to his temple.

Heather laughed. "Got it. It's looking greener today, by the way. And still some beautiful hints of purple too."

"It's my wearable performance art piece." Jason grinned. He gave her a quick tour of the house. As they reached his office they stopped outside the door, and he put both hands around hers. She was so close to him, he could practically taste her. Oh, God, how he wanted to. He thought for a moment that he might kiss her but was too nervous.

"Let's go in here," he said instead and pulled her into the office. "This is where I keep my computer and all my gadgets." He remembered to turn the light on.

"Braille is so fascinating. Can I look at your books?" she asked about the several large bound Braille books stacked on the desk.

"Sure." He let go of her hand but didn't want to. He liked holding onto her, connecting with her in a tangible way.

He heard her flipping through pages. "Can you tell me what this page says?"

"Yeah." Jason reached out and started reading from the David Sedaris book she'd selected. He placed his fingers at the top of the page. He read out loud to her, his hands flying back and forth quickly as his index fingers scanned the large page.

"It's fascinating watching you read with your fingers," she said. "Very cool. I hope you don't mind me asking about your things."

"Not at all. So I'm cool?"

"Very much so." She grabbed his hand again and excited his tactile senses.

He held onto people's elbows all the time, but interlacing fingers with someone he adored was something he'd missed. Heather's fingers felt somehow delicate and strong at the same time, and the mere contact of their flesh was tantalizing to Jason. He swallowed.

"And off to the kitchen." He led her out of the office. "I'm getting hungry. Are you?"

"I sure am," she said as they entered the kitchen.

****

"So what do you think?" he asked, smiling, but clearly looking for approval.

Heather thought that all the furniture throughout the house had clean, classic lines and was nice, yet casual. Nothing stuffy. She noticed the beautifully set table on top of the light wood dining table. The kitchen was inviting and clean, albeit rather stark like the rest of his home.

The main thing she noticed about his whole house was the lack of decoration. Nothing but white walls. Pictures scattered across the mantle in the living room, but otherwise, she didn't see any knickknacks or flowers or decorative pieces of any sort. She figured that since he couldn't see it, he didn't bother with it.

"Oh, I think your house is great. It's not huge, but it's got plenty of room and some great features. Your furniture is really nice too."

"Thanks," he said, seeming relieved. "I know it's probably kind of sparse without decorations. But I don't need that, and I figure someday I'll share it with someone who will want to do it according to her style."

Heather felt her face grow warm. "Yeah, it's a clean slate, so it would be fun to decorate."

Jason let go of her hand. "Let me finish up dinner. How much time is left on the timer?" He pointed to the oven.

"Eight minutes, thirty-two seconds."

"Just enough time to get some garlic cheese bread going." He opened the fridge and got out margarine, cheese slices, and fresh parsley.

"What can I do to help?" Heather asked.

"Everything else is done. I've got stuffed shells in the oven, a salad chilling in the fridge, and I'll make the bread now."

"Oh, wow, that all sounds fantastic."

"Hopefully it will taste good too." He sprinkled garlic into a butter mixture. "I love to cook. Do you cook much?"

Heather scrunched up her face. "I don't know if what I do can technically be called cooking."

Jason started laughing and smiled in her direction. "You do get the incredible irony of the fact that your last name is Cook, and yet you can't?" His smile was broad, absolutely melting Heather's heart. That is when he looked his best.

"Yes I do, smart-ass. Go ahead, make fun of my cruel twist of fate. It would suit me better if my last name was Gardener."

"Well that will come in handy this spring. Maybe you could help me spruce up my backyard with some plants or flowers." He cleared his throat. "That is, if you're not tired of me by then. I don't presume that we'll still be seeing each other then."

"I hope we will." She noticed that his face lit up and his mouth curled in a smile. He sliced a large loaf of Italian bread in half, lengthwise. "What can I do to help?"

"I think I've got everything under control…oh, I need a lighter. Would you mind grabbing one out of the pantry? There should be one in a basket on the left-hand side, middle row, halfway down."

"Sure." She opened the door to the small walk-in pantry. She stared in awe at the neat rows and evenly spaced canned goods, pastas, and baking items. Some of the shelves had Braille tags on them, and some of the food had tags affixed with rubber bands. "Nice pantry. Meticulous."

"Thanks," he said. "I don't mean to be anal, but please don't move anything around in there or I won't be able to find it. Then the next time you come over, I'll think I'm serving you green beans but it will be a can of soup."

She found a lighter, careful not to move anything out of its place while she grabbed it. "I understand." She stepped out of the pantry. "I guess there are a lot of things in your life that have to be pretty regimented."

"Is that bad?" He sounded as if he wasn't sure he wanted to hear the answer.

"No, that's not bad. It will just take some getting used to on my part. I'm embarrassed to say I'm a little sloppy sometimes."

The timer sounded on the oven and Jason was quick to find the button to shut it off.

"Well that's okay." He pulled out the stuffed shells and set them on the table. "Remember, I was a teenager when I went blind. My room was an homage to messiness. I constantly struggled to find things and tripped and just couldn't manage my life, so I learned to be neat and tidy. It was worth it to me." He popped the platter of cheese bread into the oven.

"Hey, if you can help me to be tidy, my mother will love you forever. Would you like me to light the candles?"

"No my dear, you sit down and just relax. Where's the lighter?"

"Right here." She put it in his hand before taking a seat at the table. He slipped it into his pocket.

He brought a bottle of wine to the table and started filling the glasses. Heather noticed that he put the tip of his finger in the glass, and when the wine hit his finger, he stopped pouring.

"I'll just go get the bread and then we're ready to eat."

"So you mentioned shooting hoops the other day on the phone...how on earth do you play basketball?"

"Well, I don't play a full-fledged game of basketball, but I can shoot hoops because I've got a device on the backboard that beeps. I just listen for the beeping, and I know where the net is."

"So that's how you do it. But are you any good?"

He grinned. "Yeah, I am pretty good, if I do say so myself. I also play a modified baseball game called beep baseball, and I coach wrestling at school. Do you play any sports?" Jason brought two filled salad plates to the table.

"I'm not the most athletic person around—I used to

dance when I was younger. But I play a little bit of golf."

"I play golf," he said with enthusiasm. "We should play a round sometime."

"You know, I've heard of blind golfers before. I would love to golf with you. But I'm not all that good."

"Well, that's okay—I won't see your lousy shots anyway. And I'm just an okay player, nothing impressive."

"I don't know that I'm ready to be beat by someone that can't even see the ball. That would be embarrassing."

"I won't tell anyone," he reassured her. "Unless you really make me mad, then I'll post it on Twitter for all of cyberspace to see." He brought out a basket full of cheese garlic bread, putting a piece on his plate and handing the basket to Heather. "Would you like some bread?"

"Love some." She took a piece.

Jason took the lighter out of his pocket. He lit one candle but struggled with the second one. Heather could see that the wick kept falling over to one side, which he couldn't. She gently moved his hand an inch to the side and it quickly ignited.

"Thank you." He blushed, and the muscles in his jaw twitched.

"Teamwork." She tried to put him at ease, and his face softened a bit. He took the seat next to her. "Everything looks and smells wonderful."

"Well, dig in, please." Jason took a bite.

"Oh, Jason, this is delicious."

"The shells?"

"Yes, just delicious. You're a wonderful cook."

"Thanks." He sounded shy.

"The salad is great too. What kind of dressing is this?"

"It's an Italian dressing I made."

"I've never made dressing in my life—I always pour it out of a bottle."

"There's nothing wrong with that. I just enjoy cooking, and I seem to have a knack for it. I like to experiment."

"I have a knack for eating." Heather took another bite.

Jason laughed. "Well it doesn't show. You're thin."

"How do you know?"

"Well, I know your arms and hands are thin, so I'm guessing the rest of you follows suit."

"It does. But if I hang around you and your cooking much longer, that could change."

"I can cook low-fat too," he said with a grin. He raised his eyebrows. "If that becomes a problem for you."

"I'll keep that in mind." She took a bite of cheese bread. *Heaven.*

****

After dinner, Heather went outside to grab the dessert she'd left in the car. Jason took the opportunity to grab his napkin and thoroughly wipe his face. He was worried that his bad aim resulted in half a jar of sauce or a glob of errant meat filling left behind on his face.

He smiled to himself, thinking of Heather's harsh tone when she reacted to a discussion they had during dinner about women not giving him a chance. She sounded angry for him—it was cute. He found nearly everything about her to be cute. This wasn't good…he was falling too fast. He sure as hell wasn't taking his mom's advice to take it slow.

He heard the door shut behind Heather and the clip clop of her heels on his floor when she walked back in. Even her footsteps sounded sexy to him. Heather seemed different from the women he'd dated in the past.

"Here it is," she said, the scent of Black Amethyst tempting him. "Where should I put it?"

"On the counter by the sink."

"Okay." The sound of a plastic container hitting the countertop sounded out, followed by her footsteps coming back to the table.

"Well, what is it?" he asked when she sat down next to him.

"French silk pie."

"Oooo, that sounds good." Jason leaned back. "I trust you baked it yourself?"

"I went to a lot of trouble to get that. I had to go to the store, pick it out, and wait in line at the checkout. It's practically homemade." She startled him with a playful slap of her napkin. "You are such a smart-ass."

"Oh, just having a little fun with you." He found her hand and grabbed it. "Are you done eating?"

"Yes, I'm stuffed. Just left a little bit of room for dessert."

"Want to go in the living room?"

"Sure, but why don't I clean this up first since you did all the cooking?"

"No, I'll do it later. Let's just enjoy ourselves." Jason tugged at her hand when he stood up. "Come on."

He heard Heather push her chair back under the table before they walked in the living room. When they reached the couch, she bent over and slipped off her shoes. "Where should I put my shoes? I don't want them in your way."

"I'll put them by the door," he said. She placed them in his hands. He felt the smooth, slick shoes and extremely high heels. "Nice sexy heels you've got here. Patent leather?"

"Yes, thank you."

Jason placed them by the front door and headed over to the fireplace. "Perfect night for a fire, don't you think?" He turned on the gas fireplace and instantly felt the heat pouring from the flames.

"Absolutely. It looks beautiful." He joined her on the couch. "I love the fire and the music playing in the background. If I didn't know better, I'd think you were trying to seduce me." She had a sultry tone in her voice, which Jason immediately picked up on.

"Oh, I am." He moved closer and put his arm around her. Her fragrance teased him. "What are you wearing?"

"A skirt, a sweater, tights…." Heather put her hand on his thigh, giving it a gentle squeeze.

He swallowed. She took his hand and kissed it, her soft, warm lips igniting passion and longing in him. Although nervous, he realized her touch brought an overwhelming sense of comfort to him.

Jason leaned in closer and put his hands on her cheeks.

He kissed her, tender at first, and then with more passion. Her lips felt silky and hot against his. He closed his eyes, overtaken by an aching inside for her. Their attraction was palpable. Sexuality poured from both of them like an electric charge.

He pulled away from the kiss, breathless. He whispered, "I've wanted to do that since the first time we had coffee together."

"What took you so long then?"

He moved his hands from her face and traced the graceful curve of her neck. He kissed her again with tenderness. "I don't know why I waited. I just wanted it to be right."

"Oh, it's right." She smiled. "I almost kissed you myself several times but didn't want to seem too aggressive."

"I'm sorry...sometimes I just worry that I'm missing some body language cues or some looks. So I didn't want to assume your feelings were the same as mine."

"Well they most certainly are."

"May I?" he asked gently, putting his hand on her thigh. He could feel her body quiver.

"Of course." Her voice was quiet, almost a whisper. His hand found the edge of her skirt above her knees. He tenderly squeezed her thigh, feeling the sheen of her tights.

He moved his fingers up her thighs, to her waist, and to her chest. Her warm, soft bountiful breasts excited him further. "My, my...what have we here?"

"That's what most guys notice on me first," she said about her extremely ample chest. "But for you, it's a surprise."

He let a broad smile spread across his face. "A wonderful surprise. I don't think I've ever felt anything quite like these." He chuckled, tenderly touching her full breasts. "And your waist is so small...you've got an incredible body, Heather."

"Thank you." She unbuttoned the top two buttons of his shirt, stroking his chest. "You're not so bad yourself,

Coach Scharp."

Her fingers felt like scorching hot velvet against his skin. He didn't know what he looked like, but thanks to all those hours he'd spent at the gym, he knew he had a flat, tight stomach and firm chest. She ran her fingers through the sprinkling of hair on his chest, and he shivered. It had been so long since anyone had touched him that way. He could feel his heart start racing, and he didn't know how long he could hold back.

"You look so sexy tonight, Jason. With your clean crisp shirt and jeans that show off your nice butt."

Jason grinned. "I called my sister-in-law before you came, and she told me what to wear."

"Smart woman." Heather initiated their kiss this time. When she pulled away, he put his hands on her face, his index finger tracing her lips.

"Your lips are so full, so sexy." He brushed his fingertips across them. "I had no idea." He moved his fingers up to her well-defined cheekbones and traced her eyebrows. She closed her eyes. He touched her eyelids and then moved over her well-structured, yet not small, nose. "Very long lashes, big eyes, great cheekbones. You're so beautiful. That may not mean much, coming from me, but you truly are."

"It means a lot," she said, and he thought he heard a tremble in her voice...tears? Maybe she sensed the poignancy of the moment. This was the first time he'd ever been able to really "see" her in any tangible way. He only saw what he touched, and he'd never touched her before. This was his first chance to see her legs, her hips, her breasts—her face. Her voice was soft when she asked, "So you like what you see?"

"Oh God, yes. I already fell completely head over heels for you, just who you are. But now I have something else to intensify those feelings...your body and your tender lips and your soft skin." He kissed her again with a renewed vigor, running his fingers through her long hair. He felt like he was on fire, desire rising from deep within and extending all the way to his fingertips. "And your hair is so silky and smooth." He pulled away. "I want you so badly. I don't know if you're ready for that or not—"

"I am," she whispered.

"Well, I don't know if I can go there yet." He looked down. Desire raged through him, but he knew his racing heart was also due to fear. "I've just...I feel so vulnerable with you because I have strong feelings, but...you scare me." He faced her again.

"What do you mean, I scare you?" She cupped his face in her hands.

"Most girls only last one or two dates before they 'just want to be friends.' The last serious girlfriend I had really...really tore me up. Things seemed to be going along fine, and I was crazy about her. But then...I don't know...she just decided she couldn't handle being with me. With my blindness." Jason swallowed. "I just can't go through that again."

Heather took a deep breath and took both of his hands in hers. He wished he could see the look on her face.

"Your blindness doesn't scare me. I'm sure it's a nuisance sometimes, and I've got to learn how to be a part of your world without screwing it up. But I'm up for that."

She kissed him gently, just a flutter of her warm lips grazing against his. He ached for her. Neither spoke for a minute. Jason could feel the sexual tension between them...it was a palpable energy. A part of him wanted so badly to react on it, but his insecurities were holding him back.

With a smile he said, "You've got me so worked up right now—I'm going to need a cold shower."

"Or how about some French Silk pie?"

"That would be perfect," he said with some relief. "Let me get it." He started to stand up, and then felt her hand on his chest, pushing him down.

"No, you did dinner, so I'm doing dessert. Sit still and I'll get us each a slice of pie."

"All right then." He ran his hand down her leg when

she stood up. "Or maybe I will still need that shower."

"Can I join you?" Heather laughed and walked out of the room.

While she got the pie, Jason grabbed a DVD off the shelf. He put it in the player and sat back down on the couch, grabbing the remote control.

"Are you finding everything okay?" he hollered. "Do you want some help?"

Standing right in front of him, Heather giggled. "You don't have to yell at me."

"Oh, sorry," Jason said with a grin. "I thought you were still in the kitchen."

"I figured as much. Here's some pie." She carefully put a plate in his hand. His fingers searched for the fork, fumbling until he found it. "Do you want something to drink?"

"No, I'm good for now." He took a bite. "Oh, this is so good."

"It's one of my favorites. Decadent." She sat down next to him.

"I rented a movie," Jason said. "Since you're an English teacher, I figured you're into literature. And this movie is about twenty years old, so you've probably seen it. But I couldn't resist, because it stars Susan Sarandon." He had a big grin on his face.

"Are you making fun of me?" She elbowed him.

"No, just having fun at your expense." Jason was clearly proud of himself. "It's *Little Women*. Is that okay?"

"Oh, I love that book and the movie too—I haven't seen it in years. Good choice!"

"Do you want to leave the lights on or would it be better with them turned out?"

"I'll turn them off. Then it's more like a theater." She got up and flicked off the switch. "Oh, the fire looks really beautiful now."

"I bet," Jason said.

She cozied up next to him. The pressure of her warm body against him felt better than anything he'd experienced in a long time. He kissed her on the cheek and put his arm around her.

"Jason, do you like watching movies? I mean, don't you have trouble following what's going on?"

"Well, yeah, sometimes it's hard. It depends on the movie. But they're starting to have more and more of them with descriptive video, DVS."

"What's that?"

"It's audio description that tells what's on the screen for people like me that can't see it. This movie's got DVS...otherwise I'd be saying through the whole thing: 'What's going on? Who's that? Where are they?' Doesn't make it much fun for either of us."

"That's really cool. Do they have that at theaters too?"

"They do, on certain movies. Most of the popular ones have it."

"So we can go to the show together?" she asked with excitement.

"I'd love to go with you to the movies." Jason grinned.

Heather wrapped her arms around him. "Have I told you what an incredible smile you have?"

"No." His smile grew broader. "Go ahead, tell me all about it."

"That's it—that's the big grin that could light up a room. It's infectious." She kissed him, and he reciprocated. "But I better stop this or we'll need that cold shower."

"So true."

"Well, then quit smiling so damn sexy like that." Heather gave him a playful nudge.

"I will do my best." He purposely frowned. He couldn't help himself though and started grinning when she laughed at him. "I can't help it—you just give me so many reasons to smile."

"Thank you," she whispered.

"Like these." His grin was mischievous while he fondled her breasts.

"Oh stop it!" She pulled away, laughing. "Start the movie."

"Okay, okay." Jason hit "play" on the remote.

The movie started and although he enjoyed it, Jason spent most of it focused on Heather. The way she felt in his arms, her scent, the softness of her hair on his cheek as she lay on his chest. In all of his years, he didn't think he'd ever felt more comfortable with any woman. He couldn't believe his good fortune.

When the movie ended, Heather rolled over on her stomach and he could tell she was looking at him when she said, "That was really good. Not as good as the book, but movies rarely are."

"Well, I'm glad you liked it." His hand caressed her cheek. "What did it feel like for you, watching yourself on the TV?"

"It's a good thing I like you...."

He kissed the top of her head. "Are you up for anything else tonight? I've got some games we can play. Or we can just talk here by the fire."

"It's almost midnight, and I'm getting tired." She yawned. "Can I take a rain check?"

"Sure," Jason said, disappointed. He didn't want the night to end. Everything felt so right and he was afraid when she walked out the door...that would be it. She would go home, talk to her friends, weigh the situation and decide that she didn't want to settle for a broken model when there were so many out there in good working condition.

"Uh...what are you doing tomorrow?" Heather asked timidly.

"I don't know...nothing planned. Just some grading, chores, that sort of thing."

"I've got some grading too, and some lesson plans to work on. But other than that, I don't really have anything planned." She sat up and put her hand on his knee. "Do you want me to come over and we can just hang out and do our work together?"

Her words fanned the flicker of hope that was burning in him and set it ablaze. He tried not to sound too eager.

"That would be great. What time do you want to come over?"

"Oh, I don't know…how about eleven o'clock?"

"Okay. We can grab a bite too, or I can make us some lunch."

"Sounds like a plan. So now I have something to look forward to tomorrow." She stood up. "Will you walk me to the door?"

"Of course." He held his hand out. She was quick to grab hold and they walked to the door together. After Heather slipped her feet into the shiny black heels, he said, "You're almost as tall as me now."

"Almost. Is my coat here in the closet?"

"Yes—"

"Here it is." She pulled it out and put it on.

Jason yawned and rubbed his eyes.

"Okay, I'm ready."

"Come here." He smiled and held both arms out.

She walked into his arms and his hug brought her in closer. They kissed…it was slow, passionate.

He finally pulled away. "You better get going." He opened the front door. "Thank you for the wonderful night. Really."

"Thank you." She kissed him on the cheek. "I'll see you tomorrow."

"Yes, tomorrow."

He waved from the doorway when he heard her car backing down the driveway, then closed the door. Walking in the kitchen, he loved that he could still smell Heather on his hands and shirt.

"Oh the pie," he said out loud to himself. He felt on the counter by the sink where he asked her to put it. Not there. He figured maybe she placed it in the fridge, so he opened the door and starting feeling around. Nothing seemed out of place. Just then, his phone chimed with a text message.

Jason grabbed the phone and ran his finger over the screen.

"Text message from Heather Cook," it read out loud to him. He grinned as it read the message out loud: *Had the best time tonight. Miss you already. Can't wait to see you and that gorgeous smile again tomorrow.*

He sat there a moment, still smiling. Then he typed a reply: *Ditto. Best date ever. Where'd you put the pie?*

Chapter Five

The next day Jason struggled to remember the last time he felt so hopeful. He breezed through his morning workout at the gym in record time, a smile dancing on his lips from start to finish. When he came home, he took a shower and threw on a V-neck T-shirt and sweatpants. He brushed his short hair carefully, hoping he looked okay.

As he walked into the great room, he realized Heather was right; even he could tell his place was little more than a "clean slate." It felt empty and...blank. Last night, when she'd been there, somehow his house had felt alive and full and warm. To fill the void, Jason turned on an R.E.M. playlist at high volume.

He sang *It's the End of the World as We Know It (And I Feel Fine)* with gusto while he unloaded the dishwasher.

"Well, you're quite the singer," Heather's voice rang out.

He jumped and nearly dropped the plate in his hands. "Crap, you scared me. Did you knock?"

"Yep, but I guess it's hard to hear when you're doing your best Michael Stipe impression," she teased. "Sorry to frighten you."

"It was a good surprise."

She touched his arm, sending jolts of energy through him. His emotions were a jumbled mess—a mixture of excitement and arousal at seeing her again tempered with worry and caution as he wondered if she was having doubts about dating him.

He pulled her close and gave her a tender kiss in greeting. When he felt her body respond to his, his worries began to dissipate. "Hello."

"Hello," she said, her tone seductive. "Good to see you again."

"Likewise." They shared a smile. "So where do you want to work—do you need a lot of space? Or a table?"

"No, I'll just be reading papers and all I need is a seat to do that."

"I'm pretty much doing the same thing," he said. "So do you want to just go in the living room and plop down on the couch?"

"That's good with me."

He poured them some drinks. "Why don't you take these in the living room, and I'll go get my papers to grade?"

"Sure," she said.

He headed down the hallway.

Heather sat down on the couch, put her large tote bag on the floor, and pulled out a pile of papers in various folders that she set on the coffee table.

Jason returned, carrying his messenger bag and a big stack of pages printed in Braille. "Where are you?"

"I'm over here," she said from her spot on the couch. Then she noticed her tote bag on the floor in his path. "Wait!"

It was too late; he tripped over her bag and his papers went flying.

"Shit!" He shook his head.

"Jason, I'm so sorry—I didn't mean to leave that in your way—"

"It's okay," he said, although his tone said otherwise. "Just…just tell me in the future if you put something on the floor."

"Okay I will, I promise." She stood up. "Let me help you pick up your papers." She started gathering papers in her hands, while he got down on his knees and swept his hands back and forth across the floor, occasionally finding some. "Jason, it's my fault, let me get them for you." She felt terrible and embarrassed for him.

"I can find them." His voice was tinged with a touch of hostility. Sighing, he sat still. "This is what it looks like when I'm searching for something, and I don't know where it is. Guess I'm not so cool now, huh?"

Heather didn't know how to respond, afraid she would say the wrong thing and anger him more. She sat back down on the couch. "I think you're cool, no matter what you're doing," she began slowly, "but on the floor on your hands and knees is not one of your better looks, and I feel awful I created this mess. I'll put the ones I picked up on the edge of the coffee table."

"Thank you," he said, still scouring for papers. "Did we get them all?"

"There's two more, to your left. By the hearth."

He found them and stood up, compiling them all in a neat stack and adding the papers to the ones on the table.

"Listen, Heather...." Jason sat down next to her and put his hand on her leg. "Don't feel awful. It just embarrassed me because I'm trying to show you how normal and independent I am, and I hate it when I do something stupid like that. It's not you, it's me."

"No, don't apologize. I should have known better—"

"Why? Because you've known a blind man for three weeks? It took me and my family years to figure out the nuances of living with this." He took her face in his hands. "This is what I meant last night when we talked. I come with some bullshit you might not want to deal with."

Heather stared intensely at Jason's boyish face. He was handsome, but not nearly so much now as when he smiled. The worry and pain were evident in his furrowed brow and the straight line of his mouth, and she wanted nothing more than to erase that.

"Jason...." She sighed, not sure what to say to make him understand. "I'm sure it will only get easier, right? Once you got the hang of things, is it so bad now?"

"No." He stroked her cheek. "I'm just so used to it...I almost can't remember what it was like to see. Now it's just a nuisance. Kind of like a scab, you forget you have it until you snag it on something and it opens back up, reminding you it's there. But you go about your day and it heals back up. Not a big deal, just an inconvenience."

"Well if you can just bear with me a little bit, and know that I'm going to rip open that scab from time to time as I learn what you need, then I don't mind the extra effort. Unless it will be too hard for you to deal with my learning curve." She took his hands from her face and held them in hers. "I'm okay with it, if you are."

"I'm okay with it, and I want so badly to believe you. But I don't want you to have some romantic notion of blind love. I mean, I have great hands, and you will probably have the best sex of your life with me...."

"Oh really?"

"Oh, yes. But I will still trip on things sometimes, and it might be embarrassing for you when my cane attracts stares. And I will never notice when you color your hair or catch your eye from across the room. I'm just afraid those things will get to you eventually."

The look of concern on his face was anguishing for Heather. She wanted to somehow, someway convince him that she was head over heels for him, sighted or not. "How shallow do you think I am? I can live with that. All I can say is that at some point, you'll have to decide if you can take a leap of faith and trust me. Because of all that you're telling me, the only thing that really matters to me is the part about the best sex of my life."

They laughed together, and Jason's eyes grew misty. He smiled with adoration at her, showing her the face she wanted to see.

"Maybe," he began, clearing his throat, "maybe now is as good a time as any to take that leap and trust you. Because I don't think I can stand being around you anymore if I don't make love to you." He grabbed her close and kissed her with more emotion, more intensity than ever before. Heather felt like she was on fire and was pretty sure he felt the same.

When they came up for air, she asked, "So you want to...?"

"Oh, hell yes," he said, breathless. "If that's okay with you—"

"Yes yes yes."

His hands moved to her thin, tight long-sleeved T-shirt and started pulling it off.

"Wait, your blinds are open."

"Let's go to the bedroom." Jason kissed her again. Their bodies were glued together when they stood up.

"Watch out for my tote bag." She took his hand and he went wide around the couch to avoid it.

"Thank you." He led her down the hallway. Right before they reached his bedroom door he let go of her hand and held his arms out. "Jump in my arms. I want to carry you in."

"Okay." She smiled, put her arms around his neck, and hopped up.

He held on tight, carried her through the doorway and gently laid her on the bed. Heather felt like a princess.

Jason climbed on top of her and resumed pulling her shirt off. He ran his fingers from her thin waist to her breasts where he discovered her new lacy, plunging bra she bought the day before on a shopping trip with Katie.

"So sexy," he said. "What color?"

"White with pink flowers." She ached with anticipation. "I bought it for you."

"I like it. A lot." He unclasped her bra and threw it on the floor, along with her shirt.

She took off his T-shirt, exposing his broad chest. He was not overly muscular, but trim and toned with good definition. While they kissed, she rubbed his chest, becoming even more attracted by the masculine contours of his muscles. Soon they were both completely naked.

Jason pulled away from her and reached into the drawer of his nightstand. "I have condoms in here." He grabbed one and handed it to her. "Look to make sure it hasn't expired. It's been a while."

"We're in luck—three more months to go." She ripped open the package.

****

They climbed out of the shower together and found

their discarded clothes. "I don't know about you, but I worked up an appetite," Jason said as they ventured down the hall.

She walked ahead of him, and he playfully grabbed her butt. She swatted at him in return. "I am hungry. Do we want to go out and grab a bite?"

"We can just stay in if you want. We can start a fire and throw something together for lunch."

"Sounds perfect and cozy. Can I help?" Heather asked as they walked in the kitchen.

Jason grinned at her. "I don't know—can you?"

"Okay, mister," she said with mock hurt. "You're on your own then. No help from me. And one more remark, and I'll go in your pantry to rearrange all your canned goods."

"Now that's going a little too far." He kissed her. "That would be naughty." He went to the pantry and grabbed a loaf of bread. "Hey, sweetheart, come pick out a soup."

Heather lit up when he called her sweetheart, and she followed behind him, putting her arms around his waist and resting her head on his back. "You feel so good." Her mind wandered back to their lovemaking...she had never had such an intense, intimate experience before. Although their first time together, Jason seemed so incredibly in tune with her every move, her every desire. They just...fit.

"So do you." He turned around and kissed the top of her head. "You don't smell like you anymore, though, since you took a shower. Now you smell like my shampoo and soap. It's weird."

"Well maybe I need to keep some of my body wash and shampoo in my purse at all times." She scanned the shelf full of various soups. "Do you like minestrone?"

"I sure do. Grab the can. If you can handle it, I'll even let you open it and pour it in the pot."

"I'm preparing to rearrange everything in here. I warned you," she said.

"Just teasing, just teasing." He pushed her out of the

pantry. "Seriously, why don't you go sit down and do some work? I'll holler when lunch is ready."

"All right." She wandered back into the living room. The pictures on the mantle caught her eye.

First, a picture of Jason with presumably his parents and brother; it looked like he was probably seventeen or eighteen. He didn't look much different, just thinner and a little gangly. Then a picture of an older couple, maybe grandparents? Another photo of Jason wearing a birthday hat and a huge grin, maybe from a few years before. There were some other guys in the picture, all laughing. In the next frame, Jason stood with his arms around a woman. She was blonde, fairly pretty.

At the end of the mantle, a picture of a much younger Jason, on the beach with a beautiful sunset behind him. Besides looking younger, he looked different...then it dawned on Heather.

He could see in that picture.

His eyes looked different—alert and focused—opened more. He seemed to look right at her from the photo, a young Jason with sight. It took her breath away.

"Hey, Jason," she asked, carrying some of the photos into the kitchen, "when's this picture from of you in a birthday hat with some guys?"

"Oh, my twenty-first birthday. I was so drunk. You'll see my brother in that picture, and then a couple of my friends."

"I spot your brother now, yeah. You guys look kind of alike. He's just a little bigger and darker." Heather hesitated and then asked, "What about this picture of you and a blonde woman?"

"Oh...." He stirred the soup and then pulled some bowls out of the cabinet above him. "I didn't realize that was still up there. That's my ex-girlfriend."

"She's pretty," Heather commented, surprised by her sudden possessive and jealous feelings.

"I'm sorry. I obviously don't look at the pictures, and I didn't even remember it was there."

"That's okay. But do you mind if I take it down?" Heather tried to sound casual but more edge appeared in her voice than she intended.

He turned to face her. "Do I detect a hint of jealousy in your voice?"

Heather rolled her eyes and crossed her arms.

Jason's brows furrowed. "Are you still there?"

"Yes and yes."

Jason smiled and walked over to her. He found her shoulder and gave it a squeeze. "There's no reason to be jealous. She broke my heart, and I never felt about her like I feel about you."

"Really?" Heather asked, wondering if it was just a line.

"Well, maybe it's just me, but I've never felt this connected, this in sync with someone. Is it just me?" he asked quietly.

"No, I feel it too." She took hold of his hand. "Which is why I don't want a picture of you and another woman on your mantle. Because I feel like we already sort of belong to each other."

"I do too." He smiled and kissed her hand. "You can throw it away, burn it, whatever."

"Thank you." She walked up next to him while he pulled the grilled cheese sandwiches out of the pan. "There's one other picture I wondered about. It's the one of you at the beach."

"That's in Gulf Shores."

"You could still see in this picture, couldn't you?"

Jason put their sandwiches on plates. "Yeah, it was the last summer I could see. I mean, I was blind in my left eye, and the right one was really blurry, but I could see colors and make out some things. What a great vacation. I can still remember that gorgeous sunset." He carried the plates to the table. "How can you tell I wasn't blind?"

"Well, your eyes are just more focused I guess. More alert. And you don't usually open your eyes all the way now."

"I don't?" he asked, sounding surprised. "Do they look

strange or something?"

"No, your eyes look fine." She felt bad for bringing it up. "Really. They just don't focus on anything."

He slowly carried two bowls of soup to the table, grinning. "Kind of like the lights are on, but nobody's home?"

"Yeah, kind of like that. But they're still pretty blue eyes. I'm sorry I said anything—"

He put his hands around her waist. "Stop worrying about hurting my feelings or whatever. I'm not a china doll. So let's get past the awkwardness and eat some lunch."

"Okay then." Heather kissed him. A long, drawn out kiss.

"Or we could skip lunch…"

"Not a chance. That's the best looking grilled cheese sandwich I've ever seen."

Chapter Six

A week had passed when Jason got an email from the principal to meet in his office before school started. He worried he was in trouble for something but couldn't figure out what it might be. When he found out Shawn received the email, too, it certainly didn't make him feel any better about it.

They made the walk to the office together, cataloging their possible crimes on the way but still uncertain.

When they walked in the office, Jason recognized the cheerful voice of Sherry, the principal's secretary. "Well, what did I do to deserve the privilege of having two handsome men at my desk this morning?"

"We were kind of hoping you'd know," Shawn said. "Mr. Johnston asked us to come see him. Are we in trouble for something?"

Sherry laughed. "Honey, I don't think so. But with you two, I can see how that would be your first thought."

"Don't lump me in with him, Sherry." Jason gave what he hoped was his most charming grin. "I'm just a poor, innocent, blind teacher, trying to make his way in the world."

Shawn jabbed Jason in the ribs. "Scharp, you are so full of sh—good morning, Mr. Johnston."

Jason heard the principal open his door.

"Mr. Mathes, Mr. Scharp, please come in."

Jason grabbed onto Shawn's elbow, and they walked into the office.

"Have a seat, please. I have something I want to ask you about. This Friday night we're having the annual Basketball Shootout fundraiser for the PTO. It generates a fair amount of money, but one of the kids had an idea that may make it even more profitable."

Jason wondered what on earth it had to do with them.

"He thought we could charge one dollar admission from everyone who wants to watch a shootout between the two of you."

"Us?" Shawn asked with surprise.

"Well yes, you're always shooting hoops after school, so we might as well put it to good use. We thought it would be fun, since the two of you are young, witty guys—I'm sure you could make it into something really entertaining. And you're both popular with the students, so we hope that will help boost attendance."

"So basically, you think people will pay a dollar to watch a blind guy shoot hoops?" Jason asked.

"Well...in a manner of speaking—"

"I think it's a great idea." Jason smiled. "Shamelessly promoting my disability to earn cash for the school. Why not?"

No one spoke.

Jason finally said, "Are you guys still here?"

"Yeah, we're here," Shawn spoke up. "I think Jason's just trying to be funny, sir. Aren't you?"

"Of course I am. I said I think it's a great idea. I don't mind showing off how us blindos do it, if it will help the PTO. And maybe it will open up people's minds a bit about blindness. I say we do it."

"Well, great then." Mr. Johnston sounded pleased. "You're sure you don't mind?"

"Me?"

"Yes, Mr. Scharp."

"No, don't mind at all. It'll be fun."

"Then here's some flyers I want you both to post all over school. Here they are, Mr. Mathes. And I look forward to seeing you put on a good show Friday night."

Jason grabbed Shawn's bony elbow and walked out of the office with him. "Have a good day, Sherry."

"Scharp, she's not even there." Shawn chuckled.

"Well, you might as well laugh at me now, because everyone else will be laughing at you Friday night when a blind guy beats you." They walked into the hallway, now busy with students heading to their lockers or class.

"Yeah, don't think that didn't cross my mind," Shawn said. "I like how he asked if you were sure you didn't mind. What about me? I'm the one that either looks like a jerk if I beat the blind guy or a fool if I lose."

"Oh, come on, it won't be that bad. We're a pretty even match, but you're better. So it'll be close, and we'll just have some fun with it."

"I'm not letting you win." Shawn squeezed Jason's shoulder.

"You better not," Jason said emphatically. "If I even think you're trying to throw it…."

"I would never do that to you. Besides, I'd rather look like a jerk than a fool." They stopped at Jason's classroom.

"So, what do the flyers say?"

Shawn laughed. "Oh, man, they're playing this up. 'Come see Coach Mathes and Coach Scharp compete against each other at the Basketball Shoot-Out. Who will win—giant Mr. Mathes or blind Mr. Scharp? Just $1 admission and you'll see for yourself! Bring your parents, friends and neighbors!'"

"Oh, Jesus." Jason chuckled. "We sound like a couple of side show freaks."

"Well, if the shoe fits…."

"Yeah, I suppose."

"I'm gonna take off for my class now—see you at lunch."

"See ya," Jason said. A student walked by him into his classroom. "Good morning, Liam." Jason followed him in.

"How'd you know it was me?" Liam asked in amazement.

Jason smiled. "I will never divulge my secrets."

****

On Friday night, Heather met up with Shawn and Jason to watch the shoot-out. Jason told her it was no big deal, but she didn't want to miss it. Things between the two of them were going better than she'd ever remembered with any other guy. And this was the first time she wasn't ignoring red flags or forcing the relationship. With Jason, everything seemed easy.

The basketball shootout was a chance for her to see Jason in his element, among students, playing ball. She was anxious to see this whole other side of him. And of course she was curious about seeing a blind man hurl a ball at a target across a gym.

While people piled in the gym, Heather said, "My God, Jason, you wouldn't believe how many people are here."

"Probably a good thing I can't see them or I'd be even more nervous."

"I'm starting to think this was a bad idea," Shawn said.

"You know you're going to beat me."

"Of course I will. And then I'll be the teacher that beat the poor blind guy."

"Hey, it's all for a good cause. And you never know. I might give you a run for your money."

"You can't run after me and you know it," Shawn joked.

Jason laughed. "Screw you."

When they were ready to do their bit, Heather kissed him from the front of the stands and watched him walk onto the court holding Shawn's elbow. Everyone started cheering and clapping. Heather smiled with pride while she watched Jason, looking sexy in his long shorts and fitted muscle tee that showed off his nice body and legs. He looked much shorter than Shawn, but also much more muscular next to Shawn's gangly frame.

"Here we have the Jolly Red Giant!" the speakers boomed as the head of the PTO raised Shawn's hand in the air. Cheering ensued. "Competing against the Blind Wonder!" Heather started laughing out loud, and more clapping followed. "They will each take turns shooting, starting closer to the net and moving further back each time. Each will shoot ten times. Whoever scores the most baskets will be declared the winner." After some discussion between the announcer and the guys: "Okay, it has been decided that the Jolly Red Giant, otherwise known as Mr. Mathes, will go first."

Jason held onto Shawn. They walked to a spot on the court in front of the net and Jason let go when Shawn started dribbling the ball.

Cheers of "Go Coach Mathes!" and general whooping rang out. Shawn took his shot and *swoosh!* It went in. The crowd cheered.

Shawn said something to Jason and bounced the ball to him. Jason started dribbling the ball in place when Heather heard some girls a row or two back saying, "I don't care if he is a teacher and blind, Mr. Scharp is just hot. Look at his body!" Heather smiled to herself. *Yeah, and he's going home with me.*

"And now," the announcer boomed, "The Blind Wonder, also known as Mr. Scharp, will take his first shot." Jason motioned to the crowd to cheer louder and they did. A smile spread across his face. He got into position and then motioned for them to quiet down.

Some of them kept yelling, though, and Jason hollered something to Shawn that Heather couldn't hear.

"Hey gang," Shawn said, grabbing the mic. "The Blind Wonder has requested silence. He looks with his ears, so he needs to hear the beeping on the backboard." After a bit of laughter they quieted down.

Jason took his shot. *Swish!*

The crowd erupted in applause and cheers as the announcer declared, "And the score is one to one!"

Heather started screaming with utter abandon, jumping up and down while waving her arms in the air. Watching Jason do that was amazing. She became aware that some students and parents were staring at her...maybe her reaction had been a little over the top. She stopped yelling and smiled at them as her cheeks burned hot.

Heather was bursting with pride. Throwing a ball into the unknown, aiming only toward a sound, couldn't be easy—but he made it look that way. Watching that made her feel like he could do anything, he was incredible. *He really can do anything.*

Until she'd seen the ball sink through the net, she hadn't realized that she underestimated him. Whatever struggles she perceived he faced were most likely in her mind, not his. Swallowing as tears tried to make their way out, Heather told herself that she would always try to remember that. Remember this moment.

Jason was no ordinary guy.

****

When the time came for the final shots, Shawn had eight points and Jason had seven.

Shawn took his place. "This is where I put the nail in the coffin on your chances of even tying," he said to Jason.

"Oh, you think so, do you?" Jason smirked. "Well, we'll see."

The crowd cheered and Jason heard the ball smack the backboard followed by groans from the crowd.

"It sounds like you dropped the nail," Jason said.

Shawn shoved the ball in his stomach. "Fuck off," Shawn whispered in Jason's ear with a smile in his voice.

"Mr. Johnston wouldn't like that kind of language." Then Jason yelled to the stands, "Who thinks the blind guy can tie it up with the freakishly tall guy?"

The crowd's cheers grew louder until Jason put his fingers to his lips.

"Go Mr. Scharp!" one last person yelled, which he distinctly recognized as Heather.

He grinned broadly, waved to her and yelled, "That's my girlfriend!"

The crowd collectively erupted in, "Awww."

Jason put his fingers to his lips again to quiet the crowd and prepared to shoot. He dribbled the ball, the steady sound of the beeper and the rhythmic sound of rubber smacking the slick wood floor putting him in "the zone."

The beeping stopped. He straightened up and the crowd started laughing. "Mathes?"

"What?" Shawn asked with fake innocence, slapping

Jason on the back. "Is there a problem?"

"Okay guys," Jason yelled out, "he's so scared of my mad basketball skills that he had to resort to cheating!" Boos and hisses and laughter erupted from the crowd.

"Oh, I'm sorry," Shawn yelled, "did I accidentally turn off the beeper? So sorry!" He turned it back on.

"You know what? I'm gonna give the Jolly Red Giant one more chance to shoot."

"What?" Shawn sounded confused.

"He gets to shoot again, but he has to wear this." Jason pulled a blindfold out of his pocket. The stands erupted in laughter and cheers. "So are you game, Mathes?"

"Sure, it can't be that hard!" Shawn approached Jason and whispered, "I will fucking kill you later."

"Come on, it will be a crowd pleaser." Jason slapped Shawn on the back and put the blindfold on him. He hollered, "No peeking, Giant!"

Shawn got into position and dribbled the ball. "Scharp?" he asked Jason, "How the hell do you do this?"

"Just ignore everything else and focus on the beeper. Visualize the net based on the sound, and throw the ball."

Shawn bounced the ball then shouted, "Here goes nothing."

Jason didn't hear the ball hit anything, until it smacked the ground. The spectators cheered anyway.

"I didn't hear it hit the backboard," he said to Shawn.

"That's because I missed the entire backboard."

"Oh. Sorry." Jason chuckled and Shawn gave him the ball.

The crowd quieted down while Jason got in place and took his final shot.

Swish!

The stands exploded in huge cheers and Shawn grabbed Jason in a strong man-hug.

The PTO president grabbed both of their hands and raised them in the air. "And it ends in a tie! Thank you to Mr. Mathes and Mr. Scharp for their efforts and entertainment. We will now proceed with the rest of the shootout."

Shawn led Jason back to his seat, and Mr. Johnston stopped to congratulate them on their efforts and let them know they'd raised more than three hundred dollars in admission fees. The news made Jason smile but not nearly as much as when he heard Heather's sweet voice in front of him, calling his name.

"Jason!" When he reached the bench, Heather jumped up and hugged him. He kissed her on the cheek, and she put a water bottle in his hand. "Hydrate, my supa-stah!"

****

Almost three weeks had passed since Jason's first date with Heather, and the weather finally began to turn around and get warmer. Jason especially cherished the warm weather, since he spent a good portion of his days walking the streets of the city and waiting at bus stops.

He sat on a bench by the front doors outside his school, enjoying the sixty-degree temperature. He wore a light jacket, checking email on his phone while he waited for Heather to pick him up. The first birds coming back for spring sang a lively tune from a tree nearby and the strong scent of fresh-cut grass wafted by on a gentle breeze. The afternoon seemed so pleasant; he imagined the sun must be shining too.

"Hey, Mr. Scharp," said a female student approaching him. "It's Jamie Newman."

"Hello, Jamie," he replied with a cheerful voice. "Just leaving cheerleading practice?" He knew as the head cheerleader she practiced every day after school.

"Yeah, I'm really worn out. You know, it looks like your bruise is about gone."

"Is it? Well good—I started wondering if it had become a permanent fixture on my face."

She laughed. "Well, see you tomorrow in class, Mr. Scharp."

"See you," he said while she walked away. He returned his attention to his email when he heard footsteps approaching the bench.

"Hi, Mr. Scharp, it's Matt Hill." Another of his students.

"What's up, Matt?"

"Not much, sir." He stopped in front of Jason.

"Hey, you did a great job on that civil rights paper. You should be proud of yourself."

"Thanks," Matt said quietly. "You're the only teacher that thinks so."

"What do you mean by that?"

"Oh, nothing," he mumbled. "I better go. Just wanted to say hey."

"No, wait a minute." Jason stuck his cane in front of Matt and blocked his way. "Tell me what you meant."

"Well...the other teachers...they don't see me the way you do."

"I hate to break it to you Matt, but I don't see you at all." Jason chuckled.

"I know. That's probably why you're so cool to me."

"What are you talking about?"

"They don't give me a fair shot. All they see is a kid with blue hair, tattoos and piercings. They think I'm a loser."

"Well, you're not a loser," Jason said emphatically. "Tattoos and piercings, eh? I would never have guessed."

"Yeah."

"Well, you can't leave me hanging like that. What do they look like? Where are they?"

Matt laughed. "I've got an Aztec eagle on the back of my neck, some starburst designs on my biceps and a really wicked abstract spider on my left forearm. I've got three eyebrow piercings, a nose ring and a lip ring."

"So you want to look just like everybody else." Jason laughed. "Those tattoos sound way cool. I wish I could see them."

"Yeah, I think you'd dig 'em."

"Seriously, though...you get trouble from your other teachers?"

"Just forget I said anything, okay?"

"No, Matt, let me help you."

"But you can't, Mr. Scharp. You don't get it. One look at me, and they think they know who I am, what I can and can't do."

"You think I don't know what that's like? Try walking around with a five foot long white stick that shouts Blind Guy."

"Yeah, I guess you do know what that's like. Maybe you should die your hair blue and that would really screw with people."

Jason grinned. "Yeah, but I don't think Mr. Johnston would go for that."

"He definitely wouldn't...he hates me."

"Why?"

"I guess because the way I look scares him."

"Would you like me to talk to him? Or some of the teachers you're having trouble with?"

"No, but thanks, sir. I just never knew that showing your individuality would make people judge you."

"You know what, Matt? There aren't a lot of things I like about being blind, that's for sure. But I like that I can't judge a book by its cover, because I can't see the cover. Hell, I can't even see the book." He chuckled. "But I know you're a smart kid, you're polite, and you're creative. I don't care how many holes you put in your body or how many tattoos you get. I like who you are, and the way you look shouldn't matter. I'm sorry if my colleagues can't get past your exterior to see you like I do." *They're probably the same teachers that object to having a blind teacher in the school.*

"You're off the hook, Mr. Scharp." Matt said with a smile in his voice.

"That's good, right?"

"Yeah, it's way good. Thanks."

"You're welcome, Matt. Let me know if you get any new ink, okay? I'd love to hear about it."

"Sure thing. G'night."

"See you tomorrow."

Jason stood up, thinking he heard what might be

Heather's car pulling up. Cars sounded different from one another, but he couldn't always tell for sure.

"I'm here, Jason," Heather's voice chimed out after she rolled down her window.

Jason grinned and headed to the car.

"Coach Scharp!" a boy's voice hollered from a distance.

Jason turned in that direction and continued walking toward the car, his cane sweeping in front of him. "Is that you, Ben?" He thought he recognized the voice of one of his wrestlers.

"Yeah, you're good." Ben sounded impressed when he caught up with Jason. "Is that your girlfriend? Because she's hot."

"Okay, Ben, thank you for complimenting my girl, but you really shouldn't talk that way to a teacher." Jason grinned.

"Sorry, Coach."

Jason got to the curb and reached out, finding the car door handle. "Okay then. Have a good night." He opened the door and climbed in.

"Hello, handsome." Heather leaned over and gave Jason a passionate kiss.

He shut the door. "Well, hello. So how was your day?"

"Oh, pretty good," she said. "Yours?"

"Fine." He sighed.

"What's wrong, baby?"

"Can I ask you something?"

"Sure."

"But you have to be completely honest."

"Well, of course I will be."

"If you have a student that's covered in tattoos or all pierced up or something...do you form opinions about that kid based on their appearance?"

"Well...I'd like to think I don't. Why? What are you talking about?"

"So you don't think it affects the way you treat them or their grades?"

"I don't think so...I hope not. But I don't know. I'm human. Maybe it affects me, and I don't even realize it. What happened?"

"I just had a conversation with a student, and unbeknownst to me, he's got blue hair and tattoos and piercings. And he told me I'm the only teacher that gives him a fair shake, because his appearance doesn't affect me."

"That's really sad."

"Well, yeah, but to be honest with you, it pisses me off. That's not fair to him." Jason faced Heather. "Before you got to know me, what did you think of me? Honestly."

"I don't know that I thought anything about you—"

"You must have had some impression of me. I'm pretty conspicuous, I know that."

"Jason, I don't know..." The car stopped at what Jason figured was a light, and he felt Heather's hand on his knee. "I just thought of you as the blind guy in my class. That was it."

He wasn't surprised, but it stung just the same. "So not thin, or young, or good looking or anything. Just blind." His heart sank. He realized, *That's how everybody sees me. Not just a guy walking down the street—a blind guy walking down the street.*

"But I didn't know you—"

"And until I talked to you, you hadn't looked past the cane to see *me*. You only saw my disability." He crossed his arms. "Maybe Matt's right. Maybe I should dye my hair blue, at least people would see something besides my blindness."

She caressed his leg. "Baby—"

"I'm not mad at you. I'm sure that's what everyone sees. But it's bullshit. And it's bullshit that Matt has teachers thinking less of him because he's into body art. Maybe the world needs more blind people—then we'd be more tolerant."

"I'm sorry if I hurt your feelings, but you said you wanted me to be completely honest. And I see who you are now. Most of the time I forget you're blind."

Jason touched her arm. "I know. I'm sorry. I didn't mean to turn this around on you. The conversation with Matt really bothered me. There must be so many kids falling through the cracks like him." He squeezed her knee. "And thank you for seeing past my cane. Most people don't take the time to do that."

"I would have missed out on a lot if I hadn't."

"We both would have." A part of him was still hurt and pissed about the whole situation, but fifteen-plus years of walking around with a long white stick had gotten him used to the idea that life wasn't always fair and he couldn't dwell on the things he couldn't control. Regardless of Heather's initial impression of him, she was here now. She was with him. That's what mattered. After his internal pep talk, he did his best to sound upbeat when he said, "Okay, let's move onto something else."

"All right...what do you want to do this weekend?"

"Oh, I don't know. Of course tomorrow night is my usual family dinner."

"Are girlfriends allowed at those?"

"Well, sure," Jason said, surprised. "Do you want to come?"

"I'd like to, but I'm sorry—I shouldn't have invited myself." He could hear embarrassment in her voice.

"No, no it's fine. I would have invited you, but I didn't know if you were ready to meet the family yet."

"Are you sure you're ready for me to meet them? I didn't mean to assume—"

"Well of course I want them to meet you. My family is great. It's just that my mom is a little over-protective sometimes." He thought about his mother's reservations about him dating Heather. Screw it. "But I would love it if you came with me."

"Okay, then, let's do it," she said with a smile in her voice. "I can't wait to meet them!"

"I'll let my mom know you're coming." He hoped he wouldn't regret this idea.

Chapter Seven

On Friday night as Jason and Heather walked together to his parents' front door, he recalled the phone conversation he'd had with his mother that morning. She hadn't sounded too thrilled when he told her Heather would be joining them.

"Hey, Mom," Jason said, his phone on speaker since he was almost afraid to hold it to his ear for this conversation. "I wanted to let you know I'm bringing Heather with me tonight."

"What?" His mom sounded surprised.

"I'm bringing Heather to dinner." He sounded more sure of himself that time.

"Well, sweetie, don't you think that's a little soon? You barely know her—"

"Mom, I've known her for more than a month now, and we've been together just about every day for the last three weeks. I don't think it's too soon at all."

"Well…."

"Well what?"

"I just hope you know what you're doing. I'll set another place at the table." She sounded resigned about the fact.

"Thank you. And Mom?"

"Yes?"

"Be nice, okay? She's been great to me, and I've never been happier."

"I'll be nice."

They reached his parents' front door, and Jason turned to Heather. "Nervous?" Because he sure as shit was.

"A little. Should I be?" He heard her bracelets clink together as they held hands.

"I love you, so they should love you too."

"You love me?"

"Well...yes." He smiled despite feeling nervous. "I do love you." She didn't respond, and her silence terrified him. "Heather? Is it...is it too soon—"

"No, Jason, it's just wonderful." He could hear the catch of tears in her voice.

"I love you too."

Jason's shoulders relaxed, and he pressed his lips to hers, taking in her warmth and her scent.

Suddenly, the door opened in front of them, and John's voice boomed, "Are you two going to stand on the porch, making out, or come in?"

****

Jason's father wore a warm smile, yet Heather suddenly felt more self-conscious and nervous than she had expected.

"Hey, Dad, we can make out anytime. So we'll go in." Jason reached out and patted his dad on the stomach. "Dad, this is Heather Cook, Heather this is my dad, John."

"So nice to meet you, Heather." John shook her hand. "Come on in."

"Nice to meet you too." Heather offered a large but nervous smile. She saw a resemblance between Jason and John, although John didn't have the same beautiful smile as his son. They walked inside, and a dog came jumping at Jason's legs.

"That is Peanut," Jason explained to Heather. "He's harmless."

"Hello, little guy." Heather bent over and petted him. He responded by slathering her with wet kisses. She laughed.

"What's funny?"

"Oh, Peanut just licked my face." Standing up, she took in the room around her. Traditional furniture but nicely decorated. There were pictures of the family all over—on tables, the walls, shelves. Heather hoped to look at them later.

"Your mom's in the kitchen, of course," John said

while they followed him. "Mark and Angie are on the way."

"Great." Jason held Heather's hand and led her to the kitchen. "Mom?" he asked when they walked in.

An attractive middle-aged woman turned around, and the adoration on her face when she looked at Jason was undeniable. "My sweet boy." Jason's mom rushed up to hug him. When she pulled away, she looked intently at Heather and said, "And you must be Heather."

"Yes, I am." She felt intimidated by the woman's watchful eye. "Nice to meet you."

"I'm Eve." They shook hands. "Glad you could join us tonight." Her tone was less believable than her words.

"What can I do to help?" Heather asked, feeling more anxious by the minute.

"Oh, nothing, dear. Everything's just about done." She smiled, and Heather saw where Jason got his broad grin. Although hers did not seem genuine at the moment. It seemed forced.

"Is the table set?" Jason asked.

"Yes, it's set. Why don't you just show Heather around?"

"Sure. What are we having? Some kind of roast?"

"Pork roast, mashed potatoes and gravy, and asparagus."

"Oh, that all sounds delicious," Heather said.

"It will be." Jason smiled. "Mom's a great cook."

"Oh, thank you, sweetie." Eve beamed at her son.

Jason took Heather's hand. "Follow me." He headed out of the kitchen. He gave her a quick tour and they were in his old bedroom, surrounded by his trophies, when they heard Mark and Angie arrive.

Heather's nerves kicked back into high gear when she and Jason headed into the great room.

"Hey, little brother," Mark's boisterous voice rang out. Although he was talking to Jason, he looked at Heather. Her face burned hot when she noticed him looking her up and down.

"Hi, Jason," Angie chimed in, smiling. "And this must

be Heather."

Heather instantly liked Angie—she seemed warm, kind, and safe, all at once. Mark, however, a big loud guy, intimidated her a bit. Yet he managed to look friendly, even while appearing to inspect her.

There was a definite resemblance between the brothers, but Mark looked like a younger carbon copy of their dad, with a goatee thrown in. Mark was taller and stockier than Jason, but there was no doubt they were brothers. They both had the same striking blue eyes. Heather was startled to see the difference in Mark's, which were infused with expression and looked directly at her.

For the first time, she had a vague sense of what it would be like for Jason to make eye contact with her. It was fascinating to see those same blue eyes locking with hers, yet disheartening for her to know Jason's never would.

"Yes guys, this is my Heather." Jason squeezed her hand. "Heather, this is my brother Mark and sister-in-law Angie."

They shook hands and Heather said to Angie, "So you're the one that helps Jason dress so well."

"Oh, yes, from time to time I've been known to give some fashion advice or go shopping." Angie chuckled.

"Well, I can see why you're so good with his clothes—you're very stylish yourself." Angie dressed fashionably and carried herself well. Her blonde swing bob was cut to a sharp point in front, complimenting her tall thin frame. She wore great eye-catching pieces of jewelry with her classic clothing.

"Oh, you're sweet." Angie smiled.

John spoke loudly from near the kitchen, "The gang's all here! Come on in, your mom's dishing up the plates now."

They all herded into the kitchen and Heather clung to Jason's side.

"Mom?" Jason asked. "Where do you want us to sit?"

"I added a chair to your left for Heather, and moved yours a bit to the right."

They found and took their seats in front of plates brimming with food. Mark and John talked with great animation and loudly. Angie greeted her mother-in-law, and they chatted.

Heather leaned over to Jason. "Do you want me to tell you where the food is on your plate?" she asked quietly.

"Yes, please." He patted her leg. She read off the "clock" arrangement to him just as he explained to her weeks ago, so he knew what he could expect to bite into. "Thanks, sweetheart."

The conversation in the room quieted down a bit as they all settled to eat.

"This all looks so delicious, Mrs. Scharp," Heather said.

"Why thank you," Eve said graciously. "Okay, Jason, your roast is at three o'clock—"

"That's okay, Mom, Heather already told me."

"Oh…okay." Eve seemed a bit put off. "Well, let's all dig in, shall we?"

Everyone started eating in silence for a bit while they busied themselves shoveling in food.

"So what's new with you guys, Mark?" Jason finally asked after swallowing a bite of roast.

"Well, I've been working my butt off." Mark cut some asparagus. "It's tough out there, selling in this economy."

"I bet. Are you making any headway?"

"I've got so many irons in the fire that something has to pop soon."

"Well good luck with that. What's new with you, Angie?" Jason faced his sister-in-law.

"Well…" she began, her face beaming. "We find out in two weeks if we're pregnant. We did IUI and now we just wait."

"Oh my goodness!" Eve nearly shrieked. "I am so excited. I would just love some grandchildren."

"Mom, we don't even know yet if we're pregnant," Mark reminded her.

"I know, but the possibility's there. Call me the minute

you get the results."

"We will," Angie reassured her.

"Just think, Dad," Jason chimed in, "we might be able to call you Grandpa soon."

"Now I don't know about that." John laughed and the others joined in. "I want you all to have kids, but I'm not so sure I'm ready to be called Grandpa."

"Doesn't matter what they call you, you'll still be a grandpa."

"So, Heather," Eve asked pointedly, "do you want children?"

"Mom," Jason groaned. Mark shot her a look too. "I don't think it's really appropriate to ask her that. We're not getting married yet or anything."

Heather noticed that he said *yet*. "Actually, it's okay," she said with a smile. "I've always wanted children. At least two."

Eve smiled in response.

"*At least* two?" Jason asked, turning to her in surprise.

"Ah, Mom," Mark moaned, "do you see what you've done? You asked her something they haven't even discussed together."

"Well, two would be fine." Heather looked at Jason. "But maybe more. If…if that's what both of us wanted." She felt her face grown warm. "That is, if that's what both my husband and I wanted."

Jason reached out and touched her arm. "Just so you know two would be plenty for me." He smiled one of those grins that always warmed Heather to her very core.

She felt completely embarrassed, like a fool in front of his family. "I'm not presuming that we'll get married, I just answered the question."

"Well, I should hope not." Eve shook her head. "It's only been a few weeks."

"I knew after our second date I wanted to marry Mark," Angie piped in. "He proposed after just nine months."

"Your mother agreed to marry me after just three

months," John added.

Heather felt almost sick. *How did this turn so wrong so fast?* "I'm not fishing for a marriage proposal—"

"Oh, Heather, I know you're not." Jason found and took her hand. She knew the panic in her voice was obvious. "Let's just drop it, okay guys? I can't believe you asked that, Mom."

"There's nothing wrong with knowing her plans for the future," Eve said.

Jason sighed. "So, Mark, when do you want me to kick your ass again in golf?"

Thank you, Jason. Thank you for saving me by changing the subject.

"*You* beat *me* at golf?" Mark chuckled. "Heather, I don't know what line of bull my little brother's been feeding to you, but he's never beaten me at golf."

The rest of dinner was lighthearted and fun. They all had a great sense of humor like Jason, and although Heather found it easy to join their banter, she wasn't quite sure what to think of Jason's mom. It was apparent she was not entirely pleased at Heather's presence, and although outwardly gracious, Heather sensed a hostility coming from her. But why? She hoped she was wrong, but she felt uncomfortable. She just really wanted to make a good impression.

After dinner, the men went into the great room and turned on the TV while the women helped clean up. Jason offered to help, but Heather insisted he go off with his dad and brother. Before he left the room, he pulled her close and kissed her. She looked over to see Eve watching with a disapproving glare.

Flustered, Heather started clearing off the table with Angie. They piled up the plates next to the sink, and chatted while Eve loaded the dishwasher and the two younger women washed and dried the other dishes. Heather learned that Angie worked as a paralegal, and Eve once held a position as an assistant to a local congressman.

"How long ago did you stop doing that?" Heather

asked.

Eve paused, looking in the distance. "When Jason started losing his sight. I wanted to be here for him, to help him and protect him as much as I could."

"And you never went back?"

"He lost his sight over about five years. Those last couple of years, he had very little vision left, which made it terribly difficult. And then it all went away. Struggling to adjust left him frustrated, and he was trying to grow into a man at the same time." Eve looked straight at Heather. "The easy-going, happy, capable man you know now didn't exist then. Not by a long shot. And by the time he was acclimated and doing better, I hadn't worked in nearly seven years. So I just decided to stay home from then on."

Heather offered a smile. "He was lucky to have you."

"Excuse me for a minute," Angie said. "I need to use the restroom. I'll be right back."

"I'll take over washing," Eve said, starting the dishwasher. She grabbed the next dirty pan and started washing it while Heather dried some knives. "So, Heather, what is it with you and Jason?"

"What do you mean?" Heather felt her face flush.

"Is this just some charity case to you? Are you dating my son to make you feel better about yourself or to help the handicapped?"

"Excuse me?" Heather was shocked to hear her say those things, and felt anger rising within her. *What kind of person does she think I am?*

****

Jason headed toward the kitchen to grab a couple of beers. He stopped just outside when he heard his mom say, "I don't want you to stop dating him after the novelty wears off and he becomes too burdensome to you. I don't want you to break his heart like all the others."

"I have no intention of doing that." Heather's voice was firm. "I am with your son because I love him."

Mom chuckled. "Oh, I'm sure they all said that. Right before they got sick of their social work project and left."

"You know, Mrs. Scharp, I think you really underestimate your son. Did you ever happen to think his blindness has nothing to do with why I'm dating him or why we would ever break up—if we do? I fell for Jason because he's a charming, funny, intelligent, sexy man. And he just happens to be blind. I wish he wasn't…for so many reasons. But I don't mind that he is. And if you think I'm going to get sick of your son because he can't see…well then you've underestimated me."

"Hey, Jace!" Mark yelled from the other room. "Where's my beer?"

Jason walked into the kitchen. He would have loved to see the look on his mother's face. "I'm getting it," he hollered back to Mark, then headed to the fridge, grabbed two beers, and turned to face the two most important women in his life. "Heather, would you please excuse my mother and me for a minute? And can you give this beer to Mark?"

"Uh, sure." She hesitated before taking the beer from Jason and leaving the room.

He faced his mother. "What are you doing? I thought I asked you to be nice. Why are you interrogating her? She's done nothing wrong—"

"I'm just trying to protect you—"

"Don't, Mom! Just don't." The last sentence came out as not much more than a whisper. "I am not a kid anymore. I don't need you to protect me, and I don't want you to screw this up for me. I really love her."

"Oh, Jason…." Her voice trailed off to a sigh, and Jason could practically hear her eyes rolling.

"Oh Jason what?"

"You can't possibly love her yet."

"So now you know not only what's best for me, but what I'm feeling too?"

"It's too soon—"

"For who? You?"

"I just want you to be careful—"

"I don't want to be careful, Mom!" He realized he had

raised his voice, but what he really had an urge to do was punch something. His whole life was about being careful, avoiding accidents, steering clear of unseen obstacles. Being careful sucked. He loosened the fist that had formed in his right hand and continued in a softer voice. "She is terrific. I wish you'd open your damn eyes and see that. Sometimes you're blinder than me." He abruptly walked out.

When he reached the great room, he was about to call Heather's name when he felt her hand slip into his. Their fingers laced in what was becoming a familiar feeling to Jason. And a comforting one.

"Let's go," he said.

"You want to go?" Heather asked.

"You're leaving?" John asked. "You can't eat and run."

"Yeah well, sorry, but it's time to go," Jason said curtly.

"What's the matter?" Mark asked, and Jason heard him stand up.

"Let's just say Mom doesn't really want us here. She apparently wants me to be alone forever and can't just be happy that I've found someone. Dad, where are our coats?" He heard Angie approaching from down the hall.

"You're leaving?" she asked with surprise.

"Jace…." John put his hand on Jason's arm.

"Yes, we're leaving." Jason's answer was brusque, and he pulled away from his dad.

"Jason," Eve said, coming into the room. "Please calm down. Don't go. Heather, I'm sorry if I offended you or upset you in any way." She sounded genuine.

"Oh, I'm fine." Heather didn't sound terribly convincing. "We can stay, Jason."

"What's going on?" John bellowed.

Eve cleared her throat. "I said some things to Heather that were probably out of line."

"Probably?" scoffed Jason.

"Okay, I overstepped my bounds as a mother and said some rude things to Heather. I'm sorry, Jason. My heart was in the right place…."

"I'm sure it was," Heather said.

Jason could feel her hand trembling in his. He was so angry with his mom for upsetting Heather and creating a problem when there shouldn't have been one.

"Sometimes, Mom," Jason said, his voice laced with anger, "I think you're afraid of losing your little boy to someone else."

"No, Jason, I'm just afraid of you getting hurt, that's all," Eve tried to explain.

"Well, I don't know what transpired between the two of you," John said, "but Heather agreed to stay and accepted your mother's apology. So don't leave in a huff."

"You at least have to stay until you drink your beer," Mark said, attempting a joke.

Jason offered a small grin. "It's always about the booze with you, isn't it?"

"It's the little things in life that make me happy."

Jason could feel the tension in the room start to alleviate.

"Why don't we play some Tripoli?" Angie suggested.

"Do you like games?" Jason asked Heather.

"Sure." Heather squeezed his hand.

"Okay, let's see if this girl can keep up with the Scharps."

****

By the time they got ready to leave, things seemed better. While they put on their jackets, Mark and Jason chatted while Eve approached Heather.

"I am sorry about earlier, but I hope you understand my concerns," she said, worry in her eyes.

"I do understand, Mrs. Scharp," Heather replied, her voice quiet. "But please know that I don't want Jason hurt any more than you do. And I do love your son. I hope with time you'll see that."

"Are you ready, Heather?" Jason turned away from Mark.

"Yes. Thank you all so much for having me. I had a great time and enjoyed meeting all of you." They replied in kind, and Heather opened the front door. "Oh, my purse." She dashed to the couch where she left it.

"Bye, everybody." Jason turned toward the partially open door and slammed into the edge of it. "Owww!" He stepped back, rubbing his face while his mom rushed to his side.

"Oh, Jason, I'm so sorry," Heather cried out. "That's my fault."

Mark said in an understanding tone, "You always have to leave doors open or shut all the way."

"I know, I know." She shook her head.

"Well if you knew, then why didn't you?" Eve's words came out as almost a hiss while she hovered over Jason.

"I just forgot—" Heather started, her eyes welling with tears.

Jason pushed his mom away and said forcefully, "It's no big deal, Mom. I run into shit all the time. Heather, it's okay." He held out his hand in her direction, and she gratefully took it, fighting back the tears.

"You could have gotten really hurt," Eve said.

"Mom, lay off it."

Heather looked down and didn't dare look at Eve. "Are you okay?" she whispered.

"I'm fine, sweetheart." He put his hand on her face. "Now we're leaving. Good night everyone."

"Good night," they all rang out.

Jason and Heather walked in silence to the car, holding hands. When they climbed in and Heather started up the car, she couldn't help but start crying from sheer embarrassment and guilt. She turned on the radio so Jason couldn't hear and tried to muffle her cries.

"Heather, are you all right?" He reached out for her arm.

"I'm fine," she squeaked through the sobs she tried stifling.

"Oh sweetheart, are you crying?" His voice was full of tenderness and concern.

She put the car in reverse and started backing down

the driveway. "No," was all she could muster.

"Yes, you are." He touched her cheek, now damp with tears. "Please don't cry. Why are you crying?"

She let the floodgates open and started sobbing out loud. "I just wanted to…make a good impression."

"You did—"

"No I…didn't," she said in between sobs. "Your mother hates me…and I just hurt you in…in front of everyone."

Jason laughed, which only made her cry harder. "My mom does not hate you. She is just overprotective and doesn't trust any girl. She acts like I'm still a little boy. That has nothing to do with you."

"You…you should have seen…the way she looked at me…after you ran into the door," she said, starting to calm down a bit. She took a big breath, looking over at Jason when they stopped at a light.

"The wrath of Mom. I remember the look. That one is seared in my brain forever. And I'm sorry. But she made a big deal out of nothing."

"It wasn't nothing. And all because I didn't think—"

"Hey, hey." He touched her leg. "Stop it, okay? We're new at this together. Remember that scab we talked about? Well, it just got pulled off a little bit. We discussed that and knew it would happen."

"But what if you were really hurt? And in front of your family…"

"Heather, I didn't get hurt. In a month I've only run into things twice because of you. That's a pretty good record, I think." He grinned, and his smile calmed her. "And do you think they've never done that before? Hell, I thought Angie was trying to kill me when she first started coming around. I fell over her purse once, and I swear it took a year for her to remember to push her chair in. I think I've got a scar from one incident." They both laughed.

Heather drove through the intersection. "Really?"

"Really. Not to mention the countless times Mark did

stuff to me when we were teenagers—he was such a slob it created a real hazard. So please relax."

"Do you think the others liked me?"

"My dad likes everyone. And I know Mark and Angie must have liked you because before we left they said they want to double date sometime soon."

"Oh, that would be fun. I liked them a lot."

"You are a seriously lousy poker player though," he taunted.

"Well it's apparent that while I studied like a good girl at school, you were playing poker, smoking cigars and drinking."

"Sometimes, yes." Jason laughed.

Heather pulled up in front of Jason's house. She looked over at him, remembering Eve's words and the look of disdain on her face. Heather wondered if Katie's concerns were right.

Dating Jason might not be so easy after all.

Chapter Eight

The next morning, Heather lay back in bed with a tray on her lap and let out a contented sigh. "Jason, dear, you are going to make me fat."

"Well, I'll still love you when you're chubby." He was cuddled up beside her with a book, and she loved the way he looked in the morning with a little bit of stubble and messy hair. "I'll just have more Heather to love."

"I'm serious. All you do is feed me your delicious cooking."

"Yes, but sweetheart, we're having lots of sex. That burns like hundreds of thousands of calories." Jason smiled.

"You are a pervert." She giggled. "I have an idea for something we could do today."

"Will it involve getting you into the bathtub again?"

"Not exactly. But you've never been to my place. Would you like to come over and see it?"

After a pause: "Sure." Jason sounded less than convincing.

"Why don't you want to?"

"I said sure," he protested.

"Yeah, but it didn't sound convincing." Heather stared at him, wondering what had suddenly taken his easy smile away.

He didn't say anything for a minute. "It's stupid and selfish, so just don't worry about it. I would love to see your place. I bet it's great." He grabbed her butt and smiled, but she could tell it wasn't genuine.

"What's stupid and selfish? What's wrong?"

Jason sighed, worry clouding his expression. "I'm just so comfortable here because I know where everything is. I know every stick of furniture, every wall, every knob or button on all my appliances. So it's easier for me here. I'm afraid I'll spend half the weekend looking like an idiot tripping over everything. But so what? I'll get to know your place too."

"I never thought of that. Is it really hard for you in new places?"

"Just makes me more dependent on you, which makes me uncomfortable. But it's just a stupid guy thing, pride. Sometimes it's hard for me to ask for help, especially from you."

"We don't have to go—"

"Yes we do. We can't stay holed up in here forever. I want to see where my beautiful lady lives, what it's like. And if that means I have to hang onto you and grope you even more than normal, well then you'll just have to deal with it." He grabbed her breasts. "Oh, I'm sorry, I didn't know these were here."

"Yeah, right."

After breakfast, they hopped in the shower together. When they got out, Heather noticed a text message on her phone from Katie:

Hello BFF! Wanna get together with us tonight? I'd like to finally meet Jason aka The Second Coming.

She laughed out loud.

"What's so funny?" Jason asked, getting dressed.

"Katie sent me a text. She called you The Second Coming. Guess I gush about you a bit."

"I think you oversold me. Here are some clothes for you." He handed over a T-shirt and sweatpants.

"Well, she's joking. I don't think I ever actually said you were a deity." She chuckled. "So anyway, she asked if we want to get together tonight with her and Dan. Would you like to?"

"Yeah, I'd love to meet your friends."

"Great! Why don't we have them over to my place? We could cook some dinner, maybe grill out—it's supposed to get up to sixty-eight degrees today."

"Yeah, whatever you want, sweetheart." He put his arms around her.

"And we could play some games. What games do you like to play?"

"You mean besides Tripoli, since you're poker illiterate?"

"Not unless I have a cheat sheet," she said with a laugh.

"What about Scrabble?"

"Oh, I can sooo kick your butt at Scrabble."

He chuckled. "You think so?"

"I'm an English teacher. I know words you've never even dreamed of," she taunted.

"Are you trash-talking me?"

"You know it. Do you have a modified game or something?"

"No, I just guess what the tiles say. Makes the game more interesting." He laughed, shaking his head. "Yeah, it's modified. It's got Braille on the tiles, along with the printed letters. And there's a plastic grid on top of the board that you put the tiles in. That way, when I'm reading the tiles, I'm not sliding them all over the board."

"Well, be sure to bring it with you then." She brushed her hair. "I'm going to text her back right now."

She typed: *Would LOVE for you to meet Jason! My place, 6:00? We'll make dinner & play games.*

A text came back right away: *I don't want to eat anything you're cooking. We can order in.*

****

A couple of hours later, they arrived at Heather's condo after loading up at the grocery store. Heather had assured Katie that Jason would be in charge of all food-related matters.

"Your condo is just beautiful," Jason teased while they carried the groceries to her building.

"Oh, shut up."

As they walked to her door, Jason heard a couple of dogs barking nearby, traffic rumbling from the busy street behind, and heavy metal music drifting from someone's open window. The aroma of soil and grass was strong in his nose.

"It smells like spring today," he said.

"Does it? Well, it's starting to look like it. There are buds on the trees and bushes. The grass is turning green. Okay, home sweet home. Let me unlock the door." She fumbled with her keys, then opened the door and led Jason through.

A rush of smells hit him...vanilla, maybe scented candles? He could smell her perfume, even from the front door. He smiled. "It smells like you in here. And vanilla."

"Those are my candles. Okay, so let's put the bags in the kitchen and then I'll show you around." She ushered him through the foyer and around a corner to the kitchen. "Here, I'll take those." She grabbed the bags from him and put them on the counter.

"So this is the kitchen?" He reached out and found the fridge.

"Yep. Um...so how do you want me to do this so you can get around?"

"We can just go room by room and show me the furniture or anything else I could run into."

She showed him the layout of the condo and placement of the furniture, giving him time to explore everything.

When they walked out of the living room, Jason clipped his head on something that moved, came back, and hit him again. He stepped back, bumped into a coffee table and steadied himself.

"Uh, is this a hanging plant that just attacked me?" Jason reached out and felt what seemed to be a pot.

"Yeah, sorry. I didn't think about that."

"That's okay. Are there any other overhead obstacles I need to watch out for?" He was irritated, not at her, but at himself for being the kind of guy that needed his girlfriend to warn him there's a hanging plant right in front of him.

"There are some candle sconces on the wall in the bedroom that stick out several inches, so I'll show you those when we get in there. Two days in a row I screwed up—"

"No you didn't." He pulled her in close to him and placed a gentle kiss on her lips. "I'm the blind one, not you. You can't know all my needs but you're trying to figure it out as you go, and you're doing a fantastic job."

"I promise I'll get better," she said with confidence.

"It takes time, getting used to the little things I need that everyone else takes for granted." He kissed her cheek. "I love you for putting up with me."

"It's not that big a deal, Jason. I just feel horrible when I miss something and you pay the price."

"I've got a thick skull and calloused shins. Don't worry."

When she finished giving Jason the tour of her little two-bedroom condo, he hugged her. "Your place is cozy and smells great, just like you."

"Why thank you, Mr. Scharp. Oh, I have to show you my little backyard. That's where the grill is you'll use for the steaks."

"You showed me where the door is, let me see if I can find it," Jason ventured. "I'll steer clear of the hanging plant." He flicked open his cane, and easily took the few steps from the love seat to the door.

"There are two steps down to my patio," Heather cautioned.

"Thanks." He stepped down and caned around. He struck something metal. "Grill?"

"That's it."

"So this is where my barbecue magic will happen." He grinned, feeling the knobs.

"Oh, my crocus plants are starting to bloom."

"Where?" He walked in her direction.

"Kneel down, they're here along the edge of the patio."

Jason felt the blooms just starting to open. He brushed his hands across the tops. "Wow, there's a lot of them."

"Yeah, I love gardening. I have tulips that will come up later, and ornamental grasses, ground cover—all kinds of stuff."

"Well, you'll have to help me out in my yard then, because I don't know the first thing about plants or flowers."

"I'd love to. Your yard is so large. I just have a tiny little area."

"We better get inside and start putting away those groceries." Jason was actually beginning to feel quite nervous. *What if they don't like me? What if they're not like Heather, and all they see is a blind guy?*

****

A couple of hours later, as it got closer to the time for their guests to arrive, it felt to Jason like it was taking forever to prepare dinner. Trying to cook in her kitchen left him beyond frustrated.

At home, he had measuring cups labeled in Braille and he knew how the knobs on the stove correlated to how much heat put out. He knew where to grab the spatula and knives and where the spices were, but at Heather's place...he had to ask for help with everything. Jason felt like that fourteen-year-old again, struggling and helpless.

And he didn't like it.

Heather did her best to help him. She couldn't read ahead in the recipe to anticipate his needs, because it was only in Braille. So she stayed nearby, doing whatever he asked.

"How much time do we have before they get here?" Jason searched on the counter with his hands.

"About fifteen minutes. What are you looking for?"

"I need to wipe my hands...I left a paper towel somewhere...." Heather handed it to him. "Thanks. So, fifteen minutes? Okay, the steaks are done marinating and I just put the steak fries in the oven. I have to finish the garlic bread. Did you say you have the salad put together?"

"Yes, you just need to make the dressing."

"That's right, shit, I forgot about that. Can you please throw the steaks on the grill while I get started on the dressing?"

"Sure, baby," Heather said. "I'll be right back."

She went outside, and he attempted to start the dressing. He found the recipe and grabbed the ingredients that they picked up at the store. But now he needed spices...where and which ones were which? He didn't know.

"Okay, I'll measure out the oil," he said out loud to himself. But while his liquid measuring cups at home were marked with tactile dots and a number for each marking, hers were just printed on. No use to him. So he figured he'd use a dry measuring cup instead...but couldn't tell what size they were. "So I have to wait for help." He began stewing, just waiting there. He grabbed his cane off the counter, opened it, and found his way to the door.

He poked his head out, saying in a brusque voice, "Heather, I really need some help in here."

"Okay, I'll be there in just a minute."

"I don't have a minute, I can't do anything until you get in here," he snapped.

"I'm sorry, Mrs. Brown," she said to someone he hadn't realized was there. "We'll have to chat later." Jason hung his head, embarrassed he'd barked at her in front of someone.

"Who's that?" Mrs. Brown asked. Jason could tell from her voice that she was an old woman. Short too.

"This is my boyfriend, Jason," Heather said.

Jason stepped out the door and waved in the elderly woman's direction. "I'm sorry, I didn't know you two were talking."

"Is he blind?" Mrs. Brown asked.

"Yes, I am," Jason answered. "Which is why I didn't see you and also why I need Heather. I need her to find something for me in the kitchen."

"Well my word," Mrs. Brown said. "Such a shame. And he's a good looking man too."

"Thank you." Jason sighed, ticked that she continued to talk about him as if he wasn't there. "Heather?"

"Good to talk to you, Mrs. Brown—I'll see you later."

She followed Jason back inside. "Wow, she acted like you couldn't even hear."

"Yeah, I get that a lot. Among other ignorant comments."

"Really?"

"Oh, sure. People telling me how amazing I am because I just crossed the damn street. People thinking I'm not capable of anything and pretty much assuming I'm helpless. I'm used to it."

"Well, I'm not used to it and it irritates me."

"Let's just forget about it," Jason said, finding his way to the kitchen. "Come on, we have to get moving."

"You were really snippy with me out there. Are you mad at me for something?"

"No, I'm just worried that we're not going to be ready in time. I don't want them to see me fumbling around in the kitchen." Looking helpless and needy in front of her friends really concerned Jason. On his own turf, he didn't need anyone's help and felt confident. Certainly not the case here.

"Okay, what do you need?"

He rattled off the spices he needed, and she helped measure to speed things up. He mixed up the dressing within a couple of minutes and put it to chill in the fridge. Then she helped him finish preparing the garlic bread.

"I have to go out and check on the steaks," he said. "If the timer goes off, that's for the fries. Take them out and put the garlic bread in."

He approached the patio door and ran into the hanging plant. Again. "Shit!"

"That one was all you—not my fault."

Jason glared at her and walked outside. After checking the steaks, he absently tossed his cane back and forth from one hand to the other, trying to calm the anxiety that was starting to take over. He heard the door open.

"How are the steaks coming along?" Heather asked, stepping on the patio.

"Fine."

"I brought you a beer." She touched his hand with it.

He offered a slight smile and took it. "Thank you, sweetheart."

"Oh, there it is!"

Confused, Jason asked, "There's what?"

"Your smile. It disappeared for a couple of hours, but I just saw a brief glimpse of it." She put her arm around him.

"I'm sorry for snapping at you." He kissed the top of her head. "I'm just spoiled at home and I forget what it's like not to have everything just the way I'm used to it. This makes me feel…blind."

"Well, you are…."

"But I don't normally feel that way. I usually just feel like…well, me. I don't give much thought to not seeing. But tonight I'm thinking about it non-stop." He took a drink. "And I'm nervous about meeting your friends."

"Well, it can't go any worse than it did for me last night." She chuckled.

He grinned. "Yeah, thanks to my mom."

"And a carelessly left open door…."

"That too."

"Katie is awesome and Dan is great too. They're going to like you a lot."

"I hope so." He wished he felt so sure. So many people he met couldn't get past his blindness to actually get to know him. But Heather didn't seem to mind, so he could only hope they wouldn't, either.

"Jason, I love you. And I just want you to be yourself and have some fun tonight."

"I will." He attempted a smile but didn't quite achieve it.

"Well, I swapped out the fries and bread in the oven when the timer went off. I better go check on the bread." Heather went back inside and within a minute, opened the patio door and hollered to Jason, "Doorbell rang. They're here."

"Do I look okay?" Jason asked.

"You look handsome as always," she reassured. "I'll go get the door."

Jason picked up the steaks, touched them to check for doneness and flipped them over. Then he walked to the patio steps, folded up his cane and put it in the pocket of his cargo pants. Taking a deep breath, he walked inside.

He heard them all clamoring in from the foyer, chatting. Then the talking stopped and Jason heard a sweet, jovial woman's voice say, "And this must finally be Jason the Magnificent!"

Jason grinned. "And you must be the famous Katie."

"The one and only." She laughed, approaching Jason. "I hope you don't mind, but I have just got to give you a hug. I feel like I know you already." She hugged him, all of what he figured was five feet two inches of her. Jason felt the large round ball that was her stomach press against him.

"Wow, you are really pregnant," he said with a chuckle, pulling away. "Unless, of course, this is your normal shape."

"Oh, thank God, no." Katie laughed. "Didn't Heather tell you I'm gorgeous and have the body of a fashion model? Minus a foot in height."

"She might have said something like that...."

"Well, it's so nice to finally meet you. Every time I talk to Heather, it's Jason this and Jason that. I was getting sick of you and I'd never even met you."

"Oh, I'm not that bad," Heather said.

"Now I see why she kept you hidden. I thought you might be her imaginary friend, but really it's because she worried I couldn't keep my hands off you, you're so damn good looking." Katie squeezed his arm.

"Excuse me," Dan piped up. "I'm right here, Katie. Your husband. Remember me?"

"Oh shit, did I say that out loud?" They all laughed.

"Dan, nice to meet you." Jason offered his hand. Dan's handshake was firm.

"Nice to meet you too, Jason. I'm glad Heather got a new man—I was getting sick of her kidnapping my wife for girls' nights out."

"Oh, sweetheart," Jason said with mischief, "were you a regular barfly? Did I get you off the streets and out of the dives?"

"Ha ha." Heather put her arm around him. "Hardly. More like a movie and Starbucks. But we did see some good chick flicks, didn't we?"

"Yes, and you cried in every one of them," Katie said, laughter in her voice.

"I can't help it if I'm sentimental and have a big heart," Heather shot back.

"That's why I love you." He smelled a burnt odor. "Did you ever get the bread out of the oven?"

"Yikes! No," Heather said, dashing into the kitchen.

"So what's the damage? Do we have any bread?"

"Uh…I think I can slice off the bottom and the rest will be okay," she said sheepishly. "I'm sorry, baby."

"No need to apologize to me, just to our poor guests who are going to go hungry."

"I told you I didn't want to eat your cooking," Katie added.

"Oh, she didn't cook it," Jason explained. "I did. She just had the responsibility of taking it out of the oven."

"Okay you two, stop ganging up on me," Heather said. "I can't have my best friend and my boyfriend against me."

Jason grinned broadly. "Katie, I bet you could tell me some great stories—"

"Don't even think about it!" Heather yelled while giggling. "Keep your mouth shut, Katie."

"Now I think I really know why she hid you." Katie touched Jason's arm. "Not just because of your good looks—because of all the dirt I have on her."

Jason felt some relief that Katie made it so easy to get along with her. He pulled out his cane. "I'm going to go check on the steaks."

"I'll come with you," said Dan.

"Sounds good." Jason reached to open the door and heard Dan open it for him.

"Here you go." Dan stepped out of Jason's way.

"Thanks," Jason mumbled. It bothered him when people took for granted that he couldn't do something simple like open a door. *But he's just trying to be nice. He's trying to help.*

"Wow, these steaks smell incredible. What did you put on them?"

"It's all in the marinade. But I can't tell you what's in it or I'd have to kill you," Jason said with a smile.

"If it's good, I can just find out from Katie. Heather will tell her anything."

"Oh, not my marinade she won't." Jason grinned. "That's a deal breaker." Dan laughed as Jason grabbed for his beer and took a drink. "Do you want a beer, Dan?"

"Sure, I'm never one to turn down a beer."

"I'll be right back with one." Jason turned to head into the house.

"No no no." Dan rushed in front of him. "I'll get it."

"Really, it's no problem." He was trying not to get pissed.

"No, you just stay here. I'll grab one." Dan walked inside the house, leaving Jason fuming. *Calm down—it's nothing personal. He just met you; he doesn't know that he's being ridiculous.*

When Dan came back, he asked, "Do you want to sit down? There's some lawn chairs over here."

"Sure, let's have a seat. I think the steaks have about five more minutes or so."

Dan pulled over the chairs and they both sat down. "So, you're a teacher?" he asked.

"Yeah, I teach high school history. And you?"

"I'm an IT specialist."

"Oh, so you're the guy I can call when I need help with my computer," Jason said with a smile, nodding his head.

"You bet. For you and Heather, free twenty-four-hour technical support." Dan took a swig of his beer. "So Katie says Heather is just crazy about you."

"Good, because I'm crazy about her too." Jason was unable to contain the smile that spread across his face. "She's pretty great."

"She's pretty hot too. She's the best looking of all my wife's friends."

"Yeah, I know I'm a lucky guy." *I might be blind, but I do have hands.* Jason got up and went to the grill, touching the center of the steaks. "I think these are done." He turned off the grill and put the steaks on a large platter.

"Here, let me take that for you." Dan picked up the steaming plate.

"I appreciate your help, but just for the record, I could have carried the steaks in." Jason hoped he didn't sound too harsh.

"I just didn't know—"

"That's all right, I understand. But now you know. When I need help, I'll ask for it. Which doesn't happen often."

"Please don't take it the wrong way. I just wanted to help. I didn't mean to offend you," Dan said, and Jason felt bad that he sounded embarrassed.

"Dan, don't worry." Jason patted him on the back. "I just don't want you to spend all night working your ass off, helping me when I don't need it. "

"Okay man." Dan sounded relieved. "Can we just start over?"

"Do-overs are fine by me." Jason smiled. "Let's eat!"
****

They enjoyed a delicious dinner—the steaks were cooked to perfection and full of flavor, the homemade steak fries were crispy and seasoned just right, the salad and dressing were a perfect match, and Heather was relieved that even the garlic bread worked out.

"I still can't believe I'm eating something other than carryout at Heather's," Katie marveled, savoring her last bite. "I mean, I've eaten here dozens of times over the years, but it's always Chinese takeout or chips and dip."

"I know, I know," Heather said. "But that's why Jason

and I are so great together—we complement each other. I always say I set a great table."

"And you do," Katie said. "It looks beautiful. Great plates, wonderful tablecloth, and I love these napkins, by the way."

"Thank you—Pier One," Heather said. Jason kissed her hand.

"Awww," Katie said. "Dan, look how cute they are together. Remember that, when we were first dating?"

"We're still cute together," Dan objected.

"You most definitely are," Heather agreed.

"Well, thank you. Of course right now I just feel fat." Katie sighed.

"Katie, your belly's not fat," Jason piped in. "It's hard like a basketball." They all laughed.

"You're right about my belly. But I feel like my face is rounder and my butt I'm sure is taking a beating."

Dan leaned over and kissed her. "You look beautiful." Heather could tell by the tender look on his face that his words were heartfelt.

"Well good, because we've still got almost three months to go, so I'm only going to get bigger."

"Well it looks like everyone's done, so I'm going to clean this up." Heather picked up plates. "Then do you guys want to crack open some wine and play Scrabble?"

"Oh, Heather, you're the Scrabble Master. Was that your idea?" Katie asked.

She grinned. "Jason brought it up first, and I was glad he chose my specialty."

"Well it sounds good to me. I just hope you don't get good tiles or we're all screwed." Katie stood up. "Let me help you."

Jason got up as well. "I'll help too." His steps were careful as he made his way to the kitchen, becoming more accustomed to the layout of her house. "Do you want me to load the dishwasher?"

"Sure, I'll rinse them off and you can put them in," Heather said. "I'm opening the dishwasher door now," she alerted him so he wouldn't run into it. "I'll put the rinsed ones on the counter above the dishwasher."

"Okay." Jason reached out and found a plate. He pulled out the bottom rack of the dishwasher and was feeling around for a spot to place it, when Heather noticed him fumbling. He felt around the rack to figure out the placement. His frustration was obvious when he said, "I'm sorry, sweetheart, I know exactly where it would go in my dishwasher, but I haven't loaded this one before."

"It's okay. Do you want me to just load it?"

"I guess you might as well." His tone resounded with defeat. "Do you need me to wash something?"

"I think pretty much everything will go in the dishwasher."

"Oh, I think your trash can is full. Why don't I take out the trash?" Heather could tell he was desperate to look competent, but she wished he could just relax and stop worrying. He seemed so tense all day, a strict departure from the usual laid-back Jason she was used to.

"Well…you don't know where the dumpster is," she said quietly.

"So tell me, and I'll find it." He pushed the trash down in the bag and pulled the bag out of the can. "Is there any more trash to put in here?"

"Yeah, hang on," Dan said. "I've got a beer bottle here."

"Dan, why don't you take out the trash?" Katie said, looking with worry at Heather.

"Jason's got it." Dan shot a look at Katie that said *don't go there.*

Jason opened his cane. "Okay, Heather, so where's the dumpster?"

"Uh…are you sure about this?"

"Yes." He sighed, a look of irritation clouding his face.

"Well, you go out the front door, take the walkway until it stops, then it's straight ahead in the middle of the parking lot. I would guess about one hundred feet."

"I'll be right back." He headed for the front of the

house.

When the door shut behind him, Katie chastised Dan. "Why wouldn't you take the trash out for him?"

"When we were outside I tried to help him with a few things he apparently didn't need help with. So he made it crystal clear he would ask for help if he needs it. I can respect that."

"Yeah, he's pretty independent," Heather said. "So what do you guys think of him?"

"Oh, Heather, he's great. You were right." Katie smiled at her friend. "And when he smiles big—wow, he could light up a room."

"He seems like a good guy, a lot of fun," Dan said.

"He is," Heather said, overjoyed that her friends liked him. "I honestly can't remember being crazier for anyone. And he's just such a good guy. I don't think there's any jerk lurking in there anywhere."

"I can usually sniff out a jerk, and Jason's no jerk," Katie said. "Remember I warned you about Richard—I didn't trust him."

"Yeah, I know. You always did say that about him."

****

Jason walked back to the condo from the dumpster, wondering, *Why does everyone doubt me?* He felt like things were going pretty well, but he didn't want to look like he was helpless, because he wasn't.

Of all the side effects of blindness, that was the one that drove him absolutely crazy. Worse than not seeing or not driving or tapping a damn cane everywhere he went, was the fact that people assumed he was helpless. God, he hated that. And worse yet, he *did* sometimes need help. That pissed him off even more and was responsible for the shotgun-like holes puncturing his self-esteem.

Jason stuck his cane in his pocket as he opened the front door and walked in.

When he reached the kitchen, Heather asked, "Did you find the dumpster okay?"

"Yes," Jason scoffed. "I'm blind. I'm not an idiot." He

couldn't believe she was being condescending to him in front of her friends.

"I know that," Heather said quietly. No one else spoke.

"I'm going to the bathroom. I'll be right back." He turned around and slammed into a wall. "Dammit!" He couldn't think of anything more mortifying or looking more helpless than running into a wall.

Heather rushed to him, putting her hand on his arm. "Are you okay?"

He pushed her away. "Yes, yes, I'm fine." He rubbed his cheek and nose. "Didn't remember that being there." The silence was deafening; he could feel their stares.

"It happens to me all the time," Dan offered.

"No it doesn't," Jason answered, full of anger. He pulled his cane back out of his pocket. "Guys, I'm sorry if I'm a little pissy tonight. I'm just really frustrated. At my house I don't run into things...I know exactly where everything is. I don't use my cane in familiar places because I don't need it. But this is the first time I've been to Heather's, and it's obvious I still need my cane in here." He shook his head. "I just wanted you to see how I really am. I didn't want you to just see me as Heather's blind boyfriend. I guess walking directly into a wall kind of fucked that up."

"No it didn't," Katie said plainly. "It just reminded me that you can't see, because all night long I keep forgetting. And so what?"

"Yeah, so what?" added Dan. "We could care less."

Patting Jason on the back, Katie said, "I just care that you've made my best friend happier than I've ever seen her. So why don't you stop worrying about making a good impression? You already have. And use your cane if you need to. Don't put it away on account of us."

"Well, thanks." Jason sighed. "I'm sorry for being testy. It's not like me." *So now they probably think I'm pathetic* and *an asshole. Why did I have to get so defensive?* "Heather?"

"Yes?" She took his hand.

"I'm sorry for snapping at you and making that rude

comment about finding the dumpster."

"It's okay."

"So, are we ready for a Scrabble showdown?" Katie asked.

"You bet," Heather said. "Jason teased me last night because I'm lousy at poker. But now I will show him my prowess with Scrabble."

"We'll see about that," Jason said. "But first I'm going to the bathroom. And look—my cane is out, so no more body slamming into walls."

****

"That was fun, don't you think?" Heather asked Jason. They waved goodbye to her friends as they drove away.

"Well for you it was—you beat the crap out of us." He squeezed her close.

"You gave me a run for my money though. I had to step it up a bit."

"Your man is no slouch," he said as they walked back into the condo. "Hey, I'm sorry if I embarrassed you with that whole being a jerk and running into a wall thing."

"I just felt bad that you were so frustrated." She looked up at Jason. She was surprised at the side of Jason she saw that day. Irritable, self-conscious, less than the usual confident guy she knew. "But you saw they didn't care."

"I know, you're right—your friends are great. And I love you so much. But can I please go home?" They both laughed.

"Of course, baby." They kissed tenderly. "I shouldn't have asked you to cook and put you in that position in an unfamiliar place and meeting people all at once."

"All's well that ends well. I just want to be somewhere that I don't have to concentrate for a little while."

"That's fine with me, as long as I can stay the night."

"Did you even remotely think I would let you come back home?" He kissed her again. "I loved waking up this morning, feeling your body beside me."

"Yeah, I could get used to cuddling with you all night."

She put her arms around his neck. "I'll go grab a bag and throw some of my things in there."

A flicker of concern flashed across his face. "Sometimes I worry that I'm dreaming, that you're not real."

"Well, if this is a dream, please don't wake me up. Because I'm with the man of my dreams, and I don't want him to disappear."

"I'm not going anywhere, Heather. Not without you."

The smile on his face warmed her heart, and Heather was glad that after a long day of frustration, he seemed like his usual self again. The Jason she'd seen earlier in the day was not easy to get along with. She left the room to grab some things for her overnight stay and thought to herself, *I hope that side of Jason doesn't show up often.*

Chapter Nine

By mid-March, their relationship settled into a comfortable place where Jason felt they knew each other pretty well and neither had scared the other away. Jason loved almost everything about Heather and was amazed to find she wasn't bothered about accommodating his needs. He knew it could sometimes be a hassle, yet nothing seemed to faze her. He figured it was a good sign that seeing her boyfriend running into walls and tripping over things hadn't driven her away. And to his delight, she appeared just as enamored of him as he was of her.

Mark and Angie invited them out to dinner for Jason's birthday. It was obvious Heather had a gift that she was anxious to give him. She had a terrible poker face—which Jason could tell without even seeing it.

They got out of the car at the restaurant, and Jason grabbed hold of Heather's arm, taking in her wonderful scent. Sometimes he felt like a crack addict, desperate for his next whiff of her.

"You know, sweetheart, I don't know if you should be wearing this sexy outfit in public. It clings to every curve."

"Trust me, it looks respectable but sultry."

"Sultry sounds good. And you're really jingly tonight."

"Jingly?"

"Yeah, something's making a jingling sound when you move."

"Oh, those are my earrings dangling. Does the sound bother you?"

"No, not at all. Just don't try sneaking up on me." He laughed. "So you've mentioned my gift a couple of times, like it's something really great. What is it, Braille porn or something?"

"Why do you need porn when you've got me? Step

up."

As they entered Bristol Seafood Grill—one of Jason's favorite restaurants—he imagined they looked good together.

"Look at you two—you look great tonight!" Angie exclaimed when they came walking in the restaurant.

I thought so. "Why thank you." He felt his sister-in-law press up against him in a hug. He hugged back. "Mark?"

"Oh, he's checking to see if our table is ready." Angie pulled away.

Jason heard a low roar of conversation from the other patrons mixed with the sound of light music in the background. And man, it smelled good…his mouth started watering.

"Hey, little brother." Mark slapped Jason on the back as he joined them. "Our table is ready. We've got a corner booth."

They followed the hostess to the high-back booth, which offered a sense of privacy. Not that Jason was planning on staring at his fellow patrons, anyway.

"It's like being in our own little room," Heather whispered to him when they sat down. He felt the starched fabric of the tablecloth.

"Here are your menus." The hostess handed them out. Jason couldn't read it, but knew what he wanted anyway. Surf-n-Turf. Center cut filet with Jumbo Lump Crab Cakes, asparagus and the pièce de résistance: Lobster Mac 'n' Cheese.

Their server came up, took their drink orders and told them the specials.

"Jace," Mark said, "do we want to start with our usual appetizer of fried calamari?"

"Of course," he nodded vigorously as his stomach started to growl. They were all chatting and took their time ordering.

Once they finally ordered, Heather asked, "Can we do presents now?"

"Fine with me," Jason said. "Mark, Angie?"

"Sure," they agreed.

Jason heard a box sliding across the table toward him from Angie. He reached out and grabbed the rather large package. "Okay, I'm going to open Mark and Angie's first, simply because I can tell you can hardly wait," he said to Heather. "Since it's my birthday, I'll enjoy making you suffer for a few more minutes."

"Fine," Heather said, and Jason could hear the pout in her voice.

He opened the gift, a new leather messenger bag and a gift card to his favorite golf course.

"Thank you so much guys." He felt the supple leather. "This is a nice bag. What color is it?"

"It's the color of an old, worn baseball glove," Mark said. "Your other bag has seen better days and instead of another canvas one, we thought we'd upgrade you."

"It's never good when your students have nicer bags than you," Heather quipped.

"True," Jason said. "I can't wait to use it."

"I'll put the box on the floor over here," Angie offered, taking it from Jason.

"Okay, sweetheart." Jason turned to Heather. "I'll put you out of your misery."

"Finally!" she exclaimed, and Jason could hear her digging in her purse.

She placed a large, thick envelope in his hands.

"Well it's not very big," he teased, and then a huge grin spread across his face when his fingers felt familiar raised bumps. "You've got my name in Braille."

"Yeah," she said. "Open it."

He opened the card and found the inside in Braille too. "I can't believe you got me a card in Braille." No one had ever done that for him. "Do you want me to read it out loud?"

"You can."

"All right... *My whole life I wanted a knight in shining armor to rescue me on a white horse and ride away into the sunset. But after years of searching, I began to think I would never find him. Then you*

127

appeared, with your amazing grin and easy laugh and made me feel complete. I wish I knew all those years that instead of a white horse, I was really looking for your white cane. Maybe then I would have found you sooner. So for your birthday, I can think of nothing better than riding into the sunset with you…to Gulf Shores. I have booked a Spring Break trip for two at a beautiful cottage on the beach. Happy Birthday Jason! All my love, Heather."

Quiet for a moment, Jason wiped a tear from his eye on the back of his hand. "I don't know what to say. I don't know what's better—the beautiful words you wrote, the fact that you cared enough to put it in Braille, or the trip. A vacation together? Seriously? That's amazing."

"Well, I know our spring breaks are at the same time, and I remembered you talking about how much you loved Gulf Shores when you were a kid. So I thought…why not go there together?"

"But that must have cost a lot of money—"

"Oh, don't you worry about that," she said, her tone firm. "Now, I know it's hard for you in unfamiliar places—"

"I'll be fine unless you dump me on the beach and take off," he said, smiling broadly again.

"Well, only if you give me a reason to abandon you."

"Me? Never. And as long as you're there with me, I'll be fine. Thank you so much, sweetheart." He opened his arms and she leaned in for a heartfelt hug and a tender kiss. He whispered in her ear, "I love you so much."

"Shit, we only got him a bag and a gift card," Mark said with mock anger.

****

Fourteen days later found them in Heather's car, headed to the Gulf Coast.

Heather was singing along to a Ray LaMontagne song when Jason stirred, catching her attention. He'd been asleep for a couple of hours. She thought he looked cute with his groggy face when he stretched.

She chuckled. "Hello sleepyhead."

He reached over and patted Heather's thigh. "Sorry I

fell asleep on you. Long car rides get a little boring when you can't see the scenery."

"That's okay." She took his hand and kissed it.

"We're almost there. I can smell the ocean."

"You can? I don't smell anything."

"Open up the window for a minute, I bet you can smell it then."

She cracked the window, and then ever so faintly, she caught a whiff of something ocean-like. "I smell it! We only have about an hour until we get to our house. We're staying in the western tip of Gulf Shores in Fort Morgan, so we have to go through the rest of town first."

"I can't wait." A smile spread across his face.

"Oh, we're coming up on the tunnel I read about. After we come out of the tunnel, we'll be getting on the Mobile Bay Bridge. It's supposed to be pretty cool."

"I vaguely remember that from coming here as a kid." The acoustics all around changed. "We're in the tunnel now?"

"Yeah, this is pretty neat. Kind of scary though."

"The sounds are bouncing off everything—it's fascinating. Is the tunnel all lit up?"

"Yeah, it's really bright." They pulled out of the tunnel. "Here's the bay! I'm finally starting to get a reward for all of this damn driving. Oh, Jason, it's beautiful. The sun is just starting to set and there's water all around. It's like we're driving on the ocean."

"Sounds cool...we're finally getting there. And then we can hit the beach."

"Yeah, but the sun's starting to set. I don't know if we can make it out to the beach tonight before it gets dark. And I really, really wanted to get my feet in the ocean."

"Uh, Heather?"

"Yeah?"

"To me, it's always dark at the beach. So you will put your feet in the ocean tonight, only I'll lead this time."

Heather smiled. "Yeah, I guess you can. Walking across a dark beach sounds scary to me, but that's what it's like for you all the time. So I'll hang onto you." She glanced at Jason, a feeling of sadness for him sweeping over her. "I don't know how you can be so confident and self-assured when you're always just walking into…nothingness, everywhere you go."

"Because you get used to it," he said, his voice matter-of-fact. "It's not a big deal. You can get used to anything, Heather. And please don't sound so…sad. That's just a small step to pity. I've never heard you sound that way about me before, and I don't really like it."

"I'm sorry." She looked at him. "But can't I empathize with you or feel sad that you can't see? Because it does make me sad. I wish so badly that you could see the ocean we're driving across, that you could see me. I would love to see you looking back at me."

Jason didn't speak for a minute, and she worried she made him angry.

He faced her. He didn't look angry, but he was often hard to read. "It makes me sad sometimes too. But I can't dwell on that, and I can't have you do that either. Because all it does is drag me down. I spent a year or more fighting anger and sadness—the worst time of my life." His words were quiet and calm, hinting at a deep melancholy. "I can't go back there. And I'm used to the way things are. There's no sense in wishing things were different because they're not, and they won't ever be. So please don't go there. It won't do either of us any good."

"Okay, I'm sorry," Heather said softly. "I will try. But I love you and if only—"

"If you love me, you can't think about the 'if onlys.' That can take us down a really fucked up path, and I've traveled there with women before. Please don't do that to us." His expression was pleading.

"All right." She rubbed his leg.

"I am sorry you're stuck with someone that can't look back at you. That must be hard, never getting the kind of eye contact that we're biologically designed to need. But I hope it's not too much to give up."

"Not at all, baby."

He found her hand and squeezed it. "Tonight we'll walk on the beach together and I'll show you what the ocean looks like to me. You'll see it isn't so bad."

****

Within an hour, they had picked up their key at the rental company's night box and were pulling onto the sand-covered driveway of their rental beach house.

"Oh, I just love it." Heather grinned from ear to ear. "It's so cute. A cozy little beach cottage. And did I tell you it has a hammock?"

"Several times." He smiled as the car came to a stop, but she detected a little apprehension. She figured it was about being in new surroundings for a week. But since it would be just the two of them, at least he wouldn't feel like he had to put on an act for anyone.

When they walked inside, Heather knew it was perfect. Nautical and tropical themes dominated the decor, with wicker furniture, seashells, and candles galore. They found the master bedroom and dropped off their bags and then explored the bungalow together with Heather pointing out what Jason would need to know.

"Any hanging plants I should be aware of?" He grinned.

Heather laughed. "None that I've seen."

"Hey, if it's okay with you, I'd like to head out to the beach now."

"Good, 'cause that's what I want to do too!"

Heather led Jason to the deck stairs and held his hand as they hit the sand. They were both barefoot, and Heather noticed how different his cane sounded when it scraped the sand versus concrete or flooring.

"So did the sun set yet?" he asked.

"Yeah, just a little bit ago. It's pretty dark when we get farther away from the house." Heather grabbed his elbow for guidance.

Jason chuckled. "That's kind of weird for a change, isn't it?"

"Yeah, it is. But I trust you. And there aren't any hanging plants out here." They both laughed. "I see some people down the beach a little bit with flashlights, but they're not supposed to use lights because of the sea turtles nesting."

"Well, they're clearly amateurs. We don't need flashlights." The sound of the waves grew louder as they got closer to the shoreline. "So are there any stars out tonight? Or the moon?"

"The sky is clear, so the stars are twinkling all above. The moon is a tiny crescent." Heather looked behind them. "Our house is just a small, glowing, welcoming little object in the distance."

"I can feel the sand changing under my feet...it's a little more compact the closer we get."

"You're right. Not quite as powdery." They walked through the darkness, up a small embankment and she had complete trust in Jason. Just about thirty feet ahead, the water hit the shore. What little Heather could see of it just looked dark and a little eerie.

"And here we are, sweetheart," Jason said when they had almost reached the water. "Are you ready to get a little wet?"

"Sure." Heather felt wet sand squish between her toes. Just then, the water splashed on their ankles and over their feet. "We're in the ocean! I can't believe it."

Jason stopped, and they stood still. Heather peered into the darkness, catching what she could see of the waves rolling in, but in the dark, she couldn't see much.

"Okay now." Jason turned her face to him. "Close your eyes—I want you to see the ocean like I do."

She closed them, and he felt to make sure.

He pulled her close, and held his arms tight around her. "Okay, keep your eyes closed. Listen closely to the waves as they come in toward us and break. Even though the water is gentle when it reaches us, you can feel its power farther out because of the intensity of the crashing sounds. When the waves get bigger, I can hear the difference."

He remained silent for a moment and let Heather hear for herself. "And feel the sand seeping between your toes...all squishy and grainy."

"I love that feeling." She kept her eyes shut and leaned into Jason.

"Me too." He kissed her temple. "And really focus on the smell. The salt in the air, the faint undertones of fish. Every now and then there's a gentle breeze off the water that floats by and rustles my hair." The wind stirred as if on cue. "Really feel that, how it tickles your face." He stood in silence again for a while. "Isn't it all so amazing? So beautiful? The sound of the surf, the sand beneath our feet, the salty air...even with your eyes closed, isn't it beautiful?"

"It is. Captivating." She snuggled in closer.

"Yes—that's a great word to describe it. You can open your eyes." She did, and saw him smiling with tenderness at her. "I might not see the ocean the same way you do, but it's still breathtaking. Don't you think?"

"I do, Jason. Thank you for showing me that." His interpretation of the ocean amazed her; just paying attention with her eyes closed made her notice so much more. "It really is beautiful, even if you can't see it."

"That's what I tried to say in the car. Just because I can't see something doesn't mean I'm not experiencing and enjoying it. The ocean is just as magnificent to me now as it was sixteen years ago when I could still see some of it."

"I get it. It's different, not necessarily worse, being blind."

"Exactly. So just keep this in mind...remember this night on the beach. Remember how much you saw with your eyes closed."

"I will. And I'll remember this too." She kissed him. Not a tender, gentle kiss... instead passionate and rough, full of fire for him. The romantic mood created by the beach made her desire for him stronger than ever. They pulled away, took a breath, and Jason pulled her towards him and kissed her again with a sensual force that worked them both into a frenzy.

"Okay," he said, breathless, "we either head back to the house or I take you right here in the sand."

"I don't want sand in my...uh...region." She kissed his neck.

"You know it drives me crazy when you do that." He pulled away. "Since you don't want sand in your hoo-ha, we're heading back. Now." He abruptly turned.

She grabbed hold, and their steps were quick while they headed back to the house.

****

By day two they had their routine down pat. Wake up, make love, hop in the shower and eat a quick breakfast of bagels or cereal on the deck. Then they threw on their swimsuits, loaded up a cooler with some drinks, grabbed their beach bag, and headed out to the surf.

They spent another relaxing day lounging on the beach. Jason woke up in the late afternoon after dozing on his beach towel. His head felt thick with the heaviness of napping in the middle of the day. He slowly shed the fog of drowsiness and reached out to Heather's towel next to him...empty.

"Heather?" He sat up. No answer. He raised his voice and called out, "Heather?"

"I'll be right there," she hollered from way up at the house.

He opened the cooler next to him and took out a Corona. After taking a swig, he stuck it back in. The thud of Heather's footsteps in the compact sand approached, accompanied by a squeaking sound he couldn't identify.

"What do you have?" Jason stood up and stretched.

"An inner tube and a raft. We just need to blow them up. I noticed a storage area under the house, so I opened it up and found these."

"Sweet. Let's get some air in them and do some floating."

They each blew one up. Jason heard several voices from the house next door. Mainly men, a couple of women.

He heard a smacking sound from time to time. "Are they playing volleyball next door again?"

"Yeah," Heather said, taking a break from blowing up the raft. "One of the guys is coming our way."

"Hey! I'm Craig," the neighbor said when he came closer.

"I'm Jason." He waved.

"And I'm Heather."

"Do you guys want to join us?" Craig asked.

"Oh, no thanks." Jason smiled. "Go ahead if you want to, Heather."

"No, but thanks for the offer." Heather smiled. "Looks like fun. But we're just going to float for a bit."

"That sounds good too," Craig said. A gentle smack, smack sound told Jason that Craig was tossing the ball back and forth between his hands. "Well, if you want to later, just come on over."

"Sure thing." Jason held up a beer. "Do you want a drink?"

"No, I'm still trying to recover from last night. Had a few too many." He chuckled. "But thanks. Well, I'll see you guys later."

"See ya." Jason heard the sound of his footsteps in the sand fade away. "Heather, I really don't mind if you want to go over and play."

"No, I don't want to." She did not convince Jason at all. He hated to think she would miss out on something in an effort to protect his feelings, but he loved that she cared that much about him.

"You're not a good liar." He started blowing up the inner tube again. Pinching it shut with his fingers he added, "Just because I can't play doesn't mean you shouldn't. I don't want to keep you from having fun."

"I want to float with you, okay?" Heather grabbed his hand. "Okay?"

"Well, good," he said with a broad smile. "But if you want to play later or some other day, do."

"I'll keep that in mind."

Within minutes, they were floating in the Gulf, their watercraft bouncing them over the waves. They held hands...Jason imagined that in the vastness of the ocean, they must look like two little dots hanging onto each other in the turbulence of the waters.

****

The next morning, Tuesday, they ate English muffins on the screened-in porch and Heather announced, "I just thought of a great idea!"

"Well, let's hear it." Jason took a sip of coffee.

"As much as I enjoy lounging on the beach for hours, we need to mix it up today."

"I agree. What do you have in mind?"

"Biking. Wouldn't that be fun?"

He chuckled, shaking his head. "Umm...I don't think I'm very good at steering around objects."

"I meant a tandem bike, knucklehead." She watched for his reaction.

He raised his eyebrows. "A tandem bike? Well, I guess that might work...."

"Of course it will work." Heather climbed on his lap, facing him. "Why wouldn't it?"

"Can I be in front?" Jason grinned.

"Not a chance in hell," she said with a giggle. "So do you want to?"

"Sure, we can give it a shot. It sounds like fun." Heather hopped up to find a bike rental place online.

****

An hour later, Heather buckled on her helmet. "Do you need help with that?" she asked while Jason fiddled with his.

"No, I've got it." Jason wiggled it to make sure it was snug.

"Okay, come with me." She put his hand on her elbow. They walked a few feet across the driveway. "The bike is bright yellow with whitewall tires. Here's your seat and handlebars. But I better get on first. I'll let you know when I'm on... Okay, climb on."

For the first time in nearly twenty years, Jason sat on a bike. He held onto the handlebars and sat on the seat, his feet still on the ground. "Wow, it seems like a lifetime since I've been on a bike."

"Well, you know what they say, you never forget how to ride a bike. Are you ready?"

"Yeah, I'm ready."

"Okay, let's go on the count of three. One, two, three!" And they were off—a little wobbly at first, but steadier after the first minute or two.

"Woo hoo!" Jason hollered at the top of his lungs. They pulled onto Alabama 180. "This is incredible." The wind rushed at him. The rattle of the bike chain and the hum of the tires crunching against the pavement all came back like a long forgotten dream. If Heather could have turned around to look at him, she'd have seen the biggest, widest, brightest smile on his face.

"So I guess you like it?" Heather yelled back to him.

"God, yes! This is a blast. I forgot how much fun riding a bike is."

They road for about twenty minutes before Heather said, "I need to take a break. There's some shade up ahead." When they stopped, Heather snapped some pictures of them with the bike. A soon as she finished, Jason put his arms around her and gave her a huge squeeze.

"I owe you this." He gave her a tender kiss.

"Well, that was nice," Heather said. "Why do you owe me that?"

"For having this great idea to ride bikes and finding a way for me to do something I haven't done for so long." He couldn't stop smiling. "This is so much fun. Thank you."

"Oh, you're welcome, baby. I had a feeling you would like it." She took a gulp of water and handed the bottle to him. "You know what I want to do with one of those pictures we just took?" Heather sounded inspired.

"What?"

"Put it on your mantel to replace the one of you and

your ex."

"Sweetheart, that would be perfect."

****

On Wednesday morning, Jason awoke to the sound of gentle showers outside. The smell of the rain, along with the sea air, created a fascinating combination. They'd slept with the windows open, so he climbed out of bed to check and see if the rain was coming in. It wasn't, so he crawled back into bed.

He could hear Heather's deep breathing next to him. Jason snuggled up to her, delighting in the feel of her silky skin next to his. He didn't feel tired, but he hated to leave her side. She seemed so much more vivid to him, more real and tangible, when their bodies were entwined. It was when he felt he could really see her in some way. So he just lay there next to her, stroking her back with gentle touches and taking her all in. Her distinct smell, the softness of her skin, the curves of her body...it all mesmerized him.

How could I be so lucky? How could this gorgeous creature want me? It seemed too good to be true. She was so patient, sweet, and kind. She made him laugh and pushed him to be even more than he dreamed. He wanted to be more for her. But his strong feelings for her terrified him. He felt so vulnerable, because he'd never let himself get that intensely close to anyone before.

She could destroy him, and he knew that. But that was also part of the allure.

"What are you doing?" Heather whispered, startling him.

"Gazing at you," he said with a smile, his voice soft. "So to speak."

"Good morning, baby." Her warm lips placed a tender kiss on his cheek.

"Good morning." He almost hated to speak, hated to ruin the quiet moment of experiencing her in slumber. "Have I told you how much I truly love you?"

"No, you haven't." A drowsy scratchiness filled her voice.

"Well, it's a lot," Jason whispered. He wanted to say so much more, because he felt so much more. But he couldn't find the words to explain what he felt.

"Well, I love you right back." She hugged him. "What's wrong? You seem sad."

"No, not sad. It's just scary to love someone as much as I love you. I keep waiting for something bad to happen."

"Well, don't. Sometimes there are happily ever afters."

"You think so?"

"I certainly hope so." Both quiet for a moment, Heather reassured him with a squeeze of his hand. "So what's on the agenda for today?"

"Well, I really want to see the old Civil War fort, Fort Morgan, before we leave. That's where the famous quote 'Damn the torpedoes. Full speed ahead!' comes from."

"I didn't know that."

"Yep. And as a history teacher, I'd be remiss if I didn't visit the site."

"Yes, you would."

"I don't care when we go, I just want to make it there before we leave."

"Well, why don't we go this morning after breakfast if the rain stops? Then we'll have the whole afternoon to lounge on the beach."

"That works for me."

Jason enjoyed checking out Fort Morgan. Being there in person to take the tour excited him, even though he already knew a lot about the fort. Before they left, he picked up some classroom literature and a T-shirt. History heaven.

Later that afternoon, the skies cleared and they played outside in the surf. They floated on the raft and inner tube, baked in the sun, and napped. Eventually their neighbors came out and starting playing volleyball again while Jason and Heather lay on their beach towels—Heather reading and Jason listening to an audio book.

"I'm a little bored out here today," Heather commented. "I can only read and nap so much."

"Do you want to go do something?" Jason paused the book, content just lying there.

"Nah. I might get in the water in a little bit."

A few minutes later, Craig yelled over to them, "Hey, Jason! Heather! Why don't you come join us? We could use some more players. Sam is still inside, hung over."

"No thanks," Heather hollered back.

"Heather, why don't you go play?" Jason urged her.

"I don't want to." Her voice was quiet.

"Yes, you do. You just said you were bored."

Heather sighed. "Are you sure you don't mind?" The concern in her voice nearly broke his heart. She was so considerate, but he knew he couldn't hold her back because of his disability.

"I don't mind." He smiled, trying to convince both of them.

"Well, okay then." She kneeled over and kissed him. "Thank you, baby. Hey, Craig," she shouted, "I'll play!" She ran off across the sand to join them.

****

"I'm glad you're gonna play with us," said Craig when she got closer. He introduced her to everyone. Heather figured them to be in their early twenties, and Craig was a pretty buff guy, along with a couple of his buddies. "Doesn't Jason want to play?"

"Uh, no, he's just relaxing."

"I get the impression he doesn't like me for some reason. I waved at him yesterday and he didn't wave back or say anything."

"Oh." Heather crossed her arms. "He didn't mean to be rude...he just didn't see you."

"He saw me—he looked right at me. And kept staring at me after that."

"Actually, Craig, he didn't see you—he's blind." Dead silence followed while everyone stared at her. She hated that...she hated that Jason was never just her boyfriend; he was always a source of fascination and curiosity.

"No shit?" He looked completely shocked. "Wow, I

didn't see that coming. Here I thought he was just being a jerk. Weird."

"Like totally blind?" A guy named Steve asked.

"Uh, yeah. Totally." It embarrassed her that they were making such a big deal out of it. She figured she better get used to it, though…people would always have reactions to his blindness. "But enough of that. Let's play volleyball!"

And they did. Heather had a blast. She'd been a teenager the last time she played volleyball, and although she wasn't very good, she had a lot of fun just trying. Her older brother used to throw volleyball parties in their back yard and this brought back those fun memories.

****

Jason checked the time on his phone: four-sixteen. Heather had been playing volleyball for over an hour. He started to get irritated when he overheard their banter.

"Good shot, Craig!" he heard Heather yell, followed by what sounded like a high five.

A couple of minutes later he heard Craig say, "Oh, nice one, Heather! See, you're getting the hang of it."

"Thanks," she responded cheerily.

Jason didn't like the tone of her voice. It sounded fun and flirty, the way she talked to him when they first met. He knew she wouldn't strike up a romance with this guy or anything, but he still didn't like it. He heard some hoots and hollers back and forth, and with each one he grew angrier and more jealous. *I should be there playing with her. I should be high-fiving her.*

"I got it," Heather shouted.

Craig hollered, "Look at that dive! You looked like Misty May. Awesome!"

With that, Jason's jealousy became too much. He couldn't stand it anymore. So he fumbled in the beach bag, found his cane and flicked it open. Then he stormed off toward the house.

After he made it about halfway to the house, Heather yelled, "Jason! Jason, what are you doing?"

He heard her but kept walking, his pace brisk while he

141

practically beat the sand with his cane.

"Man, it's too bad he can't play," he heard Craig say. "Serve!"

With every step he took, Jason became more enraged. "This is bullshit," he muttered under his breath. All his insecurities as a man and his irritation at his limitations boiled over and erupted when he reached the deck.

"God damn it!" He swung his cane with both hands like a bat, hitting one of the deck's poles. The cane snapped. He threw it as hard as he could on the ground.

"Fuck!" he seethed. "Fuck, fuck, fuck!" *That was stupid. Now I'm really screwed.*

He raced up the steps and made his way to the bedroom, feeling pieces of furniture and walls to guide his way. He threw himself on the bed and screamed into the pillow while his rage overcame him. Why did he get stuck with these shitty eyes? It was just a stupid volleyball game, but it wasn't fair that some other guy got to enjoy playing it with his girlfriend.

And it would always be like this. He couldn't hold her back; that would be selfish and unfair to her. But he didn't like it when he couldn't do something with her. It pissed him off. It never bothered him this much before, but he'd never felt so strongly for someone.

He heard the deck door open but stayed face down on the bed.

Heather's footsteps approached the bedroom and she called out, "Jason? Are you okay?" She stood in the doorway.

"Yeah, just leave me alone right now, okay?" His voice shook with anger.

"But what's wrong? Did I do something wrong?" She walked toward him.

"No, just leave me alone. Trust me, I'm an asshole right now."

"What happened to your cane?"

He groaned. "I smashed it, that's what happened to it. Just fucking get out of here. Go do something. I need to be alone."

"But what did I do? Is it because I was playing volleyball—"

He pounded his fist in the pillow. "You didn't do anything wrong, okay? I love you and I'm sorry, but I can't do this right now. Please, please give me some space so I can get my head screwed on straight." He practically shouted at her.

"Okay," she said, and Jason could hear the confusion and tears in her voice. "I'll go into town and get some souvenirs." He heard her open a drawer, and he figured she was getting some clothes on. "You're scaring me, Jason. Are you sure you're okay to be alone?"

"Yes. I'll see you later." He turned back into the pillow.

When he heard the front door shut behind her, he punched the pillow over and over again. He didn't know what to do with his uncontrolled rage. Defeated, he buried his face in the pillow, not moving. Yet his mind raced, a jumbled mess. He couldn't focus on anything in particular, just feelings of anger and hurt and pity. Self-pity. It consumed him, and he wasn't sure why. More than thirty minutes passed before he sat up and held his head in his hands.

"Okay, Scharp," he said out loud. "Get a grip. You need to stop feeling sorry for yourself and regroup."

Mark's ringtone chimed from Jason's phone. He ignored it. A minute later he got a text message.

He found the phone and checked the message from Mark: *Call me back. Heather called me & we're worried about you. Don't make me call the authorities.*

"Oh fuck." He sighed. "Can't I have a temper tantrum by myself?" He called Mark.

"Jace, what's going on?" His brother's concern rang out in his voice.

"Oh…I don't know. I'm just feeling sorry for myself, which I hate, which makes me even more pissed."

"Well, what happened? Heather called me, crying,

saying you stormed into the house and that you smashed up your cane and started yelling."

"She shouldn't have called you. I just…I just lost it for a little bit. I'm trying to calm down now."

"Why? What set you off to feel sorry for yourself? That's not like you."

"I know it's not…" His voice trailed off. "It was stupid. I encouraged her to play volleyball next door, but the more I listened to them having fun and interacting, the more pissed I got. Jealous, really. I just want to be able to play with her. Not those guys. I'm her boyfriend, and it sucks that my body keeps me from doing the things I want with her. So I guess a lot of bottled up emotions just got the better of me."

"Kind of like when your eyesight started getting really bad and you'd get upset when we couldn't include you in everything?"

"Yeah, kind of like that." Jason remembered those times…being excluded from backyard football scrimmages and video games and other things he once loved to do. When he first went blind, it sometimes felt like instead of being disabled, he had been robbed. "I don't know why it's bothering me so much. I guess because it makes me feel like less of a man, and I'm afraid she'll feel that way too."

"Oh, come on, Jace," Mark said firmly. "She loves you for who you are. It doesn't matter that you can't play volleyball. You never even liked volleyball." He chuckled.

"You're right, I didn't." Jason grinned in spite of himself. "It's just…I think she's the one for me, and I guess that's why it makes me so fucking mad that I can't be the man I want to be for her."

"You think she's the one, huh? Well that can scare the shit out of any man."

Jason sighed. "I just wish—"

"Stop right there, Jason," Mark commanded. "You told me years ago not to wish for things that are never going to change. You told me you couldn't do that and you didn't want me to do it, either."

"You're right." Jason lay back on the bed.

"Did you ever think of this? Maybe if you could see, you would have been afraid to ask out such a pretty girl. But you didn't know what she looked like, so you went for it. You're a blind guy, Jason. It's made you who you are. Maybe you'd be just another bastard if you could see. But I think you try harder and work harder and care more because relationships matter to you a lot. I think we're better brothers because of it."

"Really?"

"Really. She loves you, Jace. I can tell. Just claim temporary insanity."

"Okay," Jason said with a laugh. "Thanks bro."

"Anytime. You okay?"

Jason sighed. "Yeah, I'm good."

"Then my work here is done. Enjoy the beach!"

Jason put the phone down and sat up. His fingers traced the stitching on the bedspread as he listened to the comforting sounds of the waves outside, along with the occasional song of a seagull.

"Okay, Jace," he said out loud. "So you're blind. There will be things you can never do with Heather. Deal with it."

He got up and headed for the kitchen, determined to attempt a peace offering of a nice dinner. Turning on some Bob Marley tunes to suit the beach vibe, his mood lightened as he started cooking, even though working in the unfamiliar kitchen was like some torturous game on a reality show called *Find the Spatula—Blind Guy Edition*.

He knew he could learn to live with not being a typical boyfriend—and he better, because he didn't have a choice. She didn't seem to mind so far, so maybe she'd be okay with it too.

Besides, he figured being "normal" was probably overrated.

****

When Heather opened the door on her return from shopping, she didn't know what to expect. But she didn't expect what she saw.

145

Bob Marley music blared, and Jason sang along in the kitchen while he cooked. He turned in her direction when she walked in.

"Hi, sweetheart." He wore a sheepish grin.

"Hi," she said with an anxious tone, still fragile from their earlier encounter.

He patted a barstool. "Please come here." He turned down the music. She took a seat, and he sat down next to her, taking her hands in his own. "I am so so sorry for losing it like that. That's not like me."

"Well, what happened?" She was still unsure.

"Remember the other day on the trip here, and I told you we couldn't think about the 'if onlys'?"

She nodded. "Yes."

"Well I did. I shouldn't have, but I went there, and it brought up a lot of shit deep inside me. And I wanted you to leave, because I didn't want you to see me that way. Self-pity is not a pretty sight."

"I knew I shouldn't have played volleyball with them." She shook her head. "But you pushed me to. I thought you wanted me to."

"Are you looking at me?"

"Yes." She stared intently into his vacant eyes.

"You did nothing wrong. Nothing. I did urge you to play with them because I knew you wanted to. And it's okay that you did. I just…I just got jealous and angry because I wished I could play with you."

"I shouldn't have been so insensitive—"

"No!" he yelled. "That's what I'm trying to say to you. It's not your fault. Please understand that. There are lots of things you can do and should do that I cannot. So what? We're different people. We have different skills, different abilities. You can't cook, but I love to. You love Shakespeare—I can barely understand it. But the one thing we both have is a great love for each other. Unless I ruined that today by showing you an ugly side of me—"

"No, you didn't ruin anything. You just scared me." His earlier rage left her shaken still.

"I'm sorry, sweetheart." He squeezed her hands. "I just had to let some stuff go."

"What stuff?"

"Insecurities, fear." He looked down.

"Fear of what?"

"That you will leave. I've been burned in the past, and I worry you'll get tired of being with a blind man. That you'll want your old life back—the one that doesn't involve the nuisances of dating someone that can't see. And when you were playing volleyball, it sounded like you were having a lot of fun, which makes me wonder if you're thinking 'Wow, so nice to do something without dealing with all of Jason's bullshit.'"

"Jason, you put up with my hassles too. You are always the one who cooks because I can't. I take a long time to get ready and always make us late…we all have our hassles. So loving someone means taking the bad with the good. And I love you."

Jason's smile was grateful. "I love you too, Heather. And I'm so sorry."

"It's okay. I understand what was going through your mind now. But please don't worry about us."

"I'm really trying not to." He leaned forward and kissed her. "I could use some help finding my way around in this kitchen—can you help me with dinner?"

"Sure, as much as I can." She laughed. "Hey, what are you going to do about your cane?"

"Oh, yeah, that. Not one of my finer moments, eh?"

"No comment." Heather grinned at him.

"Well, believe it or not, Amazon actually sells them so I already ordered one and I'm having it sent next-day air. It will be here Friday."

"Wow, Amazon really does sell everything, don't they?"

"Pretty much. So…I hate doing this and I'm sorry I have to ask, but can you be my guide tomorrow?"

"Well, of course. What did you think I would do? Make you sit in the house all day?"

"Well I hoped not, but seeing how I'm the moron that smashed my own mobility device, I wouldn't blame you."

"I'm not saying I might not run you into things by accident…"

"Oh, oh I see how you are." Jason laughed. "Oops, didn't mean to run you into that wall. Oh, sorry, didn't mean to let you fall down those stairs." They laughed together.

"I'm just saying it could happen. Be prepared." Heather relaxed, realizing how tense she had been. "I'll be back to help in just a minute."

She stepped into the bedroom and sent off a quick text message to Katie: *He's fine now. Long story. U were right; this relationship's not going to be easy. But I really think he's worth it. Don't u?*

After a minute or two her phone lit up with Katie's reply: *Not for me to decide. U have to decide what u can deal with. Call me later if you want. XO*

Heather exhaled loudly, and stared up at the ceiling, her eyes tracing some small cracks above. Another sigh escaped and she whispered, "But I love him so much."

Chapter Ten

Over the next couple of days, Jason's episode became a distant memory. They thoroughly enjoyed hiking in the Bon Secour nature preserve. On a rainy day they caught a movie and on Friday went to The Track amusement park to ride go-karts. Not sure if the staff would be too keen on letting a blind guy drive, Heather climbed in the driver's seat, but let Jason steer from the passenger seat while she worked the gas pedal. He had a blast keeping it between the guardrails as she shouted, "A little to the right...now left! More left! Straighten it out...now right!"

For their last night in Gulf Shores, Jason suggested they have a little picnic and watch the sunset. Heather thought it was a perfect idea.

Jason cranked up some Jimmy Buffett tunes while they got their sunset picnic snacks together. The wine chilled in a bucket and Heather found a basket to fill with fruit, cheese and crackers. They made a nice little picnic area outside near the water and cracked open the wine.

Heather took a sip. "Delicious. Good choice."

"Yeah, I thought you would like that since you prefer sweeter wines." Jason had his arm around her. They faced the ocean. He turned on a romantic playlist he'd made that he knew Heather would appreciate. "Your Body is a Wonderland" by John Mayer floated quietly through the air. "So is the sun starting to set yet?"

"It is. I was just looking at how beautiful it looks out there with the water against the setting sun."

"Please describe it to me," he whispered.

"The sun looks like a ball of fire, bright molten orange in the center. Coming out from it are intense pinks near the center and then it fades out to fingers of pink pastels against a darkening blue sky. It looks like the sun is just barely hanging above the ocean, getting ready to pass below it."

"Sounds gorgeous." He squeezed Heather. "Thank you."

"You're welcome, baby." They sat together in a comfortable silence and Jason enjoyed the feeling of Heather leaning into him. He was relieved his pity tantrum earlier in the week seemed to be forgotten.

She rested her head on his shoulder and described the sun continuing its slow, dramatic descent. Her low voice was soft as she painted a mental picture for Jason in between sips of wine and bites of cheese. He didn't say anything, just held her close with his eyes closed.

"And the sun is virtually gone now….just the faintest hints of orange and a smattering of pale pink left behind."

"Your descriptions were so good," he said, breaking his silence. "I could visualize the sun while it set. I felt like I could really see it with you."

"Good." She kissed his cheek.

"I'm glad you're an English teacher. That probably helps. If you were a math teacher, the most I'd get out of you is a formula or algorithm here and there."

"Is that why you're with me?" she asked playfully. "For my descriptive words? Are you a description whore?"

"Actually, I'm with you because I need a ride from time to time."

"Oh, shut up." She giggled.

"That, and you smell good."

****

Heather returned home the next night at around eight-thirty after dropping Jason off at his place. She lugged her heavy bag up the front step and noticed a covered vase on the little porch.

"What in the world?" she said out loud.

She put down her bag and grabbed the flowers, tearing off the wrapping to expose a dozen beautiful yellow and apricot colored roses. She grabbed the card and opened the envelope.

Heather,

I can't thank you enough for the best vacation of my life. The sand, the sun, the surf and the love of my life. What more could I ask for?

Yours,

Jason

Heather smiled as her eyes grew misty. *I could get used to this.*

Just then, her neighbor's door across the porch opened—Mrs. Brown.

"I thought I heard something out here," Mrs. Brown said. "Oh, you got flowers. How lovely."

"Thank you." Heather admired the bouquet.

"I think he's a keeper, even though he can't see a damned thing," she muttered, turning back toward her door. "Tell that blind boy of yours I said well done."

Heather could hardly believe what she heard. But she figured that once you're in your eighties, you can pretty much say whatever you want and get away with it. And in her odd, offensive way, Mrs. Brown had complimented Jason.

"Uh...I will, Mrs. Brown." Heather unlocked her door. She took the flowers and her bag inside, then called Jason right away.

"Aren't you sick of me yet?" he answered.

"Oh, you are so sweet, Jason." She smiled.

"Whatever do you mean?"

"You know what I'm talking about. The flowers are beautiful, just gorgeous."

"I'm glad you like them."

"I love them. It's been years since anyone got me flowers. Thank you, baby."

"Well thank you for the trip."

"It feels funny without you. I miss you already."

"You too, huh?" He chuckled. "Glad I'm not the only one feeling lonely right now."

"So when can I see you tomorrow?"

"What time are you getting up?"

"Why don't I call you when I wake up?" Heather suggested. "I just need to throw some laundry in and shower, and then I'll come over."

"How about you bring your laundry over here, and we'll do ours together? And I can make breakfast."

"Mr. Scharp, are you proposing that we mix our unmentionables together?"

"Yes, I believe that I am. Do you think our relationship has reached the point that our underwear can cohabitate in the washer?"

Heather could picture an adorable grin on his face as she climbed into her bed. "I think it has, my dear," she said with a laugh, followed by a yawn. She was exhausted.

As much as she hated to admit it, it taxed her to be "on" all the time for Jason when they were in new surroundings. Tonight she wouldn't be looking for steps or obstacles or describing anything to anyone. It would be nice to only be responsible for herself. She could really, truly relax.

"Sounds like you need to go to bed. Sweet dreams."

She was already asleep.

****

The week after their trip, things got back to their normal routine, with one exception. Heather announced the next weekend that she was abandoning Black Amethyst for her spring and summer scent, Bali Mango.

"No more Black Amethyst?" Jason asked with disappointment.

"Nope. Sorry. It will now be Bali Mango. It's a lighter, more summery fragrance."

"Well, shit, I won't even recognize you anymore." He chuckled.

"You'll get used to the new one. It will be like a sighted guy when a girl changes her hair color. It's like a whole new woman. You'll feel like you've got a new gal."

"I guess, but I like the one I've got." He fondled her breast and grinned.

"Well, I'll be the same except for the way I smell."

The next morning they were getting ready to meet Mark and Angie for golf when Jason caught a whiff of her new perfume. "Excuse me, miss, but have you seen my girlfriend? She's a beautiful girl that looks like Susan Sarandon and smells like this great fragrance called Black Amethyst."

"Ha ha." She nudged him. "Very funny. So you don't like the way this one smells?"

"Oh, sweetheart, I'm just kidding." He reached out and found her shoulder, giving it a squeeze. "You smell good. Just not like I'm used to. Give it a few days, and it will start to smell like Heather."

"Okay. In the meantime, I am a mysterious sexy woman, you naughty boy."

"Ooh, I like that. But my girlfriend's not gonna be happy about it."

"All right, smart ass, let's hit the road," she said.

Jason laughed, pleased with himself. "You want me to go with you? Because my girlfriend will really not like that." He laughed even harder and grabbed their golf bags at the front door.

"Stop!" she insisted, but he loved the giggle that colored her voice.

They arrived at their ten o'clock tee time with Mark and Angie. Jason was looking forward to his first game of golf with Heather.

When their golf carts stopped at the first tee, they were joking and laughing.

"So, what do you need me to do as your partner?" Heather asked Jason while they walked to the back of the cart.

"Basically, function as my eyes and tell me what I need to know to make the shot," he said, finding his clubs. "For instance, I've played this course before but it's my first time in months, so I need a refresher. How many yards?"

"Umm…326 yards."

"Par four?" he asked, selecting his club.

"Yes."

"Okay, I remember the layout of this hole, but if I don't know, then I'll need you to describe it to me."

"I can do that." Heather pulled out her club.

"And of course you'll need to guide me, since I'm not using my cane out here. Oh, and you need to watch where my ball lands so you can find it."

"Wow, I think I'm going to charge for my services."

"Maybe I could make you a nice dinner?"

"You were going to do that anyway. Nice try."

"Screw it, I'll have Mark coach me—he's free." Jason grinned.

"Okay, I'll give you the girlfriend discount. It's gonna cost you a kiss."

"I can definitely afford that." He leaned in, kissing her. "And I can't forget to tip you." Jason kissed her again.

"Hey hey hey," Mark objected. "Is this a make-out session or are we playing golf?"

"Sorry, just paying my coach." Jason took hold of Heather's elbow and nudged her to approach the tee. He took a couple of practice swings to loosen up, noticing the distinct aroma of freshly cut grass and feeling the warmth of the sun beating down on the left side of his face.

"Aren't you playing, Angie?" Heather asked.

"Oh no, I'm just along for the ride," Angie said with a smile. "Sports aren't exactly my thing."

"Shopping is her thing," Mark joked. "She could win a gold medal for that." They all laughed.

"All right, Heather." Jason took a tee and ball out of his pocket. "I need you to point me in the right direction when I tee up."

"Okay, baby," she replied, putting her hands on his hips. "I'm going to turn you just a smidge." She twisted him a bit. "That looks good."

"Here goes nothing." Jason whacked the ball. The distinctive sound of club hitting ball made a pleasant *ping!* in his ears. "Well it felt good, but how does it look?"

"Wow, Jace, nice one." Mark slapped his brother on the back. "It landed on the edge of the greens. You might get a birdie on this one."

"Thanks." Jason held his hand out. "Heather?"

"Right here." She took his hand and placed it on her arm. "That was impressive."

"Well, I'm no Tiger Woods, but I'm decent." They walked away from the tee. "Who's next?"

"I'm teeing up," Mark said. Jason heard the swish of Mark's club slicing through the air and then—*ping!* "I might have got a little bit past you Jason, but they're close."

"Good shot, dear," Angie said.

"Okay, I'm up." Heather's voice was unsure. "Jason, remember I told you I wasn't good at golf? Well for once, I'm glad you can't see."

Jason laughed. "Endorsing my blindness for your own personal needs. Nice."

"Well…" She giggled as she set up for the shot and then took a swing.

"I heard you hit the ball, that's a start." Jason leaned on his golf club. "So…?"

"I hit it straight, that's good. Just not very far."

"Oh, you did fine," Mark said. "Let's go!"

****

The rest of the game went pretty much the same, with Mark edging out Jason for the lead and Heather lagging behind quite a bit. But she felt better when the guys complimented her on a good first job of coaching Jason. Mark helped too, teaching Heather what she needed to do, since he had years of experience assisting his brother. Heather was amazed at Jason's skill level. And he seemed to thrive on the physical aspect of the sport.

They enjoyed drinks and lunch at the clubhouse after their round of golf. Jason's hand rested on Heather's thigh while they sat at the table, chatting after finishing their meals.

He leaned into her, whispering, "I like this little golf skirt on you."

"Well, I figure I better look good because my game is so bad."

"Oh, sweetheart, you weren't that bad." He touched her arm.

"You can't even see the ball or the course and you killed me. But it's all about having fun, and I had a great time."

"Well, good, because I like golfing with you."

"Me too, baby." Heather looked at his handsome, boyish face. His blank eyes faced her, and she yearned so badly to see him looking back. For their eyes to connect, to be seen by him. She missed that more than she expected. Such a small thing but an important aspect of a relationship that she'd always taken for granted. She felt cheated.

Mark cleared his throat. "Can we interrupt you two lovebirds for a minute?"

"If you must," Jason said.

Heather smiled at Mark, shrugging off the sadness that hung over her.

Mark put his arm around Angie. "Jason, Heather—we want to share some news with you."

"What?"

"Well, Jace," Mark said with a huge grin, "you're going to be an uncle!"

"Seriously?" Jason's voice displayed disbelief. "Angie—you're pregnant?"

"Yes, I am," she gushed.

"Oh congratulations!" Heather cried out.

Jason stood up. "Ang, this calls for a hug." They embraced, and she giggled with joy. "This is amazing. Mark, good job! High five?" He held his hand up in the air, and Mark smacked it. "I am so excited for you both. I know you've been trying for so long. Here I finally found a woman to put up with me, and now my big brother's gonna be a daddy. Things are definitely looking up for the Scharp boys."

Chapter Eleven

It was the beginning of May, and Jason was glad they only had three more weeks of their night class left. He looked forward to freeing up those two nights a week, and then just one week after that, work was over for the summer.

In the morning Jason walked to the bus stop and his mind rushed with thoughts of all the fun they would have over the summer. No work, just playtime with his girl.

Midway through the day, he got a text from Heather saying she didn't feel well and wouldn't be going to class that night. After the lecture, he rushed to her place in a cab and found that she was getting worse, not better.

Based on where the pain was, Jason thought it sounded like appendicitis. He found some of her clothes, helped her dress, and called Mark to take them to the hospital. It frustrated him that he couldn't just drive his own girlfriend to the hospital, and he was irritated again when he had to ask Mark to fill out all the forms. But he had stepped up and done everything he could to take care of her, and he tried to convince himself he was okay with that.

Now he sat alone, clinging to a paper coffee cup with *The Tonight Show* blaring from a TV in the corner, while the doctor performed an emergency appendectomy on Heather. Nearly as nerve-wracking for him was the fact that he would be meeting her mother, Linda, for the first time. He'd called her a half hour earlier to let her know, and she was on her way.

When she asked how she'd find him, he'd chuckled and answered, "It's a pretty good bet I'm the only guy in the waiting room with a long white cane."

While he waited, it dawned on him that he needed to

line up substitutes for both of them for the next day. He contacted their principals and then tried to relax. He sat drinking his coffee, fixing his eyes in the direction of the TV. Boredom, nerves, and exhaustion claimed him.

He heard light footsteps coming down the hall and onto the carpeted waiting room area.

"Jason?" an older version of Heather's voice asked.

"Mrs. Marx?" He stood up.

"Oh, please call me Linda. Give me a hug." She embraced Jason. "Thank you so much for calling me."

"Well, Heather said hospitals are difficult for you so she didn't want to call. But once they decided to operate, I thought you'd want to know."

"I'm so glad you called. Of course I want to be here for her."

"I have to say, your voice is so similar to Heather's...it's uncanny."

"You know, I never thought about that, but I guess we do sound alike."

Jason gestured to the empty seat next to his. "Please take a seat. Would you like some coffee?"

"Sure, that sounds wonderful actually. But I can get it—"

"No, just sit and I'll be right back. Do you like cream or sugar?"

"Sugar please. Are you sure you can—"

"Yes, it's no problem. I'll see you in a few minutes." He carefully counted his steps while his cane tapped back and forth down the halls. Mark had shown him where the coffee was before he left, and although Jason knew coffee was a small thing, the gesture would show Linda her daughter's boyfriend was capable. He wanted Linda to see him as the confident, self-sufficient, strong man Heather saw. He only had one chance for a first impression and really didn't want Linda to feel her daughter made a mistake by being with him.

Coffee wasn't a big deal, but it was something.

He returned a few minutes later, holding out the coffee

to her. "I didn't know if you like Equal or sugar, or whatever. So I grabbed a couple of packets from each bin." He held his hand out, and she took them.

"Well that was thoughtful, Jason," she said with a smile in her voice. "So you're the man Heather has been keeping from me."

"Yeah, I'm sorry we had to meet under these circumstances." Heather wasn't all that close to her mom and didn't see her often but kept telling Jason she wanted them to meet soon.

"Me too," Linda said. "I know Heather's busy, and I'm afraid I'm just not a priority to her. But it's my fault, I suppose."

Jason didn't know what to say. Heather never said anything negative about her mom. She never said much at all. "What do you mean?"

"Well…" Linda sighed. "I think our relationship started to deteriorate when her sister Anna got sick. You see, when you've got a child that is ill and needs your help…all of your attention and energy is focused on that child. On getting her well, on making her comfortable. And in all of that with Anna…I think Heather got a little lost in the shuffle." She took a drink of coffee. "God knows I never meant for that to happen, but it did. Heather was old enough to dress herself, make a bowl of cereal, do homework on her own. So she did. She did all of those things by herself while Doug and I cared for Anna."

"I can understand that." Jason wondered if that happened to Mark while Jason was going blind.

"Well, it's understandable, but it doesn't make it right. Or fair. And I don't think Heather ever got over that. I don't know if she holds a grudge…I just think it put a lot of distance between us, and we never recovered."

"I'm sorry about Anna and about losing a part of Heather too," he said with genuine concern.

"Thank you, Jason. Heather told me you're a good man."

Jason smiled, uncomfortable with the attention. "Well,

she makes me want to be a better man. She's pretty fantastic herself."

Linda patted his knee. "I have to agree."

They chatted more, mainly small talk, in an effort to abate their nerves and fill the silence.

After about ten minutes passed, Jason heard brisk, purposeful footsteps approach the waiting room. "For Heather Cook?" a man asked of the waiting room.

"That's us." Jason stood up and the man walked over to them.

"I'm Dr. Weir."

"I'm Jason Scharp, Heather's boyfriend." Jason offered his hand. Dr. Weir shook it.

"And I'm her mother, Linda Marx." She stood up.

"Nice to meet you both. Heather is out of surgery. She did great, everything's fine. The appendix didn't burst so we got it out in time."

"Great." He loosened the tight grip on his cane; he hadn't realized how tense he'd become.

"If we'd gotten in there an hour or two later, we might not have been so lucky."

"So can we see her?"

"She's in recovery now, but we'll move her to room three-forty-two shortly. You can wait for her there, and you'll see her the minute she's wheeled in. It's just down that way, follow the signs until you see it."

Oh, okay. I'll head wherever "that way" is and sure, I'll follow the signs. Thanks, Doc.

"Thank you so much, Doctor," Linda said while he walked away.

"May I take your arm and follow your lead?" Jason wished he didn't have to ask Heather's mom for help. Humiliating. So much for getting her coffee.

"Certainly."

"Thanks." He reached out and found her arm.

Linda didn't say much while they walked, which enabled Jason to count steps so he could make his way back to the elevator and coffee later. When they reached her room, Jason felt by the doorframe and found the room number in Braille. 342.

Walking inside, Jason felt a little more relieved, one step closer to seeing Heather. He knew she was okay, but he would feel better when she was in front of him. Linda and Jason chatted while they waited. He found she had a good sense of humor like Heather. He wondered if her father did too.

There was a long silence, and Jason finally decided to just throw it all out there and see what she thought of her daughter dating a guy like him. If there was a problem, he might as well find out now.

"Linda, I get that I'm probably not the suitor that a mother wishes for. But blindness is not the big deal that most people seem to think it is. My life is pretty normal. My disability is just a nuisance, really. And I promise you that I'll take care of your daughter in every way I can and I'll be good to her."

She didn't speak for a moment and it was one of those times Jason felt at a serious disadvantage since he could glean nothing from her silence. What he wouldn't give sometimes to see a person's expression. To read someone's face.

She patted his hand. "I admit I was a little shocked when she told me, and I had my worries. But from what I hear, you're the perfect guy for her, and the only thing I care about is that she's happy."

"Thank you, Linda." He rubbed his sweaty palms on his pants. "I appreciate your candidness."

"You're welcome."

He heard a sound down the hall. "They're wheeling someone this way—I hope it's her."

Sure enough, they wheeled in Heather's bed. "Okay, Heather, we're in your room now." The nurse pushed the bed into position. "You've got some visitors waiting for you." The nurse turned to Jason and Linda. "She's still pretty groggy and a little out of it. She'll sleep good tonight. My name is Courtney, and I'll be her nurse. Here's the call button if you need anything at all." With that, she left the room.

"Oh, my poor baby." Linda sounded upset. "You look so pitiful."

"Mom?" Heather said, her voice sounding a tad drunk. "Mom, you're here." She sounded happy, albeit fuzzy. "I didn't want you to have to come to the hospital—"

"Well that's just ridiculous," Linda scolded her. "I had to be here with my girl."

"Where's Jason?" she asked, slurring her words.

"Sweetheart, I'm right here." He followed the bed rails and made his way around the other side of the bed. He found her hand, which had an IV in it.

"Hi, baby."

"I'm so glad to see you're okay. You scared the shit out of me." His eyes grew misty as he swallowed. The strong emotions coursing through him took him by surprise. He stroked her cheek. "How are you feeling?"

"I feel like I'm drugged. I guess I am, huh?" She giggled.

"Are you in any pain?" Linda asked.

"Not now. I feel better than when I came in…" Her voice trailed off.

"I think she's asleep," Linda said.

"No…I'm not," Heather said quietly and slowly. "So you two have met."

"Yes we have." Jason chuckled.

"How did that go?" she mumbled.

"I think he's wonderful." Linda smiled and patted her daughter's hand.

"I told you…" Her voice trailed off again. Within seconds Jason heard snoring.

"Okay, now she must really be asleep," Jason whispered, smiling.

"She is," confirmed Linda.

Jason let go of her hand, which woke her up.

"Baby, don't leave," she moaned.

"Oh, sweetheart, I'm not going anywhere," he said

with tenderness. "I just want to sit down."

"Can you sit on the bed with me and hold my hand?"

"I don't want to hurt you...I don't know if that's a good idea—"

"Why don't I push a chair up next to the bed?" Linda suggested.

"Yes, that would be great." She pushed the chair up and he sat down, never letting go of Heather's hand. "Will that work, Heather?"

"She's asleep again," Linda said quietly. "You know, it's after midnight. If we give it a few minutes she'll probably fall into a deep enough sleep that you can leave."

"I'm going to stay here."

"Oh, Jason, she'll just be sleeping."

"Well I want to be here whenever she wakes up."

"You're not going to get any sleep—"

"That's okay. I need to be here for her." Finality rang from his voice.

"All right then. Is there anything I can get for you before I leave? Or that I can bring you in the morning when I come back?"

"There is one thing. Can you put my hand on the nurse call button so I know where it is in case we need her?" Linda showed him. "Thanks."

"She looks so pale and weak," she said.

"I bet." He stroked his thumb back and forth on her hand.

"I'm glad I got to meet you, Jason."

He offered a weary smile. "Yeah, me too."

"I'll see you in the morning. Try to get some sleep."

She left the room and Jason sighed with relief. Heather was safe, and he'd survived the first meeting with one of her parents.

****

"Jason?" Heather whispered. "Are you awake?"

He suddenly sat upright, a bit disoriented. Where was he? "Heather?"

"I'm right here. I can't believe you stayed all night."

163

The hospital. Sometimes he struggled to remember where he was if he woke up in a strange place, because he couldn't glance around the room to see. He'd slept by leaning on the bed rails. Not very comfortable. And he woke many times hearing strange noises, from nurses coming in to check vitals and that sort of thing.

"Well of course I stayed all night. I told you I wouldn't go anywhere." He offered a small smile, still half asleep. "How do you feel, sweetheart?"

"I'm in a little bit of pain, but nothing like yesterday."

"Why don't we buzz the nurse and see if they can give you something more for the pain?"

"No, it's not bad. It's definitely tolerable."

"Well you don't sound all loopy like you did last night." Jason grinned and stood up. He let go of her hand that he'd held all night and stretched.

"I vaguely remember talking with you. And my mom was here, right?"

"Yes, she was." Jason checked his watch. Ten after seven.

"Oh no, I need to call my principal," Heather said in a panic.

"No you don't. I took care of it." Jason pulled his phone out of his pocket and found two new text messages and a new email. "Listen."

He tapped the email from her principal, which his phone read aloud. "Mr. Scharp, I received your messages last night and will arrange a substitute for today and the rest of the week. Please tell Heather we're thinking of her and wish her a speedy recovery."

"See?" Jason smiled. "It's taken care of."

"Wow, you really did take care of everything, didn't you?" The admiration in her voice was obvious. "You helped me get dressed, got me here, contacted my mom, lined up a substitute…you're amazing."

"Well, I try." He grinned and leaned over to kiss her cheek. He couldn't shake a thought that had been on his mind since last night. He wasn't sure what Heather would think, but decided he'd find out. "Heather?"

"Yes?"

"There's something I keep thinking about." He leaned on the rails of her bed and took a deep breath. "The doctor said last night that if we would have gotten you here an hour or two later, your appendix might have ruptured. It would have been a much more serious situation."

"Really?"

"Yeah, and it got me to thinking. It really bothered me that I didn't know until yesterday afternoon that you were sick. What if I hadn't insisted on coming over?"

"Well...but you did."

"What I'm trying to say is, if we lived together, I would have known first thing in the morning you were sick. I would have taken you in then. I want to always be there for you, to take care of you. And you take care of me. So...what I'm trying to ask is...would you consider moving in with me?"

"You want me to move in with you?"

What is that in her voice? He wasn't sure. "Well, yes. On vacation...it just felt right. Ever since we got back from Gulf Shores, I miss you every night we're not together. And I miss waking up with you in my arms, being with you first thing in the morning, eating breakfast with you." He waited, worried he was pushing too much too soon.

"You want to live together? Really?"

When he heard the enthusiasm and excitement in her voice, any worries Jason had melted away. "So is that a yes?"

"Oh, it sure is! I would kiss you, but I need my toothbrush first."

"Will it hurt if I hug you?"

"Just don't lean on my stomach and I think we'll be okay."

They hugged and Jason kissed the top of her head. "You know, you don't smell much like yourself today. You smell like hospital gown and medicine. But I still love you."

"If only you could see me in this fashionable frock I'm

wearing. No makeup, teeth un-brushed…I'm quite the catch."

"Actually, Heather, you are." He stroked her hair. "I have to get some coffee. I'm dying here. I wonder when they're going to bring your breakfast?"

"I don't know, I'm pretty hungry. I didn't eat anything yesterday."

"Well, I'll go get some coffee and if I wander around long enough, I'll eventually stumble into the nurses' station. I'll find out when you're getting breakfast, okay?"

"Okay. Thank you." He started out of the room and Heather said, "Jason?"

"Yes?"

"When I move in, can I bring some of my stuff? I mean, I don't want to feel like I'm just living in your house, although technically I will be. I want it to feel like our place. So I want to add some personality, some touches of me."

"Of course you can. That's what I hoped you would do. Right now it's just a house, and I'd like you to turn it into a home for us."

"I love you, Jason Scharp." She laughed. "Ow…it hurts when I laugh."

"I love you too, Heather Cook." He smiled as he walked out the door.

****

Mark and Jason sat in a booth at Pasta House, one of their favorite local restaurants, waiting for their food to arrive. Mark had picked Jason up from the hospital so he could take a quick shower, change clothes, and grab some lunch before heading back to the hospital. Jason felt refreshed after cleaning up, though he was still tired. And hungry. He had been craving the locally famous Pasta House Salad, a blend of lettuce, artichoke hearts, red onions, parmesan and pimento, and was digging in like he hadn't eaten in days.

Mark recounted to Jason a funny story about his sales call that morning, which got them both laughing. Mark was a natural-born salesman—outgoing, friendly, and great with people. Persuasive too.

He'd just finished the story when the waitress brought their entrees. Jason could feel the steam rising off his bowl of Pasta con Broccoli. As soon as she left, they both dug in.

Jason had been bothered by what Linda said to him the night before about Heather being neglected. He wanted to talk to Mark about it but was a little apprehensive. He decided now was as good a time as any to bring it up.

"Hey, Mark, can I ask you something?" he asked, his voice quiet.

"What's that?" Mark asked, taking a bite of his meatball sub.

"Well, I don't think I ever told you, but Heather had a sister that died of cancer as a girl."

"No, you're kidding me? That's awful."

"Yeah, it is. Last night Heather's mom told me that when Anna became sick, all of their energy focused on taking care of her, and Heather got kind of lost in the shuffle. She said they didn't mean for it to happen, but it did." Jason took a bite of pasta. "So it got me to thinking…I never considered what you went through when I went blind. Everyone was busy helping me, caring for me…did you get lost too?"

Mark didn't reply right away, and Jason heard him put his fork down. "You went through hell. What I went through was nothing."

Jason shook his head. "Of course it was a shitty time for me, but I'm wondering how rough you had it."

"Jason, why are you asking me this? We're talking fifteen, twenty years ago." Mark shifted in his seat.

"Because you're my brother and I want to know what it did to you. I've been so selfish all these years I never even asked."

"You're not selfish—"

"Sometimes I think I am. I can't see beyond myself, so I think I get wrapped up in my own little world." Jason took another bite and chewed it slowly before he asked again, "So what did my blindness do to you?"

"Well, you keep asking and asking," Mark sounded irritated, "so I'll tell you. It sucked. I hated it, okay?"

Mark's harsh words surprised Jason, since he'd never said a word about it before. But he'd asked. "How so?"

"It was like I didn't exist for a couple of years. Always 'Jason this, poor Jason that. We can't because of Jason.'"

"Really?"

"Yes." Mark sighed.

"Why didn't you ever say anything?"

"Why would I? You lost your eyesight, for God's sake. I only lost some attention." Jason didn't know what to say. Mark continued. "Do you want to know the worst part? For a while I hated you. I mean, really loathed you. Because your blindness changed everything. So instead of being mad at the circumstance, I got mad at you."

"Well that's just the mind of a teenager, lashing out—"

"I know, but you were *my brother*. What happened wasn't your fault but I blamed you anyway. And do you know what I used to do? I used to leave doors open on purpose, leave stuff lying on the floor, that sort of thing…just so you would trip or run into things." Mark's voice wavered. "I don't know if I wanted to hurt you or just get attention. Probably a little of both. Because whenever I did that, Mom and Dad would jump my ass, but at least they noticed me. Jason, I am so sorry I did that to you. It was despicable, unforgivable."

A little stunned, Jason offered a small smile. "Well, I'm sure I did plenty of tripping and falling without your help."

"I guess. Do you remember that time I scored a touchdown in my senior year?"

"Uh…no, I don't, I'm sorry."

"Well, I played defense, so I didn't have a lot of opportunities to score. But you and Dad were at the game, and I intercepted a pass and ran it back for a touchdown. The only time I got a touchdown in four years of playing football. I was so excited, so thrilled that Dad was there to see it. Maybe then he would finally notice me."

"So did he?" Jason sure hoped so.

"No, he missed it," Mark said quietly.

"How did he miss it?"

"Because he had to help you find the bathroom, and that's where he was when I made the play." They both stopped eating while they shared an uncomfortable silence.

Jason felt miserable. "I never knew about that. I'm so sorry Dad missed your big moment because of me."

"But don't you see? It wasn't your fault, so you don't owe me an apology. As pissed as I was, I felt bad that at fifteen years old, you couldn't just go take a leak without someone taking you there. So I felt so conflicted…upset for myself but guilty for feeling that way."

"I don't blame you for feeling that way—"

"But I do. All these years and I still struggle with that. I felt like nobody gave a shit about me, but at least I could see. I wouldn't want to trade places with you for anything."

"It's not that terrible. Sounds like you went through some bad shit too. When did it start to get better?"

"I don't know…even when things got easier for you, for a long time you always went crying to Mom."

"What are you talking about?" Jason asked, feeling the defensiveness rising in the pit of his stomach. He took another bite of salad.

"Oh, you used to complain to Mom, and she always took your side. Her poor little Jason."

"And what do you mean by 'poor little Jason'?" Now he was getting pissed.

"Nothing." Mark sighed. "I don't mean anything."

"Well, you meant something by it." Jason leaned forward, his elbows on the table. "What did you mean?"

"Nothing, I was just relaying how it felt to me all those years ago." Mark's voice was strained.

"Is that how you see me, Mark? As poor blind Jason?" He had never heard Mark talk about him that way before; it was unsettling. Mark was the one person he thought truly saw him just as Jason, without seeing his disability.

"Oh Jesus, let's just drop it," Mark said, exasperation evident in his voice.

"Well, do you?"

"No, of course not—I can't even believe you're asking me that."

"Well you're the one that said it—"

"I never said I felt that way, but back then, that's how I thought they treated you." Mark patted Jason's shoulder. "So chill out, okay? You asked when it got better, and I'm trying to tell you. To be honest with you, it wasn't until I left for college. Then I had some distance from the situation, and when I came home to visit or for the summer, I was just glad to see you and hang out. And in my years away, Mom and Dad stopped hovering around you so much."

Jason remembered feeling lost when Mark was away at school. Lonely without his big brother, his best friend. "Shit, Mark." Jason sighed. "I'm sorry I started this. I didn't mean to drag up all kinds of old stuff to make us both feel bad. But I'm glad I know now what you went through. I had no idea, and I'm sorry I never asked. Losing my sight didn't only affect me, it affected our whole family. I guess I'm just lucky you got past it and still want to hang out with me."

"You're my best friend, Jason. Of course I want to hang out with you. It just made things hard on everyone for a while. So can we please start this lunch over?"

"Fist bump?" Jason held his fist out to Mark, who promptly tapped it with his own.

"You know what? I think we just condensed fifteen years of therapy into one lunch." Mark chuckled.

Jason laughed with him. "I think you're right." He took a drink of his iced tea. "And seriously, you set me up to run into shit? That is just wrong. I imagine I've got scars with your name on them." He continued laughing.

"It's not funny, Jace."

"Well it wouldn't have been funny if I got seriously hurt, but since I didn't, in hindsight it's pretty damn amusing."

"Maybe a little. Do not ever tell Mom and Dad

though. Oh my God, they would disown me."

"I'll keep my mouth shut...for a price." Jason managed to keep a straight face for a moment before he burst into a huge grin. "Really though, I won't say anything. They *would* disown you."

"Oh, I know they would," Mark said as he took the last bite of his meal.

"And don't feel so bad about it. You also looked out for me all the time. Remember that time you beat up Tom and Brad?"

"Oh, yeah, I forgot about that. Those little fuckers took your cane. Who does that? I mean, seriously, would they have thrown a guy out of a wheelchair too?"

"Not after you got a hold of them."

"Yeah, I busted Brad's nose. Man, that still pisses me off."

"I sometimes wonder what I would have done if you hadn't shown up."

"But I did."

"How did you see what was going on, anyway? Your bus from the high school got home an hour before mine. Why weren't you in the house?"

"What's with you and all the questions today?"

"Well, I never thought about it before. It was great timing."

"I wasn't in the house because I was watching for you, making sure you got home okay."

"Really? Glad you decided to look out for me that day."

Mark's voice was quiet. "I did it every day, Jace."

"What?"

"Every day, I walked or rode my bike down close to the bus stop." He added quietly, "When your eyes started getting really bad, I was worried about you."

Emotion rose in Jason's throat and he swallowed. He'd never loved his brother more than at that moment. "I can't believe you did that for me."

"It was no big deal—"

"Yes, Mark, it was. Thank you."

"You're welcome," Mark said with a smile in his voice. "That's what brothers are for. When they're not busy booby-trapping the house for you." They both laughed, breaking the serious moment.

"So how is Angie feeling?"

"Super tired, a little nauseous now and then. But overall not too terrible."

"I can't believe you're going to be a dad."

"Me neither, trust me. It took so long...I was starting to think maybe I'd never get to have kids. But now it's happening, and I'm excited and scared shitless all at the same time. And you'll be an uncle!"

"I can't wait. But you better not do any of that Wiley Coyote booby-trap stuff to me when I'm holding your baby."

"I should have never told you about that." Mark grinned. "You're going to hold it over my head forever."

"Not forever, just a couple of decades. So you're having a baby, and I've got some good news too."

"What's that?"

"Heather's going to move in with me." Jason grinned from ear to ear.

"Really? That's terrific. When is she moving in?"

"I guess right away. We talked about it today, so I think when she comes home from the hospital I'll bring her to my place. Then when she's up to it we can go get her stuff."

"Well, let me know when and I'll come help move her."

"That would be great. I can ask Shawn too and rent a U-Haul or something."

"I don't do manual labor in extreme heat or rain. So plan accordingly," Mark joked.

"We'll keep that in mind." Jason took his final bite of lunch. "Are you done eating? I need to get back to the hospital."

"What you really need is a nap. You've got bags and

circles under your eyes."

"I'm fine. I just want to be with Heather. She must be bored out of her mind. Oh hey, can we stop at Walgreens and pick up a couple of magazines for her?"

"Sure, I don't have a job or anything...."

"Well, since some days you're out on the golf course, I wonder."

"Good point. Walgreens, you say?"

Chapter Twelve

When Jason brought Heather home from the hospital, he brought her to the home they would now share. He took care of her while she recuperated and two weeks later, instead of just keeping some clothes and essentials at the house, they officially moved her in.

Both Shawn and Mark were more than willing to help. This was a big step, and everyone seemed so excited for them. Well, everyone except for Jason's mother. He knew she still had reservations about Heather, but even she reluctantly admitted to Jason that they seemed very happy together. And they had been together for more than four months—a record for him.

A couple days after the move, Heather finished phase one of the house transformation.

"Well," she said to Jason that evening as she hung the final piece of artwork on the living room wall, "I'm done. What do you think of the renovation?"

"I think it all looks fantastic." Jason sat on the couch, reading a book. He pointed to the wall across from him. "That picture in particular is my favorite."

"Jason." She laughed and plopped down next to him. "There's not even anything there. Very funny."

"Well, what do you expect me to say? As far as I can tell, you've just put a bunch of stuff on the tables and counters and all over the place for me to knock over. I'm sure it looks great, but to me, it's just a bunch of accidents waiting to happen."

"It does look great, so there." She turned her back to him.

"Thank you for turning our house into a home." He kissed her neck.

"You're welcome." She smiled, turning back around to

face him. "It really is nice. It looked nice before, just a little too sterile. Now it has character."

"You know, I hope you didn't completely fill the mantle because I've got one thing to give you." Jason stood up. "Wait here."

"What are you talking about?" Heather asked, and he could hear the curiosity in her voice.

He loved surprising her and couldn't stop smiling when he walked back to the bedroom and returned with a sloppily wrapped package. "I'm not the best at wrapping gifts, but it's the thought that counts, right?"

"Of course," she said when he handed it to her. She quickly unwrapped it. Jason hoped the framed picture of the two of them on the beach in Gulf Shores looked something like he imagined. The frame was covered with shells and raffia. "Oh, Jason, I love it! Thank you so much, baby."

"You're welcome, sweetheart."

"And I'm going to put it right on the center of the mantle." She placed it there and stepped back. "It's perfect. Now it's our home."

"It feels perfect, doesn't it?"

"Without a doubt." Heather sat back down next to him and he put his arm around her.

"And now that school is out, we have the whole summer to spend together."

"I know. I'm so excited," she said. "I want to start planting some stuff out back. We can barbecue all the time…hey, you know what I'd love to do?"

"What's that?" Jason snuggled in closer to her.

"Can we have a party? It wouldn't be a house warming party since you already lived here, so maybe we could call it a moving in party. It will be a great chance to meet each other's friends."

"That sounds like a stellar idea, Ms. Cook. Count me in! When do you want to have it?"

"Maybe in a few weeks…I'd like to paint some walls, get some stuff done in the backyard, and we need time to get it all organized."

"Okay. I'll have to come up with a menu…."

"Whatever you make, I'm sure it will be delicious. And we have to make a party music playlist."

"I can help with that."

"This is going to be so much fun." Her phone started ringing and Jason recognized by the ringtone it was Katie. "Hey chick! How are you?"

Jason tried to piece together the conversation while only hearing Heather's end.

"What? Are you kidding me? …Okay, okay, I'll come right up. I'll bring Jason too, if he wants to come. …Yeah, I'll bring my camera. Oh my gosh, this is so exciting! I'll see you in a bit. Breathe." She hung up.

"What's going on?" Jason asked. "Where are we going?"

"The hospital—she's in labor. It's happening. My best friend is having her baby!"

"That's terrific!"

"So you can come up with me if you want, but it might be a long night. You never know, especially with a first baby. If you want to stay at home, I don't blame you."

"No, I'll go. This is a big deal—I want to be there with you."

"I can't believe this time has finally come." Heather threw her arms around Jason.

"Maybe someday it will be our turn."

"I sure hope so. Let's get going."

****

"It's a girl!" Dan ran into the waiting room.

Cheers erupted from Dan and Katie's parents, and from Heather and Jason. After waiting several hours, they now shared high fives, hugs and tears.

"So what's her name?" Heather asked.

"Abigail Katherine," Dan said, beaming.

Heather had never seen him so happy. "Oh, that's sweet. When can we go see her?"

"It shouldn't be too much longer. I need to get back to Katie." He took off back down the hall.

"Wow, little Abigail." Heather grinned at Jason. "I would love to have a girl someday."

"And what if we have a boy?" Jason asked.

Heather noted that he said we, not you. "Oh, I'd like a boy too. But I have to have at least one girl. To do her hair, and dress her up, and hopefully share a bond that I just don't have with my mom."

"You know, that first night you went to dinner at my parents' house, you said you wanted at least two kids. There's no way I want more than two. Even one is fine with me."

"Well...I would be okay with two. But not one. I don't want an only child."

"I can understand that."

"How..." Heather chose her words carefully. "How do you think you would do with a baby? I mean, do you think you can figure out some ways to help care for one?"

"Well, I'm sure I can...but I don't know how I would do everything. And I'm guessing there are some things I'll have trouble with, but that's where you would come in." He didn't sound angry, just matter-of-fact.

Heather was quiet, considering this. She never thought about it before, but Jason's blindness might really create a problem when it came to babies. A feeling of uncertainty and worry crept over her.

"Heather?" Jason asked, sounding concerned. "Sweetheart, I can't see your face...what are you thinking?" He reached out for her hand and when she took hold, he held on tight.

"Oh, I just never thought about that before. I'm kind of thinking things through in my mind."

"Like having a baby with a blind man?" His voice was quiet.

"Well...yes. It's something I've never had to consider before now."

"So it's something you have to consider? As in, you may not want to?" In his voice, the hurt was obvious.

"Jason, no...it's just the first time it came up, and I

realize this might be a big struggle."

"Too much for you to overcome?"

She didn't answer immediately.

"Apparently." His voice exuded anger.

"I didn't say that—"

"Maybe you didn't say so, but your silence spoke volumes." He dropped her hand and abruptly stood up. "I'm going to get some coffee. Do you want some?"

"Jason, wait," she pleaded quietly, not wanting to cause a scene. She grabbed his hand and tugged, encouraging him to sit down. He did. "Just because I said it might be a struggle doesn't mean it's not worth the effort."

"But you're not sure about it, are you?"

"I'm sure about us. Isn't that what really matters?" She tried to gauge his facial expression.

"Well, that's a great start." He swallowed. "But caring for a baby is a big deal—it even scares sighted people. And I'm capable of an awful lot, Heather, but I'm not going to sit here and say that I'll be able to change diapers and all that when I don't know for sure."

"Fair enough. Jason, I love you. Please don't get angry with me for having logical concerns."

"I love you too." He sighed. "I just…I sometimes feel more blind with you. I think it's because I feel I have to be normal and just like a sighted guy, and if I try to pretend that I am, it only leads to failure."

"I don't expect that of you—"

"But I put that pressure on myself. And now with kids…that's daunting. I can't fake my way through that."

"We'll work it out, okay?" Heather kissed him with tenderness, noticing that his face looked strained. "Please…forget I even brought it up."

"Okay." He seemed to soften a bit. "So do you want a coffee?"

"No, but I might take a sip or two of yours."

"But I drink my coffee black…."

"It's two in the morning. Black would be fine right now if I'm going to keep my eyes open at all."

"Okay." He offered a small smile. "I'll be right back." He walked away, his cane tapping down the hallway.

Heather took a deep breath. Could they really work it out?

****

Jason listened to his footsteps echo in the hallway of the hospital, his mind reeling. It always came back to the same thing. His worthless, shitty eyes. Ever since he'd been with Heather, he worried about her leaving him because of his blindness. Now she'd moved in, things seemed great, and bam! There it was. He couldn't escape it.

He'd always wanted to be a dad. Now Mark was going to be one, and Jason wanted nothing more than to have their kids grow up together. But how would he be a dad? How would he manage it? What if that was the one thing in his life that no amount of technology or tools could help him succeed at? *What if Heather decides she wants a man that's whole and leaves me?*

"We'll work it out," she'd said. *She loves me.* Although fear and worry gripped him, he clung to the hope that this time it was different. She was different.

Wasn't she?

****

Jason was careful not to bring up the topic of babies again while their summer started with great promise. For a housewarming gift Mark and Angie splurged and gave them a tandem bike. Mark said the look on Jason's face in the Gulf Shores picture was priceless, and he wanted to give them something that would bring that much joy over and over again.

So they got into the habit of riding most mornings, at least four days a week. They rode different places but favored the Katy Trail. The sights and sounds of nature surrounded them as the wind rushed by. Jason loved the low hum of gravel under the tires, crunching leaves, and tweeting birds. Sometimes if the wind was particularly gusty, the sound of it blowing through the trees reminded him of the ocean waves in Gulf Shores.

When they stopped to take a drink or rest, Heather described their surroundings in detail—wildflowers, critters scampering about and the sun shimmering on the Missouri River. All the remarkable smells that surrounded them intrigued Jason and formed a picture in his mind while they rode down the trail, which ran alongside the river for much of the journey.

The days they didn't ride, Jason would head to the gym and work out. Heather went with him once or twice but explained she wasn't a big fan of organized exercise. Sometimes he could get her to guide him on a short jog around the neighborhood—he was always trying to find an outlet for his energy. Beep baseball practices and games in the summer certainly helped.

Their subdivision had a pool, so they spent a lot of time there. Often they would hit the bike trail early in the morning, before the Midwestern heat and humidity set in, and would make it to the pool afterward to cool off.

Then they often just lounged around the house or worked on one of the many projects Heather had planned. They would head to Home Depot to buy more flowers or bushes or trees. Jason dug plenty of holes that summer and helped with whatever else he could, but she did most of it on her own. It sounded to Jason like the yard was starting to look good, but what did he know?

Evenings were spent barbecuing with Mark and Angie, his parents, Katie and Dan, or Shawn and whatever random girl he was dating that week. Sometimes they'd catch a movie or go out to dinner. They played golf when Mark's schedule allowed.

They had fun double dating with Mark and Angie and sometimes went bowling to get out of the heat. Jason wasn't that great at it, but as long as he was lined up okay before he threw the ball, he wasn't too bad. He would line up by leaning his leg against the ball return and then take a couple of steps to the side to reach the center of the lane.

One night, the guy in the lane next to them asked about halfway through their game, "Excuse me, sir...are you blind?"

"Yeah, I am." Jason grabbed onto Heather's arm and she led him back toward his seat.

"So you're telling me that a blind guy in the next lane is bowling a higher fucking score than me?"

Jason laughed. "Hell, I don't know—I can't see your scoreboard."

"Well, you *are* beating me." The guy laughed. "Jeez, I think I should just go home."

"Maybe you should close your eyes, see if it helps," Jason said with a grin.

They were having such a wonderful summer off together, getting to know each other better every day. Besides the growing landscape in the backyard, she decided the house needed some color inside. Jason granted her total artistic freedom. He couldn't care less—he'd never see any of it, anyway. After inspecting paint cards for more than a week, she finally settled on the colors she thought would be perfect.

They were eating a delicious breakfast he'd cooked of Eggs Benedict while she rattled off the colors she'd chosen for the office (yellow), master bedroom (celery green), and kitchen (bluish gray).

"And I'm thinking taupe for the living room." She took a bite of the eggs. "What do you think?"

"What color is taupe?" He took his last bite.

"You don't know what taupe is?"

He chuckled. "Sweetheart, I was fourteen years old when I went blind. I can assure you that the vast majority of straight fourteen-year-old boys don't know what taupe is."

"Well, I guess so. It's kind of a brownish-gray color. It's a warm, soothing neutral color."

"Works for me. All the colors sound good."

"Are you sure?" She sounded uncertain. "I mean, it's your house. I don't want to change it to something you don't like."

"As sure as a blind man can be about colors of paint."

He grinned. Reaching out and touching her hand he added, "Sorry I can't be more help to you, but I trust your judgment."

"Well, like you said, you couldn't care less. You're fine with off-white walls. I'm the one that wants to add some color, so I don't mind doing the work." She kissed him. "Besides…you'd make a lousy painter."

****

By the end of June, shade and ornamental trees filled the yard along with flower beds, and Heather even planted an herb garden so Jason could get fresh herbs right from the backyard. She bought little stakes that he placed Braille labels onto, so it would be easy for him to find the herb he wanted.

Heather also took Jason into account when she designed the landscaping. She didn't put any trees in the center of the yard, so he was free to walk straight out to the flower garden in the back, without fear of running into an oak or Bradford pear. And since Jason was so athletic, she wanted to keep most of the yard free and open if he wanted to practice beep baseball or anything else.

When choosing what to plant, Heather picked extremely fragrant varieties whenever possible. That way, Jason could appreciate the smells of the landscaping, even if he couldn't see it.

He bought a basketball hoop and Shawn helped him set it up. Once he added the beeper to the backboard, he was ready to go. So when it wasn't incredibly hot, he spent a lot of time shooting hoops with Shawn or Mark and sometimes even Heather. When he couldn't scrounge up a partner, he'd take some shots, but it didn't take long before he tired of searching for a ball he couldn't see.

Although the summer was shaping up to be a lot of fun and living together was going well, it was not without its hiccups. Jason loved that Heather was so excited about redecorating, but it left the house in a constant state of upheaval. For anyone, it would be disruptive. For Jason, it was torturous.

Every time he turned around, it seemed another room became a construction zone, which to a blind man meant just plain dangerous. And he was still trying to get used to the new pieces of furniture and all the decorative pieces Heather added throughout the house. It seemed as if every day Jason knocked something off a table or countertop. So accustomed to the old layout and placement of everything in the house, he would forget the new candle on the end table or the flower arrangement on the bathroom counter.

So far he hadn't broken anything. Yet.

One Saturday morning after they'd finished breakfast, Jason got up from the table where Heather had her nose buried in a book. He filled up his cup of coffee. "I'm going to fire up the computer and make my grocery list."

"Okay, baby," she said. "By the way, you'll need to stay out of the living room tomorrow."

"Why?"

"Because I'm going to paint it. I'm picking up the paint later today so I'm ready to get started first thing in the morning."

"Aaaagh," he moaned. "First the bedroom, then the office and now the living room. The living room connects the kitchen to the hallway...maybe I'll just go hang out at my parents'."

"Yeah, that might be a good idea. I know all this painting has been a hassle, but it's going to look great when it's done." Heather walked over to him and rubbed his shoulders.

"I'm sure it will. Ooo, that feels good. Hey, don't forget you said you want to go grocery shopping with me today instead of Mom."

"Oh, that's right. When do you want to leave?"

"I don't know, maybe an hour or so."

"Okay, I'm going to get ready now. But we can't leave too late. I've got lunch with some of the girls from work at one o'clock."

"Well, when we get home with the groceries, I need you to help me put Braille tags on some of it before I can put it away."

"Oh yeah, I forgot about that. Well, we better leave as soon as we can. I'm going to get dressed."

"So much for a relaxing cup of Joe." Jason headed off to get started on his grocery list.

****

When they got back from the grocery store, Jason could tell Heather was scrambling and rushed. He trailed behind her while she hurried into the house, both of them with arms full of groceries.

"I've got to leave in five minutes," she said with desperation. He heard the refrigerator door open and it sounded like she was stuffing things inside.

"Wait, wait—are you putting things in the fridge?" Jason dropped his bags on the counter.

"Yeah, I'll put the cold stuff in, but then I have to get going."

"Are you putting it where it belongs so I can find it?"

"Uh…shit, no. But I'll fix it all when I get home."

Jason leaned against the counter. "Heather, you're supposed to help me tag the canned goods and other stuff I can't distinguish."

"I will, baby, I will. Just not until after I get back from lunch. I have to go change my clothes now." She took off down the hall at a brisk pace.

Jason shook his head and tried to calm the anger that threatened to boil over. He went to the bedroom. "You were the one that said you wanted to start shopping with me. Well, part of shopping with me is helping me put it away."

"Are you talking to me?" Heather yelled from the bathroom. "I can't really hear you. I've got the water running."

Jason walked to the bathroom doorway. "Can you hear me?"

"Yes." He could tell she was brushing her teeth.

"Why did you say you want to go shopping with me if you're not going to help finish the job?"

"Baby, I didn't know it would take that long at the store. We just ran out of time."

"You don't get it." He crossed his arms and leaned against the wall. "So now you just crammed a bunch of things in the fridge, so I can't find anything, and everything else is just going to stay on the counters?"

He heard the water shut off, and Heather touched his arm. "I'm sorry, but you are not a fast shopper. I've never done a whole week's worth of shopping with you, and it just took longer than I thought. Next time I'll know."

"I know I'm slow, I know it's probably a complete pain in the ass to you—"

"Jason, I'm in the bedroom now."

He was beyond irritated now. "Can you please let me know if you're leaving the room?"

"Okay."

"Heather, do you realize how hard it is for me to ask for help? I don't like to do that, but I'm telling you now that I need your help, and you're blowing me off for some lunch."

"Now that's not fair. I'm not blowing you off. I'm just under a time constraint."

"Well, you shouldn't have offered to help me if you weren't going to follow through. My mom's been taking me shopping for years, and she would have done it again today except you said you wanted to."

"Baby, I'm sorry, okay? But I don't get what the big deal is. We'll do it when I get home."

"The big deal is that you made a commitment, and if you say you're going to help, you should. What's next? Are you going to leave me stranded somewhere when you say you're going to pick me up, just because you've got plans?"

"Now that's just being hurtful." Heather sounded angry. "I do things for you all the time and you know it. But I'm new at this, so cut me some slack. Just wait a few hours and I'll take care of it."

"You don't do things for me all the time! You offer to give me rides and pick out my clothes sometimes and stuff like that, but not often, and I rarely ask for those things. I don't need you to do that—I got by on my own just fine before you." He knew he shouldn't have let her help him. It was hard enough relying on your girlfriend and feeling like a stupid little kid, but now she wasn't even going to finish the job.

"If you don't need my help, then put the damned groceries away by yourself."

"Damn it, Heather, you're missing the point. This is one thing you know I need help with. I need to know I can rely on you. I should have just gone with Mom—"

"Oh, I'm sure she would just love this. Me dropping the ball for her precious Jason." He heard the clip clop of different shoes while she slipped them on and the rustling of her purse. "Since I'm such a lousy girlfriend, why don't you call your mommy and see if she'll come over and take care of it for you?"

"Fuck you."

"Nice, Jason. I'm leaving the room now," she practically hissed. He could hear the anger in her footsteps when she stormed into the kitchen, followed by the jingle of her keys and more angry steps as she headed to the front door. "I'm heading out. I'll be back after lunch and a trip to Home Depot to pick up paint." She accentuated her statement by slamming the door behind her.

Jason stood in the bedroom, still fuming. *Why does she have to throw my neediness in my face?*

He sat down on the bed to find it covered with all kinds of Heather's stuff. Clothes, shoes, purses…he couldn't tell for sure what was there.

"This is bullshit," he muttered.

He went in the kitchen and grabbed a beer out of the fridge after fumbling around to find it behind the stuff she piled in. Then he plopped down on the couch and turned on some music. Nine Inch Nails suited his mood at the moment and he turned it up high, closed his eyes and attempted to calm himself down.

It was hard to deal with a frustration that would never

go away. His circumstances would never change. It was bad enough needing help, but worse when it was coming from his lover. How could he feel like a strong, macho guy when his girlfriend had to help him distinguish between a can of peas and chicken broth?

His churning thoughts were interrupted by the ring of his doorbell. He muted the stereo then walked to the door.

"Who is it?" he asked.

"Kennedy!" shouted the five-year-old neighbor girl who seemed to have adopted him. She lived next door with her mom and thought he was just the greatest. He didn't see much of her during the winter, but now with summertime, he ran into her a lot.

Damn. This is the last thing I need right now. He considered telling her he was busy and then decided that maybe a visit from a sweet little five-year-old was exactly what he needed. He opened the door.

"How's my favorite little girl?" He swung the door open.

"Good. My mom said it was okay if I came over to see if you can play. Can you play?"

Jason chuckled. "With you, of course. Come on in."

"Ooo, you've got all kinds of new pretty stuff in here."

"Yes, Heather's been decorating." The mere mention of her name brought back their fight in his mind.

"She did a good job."

"That's what I hear. So, what do you want to do? Do you want to play in the backyard? Or watch a movie?"

"Let's go in the backyard! Can you teach me how to play basketball like you do?"

"I can try." Her enthusiasm was a joy.

They walked through the kitchen and Kennedy asked, "How come your kitchen is so messy with food everywhere?"

Jason wanted to say, *because my girlfriend was being selfish*, but he bit his tongue. "Well, I need help putting the food away because I can't see the packages to know what's in them. Heather planned to help me, but she had to leave."

187

"I can help you."

"Can you read? You're not even in kindergarten yet, are you?"

"No, but I know all my letters."

Hmmm. Maybe she can help. "Are you sure you want to help?"

"Yes! What do I do?"

"Okay, just a minute." Jason grabbed his box of Braille index card tags from the top of the fridge. He had them filed by category. He reached over to the counter and found a box of cereal. "Can you read the big letters on here for me?"

"It's Raisin Bran. I know 'cause my mom eats it all the time."

"Great. Thank you, Kennedy." He found his Braille tag for Raisin Bran and attached it to the box with a rubber band. "What about this one?"

"H-o-n-e-y N-u-t C-h-e-e-r-i-o-s."

"Honey Nut Cheerios." Jason attached the tag.

"Can I see that?"

"What?"

"That."

Poor kid was probably pointing. "Sweetie, I can't see if you're pointing to something."

"Oh." She giggled. "I forgot. The paper you put on the cereal."

"Sure." He held the box out for her.

She felt the Braille letters with her fingers. "What are those bumps?"

"That's how I read," he explained. "I can't see letters, so I have to feel them. Each of those little blocks of bumps are letters. It's called Braille. See," he said, holding up another card, "this one says 'Green Beans.'"

"You read with your fingers? That's so cool." Her voice filled with awe. "I'm gonna tell my friends at preschool that you can read with your fingers. They can't do that."

Jason laughed. "I think you're probably right."

"There's green beans right there if you wanna put that paper on."

Jason smiled, wondering where "right there" was. He wasn't surprised a five-year-old didn't get it; every day he got similar directions from adults. "Can you give them to me?"

"Yep." She put the can in his hand.

They continued, with Kennedy reading off the labels and Jason putting things away in the pantry until they finished.

"Thank you so much, sweetie." Jason patted her on the head. "You were a big help."

"I can't believe you read with your fingers. Can you teach me that?"

He grinned. "Well, I think you need to learn to read printed letters on a page first, okay?"

After Jason made them some lunch, they went outside, and he did his best to show her how to dribble and shoot hoops. She started to kind of get the hang of dribbling, but the hoop towered too high for her. So he cheated and held her up so she could drop the ball right in. Kennedy giggled with glee, unconcerned that she had to be held up to get a basket.

He wished he could be so carefree about needing help.

After a few of those, Jason put her back on the ground. "You're making my arms tired, kiddo."

"Can we go look at all those pretty flowers out there?" she asked.

"Sure." Jason grabbed his cane from against the sliding glass doors where it rested. Kennedy took his left hand and they headed to the back of the yard. He showed her where the jasmine, summer lilac and lavender plants were.

"They smell good," Kennedy said. "How do you know where the different plants are?"

"Because I can smell them and tell them apart that way."

"So you read with your fingers and see with your nose." Kennedy giggled.

"Yeah, I guess I do, don't I?" Jason laughed with her.

"Hi guys!" her mom, Tina, shouted from the yard next door. He felt Kennedy's little hand grab his.

"Hi, Mommy! Jason's showing me the flowers. There's lavender and jasmine and stuff."

"Great, sweetie," she said, approaching the fence. Jason and Kennedy headed her way. "Why don't you send her back home? She'll stay forever if you let her."

"I love her company. It's fine," Jason assured.

"Mommy, guess what?" Kennedy bubbled with enthusiasm.

"What, sweetie?"

"Jason can read with his fingers and see with his nose!"

Jason felt his cheeks grow warm. "She saw Braille, and I explained how I read."

"And he can tell what the flowers are by smelling them."

"Impressive." Tina said with a smile in her voice. "Hey, Kennedy, I think it's time to head home. I'm sure Jason has other things to do today."

"Aww, okay, Mommy." Kennedy grabbed onto his leg and he picked her up. "But he's so much fun. He showed me how to get a ball through the hoop. Hi, Heather!"

Jason turned around.

"Hi, Kennedy," Heather called from the patio. "Hello, Tina."

****

Heather watched Jason holding Kennedy in his arms and thought he looked like a natural. Anytime she saw him with Kennedy, it reinforced for her what a great dad he would be. But how would he chase after a toddler? Change a diaper? See if it's about to shove something it shouldn't into its mouth?

"Hi," Tina replied with a smile. She turned back to Kennedy. "Okay girl, let's go home." She grabbed Kennedy out of Jason's arms and carried her over the fence. "Tell Jason thank you."

"Thank you for playing with me and for grilled

cheese."

"You're welcome." He grinned broadly. "I'll see you soon."

"No you won't—you can't see anything."

"Kennedy!" Tina said in embarrassment.

"You're right." Jason laughed. "How about…smell you later?"

Kennedy giggled hysterically. "Smell you later! That's funny, Jason."

"Bye."

Jason headed back toward the house. "Heather?"

"Right here on the patio."

He walked up to her and she reached out, grabbing his hand. Neither one spoke for a minute.

"Who helped you with the groceries?" she asked.

"Kennedy. She can't read, but she read the letters off to me."

"Oh." It was obvious they were both waiting for the other to apologize. Wanting to end the thick tension, Heather finally said, "Jason, I'm sorry you feel like I let you down."

"You did let me down. You have no idea how much I hate that I need your help, but I needed you." He shook his head. "You can't pick and choose when you're going to be my partner. Being my partner means sometimes doing time-consuming, annoying tasks like that. I'm sorry, but that's just part of being with me."

Heather sighed. "I know that. But does that mean I should skip my plans with friends for something that wasn't necessary at that exact moment?"

"But you were the one that offered. And what's all that crap on the bed? You left a mess in the kitchen and a mess in the bedroom." Jason crossed his arms.

Heather felt a great deal of pressure. It was a lot. His life seemed so regimented and structured, and sometimes it felt like too much. He was definitely worth it, but it was hard to get used to. She wanted to tell him how she felt: that he just needed to loosen up a bit. But she thought he would worry she might leave or want out. So instead she quietly said, "I was in a hurry and didn't want to leave that stuff anywhere that you could stumble over it. So I just threw it all on the bed."

He sighed. "Being organized is how I cope with this blindness shit. Structure makes me feel like I'm in control of at least this small piece of my world, and it stresses me out to feel like I don't know where things are in my own house. The fact that I need your help sometimes is embarrassing enough. So please don't offer if you can't really help, okay?"

"Okay, I'm sorry for that. I didn't mean to stress you out, Jason. But I get stressed too, when everything has to be done just so and when you want it. Can you relax, just a little bit? Every couple that moves in together has conflicts. We're two different people. We're going to do things two different ways. We need to find a happy medium."

After a pause he said, "I think you're probably right."

"And you have no reason to be embarrassed for needing help every now and then. This is me, Jason, the woman who loves you so much."

"But that's what makes it even harder sometimes. I want to feel like the big man, the protector, the hero. Not the guy who can't put away his own groceries."

Heather chuckled.

"It's not funny, Heather."

"What do you think this is? The 1800s or something? I don't need a protector. I can take care of myself. Besides, when I got appendicitis—you were completely my protector. You swooped in, got me dressed, got me to the hospital, and nursed me when I came home. So you are the hero, okay?"

His shoulders relaxed a bit.

"What I really need is to feel safe emotionally, mentally. And I feel that with you, so much." She put her arms around his neck. "Don't you get that?"

His voice quiet, he said, "I get that now."

"So can we please end this argument? I don't like

fighting with you—I couldn't even enjoy my lunch because I was so upset."

"I don't like it either." Jason rested his forehead on hers. "I'm sorry for the horrible way I talked to you."

"Okay. And I'm sorry for the mommy comment—"

"Yes, so not cool, sweetheart. That one hurt."

"I know, I meant for it to hurt because you hurt me. But I knew as soon as I said it that I went too far."

"Truce?"

"Truce." She kissed him. "Do you still want me to organize the stuff in the fridge?"

"Yeah, that would be great."

"Then maybe some hot make-up sex?" There was mischief in her voice.

"Well in that case, the groceries can wait," Jason said eagerly.

"Oh no, Mr. Scharp. We're doing the food now because you lost your mind over it, so it's not going to wait. Your loins can wait."

"I didn't lose my mind." They walked inside. "Well, maybe just a little bit."

"Uh-huh," Heather reached the fridge. "I'll take everything out that I put in, and I'll let you put it in where you want."

"And then I'll put something in you—"

"Stop!" She laughed when he hugged her from behind. "Focus, Jason, focus."

While Heather helped him put each item in the fridge in the exact spot where he could find it, she felt for a moment like a new recruit on duty being trained by a strict drill sergeant.

But just for a moment.

Chapter Thirteen

Heather finished painting all the rooms by the first week of July. It was a lot of work and disruption at the house, but it was finally done and they were both relieved. For different reasons.

One morning after they returned from a bike ride, Heather went inside to take a shower, and Jason told her he'd come inside after unloading the bike. It had taken him painstaking hours to figure out how to do it by himself when they first got the bike, causing another tense argument since Heather could do it in a matter of minutes. But he'd figured it out, like he did most things.

She cleaned up, changed clothes, threw her hair in a ponytail, and put on some mascara and lip gloss.

Jason came in, sweaty but looking sexy, and headed straight to the shower.

When he came back out in the living room a few minutes later, pulling on a T-shirt, he hollered, "Heather?"

"I'm right here," she hollered back, smiling, just a couple feet in front of him on the couch.

"Oh sure, mock me." He grinned. "So what's on the agenda today?"

"Well, I'm going shopping for the last few finishing touches to complete the renovation before our party. I need to find some pillows and a throw for the living room. Maybe add a few pillows to the bed too."

"We already have seven decorative pillows on the bed."

"You counted them?"

"I count everything, sweetheart." He ran his fingers through his wet hair. "Steps, doorways, cabinets—that's how I find things. And I know there are seven pillows on the bed because when I put them back on the bed or take them off, I'm done when I get to seven."

"Well, when you put it that way, maybe we don't need more for the bed. But we do need throw pillows for the couch, to add a splash of color."

"I'll tell you what else we need. One of those hanging caddies for the shower to hold the six bottles you added when you moved in. Why the hell do you need six bottles of stuff in the shower?"

"Oh, you found those, huh?" She grinned.

"My foot found them in the corner of the shower. What is all that stuff?"

"They make me beautiful and silky in all the right places."

"Well then it works, 'cause your places are all silky." He grinned. "So where are you going shopping?"

"I thought I'd go to the mall."

"Can I come with you?" He sat down next to her on the couch.

"Well, sure."

"I mean, if you don't mind me tagging along. I could use some new tennis shoes."

"Isn't the mall boring for you?"

"Well, sometimes…but the mall can be kind of cool. Good for people watching and just a lot going on."

"People watching? Gonna scope for babes?" She laughed.

"Well of course I didn't mean that literally. Eavesdropping would be closer to what I do."

"I'd like the company—this will be fun. How about if we shop and then grab a bite for lunch?"

"Sounds good to me."

She put her hands on his face and kissed him. "The mall and my boyfriend—my two greatest loves. What could be better?"

****

Their first stop in the mall was for Jason's shoes. Jason took it in stride, laughing it off, after enduring the typical ignorance of a sales lady that insisted on directing questions to Heather on Jason's behalf: "What size shoe does he wear?" "How would he like to pay?"

After all, Jason figured, it was only logical to assume that people who couldn't see, couldn't talk either. And it never failed to amuse him that people must somehow think the eyes and the ears were connected, since he was hollered at more than the average person, as if talking louder will somehow make up for his lack of vision.

They decided to grab some Chinese in the food court, and after enjoying a quick lunch together, they resumed the pillow quest. They walked through the mall, and Jason held onto Heather's arm until he clipped his shoulder on a window display that jutted out from the wall. She felt awful and apologized profusely, but Jason just shook it off—bumping into things was nothing new for him.

But after that, he pulled out his cane. He had put it away in an effort to protect Heather from the stares of other people. The stares didn't bother him; he couldn't see them. But although she'd never said anything, he worried what it must be like for her when heads turned at the sight and sound of his white stick.

Two hours later, after shopping at five stores and weaving around piles of pillows, Heather was thrilled when she found the perfect ones.

"Oh, I think they're perfect too." Jason grinned at her.

"You are such a smart ass, you know that?"

He was relieved that the tense moments they'd been having lately seemed to be forgotten. But he was left wondering how long they would be playing this delicate game of accommodating each other.

When would he be comfortable with really being a blind guy around her? And when would she get his needs and understand when he needed help, and when she should leave him alone?

While they rode home in the car, Heather singing along to the music of Ben Folds, he wondered how she was supposed to know those things…when he didn't know himself.

****

Moving-In Party night had finally arrived. They cleaned the house until everything absolutely shone.

Once dressed and ready to go, Heather lit candles all around the house and walked through one last time to check everything. With the candles lit, the place seemed to glow. Heather liked what she saw—it looked spectacular. The paint turned out just like she hoped, and the house as a whole looked warm, inviting, and much more like a home with the added touches she made.

Heading toward the kitchen, she stopped to watch Jason. He wore a bright orange short-sleeved button-down linen blend shirt with khaki shorts. As always, he looked crisp and clean and adorable. She noticed his hands as he arranged food on platters—he had great hands. Strong, graceful, and so intuitive…a replacement for his eyes. She admired the way his long fingers worked like finely tuned instruments.

"Heather?" He turned in her direction.

"Yeah, it's me." She walked up to him.

"What were you doing?"

"Just watching you." She rubbed her hand on his back. "You look so handsome tonight, baby."

He smiled. "Thank you, sweetheart. What are you wearing?"

"A sundress. White and yellow flowered. And bejeweled white flip flops."

"Gotta have bejeweled flip flops." He grinned. "Your outfit sounds cute. Let me see." He wiped his hands on a paper towel and found the sundress tied at her neck. "Oh, easy access. I like." He smiled broadly, looking as handsome as ever. His hands moved down the front and felt the low cut neckline. "Are you scouting for new boyfriends tonight?"

"No, just trying to look pretty for the one I've got," she said, her voice soft. She put her arms around his neck. They kissed. Then again. She closed her eyes.

"I love you, Susan—I mean Heather." He chuckled.

Heather swatted his butt. "Very funny. Hey, don't forget I've got candles lit all over the place, so be careful. There's one at the end of the kitchen counter."

"Thanks for the reminder. I'll try not to burn down the house before the party starts."

****

Guests started arriving just after seven-thirty and they seemed to come in droves. First Mark and Angie, whose pregnancy Jason figured must be really starting to show, since he could barely wrap his arms around her in a hug. Shawn and a random date followed just a couple of minutes after them.

Next to arrive was Heather's friend from work, Christina. Heather was giving her the grand tour when the doorbell rang.

"I'll get it," Jason hollered, heading to the front door. He opened it.

"Uh…is this Heather's place?" asked a woman's voice.

"It sure is, I'm Jason, come on in." He stepped out of the way. "And you are…?"

"I'm Jenny and this is my husband David."

"Nice to meet you both." Jason extended his hand to shake. There was a pause…Jason wasn't sure what was going on. He started to put his hand down when he felt a man's hand grab it in a firm shake.

"Nice to meet you too," David said.

Ah, the I-just-realized-you're-blind voice. Awkward first meetings are my specialty. "Heather's back here in the kitchen, just follow me. So how do you know Heather?"

"We met in college," Jenny explained.

They rounded the corner into the kitchen, and Heather saw them. "Jenny! David! It's been forever." She rushed up and hugged her friends. "So, you met Jason."

"Yes, we did," Jenny said, and Jason detected an uneasy tone in her voice.

"Hey, sweetheart," Jason piped in, "I'm going to go outside for a minute and see if Mark and Shawn are done setting up for horseshoes."

198

"Okay," Heather said, and he could tell she'd already turned her attention back to her friends.

A few minutes later, Jason was outside drinking a beer and laughing with Mark when he heard Heather say, "You've got more guests, Jason." He turned to them.

"Scharp, I'm surprised you found a woman to put up with you," said a man he recognized as Josh, one of his co-workers.

"Josh." Jason grinned. "Screw you, okay? Not only did I find a woman, but I hear she's even hot." They hugged.

"She is hot, but so is my Jayne. You remember Jayne?"

"Yes, of course. How are you?" Jason asked.

She hugged him. "I'm great, thanks for having us," Jayne said, and Jason remembered her bubbly voice.

"And you've both met Heather?" Jason asked.

"We sure have," Josh said. "Now Jason, since you've got a beautiful girl of your own, can I trust you to not flirt with Jayne this time?" Josh turned to Heather. "The first time he met Jayne, I caught him telling her how great he is with his hands."

They all laughed.

"She's safe, don't worry. I've got all I ever need right here." Jason kissed Heather on the cheek.

"Okay, just checking." Josh chuckled.

"But I see you didn't take my advice, Jayne." Jason faced her. "I told you he was no good and to run the other way."

"What?" Josh objected.

"No, Josh, Jason didn't say that." Jayne laughed. "He told me you're a great guy and you deserved a good woman like me."

"And," Jason said, shaking his head, "I also said if he knew that, he'd get a big head. Now you've done it."

"Well, thanks." Josh slapped Jason on the back. The doorbell rang.

"I'll grab that. Hey, Heather, Josh is an English teacher like you, so you guys should chat and talk your literary lingo with each other." He took off for the door.

****

Heather talked with them for a couple of minutes and found both Josh and Jayne to be really warm, fun people. They were an adorable couple; Jason was lucky to have such good friends.

Within thirty minutes, all of the guests had arrived. Even Katie and Dan came with little four-week-old baby Abby. Tina from next door came over, as well as Joe, an old friend that had known Jason since they were kids. At one point, Heather played horseshoes, and Joe was on her side, just the two of them.

"You know, Heather," he said, "Jason sure seems happy with you. I've never seen him this happy."

"Oh, that's sweet to say." Heather smiled. "He makes me pretty happy too."

"We've been friends since the first grade, and I've watched him through some tough times. It's good to see him with a great girl."

"So you two were friends when he went blind?"

"Yeah, we were buddies before his eyes ever started acting up. That was a scary thing, watching your friend lose his sight."

"I bet. So tell me—what was he like before?"

"Before he went blind? Well, crazy funny like he is now. But he ran everywhere, all over the place. Kid couldn't sit still and was kind of fearless. We always played baseball or ran from house to house, played in the creek, you name it. My mom used to call him Speedy Gonzalez."

"Oh yeah?" Heather chuckled, trying to picture a young Jason running around.

"Yeah, but when he started losing his sight, that got him hurt a lot. It took a while for him to learn to slow down. And he didn't want anything to do with a cane, I remember that."

"Really?"

"Oh, he resisted it big time. I think because he could still see a little bit, so in his mind, he didn't need it. Canes were for people who were totally blind, not for him. But it made for a lot of problems, because he would get hurt and people didn't understand why he seemed so clumsy and awkward. He just looked kind of drunk sometimes, you know? Once he lost all the sight in his left eye and the right one was really bad, he finally caved in and started using it all the time."

"Did it make a big difference?"

"Hell yes—like night and day. He regained some confidence and didn't rely on me or the other knuckleheads to help him. Jason wasn't Speedy Gonzalez anymore, but he was independent again. That was a big deal. And people could tell at one glance, there's a blind guy, and they would get out of his way. Plus when I went out with him, I called his cane our Golden Ticket." He laughed.

Heather smiled, curious. "What do you mean?"

"Oh, people would let us cut to the front of just about any line. It was awesome." They both laughed. "At first Jason didn't like that, but I convinced him to consider it a special perk. Plus, if he got us bumped up in line, I'd pay his way to whatever we were doing—food, movies, whatever."

"That's terrible." Heather laughed some more.

"I know, right? But we were just kids. We had fun with a bad situation."

"Heather?" Jason queried from the patio.

"I'm out here, playing horse shoes," she yelled.

"Can you make another batch of margaritas?" Since he made all the food, she was in charge of booze.

"Well, we're playing teams."

"I'll play in your spot." Jason headed toward them.

"Hold up, guys," Joe said to the men on the other side, David and Shawn. He motioned in the direction of Jason.

"You play horseshoes?" Heather asked with a grin.

"Oh, you doubt me, do you?" Jason walked up to her.

"Actually, I'm learning to never doubt you, baby."

"Hey, Jace." Joe gave Jason a light smack on the stomach.

"Hey man." Jason smiled. "So have you been telling

Heather tales of corruption about me?"

"Never. That stuff's in the vault, man." They laughed. "So you want to take Heather's place? Isn't that a little dangerous?"

"Maybe for the guys on the other side, but not for us." Jason chuckled. "Joe, can you please grab the beeper off the basketball hoop? It's just fastened with Velcro. We'll put it on the horseshoe stake."

"I'll get it," Joe said, taking off for the patio.

"Who are we playing against?" Jason asked Heather.

"Shawn and David."

"Hey Shawn, David!" Jason hollered. "I'm gonna play for Heather. Joe's putting my beeper on the stake so I know where to throw. But I recommend you step way to the side when it's my turn."

"No problem, man," Shawn yelled back.

Joe started fastening the beeper box to the stake. "Okay, it's your turn now. I'll turn it on."

The beeping started, and the guests quieted down. Jason yelled, "Hey, did everybody stop to watch the blind guy hurl heavy, dangerous horseshoes across the yard?"

"We sure as hell did." Mark laughed.

"Well, I never said I was good." Jason threw the horseshoe. The clank of metal hitting metal rang out. "Did I get it?"

"No," Shawn said, "it hit the outside edge. Good shot though."

"Okay, well, you have this under control, so I'll go make margaritas." Heather kissed Jason on the cheek.

She went inside and started to put ice in the blender. Katie came inside with the baby. "Oh, let me see little Abby."

"You can hold her for a minute, but then I need to go feed her." Katie handed the baby over.

"She is so precious." Heather was enamored with her. She gently rocked Abby in her arms. "I think she looks a lot like you."

"I think so too." Katie grinned.

"And I have to say, Katie, you look fantastic. Have you lost all the baby weight?"

"Not all, but close. It's just redistributed to different parts now. Parts I don't want extra weight on." They both chuckled. "I better feed her. Is there a room I can go to nurse?"

"How about the spare bedroom?" Heather led her down the hallway.

"Heather, the house looks fantastic since you decorated. The colors are great."

"Thank you." Heather flicked on the bedroom lights. "I had a lot of fun, picking everything out."

"What are you doing with your place?"

"Well, I'm just hanging on to it for now. I hate to sell it until I have a ring on my finger."

"I don't blame you, I wouldn't either. Speaking of rings...do you think that's where this is headed?"

"Well, I think it is. I hope so, anyway. We talk about things like it's forever."

"What about kids?" Katie asked in a hushed tone while the baby starting nursing. "I know Jason's very independent, but there's a big difference between being independent and caring for a child. Don't you think you'll do most of the work by yourself?"

"I don't know." Heather sat on the bed next to Katie. She sighed. "When you delivered Abby, he and I got into an argument about that at the hospital."

"You did?" Katie seemed surprised.

Heather looked at her friend with sadness as tears threatened to come to the surface. "Yeah, we did. He admitted it might be hard for him, and he couldn't promise me anything because he didn't know. And I have to tell you, it scared me, thinking about it."

"In what way?"

"In many ways...the fact that I might be basically like a single parent, at least while they're little. And that maybe I won't ever feel like I can completely trust him with a baby. I mean, maybe I can, but what if I can't? What if it's too hard for him to find a way to compensate, and I'm left holding the bag? It's the first time his blindness has ever truly worried me. And I know there are blind parents out there, but…I don't know how they do it. I don't want all the burden of caring for a baby to fall solely on me, along with keeping perfect order around here for Jason. That's a lot to handle." Tears stung her eyes, and Katie pointed to the hallway. Heather turned around. Jason stood there, a pained expression on his face.

"Jason…" Her voice was shaky.

"I was just looking for you," he said quietly.

"Katie's nursing the baby, and we were just talking." Heather hoped Jason hadn't heard, but could tell by the look on his face that he had.

"Yeah, I heard." The hurt in his voice made Heather sick to her stomach. "I'm going to head back outside. Please bring some margaritas out when you're done…talking."

Wiping her eyes, Heather shot a helpless look at Katie. Jason brusquely turned around and headed down the hallway. Heather went after him.

"Jason, wait." She touched his arm and he recoiled from her grasp.

"I'm not having this conversation right now." He spun around to face her. "We've got a backyard full of guests, and we need to tend to them. Not to your bullshit worries about perceived problems I might have with a hypothetical baby that doesn't exist."

"Jason—"

"I just have one thing to ask you, and then I don't want to talk about it anymore. You've said you definitely want to have children. So if you can't trust me with a baby and you don't want to feel like a single parent—why are you with me?"

"It's not that simple—"

"Well it sounds to me like your claims to not be bothered by my blindness are all a fucking lie. And I don't understand why you moved in with me if you're so damned scared to have me as the father of your children."

"Because I love you. Because I want to be with you forever—"

"Oh, do you? What about when it's time to have kids? Then what?"

"Then I'll deal with it, we'll figure it out. I just voiced my concerns to Katie. I didn't say I didn't want to have children with you. I would love to make babies with you. But yes, I'm worried about how our life would be. About how much responsibility will fall on me."

"You just said outside that you're learning to never doubt me. Well I'm hearing plenty of doubts." The sliding glass doors opened. Jason whispered, "I'm done talking about this for now."

"Hey, Jace, where are you?" Mark hollered, walking through the living room and spotting them in the hallway. He caught Heather's teary eyes, and she looked down. "Is everything okay?"

"Fine," Jason said, producing an impressive fake smile. "I was just heading back out." He walked past his brother.

Mark looked at Heather, who eventually looked up at him. "I'll be right out, Jason," he said as his brother walked out the door. He turned to Heather. "What's wrong?"

She walked to the kitchen, and Mark followed. "It's complicated." Her voice not much more than a whisper. She leaned against the kitchen counter.

"Well I'm a fairly smart guy—try me."

Heather looked him in the eye. "It's just something between Jason and me."

"Okay." Mark stepped back. "But you were crying, and Jason looked upset. He's my brother. If there's something going on that I could help with, just say the word."

"Thanks, Mark." Heather smiled. "We'll work it out."

Their eyes caught for a moment before he said, "Okay," and walked back outside.

She finished mixing the margaritas and rushed outside.

"Where the hell have you been?" Shawn joked from the patio in front of her, with a basketball in his hands.

Jason stood a few feet away. "We thought you were taking a nap or something."

"No, I was just with my friend who's nursing her baby." She smiled at the half-truth. "Hey," she said to Jason, giving him a gentle rub on his back.

He tensed up. "Hey."

"I'm sorry," she whispered in his ear. "I'm sorry I don't have the confidence about this that you do. But please give me time…I'll get there."

Shawn saw them conversing quietly and said, "Hey, Scharp, I'm going to get another beer and check on my lady. Be back in a minute."

Jason closed his eyes and whispered back, "I said I didn't want to talk about it now."

"But I don't like it when you're mad at me—"

"I'm not mad, I'm scared. You have doubts and that scares the shit out of me," he continued to whisper.

"Baby, I love you—"

"I love you too. That's why it hurts so fucking bad that you don't believe in me."

"You can do so much, but you do have limitations— I'd be stupid not to consider that. But I never said it was insurmountable or a deal breaker."

"Yeah, well you never said it wasn't, either."

"I believe in us, we'll figure it out," she whispered, trying to convince herself as much as him. She gave him a gentle kiss. He kissed her back.

"Please don't give up on me," Jason whispered. "I'll be a really good dad someday." His desperation nearly broke her heart.

****

The party lasted until after midnight, when Jason pushed Shawn and his date out the door.

"Ah, quiet," he said when the sound of their car disappeared down the road. "Heather?"

"Right here sitting on the couch, baby." She smiled at him with her feet propped on the coffee table. She moved her feet out of his way when he walked by and sat next to her.

"Well, I think our first party was a success, don't you?"

"Very much so." She patted his thigh. "We make a great team."

"We do." His voice was quiet and he looked down. "I need to ask you something."

"What's that?"

"Are you having doubts about being with me?"

"No," she was quick to answer.

"But if you definitely want kids and you're not sure you want to have kids with someone who's blind...then how do I fit in your life?"

"I never said I don't want kids with someone who's blind. I said it was something to think about, to figure out how we will cope with that. You surprise me with what you're capable of every day." She heard a song playing in the background by Brett Dennen, an artist they both loved. *Darlin' Do Not Fear* was all about not being afraid of the unknown. Listening to the lyrics, she suddenly felt inspired and determined to stop over-thinking things.

"The song that's playing is just perfect." Heather took Jason's hands. "Just like you took that leap of faith with me and decided to trust someone again...well, I'm going to take a leap of faith and believe that you will be able to figure out the dad thing. That together we'll figure out a way to make parenthood work for us." She sounded sure of herself and felt it too. Why stress over something unknown when what she did know was that she loved Jason more than any man she'd ever known? She felt like a weight lifted off her.

"Really?" he asked, smiling.

"Really." She kissed him, and he kissed her back with enthusiasm.

"I don't want you to say anything just because you think I want to hear it."

"I'm not, Jason. I just decided I'm sick of worrying about it. So I'm not going to. Like the song said, I'm going to stop being afraid of something that may or may not be a problem. I'm just going to believe that we're such a good team we can do this. I believe in us."

"So do I," he said with a sense of relief. "I told you before, I don't know how much I can do, but you know I don't give up easily. And I'll do anything in my power for you."

"I know you will."

Jason kissed her neck. "Let's clean up the mess tomorrow. I just want to take you to bed right now and explore every inch of your body with my lips."

"Jason?" Her voice was soft as her hands rested on his face.

"Yes?"

"You are everything to me." She gazed at him and felt an overwhelming sense of love and security.

"As you are to me." His lips brushed her ear lobe, then her cheek and finally, her lips. "I must have you, now."

"Okay." She smiled. "I'm yours."

They walked to the bedroom holding hands and she thought to herself, *I do believe everything will work out. Really.* She squeezed Jason's hand, and he smiled in response.

It has to.

Chapter Fourteen

Late July meant the end of Jason's beep baseball season. Over the summer he played in several tournaments, and Heather drove him to all of them—Wichita, Chicago area, Topeka, and the last one was scheduled for Indy. Not only would Heather go to this one but so would his parents and Mark and Angie.

Heather knew absolutely nothing about beep baseball until Jason educated her. Each team had a sighted pitcher who pitched to his own team. The ball beeped so the visually impaired players could hear it coming and locate where it was. If they hit the ball, one of the two bases started beeping, and the batter ran to that base. If the player made it to the base before the other team got the ball, then they scored. The bases were soft foam pedestals that the players could run into, located at what were normally first and third base.

At his first game of the season, it was thrilling for Heather to find out he was kind of the star of the team. He was by far the best fielder and a strong hitter too. Maybe Jason had an advantage because he played baseball for six years as a kid before his eyesight got too bad, whereas some of the players were born with a vision impairment and never got to play real ball. Or maybe it was just because of his natural athleticism and fearlessness.

The first time Heather saw him hit the ball and take off running for the beeping base, it gave her chills. It dawned on her she never saw him move that fast or run at all. When he walked with his cane, his pace was moderate, deliberate. Or if he held onto someone's arm, he followed their lead. But out there on the ball field…he became the Speedy Gonzalez his friend Joe described. He was like that kid again, running with abandon.

While Jason played ball, and for a while afterward, he was positively effervescent. The smile on his face when he made a play was the very definition of joy. Funny how something like baseball could arouse such emotion in both the players and the people watching them. But in many ways, Jason became the kid again whose childhood was cruelly cut short, the man his limitations didn't always allow him to be in the real world. On the beep ball field, he wasn't a blind guy…he was just another ball player.

After his first game, Heather ran down from the stands to greet him on the field.

"Jason!" she yelled, smiling when he turned at the sound of her voice and waved in her direction. She waved back before she realized what she'd done and put her hand down. He looked sexy in his ball uniform. He pulled out his cane and headed toward her when she approached. "Jason, I'm right here."

"I knew it was one of my adoring fans." He grinned, and she threw her arms around him in a hug. "Oh, sweetheart, I'm all sweaty and gross."

"I don't care." Heather kissed him.

"So, what did you think?"

"I think I've never seen you so exhilarated and so…free. It was fantastic!"

"It is, isn't it? I mean it's not real baseball."

"No, it's harder. In real baseball the players can see the ball."

"Let's head to the car—I want some A/C." He grabbed her elbow, and they headed to the parking lot.

"So…why didn't you tell me you're like, the star player?"

"Well, I don't know about that…."

"Oh, come on," she groaned. "You know you are."

"Maybe I am," he admitted sheepishly. "But I didn't want to brag or anything."

"I thought I would lose my mind when you caught that ball in the air! I mean, how often does that happen?"

"Pretty much never. I think I've only ever done it twice

before. Normally we get it after it hits the ground. That was sweet, wasn't it?"

"My baby is a supah-stah!" They both laughed. "And did I mention that you look hot in your uniform?"

He chuckled. "You said some things."

When the time came for the road trip to Indianapolis, Heather was a little worried about going with Jason's parents. Specifically, with Eve. She was by no means Heather's biggest fan, and Heather knew she couldn't do anything about it. There was nothing personal in Eve's distrust of Heather, just an overall distrust of women who dated her son. So how could Heather combat that? But she tried to be optimistic and hope maybe this trip would help things. Spending almost three full days together would maybe give Eve a chance to know her better.

****

When they arrived at Jason's parents' home, it was agreed that Jason and Heather would sit in the third row of John's SUV to give the pregnant lady more legroom. So they climbed all the way in back, and everyone else followed.

"Wow, this is…cozy." Jason squeezed Heather's leg. It was a tight fit. Jason had a passing thought…could he get claustrophobia even if he couldn't see the confines of the space? Probably not. So he focused on fiddling with the air vents above them. He asked Heather, "Are you getting enough on you?"

"Yeah, baby, thanks." She rested her head on his shoulder. "This is going to be a long ride. Maybe I'll just sleep for a while."

"That's fine with me. For once you can do that, since you're not driving."

He pulled his earphones out of his bag and noticed Heather's breathing had already slowed. As he scrolled through the menu on his phone, listening for the title of the book he wanted to hear, he heard his mom say, "They do look cute together there in the back, don't they?"

Jason smiled to himself.

****

When the car came to a stop, Heather lifted her head off Jason's shoulder. He pulled out his earphones. "Are you awake, sleepyhead?"

"Yes." She yawned. "Where are we?"

"Uh, let me see…" He looked toward the window. "You know, I'm not sure. Looks exactly like my parents' driveway to me."

"Just for the record, I'm rolling my eyes. Why do I even put up with you?"

"Because I'm irresistible."

"Oh, that's right," she said. Jason leaned over and kissed her.

"We're in some little Podunk town not far from Effingham," Mark said. "Stopping for the mother of my unborn child to pee. Again."

They all climbed out, took a bathroom break and bought some snacks. When they got settled back in the car and on the road again, Eve said, "Hey kids, instead of everyone doing their own thing, why don't we interact more? Road trips are times to share together. You guys are all on your iPod thingies or whatever. When you were kids we used to play games and things like that in the car."

"That's because there was nothing else to do in a car back in 1987," Jason said.

"Well, I still think we should make this more fun."

"Yeah, Jason," Mark said. "Mom's right. Here's a game you'll enjoy in particular. Let's play 'I Spy.'" He laughed out loud at his own joke.

"Sure, Mark." Jason grinned, taking the bait. "I'll go first. I spy something that looks like an asshole."

The two brothers and their ladies all busted out laughing.

"Boys, that's not funny." Eve was clearly not amused. "Angie, I hope you have a girl and not a boy. Do you see what I have to put up with?"

"I'm sorry, Mom." Mark was still laughing. "I couldn't resist. What do you want us to play in the car?"

"Oh, I know," Jason said with excitement. "We could all sing *Kumbaya My Lord.*"

Mark continued laughing and slapped Jason's shoulder in amusement.

"Boys," John piped up. "That's enough. Your mother has a good point."

"Sorry, Mom." Jason and Heather continued laughing in the back seat. "What do you have in mind?"

"I don't know, I just thought we'd enjoy each other's company a little bit more." Eve sounded deflated.

"Mom, it's not like I can play any road games. I suck at I Spy, or finding license plates, or anything else that requires looking out the window."

"Of course I know that. Couldn't we just talk?"

"Well, Heather and I are way back here and it's kind of hard to hear. And we've got more than two days of togetherness...I think we'll have plenty of bonding time."

Mark jumped in. "Why don't we all just watch a movie together? I brought some along, and a lot of these are classics you've already seen, Jace, so you won't need a play-by-play of the action."

"A movie sounds good," Heather agreed.

"What have you got?" Jason asked.

"Let me see..." Mark said. "Oh, here's a perfect one! How about *This is Spinal Tap*?"

"Yeah," Angie said. "That's so funny."

"One of my all-time favorites," Jason said. "Heather?"

"It's wicked good—count me in."

"Okay then, I'll load it up," Mark said.

Eve sighed. "I'm taking a nap."

****

After two more bathroom breaks for Angie and about three more hours of driving, they arrived in Indianapolis. They all agreed to take a few minutes to settle in their rooms at the JW Marriott hotel and then meet downstairs at the restaurant.

Jason put their suitcase on the luggage stand, and Heather showed him the layout of the room. She gushed about the décor and great view of the city. He took her word for it.

After leaning his cane against the wall, he put his arms around her. "Why don't we give the mattress a spin and see what we think?" He relished the contact of their bodies pressed against one another and kissed her.

"That sounds fantastic, but we have to meet your family downstairs. How about right after we're done eating, we'll say we're beat from the trip and want to make it an early night. Then we can come up to…finish this."

Jason sighed. "If we must."

****

During dinner, they enjoyed a fun and light mood along with delectable food. The upscale Italian restaurant didn't disappoint. Heather and Jason both got light salads to start, and then he got a perfectly pan-seared bass while Heather enjoyed the melt-in-your-mouth chicken parmesan.

Genuinely friendly toward Heather, Eve came across as a nice woman and funny like the rest of the family. For the first time, she seemed to warm up to Heather, who was optimistic that maybe this weekend would be a turning point. But she was careful not to get too ahead of herself. It was only one meal, after all.

"So how are you feeling these days, Angie?" Heather asked between bites of her decadent dish.

"Actually, pretty good. The morning sickness is gone, and I have a lot more energy now. Just three months to go."

"Hey guys." Mark grinned at his wife. "We've got something to share with you. We couldn't wait anymore—we found out the sex."

"What is it?" Eve asked, bursting at the seams.

With a huge smile on her face, Angie said, "A girl."

"A girl!" Eve and John cheered in unison. Everyone laughed.

"Finally a girl in our family," Eve said.

"Wow, a niece." A small smile turned up the corners of Jason's mouth.

"I can't wait to dress her up in frilly things," Eve said.

"Me too," Angie chimed in.

"She's going to be spoiled rotten," John said, and everyone agreed. Heather felt lucky to be surrounded by so many faces filled with joy.

"So, Jason." John looked at his youngest son. "Are you nervous about the games tomorrow?"

"No, not nervous. Excited. But this isn't the World Series or anything, just a tournament. I'll play my best and have fun—that's all I can do."

"Well, I'm anxious to see it." John pushed his clean plate out of the way.

Jason took a drink of his wine. "Hey, guys, while we're on the topic of my ballgame, I want to say thanks to everyone for coming all this way just to watch me play. You have always been supportive of this crazy sport of mine, and it means a lot to me. So thanks."

"Well, you need a big cheering section," Angie said. "Poor Heather's been the sole cheerleader for most of the season."

"And a great cheerleader she's been." Jason smiled at Heather, squeezing her hand. He set his glass down and she noticed it teetering, half of it resting on his napkin, so she nudged it the rest of the way onto the table.

"Oh, I love watching you play." She smiled. "You're phenomenal out there and the look of excitement on your face is worth the long miles."

"Thank you, sweetheart." One of his trademark grins spread across his face. "Did I ever tell you guys about the time Mark thought he'd give beep baseball a shot?"

"We don't have to talk about that." Mark laughed.

"I never heard this story," Angie said. "Do tell."

"Well, he thought he could do as good a job as me," Jason explained, "so I blindfolded him and our pitcher started throwing balls. Many of them. How many would you say, Mark? Twenty?"

"No, probably fifteen," he said sheepishly.

"Okay, I'll give you that. And he couldn't hit any of

them. Keep in mind, our pitcher is really good, and his whole job is to make sure he's throwing so you can hit it. But Mark still couldn't make contact, so they brought out a tee for him."

Angie giggled. "Like the little four-year-olds use?"

"Yep, just like that," Jason said with glee. "It still took him several swings to hit it."

"I would love to have seen that." John's deep laugh rang out.

"Me too, Dad, me too." Jason laughed. "But that's not all. When he finally hit the ball off the tee, he headed for first base. From the way they described it to me, he made it about halfway before he started veering off the baseline and then when they yelled at him to go to the right, he tripped over his own feet and fell."

The whole table laughed hysterically. "Sure, laugh it up." Mark blushed. "But I'd like to see any of you try."

"No thanks," Heather said. "I'll stick to the stands."

"I don't know how you do it, Jace." Mark shook his head. "That was tough."

"Well, I've had lots of practice. And it's apparent I'm more coordinated and athletic than you."

"Oh, screw off."

Jason took his last bite and leaned over to Heather. "Are you done eating?"

"Yep," she said. He squeezed her thigh under the table.

"Well, I think we're going to make it an early night, gang," Jason said. "I'm tired from the trip and need to rest up for the games tomorrow."

"I don't buy that for a minute." Mark grinned. "You want to take that pretty lady of yours upstairs and get your money's worth in that room." Heather's face turned red.

"Oh, Mark," Eve scolded.

Jason chuckled. "I have no idea what you're talking about."

"Uh huh," Mark said.

Within a few minutes, after arguing about who was

going to pay the bill (John won), they all went their separate ways for the night. When Heather and Jason reached their room, she said, "Now we can finish what we started earlier."

"Oh, testing the mattress, eh?" Jason chuckled. They walked into the room and Heather flicked on the light switch. "Wait—Heather?"

"What?"

"Is it really dark in here when the lights are off?"

"Yeah, pretty much pitch black. Why?"

"Turn the lights off. I want you to see what I'm seeing while we're in bed."

"Oh, really?" she said with naughtiness.

"Your hands will have to grope me and your lips will have to find all the right places," he whispered while he took his clothes off.

"But I like to look at you." She admired his flat abs and broad, toned chest.

"You can look at me—just not with your eyes." He climbed under the covers.

"Fair enough," she said with a grin, flicking off the lights and joining him.

Their lovemaking was even more intense, more sensual than normal. The darkness enveloped them in a world dominated with touches. And taste. Heather loved the taste of his skin, the manly smell of his body. It was intoxicating.

She realized that although she'd been with men in the past, she'd never experienced the raw animal passion she felt with Jason. He was an incredibly caring and unselfish lover. She took great pleasure in the delights of his tongue and his fingers.

"Oh my, what great fingers you have," she moaned after they finished.

"I knew all that Braille would eventually pay off." His breathing was heavy. He lay down beside her, their legs still entangled. "I'm not sure, but I think your G spot has an actual Braille G there." They both laughed.

She snuggled in closer to him, kissing his chest. "I kind

of liked it in the dark."

"In bed is one place where no vision is required. In fact, I think it gets in the way."

"You might be right. That was amazing." She closed her eyes. "You're an extremely good lover, have I ever told you that?"

"Not so much in words, but your body has given me some indications of that," he said with mischief in his voice. "You're pretty damn good yourself, Ms. Cook."

"Thank you. Have you ever had sex this good?"

"No, sweetheart, never. Everything's just better with you."

They fell asleep in each other's arms, succumbing to the deep slumber that only security and contentment can bring.

****

At the game the next day, Heather sat between Eve and Mark in the stands, excited and yet nervous. Jason loved the game so much, she really hoped his team would win. Or at least play well.

His team was hitting first. When it was Jason's turn at bat and he headed to the plate, Heather yelled, "Go Jason!" at the top of her lungs.

Mark cracked up laughing, ribbing her, but it thrilled Heather to see Jason wave in her direction. She started to wave back and then caught herself.

"Waving at a blind man, eh Heather?" Mark teased in a fun, brotherly sort of way.

"Oh hush," Heather said, laughing at herself. She resisted the urge to yell more encouragement to Jason, because in beep baseball, the spectators have to remain quiet until after the play is over so the players can hear the ball.

Jason let the first ball go by. He swung and missed the second one. On the third pitch he popped the ball way into the outfield and took off running at full speed. He was fast! Dirt clouds flew up around him, and he easily reached the base before the opposing team got the ball.

"Go Jason, go Jason, go Jason!" Heather cheered. Angie joined in with her. One of the coaches led him back to the bench, and Jason smiled that gorgeous grin Heather could never get enough of.

Eve smiled with pride. "He really is good, isn't he?"

"Yeah, he is," Mark agreed, looking proud himself. "Of course we all know I could have hit that."

"Oh sure, son," John said with a laugh. "If we put the ball on a tee."

Jason did a great job fielding and got several outs during the game. He scored every time at bat except for once, when he got a hit the opposing team caught before he made it to base. Being fiercely competitive, he seemed pretty pissed.

Jason's team won the first game by a narrow margin, so they would play a second game later. That gave them a break for a bit, before playing the winner of the next game.

Heather went down to the dugout and brought Jason up to the stands. He shared congratulations, slaps on the back and hugs all around with his family. He basked in the glory of the victory while they discussed the game and the plays that Jason made in detail.

Heather was all smiles, enraptured while she listened to him tell his stories from the field. She rested her hand on Jason's thigh and cozied up next to him when he put his arm around her. When he was done talking, he leaned over and kissed her. Out of the corner of her eye, Heather caught Eve watching them.

"Heather, why don't we grab some lunch for everyone?" Eve asked.

"Okay," Heather said, surprised that Eve wanted her help with anything. They decided to get an assortment of hot dogs and pretzels, and a Coke for Jason.

When Eve and Heather reached the concession stand, they found themselves standing in a fairly long line of people. At least the shade of the awning offered a reprieve from the hot sun.

"Heather." Eve cleared her throat. "I know we didn't

exactly get off on the right foot with each other. But it's been several months now, and I want to take this opportunity to apologize and let you know that I do believe you're sincere about being with Jason."

"Well, thank you," Heather said in absolute shock.

"I've been watching you two, especially on this trip. Just seeing you together now in the stands…it shows me how much love you really do share." Eve looked at Heather with gratitude. "It means the world to me that Jason is so happy. And you have an awful lot to do with that."

"Well, he makes me happy too." Heather was still in disbelief.

Eve patted Heather on the back. "When I'm wrong, I admit it, and I was wrong to doubt you. It's just…when you're a parent, you want to protect your children from the bad things in this world. And Jason's life has been hard at times, very difficult, and I couldn't do much about it. As a parent, that kills you. So when it came to women, I guess I felt I could intervene in some way, maybe prevent him from getting hurt. But he's right, he's a grown man, I can't keep treating him like a boy. So I'm glad he's got you by his side." She smiled and Heather was delighted to see on her face the same big, broad beautiful smile that she passed down to her youngest son.

When they got back to the stands, they passed out the food, and Heather took her seat next to Jason.

"Hey, sweetheart." Jason patted her leg. "I thought I smelled Bali Mango."

"Yeah, along with a nice dose of sweat," she said. "I'm putting your Coke in the cup holder in front of you." Jason reached out to find it, but searched too high. "Lower, baby."

He grasped it and took a drink. "Thanks."

Heather wished he could see the look of astonishment and pleasure still on her face from the conversation she'd had with Eve.

Since he couldn't, she whispered in his ear. "You won't believe what your mom said to me."

"What?" he whispered back.

"She apologized for doubting me and thanked me for making you so happy. She said she's glad you have me."

A smile spread across his face. "I told you she'd come around."

Chapter Fifteen

It took three weeks or so to get back into some sort of routine after school started. Although Heather offered to drive Jason to work every day, he insisted on taking the bus unless rain poured from the sky.

So most days they left the house about the same time, Jason's cane tapping down the sidewalk to the bus stop while Heather drove by him. She had fun rolling down her window to belt out a whistle or cat call, just to make him laugh.

Their uniform for the summer had been shorts and T-shirts, and although Jason looked great in anything, Heather enjoyed seeing him look preppy again since they were back at work. She thought he looked cute with his leather messenger bag slung across his body wearing khakis and various button-down or Polo shirts.

She missed the lazy days of their summer, but life with Jason was pretty good even when they were working. Some afternoons she'd make it home before him and other times, if she stayed for a late meeting, he would be there when she got home and something would already smell delicious in the kitchen.

****

On a weekend in September, they agreed to babysit for Katie and Dan. Little Abby was three months old, and this was the first time they decided to leave her with anyone besides Grandma. Katie seemed a little nervous.

"So I showed you where everything is, right?" Katie asked.

"Yes you did," Heather said. "Bottles, diapers, binkies, jammies, everything. I have your number in the unlikely event that I would need to call you about something. I know her bedtime and how many times you like to burp her. Just go have fun."

"You know, Katie," Jason offered, "if you're worried about leaving her, you could always stay here with Heather while Dan and I hit the town."

Dan laughed.

"Oh, shut it, Jason." She startled him with a playful slap on the arm. "We're leaving. I'm fine. No having sex in our bed, you crazy teenagers."

It was Jason's turn to laugh. "But the couch is okay?"

"It's leather. Don't even think about it."

Then they were out the door, and Heather busied herself holding Abby and babbling on in baby talk. Jason was fairly certain he could find a better way to spend his Saturday night, but Heather had begged him to join her.

"Excuse me," he said, "I know you're in the middle of an important conversation, but can you turn the TV on?"

"Don't you want to play with the baby?"

"Well, she doesn't really do much yet."

Heather turned on the TV. "She smiles and makes the cutest faces…"

"I'll take your word on that. I'm sure she's making an adorable face right now."

"Actually, she is. But she giggles now too, and smells so good."

"That I'll give you," he said, reaching over next to him on the couch and finding Abby's shoulder and then rubbing her cheek. "She does have that great baby smell. What is that, anyway? Lotion?"

"It's all that stuff…baby wash, shampoo, lotion, powder."

"I could smell it the minute we walked in here. I guess that's what Mark and Angie's place will smell like soon. Wow, her skin is so soft. Unbelievably smooth."

"I know, I love it. Do you want to hold her?"

"I don't know. Babies are just kind of squirmy, and they don't talk, which means I don't have any way to get feedback from them. I can't see if she's smiling at me or about to cry."

"Well, I'll tell you," Heather said in a soft voice. "When we have kids you'll hold them a lot, won't you?"

"Oh, is that what tonight's about?" Jason asked, his voice ripe with irritation. "Is this some kind of test or something to see how I can handle a baby?"

"Jason, that's not fair. This isn't a test. I just thought it would be fun for us to babysit together tonight. What girl doesn't like to see her man hold a baby?"

"Fine, I'll hold her if that's what you want."

"Well you don't have to—"

"Just give her to me, okay?" He held his hands out and felt a warm bundle placed into them.

"Do you have her?" Heather asked.

"Yeah." He put her up against his shoulder. "Wow, she smells so sweet. And she feels like a heavy football or sack of flour or something." Abby made some cooing sounds and a big grin spread across his face.

"Isn't she wonderful?" Heather whispered.

"She's not too bad," he said with a smile, laying her face-up on his lap. "Is this okay?"

"Yep, that's good. She's looking right at you."

"Who's that funny looking guy, huh Abby?" he said in a sweet baby voice. "It's your 'Uncle Jason,' or that's what they call me anyway. But I'm not really your uncle. I'm just sleeping with your mommy's best friend."

"Jason!"

He laughed. "Like she knows what I'm saying."

"Oh, Jason, she's smiling so big at you right now, reacting to your laughter."

"Can I...can I see?" he asked, his tone timid.

"Sure, you won't break her."

He reached down and felt her chin and then her mouth, wide open and full of slobber. She giggled. Jason turned to Heather. "Did you hear that?"

"Yeah, she likes you."

"Uncle Jason is the best," he said in a singsong voice, and Abby giggled again. He had one hand on her face and could feel her cheeks rise up when she smiled bigger. "Her head is incredibly tiny."

"Everything on her is tiny."

Jason found her fingers and she grabbed onto him. He couldn't stop smiling. "What little fingers you have, Abby." She started wriggling around and Jason quickly held her with both hands again. "What's she doing?"

"She's kicking and wiggling. Just baby stuff." Heather put her arm around Jason.

"I'm afraid I might drop her."

"I'm right here, baby, you're fine. She's fine. Just enjoy her." She patted his leg. "Seeing you hold a baby…it's stirring up some strong emotions."

"Oh, yeah?" He smiled. "Uh, I think she's doing something in her diaper…I felt something. Your turn." He picked her up from his lap and held her out to Heather.

Heather grabbed her. "Is that how it's going to be with ours? Bowel movement—here you go, Heather."

"You betcha," he said with a grin. "Can you turn on something I might be interested in?"

"Back to the TV, huh? Fine." She flipped through the channels and found a documentary on the History Channel about Lewis and Clark. "Will that work for you?"

"Perfect. But is there something else you'd rather watch?"

"I'm going to play with the baby. And as soon as she's done filling her diaper, I'm going to change her."

A few minutes later Jason was engrossed in the show, and Heather asked, "Do you want to go with me to change her?"

"Not really." Heather didn't respond, but even without seeing the expression on her face, he could sense that was not the answer she wanted to hear. Sighing, he said, "If you want me to I will."

"Great!"

So he grabbed onto her elbow and they walked to the baby's room. The smell of baby powder grew even stronger.

"They've got it decorated so cute in here," Heather

said. "Okay, cutie pie, let's get you changed."

Jason stood next to Heather, feeling more than out-of-place.

"Here's a diaper." She touched his hand with it. "Give it to me when I ask for it, okay?"

"I can handle that."

"Can you open it up for me, so it's ready?" She undid the snaps in Abby's pants.

"Sure." He pulled the sides of the diaper open. A sudden pungent aroma hit Jason's nose. "Oh yeah, that's poop all right."

"It's been a while since I've done this," Heather admitted. "Let's get you all cleaned up. Jeez, she's really wiggling around. You little stinker, hold still, Abby. Diaper, please."

"Here." Jason handed it over.

"Thanks. I've got her all cleaned up now—do you want to put the fresh diaper on her?"

"No. I'm not going to experiment with someone else's baby."

"Okay." Heather sounded discouraged. Jason heard Heather snapping Abby's pants back up. "There you go, Abby. All clean." She turned to Jason. "Can you please take her while I go wash my hands?"

Jason held out his hands and felt the bag of sweet-smelling flour in his hands again. He didn't dare walk anywhere, not knowing the room at all, so he just stood there with her. She started whimpering.

"What's wrong, Abby?" he cooed to her in a soothing, soft voice. He kissed her cheek. "Uncle Jason's got you, no need to fuss." The whimper turned to a cry. He started bouncing her up and down, but she cried more. "Heather?" he hollered.

"Coming," she said from down the hallway and was soon in the bedroom. "Oh, her leg's caught up." She pulled Abby's leg free from where it was pinned up against Jason's chest and she stopped crying.

"Is she okay?" Jason asked, concerned.

"Oh, she's fine. Her leg just got kind of wedged up against you, and she couldn't get it free."

"I'm sorry, I didn't know—"

"Jason, it's no big deal."

"Here, take her." He held the baby out in front of him. Heather grabbed Abby from his arms.

Jason didn't want Heather to be worried about his abilities as a father any more than she already was. *Way to go, Scharp.* "You know, I'm sure I'll get better when I get more practice around our babies."

"I'm sure you will too," Heather said quietly. "Take my arm. We'll go back in the living room."

****

Jason went back to watching his show, and Heather played with Abby, but her mind churned. Abby's leg getting bunched up was no big deal at all, but it was a small example of how challenging raising a baby was going to be for Jason. Diaper changing alone was going to be difficult—maybe wet diapers would be easier, but the poopy ones could even be tricky for someone sighted to change on an active baby.

Jason wouldn't even be able to see what a baby was doing without using one of his hands to keep track of her. That would only leave one hand to do everything else— hold her legs up, wipe, and put a diaper on.

A feeling of trepidation crept over her. She knew Jason excelled at finding his own ways of doing things, and there were plenty of successful blind parents in the world, so it was possible. But at the moment, it just seemed so daunting.

"Something's wrong," Jason said during a commercial break.

"With what?"

"With you." He faced her. "You never ever go this long without talking to me."

"Nothing's wrong," she lied.

"It's the whole having a baby with me thing again, isn't it?"

"No," she lied again.

"I can tell when you're not being honest with me, Heather." He sighed.

"I told you I got past that, and I did. But it doesn't mean I don't ever think about what it's going to be like."

"I'm not even a dad yet, and you're already doubting me."

"Jason, I know you'll figure it out."

"And what if there are some things I just can't 'figure out?'"

"Well if you can't—"

"Then you'll be left holding the bag. I know. I've heard it from you before."

"I was going to say if you can't, then we'll figure it out together." She knew she didn't sound terribly convincing, but she tried her best. She did want to believe they could make it work. She thought they could. It just seemed like in the beginning it would require a lot of effort and ingenuity.

"You told me this wasn't an issue for you anymore." He closed his eyes and shook his head.

"It's not, okay? You brought it up, not me."

"It was just a little thing with her leg—"

"I know, Jason. It's okay. Just stop. Quit putting words in my mouth."

He didn't speak for a minute. "Just because you don't say the words doesn't mean you're not thinking them."

He was right, and she knew that. But what more could she say? "Jason, I want to have kids with you someday. I don't know what else you want me to say."

"That you believe in me. And that even though I don't know how or if I can do everything you'd like me to do as a father, you'll be okay with it."

"I will be okay with it." It took all of her strength to sound convincing. He didn't respond, but Heather could tell he relaxed a bit. "I'm going to feed her and put her down for the night."

She left the room with Abby. Why couldn't this just be easy? She'd found the perfect man and was happier than she'd ever been. But she wanted kids. And she wanted a husband who could share in the caregiving. She didn't want to be the only one caring for their babies. It wasn't fair. What if she ended up resenting Jason if she was stuck doing most of the work while trying to keep everything in the house in its precise location?

It wasn't fair that the person she wanted to share her life with got screwed in the gene department.

What she really wanted was for Jason to be able to see. Was that so much to ask?

During the next couple of weeks, they didn't bring up children again, and they both made a point to avoid the topic. Heather loved seeing Abby in Jason's arms and the way he lit up when she giggled and cooed. She knew he would be a great dad—he was so good with Kennedy and his students. But she figured the infancy and toddler years would present his biggest struggle. So she just didn't think about it.

****

Jason walked in the house after work one day in late September and wondered if Heather was home already. Then he heard sounds coming from the kitchen...and did he actually smell cooking food?

"Hey, sweetheart, I'm home." He put his cane and bag in the corner and took off his shoes.

"I'm in the kitchen," she yelled.

He walked into the kitchen. "Where's my sexy gal?"

"I'm at the stove, baby," she said, and he heard the sound of a wooden spoon stirring in a pan.

"Why are you at the stove? You're scaring me, sweetheart," he said with a smile, touching her on the back.

"Very funny." She turned around. "I'm just heating up—what happened to your head?"

"Oh yeah, that." He reached up to feel the large gash on his forehead that oozed blood. "A tree limb. That house near the corner has a tree that overhangs into the sidewalk and I clipped it pretty good. Must have strong, thick branches."

"Too bad your cane can't detect things overhead. We need to ask them to trim their tree. Here, let me clean that off for you."

"How bad does it look?"

"Well, it's right in the center of your forehead, so it's pretty noticeable. The cut's not deep though. You're lucky it didn't get you in the eye."

"Couldn't have done too much damage to something that doesn't work." He chuckled.

"But it would have hurt a lot more." Her touch was gentle while she rubbed the cut with a wet paper towel. He heard the clinking sound of what he guessed were metal bracelets sliding down her arm.

"True. So what on earth are you doing in the kitchen? Do I smell something cooking?"

"Yes, don't look so shocked."

"I would say it's more alarm than shock."

"I'm just heating up some sauce to dip breadsticks in. I stopped and got a frozen pizza and breadsticks. Even I can't screw that up."

"I would hope not," he said, standing next to her. "Do you want some help?"

"No, I've got it under control." She sounded proud of herself.

"Okay." He had flashbacks of some burnt cinnamon rolls she made in Gulf Shores. "Why don't I set the table?"

"I already did."

"Wow, you're just being little Suzy Homemaker, aren't you?" He headed to the fridge.

"Well, let's not get ahead of ourselves."

"I'm going to get a beer and sit on the couch then." He reached inside for a Corona. Instead of finding the beer, he found a package of…something. He picked that up, expecting to find his beer behind it but no; something large and round in a plastic bag lay there. Lettuce maybe? "Heather, did you go to the store and throw a bunch of stuff in the fridge?"

"Oh, yeah, just a few things."

He shook his head. "You can't do that, okay? I've told you that over and over. I can't see what's in there, I only know how to find things because everything has a place. If you move things around, I can't find anything."

"I'm sorry, it's just a few things, baby. I planned to put them away in the right place for you later—I was just in a hurry to get dinner going. I'll get you a beer."

"I just wanted to grab myself a beer out of the fridge…" He held his tongue and shook his head. She didn't get it sometimes, how something simple like moving the stuff around in there turned him from someone self-sufficient into…a blind man. She brought his disability front and center at times when it didn't need to be anything more than a side note.

She put a beer in his hand. "I'm sorry—I meant to get it straightened up before you got home."

"Sweetheart, I know you didn't mean to do it, but it happens a lot. And yes, it's a pain in the ass, but this is how I function. Can you please try to make more of an effort?"

"Yes." Her voice dropped low as she headed back to the stove.

"I'm not mad." He put his hand on her shoulder. "It's just frustrating."

"I know Jason, I know." Her voice told Jason she was frustrated too. "I'll do better."

****

Although she knew he couldn't see it, she took joy in letting her irritation out by glaring at him.

He turned away and started to head to the living room. He stopped and leaned against the counter. "I'm sorry I'm not easier to live with. Thank you for all you do to accommodate your annoying boyfriend."

"You're welcome."

"I'll try not to be so hard on you. I know you're trying, and I love you for it."

Still left with the feeling like she had once again been scolded by the drill sergeant, she noticed a small smile playing at his lips and his expression showed he clearly adored her. The powder blue polo he wore intensified the blue of his eyes. He was so damn sexy. She walked over and kissed him.

"I love you too. But I'm still getting used to all this…I really will get the hang of it. Now go relax and let me finish dinner for once."

"Okay, but just for the record, I'm not a fan of blackened pizza," he said, leaving the room.

****

"Is something wrong?" Heather asked, looking over at Jason beside her in the car on their way to work that Friday. The cloudy skies spit rain off and on, so she convinced Jason to let her give him a ride. "You look like you don't feel well. You're pale."

"Really? No, I feel fine."

He didn't look fine. Heather pulled into Jason's school parking lot. "I hope you're not getting sick. I'm looking forward to going out for my birthday tonight with Katie and Dan."

"Oh, don't worry about it, birthday girl." He flashed a grin.

"I'm just barely going to make it to work on time. We should have left a lot earlier."

"If you want, I can just open the door and jump out so you don't have to stop the car," Jason offered with a sarcastic smirk.

"Yes, that would be great." She gave him a playful smack on the leg. "We're in your school parking lot, but there's a bus in front of the walkway where I normally drop you off. Can you find your way if I pull up behind it?"

"Sure." He pulled his cane out of his bag. "How far away from the center of the walkway are we?"

"I guess about twenty-five or thirty feet."

"Okay, I got it. Thanks, sweetheart." He gave her a quick kiss. "So you'll pick me up tonight?"

"Yeah, I'll call you when I'm on the way."

He climbed out of the car, flicked open his cane and started making his way along the damp sidewalk. The rain had stopped. Normally when she dropped him off, students weren't there yet, but since they'd arrived later today, the walkway teemed with kids. Heather noticed how they moved out of his way…it kind of looked like the parting of the Red Sea. A boy came up to him and tapped his shoulder, said something, and Jason smiled. *What a cute guy I have*, she thought.

Jason seemed to know the sound of her car and stopped and waved in her direction as she left.

****

All day long Jason felt distracted, unable to focus. All he could think about was the surprise he'd planned for Heather's birthday. Obviously, she had picked up on the fact that something wasn't right that morning. Jason figured his nerves made him look like he was about to vomit. It wasn't too far off the mark. He was pretty sure she'd like her gift, but…well, he just tried not to think about it.

While he led a scattered lesson in his last class, one of his students said, "Mr. Scharp, it's Jenny. Is something wrong?"

"What do you mean?" he asked, sitting on the edge of his desk.

"You're acting kind of…strange today. Like you're a million miles away or something."

"Yeah," said a male student. "You're kind of spaced out."

"Is that Ian?" Jason asked.

"Yeah, it's Ian." He taught all his students to say their names first when they talked, since he couldn't possibly recognize all of their voices.

"Well, you're always kind of spaced out, Ian, so how would you even know?" Jason joked, and the class laughed.

When the laughs died down, Ian retorted, "So you know if even *I* can tell you're acting weird, it must be true!"

"Sorry, guys, I didn't think it was that obvious." Jason stood back up and walked to the podium in the front of his room. "I'll let you in on a little secret." The room resounded with excited murmurs. "Tonight I'm going to ask my girlfriend to marry me." He heard gasps, *whoas*, *awws*.

"*You* have a girlfriend?" asked a boy that Jason recognized to be Sam.

"Okay, Sam," Jason chuckled, "why wouldn't I have a girlfriend?"

"Well…'cause…" Sam mumbled.

"Because I'm too ugly?"

"No," Sam said while everyone laughed.

"Because I'm too old?"

"Uh no."

"Oh, well then. Must have something to do with my defective eyeballs, huh?" Sam didn't respond. "Well I've got news for you kids—blind people get married and have kids. Which means…oh my God…blind people *do it!*"

They all started laughing hysterically. Didn't take much to reduce fifteen-year-olds to giggle boxes. Jason grinned. "You don't need eyes for everything, kids." When their laughter died down, he checked his watch and continued. "So anyway, that's why I'm acting like an idiot today, because I'm nervous about proposing tonight. Sorry guys. Okay, we've only got a couple of minutes left, so let's close our books and talk amongst yourselves."

Jason went back to his desk and checked his email. When the bell rang, he told his students to have a good weekend, cherishing the silence after they all shuffled out. But that's when the nerves really kicked in. It was time to set the plan into motion, so he sent a text to Heather, telling her he had to head up to the college to sign some papers, and to meet him there at the coffee shop at four-thirty.

Little did she know what would happen when she got there.

****

Jason sat in the coffee shop at a table near the front, waiting for Heather. It was right at four-thirty. Students filled the shop, and he passed the time by eavesdropping on conversations, many of them making plans for the night.

One girl relayed tales to another about her rotten boyfriend; at a nearby table he heard a couple on what sounded like an early or maybe even first date. He smiled to himself, remembering the first time he joined Heather here. It seemed like only yesterday, yet in many ways it was hard to remember his life without her.

He was sweating profusely and knew exactly what the expression "butterflies in your stomach" meant, because he felt them. But they actually felt more like large, rabid bats. He checked his pocket for about the fifteenth time, and yes, the ring box was still there. He reached out on the table until his fingers felt the cup of coffee that he ordered for her, just the way she liked it—caramel macchiato latte with extra vanilla.

The door of the shop opened, and he recognized Heather from the brisk, firm clack, clack of her heels when they hit the tile floor. He held his hand up and waved when the footsteps came toward him.

"Hey, baby." Her fragrance suddenly surrounded him. Her familiar scent was, for Jason, like catching a glimpse of her. He felt her lips press against his in a kiss.

"Hi, birthday girl." He smiled while she took the seat across from him.

"I really think you're getting sick. You're sweating." Concern filled her voice.

"No, I'm fine, it's just warm in here." *And I'm about to have a panic attack.* He pointed to her cup. "I got you a coffee."

"Oh, thanks. I'll take it with me...we can only stay a few more minutes since we have to get home and change for dinner."

"Well, that should be enough time." He swallowed.

"Enough time for what?"

"Nothing." His hand clutched the lump in his pocket. "So, how was your day?"

"Fine, nothing out of the ordinary. How about yours?"

"Okay, a good day."

"So what papers did you have to sign here?"

235

"Well, sweetheart, I've got a confession to make. There were no papers to sign."

"What? Why are you acting so weird?"

He held out his hand and when she took hold, Jason realized how well he knew her hand. The size, shape, contours, softness…and how well it seemed to be a perfect fit in his own. "I just made that up about signing papers so you would meet me here. Do you remember the first time we came here together?"

"Of course I do," she said with a smile, though there was confusion in her tone.

"Do you remember that I asked you if there was a Mr. Heather?"

She giggled "Yes…"

"Well, I wanted you to meet me here because this is where it all began for us. This is where 'Heather and Jason' started. Even that very first day, I sensed something special between us. There was a connection I'd never felt with anyone before. It felt like I was home."

"I felt it too."

He squeezed her hand. "I thought your birthday would be the perfect time to do this."

"Do what?"

"I know I come with some extra baggage, but I also know that a love like ours doesn't happen every day. I want to spend the rest of my life waking up next to you and falling asleep at night with you in my arms. I want to say things that make you smile and put that giggle in your voice until the day I die. I love you more than words can ever say. So what I'm asking you, sweetheart, is…can I be Mr. Heather?" He pulled the ring out of his pocket and got down on one knee in front of her. "Will you marry me?"

It seemed like an eternity to Jason until Heather's voice squeaked out from behind her tears.

"Yes! Of course I will." She put her arms around his neck and the patrons began to cheer, clap, and whistle. Jason stood up. They embraced in a hug and kissed.

When they sat back down, Jason wiped tears from his

eyes with the back of his hand and pulled the ring out of the box. "Do you like it? Because if not, we can exchange it and get something else."

"Don't even think about it—this ring is absolutely gorgeous."

Jason smiled with relief and utter joy. "Would you like me to put it on you?"

"Please do. Oh my God, I think you spent way too much on this."

"Nothing is too much for you, Mrs. Scharp." He slipped the ring on her finger. "Well?"

"It takes my breath away." Her voice was just a whisper. "I can't stop staring at it—it's so sparkly, it's dazzling. How long did you have this?"

"A couple of days. Angie and Mark helped me pick it out."

"It's perfect, Jason. And it fits too."

"We guessed at your ring size. I'm so glad you like it— let me see it on you." He felt the ring on her hand, which seemed large on her delicate finger.

"Heather Scharp," she said, trying out the name. "This is the best birthday gift ever. I get to be your wife."

"And I get to be your husband." He kissed her hand. "Thank God you said yes, otherwise everyone here at the coffee shop would have seen this poor guy get his heart stomped on."

"Did you even doubt it for a second?"

"I was pretty sure, but it's a scary thing, proposing. I've been a wreck all day."

"So that's why you've been acting so weird and looking like you might throw up."

"Yep, that's why." They laughed together.

"I can't believe it—we're getting married!"

****

After a great dinner with Katie and Dan to celebrate both Heather's birthday and the new engagement, Heather wasted no time getting started with wedding plans. The next day she met her mom and Katie for lunch, and they headed out to do some dress shopping and to discuss locations, themes, and a multitude of other details that Jason tuned out when Heather told him.

Jason returned home that afternoon to an empty house after a good workout. He turned on some music that played softly in the background while he graded papers. Jack Johnson's easy musical vibe went right along with his beer and the quiet afternoon. As he typed notes about a student's paper, it hit him: *I am getting married. I am going to be somebody's husband. The life I always dreamed of but feared might not happen, is actually happening.*

Jason took a drink from his beer and instead of feeling fear or anxiety about the future, he felt thrilled. Eight months ago it was just him, and he seemed to be killing time, waiting for something. Waiting for someone.

Heather was the culmination of dreams he harbored for years but stifled, because he just didn't know how realistic those dreams were. And now they were coming true, with the most amazing, sexy, fun, tender, patient woman he'd ever met.

Unable to believe his good fortune, Jason actually started tearing up. The ring set him back a bit, but he would have bought her the moon if he could. He had this lovely person to come home to every night and felt loved to his very core. Together, they felt safe and intimate and complete.

He wiped his eyes and laughed at himself for being so sentimental. But for a guy rejected more often than not, this was a huge deal. She accepted him, regardless of his physical limitations. She saw him for who he was.

The past twenty-four hours overflowed with tension, absolute joy and excitement, and now…peace. Jason headed off to the bedroom, ready for a nap. When he curled up on the bed, he smelled Heather's pillow and smiled at her unique scent ingrained in the fabric. Then he drifted off to sleep, more relaxed and content than he'd felt in what seemed like a lifetime.

Chapter Sixteen

Halfway through October, life for Jason was hectic, happy and passing by at a lightning pace. It was getting close to the end of the quarter at school, so there was a lot of grading going on for both of them. Most days after school, Jason coached wrestling. The official start of the season was the last weekend in October, so he and Shawn pushed their team to get ready. While wrestling occupied Jason, Heather happily busied herself with planning their wedding.

They decided to get married in the summer since they would both be off work. They set the June date, and then Jason was happy to step back while Heather immersed herself deep in the midst of arranging everything. He didn't care about any of it, except for the music and food. He insisted on being involved with those two things, but everything else—he could care less. So he gave her free rein to do what she wanted; it was the perfect arrangement.

****

It was late one afternoon as Jason stood in the doorway of his classroom, glad to make it to the last period of the day. Then wrestling practice and home to Heather.

"Hey, Mr. Scharp," a female student greeted him as she walked into the classroom.

"Is that Missy or Candace?" he asked.

"Candace."

"Good afternoon, Candace. I have a lot of trouble telling you two apart."

"Well you wouldn't if you could see us." She giggled. "I'm black, she's white."

Jason laughed. "Could've fooled me."

Down the hallway, Jason heard what sounded like a confrontation.

"It wasn't me, Mrs. James," he heard a familiar boy's voice saying. "I didn't do it!"

"I don't believe that for one second, Matt. This time, it's the principal's office." Mrs. James was not known for being one of the nicer teachers in the school. And Jason had the distinct pleasure of being ostracized by her from day one, when she railed in the staff meeting about how a blind person shouldn't be teaching.

"Mrs. James, please don't," the boy pleaded. Jason thought it was Matt Hill, the blue-haired boy. He opened his cane and headed toward Mrs. James' classroom at a brisk pace.

"Hey, everything okay?" he asked when he got closer. "Something I can help with?"

"Mr. Scharp, it's Matt Hill—" the boy started.

"Everything is under control, Mr. Scharp," Mrs. James said.

"What's going on?" Jason asked, irritated by her condescending tone.

"Someone drew a picture on her chalkboard of a witch with Wicked Witch of the West Hall written underneath it," Matt explained. "She thinks I did it."

Jason held the laughter in check that desperately wanted to come out. Some artistic student had a great sense of humor. "Did you see him doing it?" he asked Mrs. James.

"Mr. Scharp, I don't need to see someone doing something to know who did it. You, of all people, should know that."

"I didn't do it, Mr. Scharp, I swear it," Matt begged. "I can't even draw."

"Mrs. James, can we step aside for just a minute?" Jason walked a few feet down the hall. He heard her steps reach him. "What makes you think he did it?"

"Because he's a troublemaker."

"Well, I think he's a great kid. I've never had any troubles with him."

"Lucky you, Mr. Scharp. He's a hoodlum."

"Why, because he's got tattoos? That makes him a trouble maker?"

"I am going to escort him to the principal's office. This is none of your business." She raised her voice so that Matt could hear.

Jason knew she was right; it really was none of his business. But he wasn't going to stand by while a kid was unfairly stereotyped, either. "Looking out for students is my business. It is my job to motivate and educate these kids. And if I think someone is getting in the way of that, you better believe it's my business." His voice was raised too, and he could sense a crowd gathering.

"Hey, Scharp, what's going on?" Shawn asked, his voice towering from above.

"Your buddy here is interfering with my discipline of a student," Mrs. James pronounced.

"I don't have a problem with you disciplining a student," Jason said, "but I do have a problem with people being stereotyped and treated unfairly." He heard students murmuring as the last period bell rang.

"Everyone, get to your classrooms," Shawn barked. He turned back to Jason and Mrs. James. "Why don't you two take the student in question to the office and take care of this? I'll get your classes started, okay?"

Just then, Mr. Johnston's booming voice rang out. "What's going on here?"

"He is trying to usurp my authority!" Mrs. James said, and Jason imagined her bony finger pointing at him with rage.

"I'm trying to make sure the students are being treated fairly—"

"Is this the student?" Mr. Johnston asked.

"Yes sir," Matt answered quietly.

"All of you, come to my office." On the way there, Jason wondered if Mrs. James actually looked like a witch or just acted like one. He decided he would take poetic license and picture her skin with a green hue just like the famous witch from *The Wizard of Oz*. It was his image; he could envision her any way he wanted.

When they arrived at the office, Mr. Johnston said, "Matt, you sit out here. I'll be with you in a minute. Mr. Scharp, Mrs. James—in my office." He slammed the door shut behind them. "Would someone like to explain to me what on earth is going on?"

"Someone drew a picture on my blackboard of a witch and wrote 'Wicked Witch of the West Hall' under it."

"And she just assumed that Matt did it," Jason said.

"He's a troublemaker. He looked me right in the eye and laughed. He even sneered at me."

"Oh, so laughter and sneers are now evidence of guilt?"

"Mr. Scharp," Mr. Johnston interjected, "how did you get involved in this?"

"Yes, how did you?" Mrs. James snickered.

"I overheard their conversation. So I just asked what happened."

Mr. Johnston sighed. "It isn't your place to interfere with another teacher's disciplinary actions."

"Well, I know firsthand that Matt is a good kid. I've had him in two of my classes, and I've never had a problem with him."

"He's in detention on a routine basis—"

"I happen to know that he doesn't get a fair shake with all the teachers. People look at him, see the tattoos, the blue hair—"

"It's purple now," Mrs. James said with what Jason decided was a cackle in her voice.

"Whatever. But you all see that and assume he's a troublemaker. Well I don't. All the kids are on equal footing with me."

"What makes you think he's been unfairly stereotyped?" Mr. Johnston asked.

"Well, he's talked to me about it before, and I find it hard to believe that a kid that's never given me trouble would be such a menace to everyone else. Something doesn't add up."

"I've personally had issues with his behavior."

"Are you sure it's not your expectations causing you to make assumptions about him?" No one responded. "Why don't we ask the art teacher if that looks like his handiwork on your chalkboard?"

"I will do no such thing," Mrs. James said. "I know he did it. And no, I'm not stereotyping him."

"I know firsthand that you stereotype people. You did it to me the day you met me. You still do." His voice was raised now.

"What are you talking about?" Mr. Johnston asked.

"My very first day here, I'm sure you remember, Elizabeth, how strong your objections were to my being here. I believe your words were, 'It is impossible for a blind person to be an effective teacher.'"

"Well, I still don't see how you can properly—"

"Have you ever observed my classes?" No response. "Mr. Johnston, you have. Am I a capable teacher? Am I effective?"

"You know I think you're an excellent teacher. We're lucky to have you," Mr. Johnston confirmed.

"But you need all sorts of extra help." Mrs. James's voice was cold. "You monopolize the teacher's aide. You don't pull your weight like the rest of us when it comes to lunch duty or bus duty."

"I don't overuse the teacher's aide—I only use her for tests. Everything else the students do is emailed to me, and I grade it myself. Besides, there's a little something called the Americans with Disabilities Act that ensures those sorts of reasonable accommodations in the workplace. And no, I don't do lunch or bus duty, but I try to make up for it by always typing the minutes of our staff meetings, working on the dance planning committee, and helping to organize the pep rallies. I don't see you doing any of those things. But then again, I am just a blind guy, so maybe I missed you."

"I still don't think there's any way that you can properly teach. I don't think it's fair to the students to have a teacher that can't give them a full experience."

"Well maybe I think you're too damn old and out of touch to teach."

"Excuse me?"

"I might not be able to see my students, but I understand them. I get them. You don't even care anymore. No wonder they call you the Wicked Witch of the West Hall."

"Jason—" Mr. Johnston interrupted.

"Mr. Scharp," Elizabeth raised her voice, "why are you making this personal? I don't have a problem with you personally—"

"Then why do you always ignore me in the hallways? I'm blind, Elizabeth, I'm not deaf or stupid. You walk right by me and completely ignore me. There was even one time you were in the teacher's lounge while I was in there for about thirty minutes. You never said a word to me, but I knew you were there."

"Is that true?" Mr. Johnston asked.

"I don't recall any of that…I don't know." Her tone was much more subdued now.

Mr. Johnston sighed. "Be that as it may, that has nothing to do with the boy sitting outside my door."

"It has everything to do with him." Jason was fired up. "Don't you see? She's doing to him what she did to me. She took one look at my useless eyes and decided in that moment that she knew what I was or wasn't capable of. And after seven years of being here, she still makes false assumptions about my teaching and the help I need or how I contribute." Jason shook his head. "She's doing the same thing to Matt. I think maybe both of you are. You see his exterior, and you think you know him. You didn't even give him a chance. Well, I'm telling you that I know a completely different kid, and he's worth fighting for."

There was an awkward silence. It was one of those times Jason truly wished he could read the expressions on someone's face. He knew he was out of line and was worried there would be real repercussions.

Mr. Johnston finally spoke. "Elizabeth, is there any

chance that it may have been one of the other students? I mean, we're all human here. If we have trouble with a student, we tend to expect more trouble. So I can see how you thought it was him, but we don't have any way to prove that, do we?"

"He sneered at me!" She turned to Jason. "You didn't see his smug little face. I did."

"Maybe he just thought it was funny," Jason said.

"I bet you think it's funny, don't you?"

"Actually, I do. I don't condone the behavior, but I do wish I could see the picture." He couldn't resist a grin.

"Jason, I don't think that's a productive response." Mr. Johnston stood up. "You've got classes in session. I'm not going to stand here and listen to you two bicker. I expect the two of you to be professional to one another, and I don't ever want to hear about a public squabble between you again. Do you understand me?"

"Yes," they both said.

"Jason, you may leave. Tell Matt to hurry to last period. Elizabeth, please stay for a moment." Jason walked out of the office, wondering if anyone overheard their heated conversation, and wishing like hell he could stay behind and be a fly on the wall.

"Matt?"

"Yes, Mr. Scharp?" Matt was apparently sitting outside the door, right where they'd left him.

"You need to get to class." Jason headed out of the office and heard Matt's feet rushing behind him.

When they got into the hallway, Matt asked, "So I'm not in trouble?"

"No, you're not." Jason stopped. "Is there anyone within earshot?"

"No sir."

"Okay, I just stuck my neck out for you and got bitched at for it. It really wasn't my place to interfere." Jason put his hand on Matt's shoulder. "So you better not disappoint me."

"I won't, Mr. Scharp, I promise."

"I mean it, Matt. You told me that no one gives you a fair shake. But that means if you've screwed around in the past, you better stop. Because if they give you this chance and you prove me wrong…well you're never gonna get another chance. They'll be all over you then. And so will I."

"I understand. And sir…I overheard some of what you said in there."

Shit. "It got a little more heated than it should have."

"I heard you say that I'm worth fighting for. You really believe that?"

"Of course I do. Do you think I would have stuck my neck out just to fight with the Wicked Witch of the West Hall?"

Matt chuckled. "I guess not, Mr. Scharp."

Jason started walking again, cane swinging. "Let's go. We're late."

"Yes sir."

"And your hair's purple now, huh?"

"Yeah."

"Well next time let me know when you change it. Now they know I'm color blind, too."

****

On Saturday, Jason and Heather bustled about, getting ready to attend a wedding. It was for one of Heather's colleagues, Tracy, and Heather was using this as an opportunity to get ideas of what or what not to do at their own wedding.

"So, I thought I'd wear this—is it okay?" Jason asked, walking out of the closet holding a suit, shirt and tie.

"It's fine, but do you mind if I see if there's anything else I like better?" Heather asked from the bathroom.

"Be my guest." He laid the clothes on the bed. "I'm going to shave and get in the shower."

"Okay, I'll go scope out your closet." She patted his stomach when she passed by him.

Jason went to the sink, lathered up with shaving cream, and reached for his razor. Not there. He always kept it to the right of his sink, by the mirror. *Did I knock it off?* He pawed around, looking for it on the floor, the counter, the sink. Nothing.

"Heather?"

"Yes?" she asked from inside the closet.

"Have you seen my razor? It's not where I keep it."

"Oh, I just used it to shave my legs…it should be there."

Jason took a deep breath, irritation rising in him like the nearly boiling water in a teapot. "Well it's not, and I need it now."

Heather came into the bathroom. "It's right here by my sink." She handed it to him.

"And how the hell was I supposed to know that?" he snapped.

"Baby, I'm sorry, I thought I put it back where I got it. It was literally only ten inches away."

"Well it might as well be in the backyard, because I couldn't see it. Here I was, checking on the floor, thinking I'd dropped it or something—and it was just your carelessness instead."

"Oh, so I'm careless? I said I was sorry." Resentment colored her voice.

"Dammit, Heather, you can't do that! You have no idea how frustrating it is to know where something should be, and it's not. I can't see ten inches away—I only see what I touch. When you move stuff, it's like it doesn't exist anymore, even if it's in plain sight. Why can't you understand this?"

"I do understand that. And I work so hard at being neat and tidy and putting things back where they belong. But I am not perfect. I make mistakes…I'm doing the best I can."

"Well, it's not good enough," he spat, slamming down the razor.

Silent for a moment, Heather took a deep breath. "I'm sorry I'm such a disappointment." Her voice was subdued. "But I don't think you have any idea of the sacrifices I make for you. I am not naturally a neat person—I'm disorganized, I tend to make clutter. But for you, I have been diligent to go against my nature to fit your needs."

"Oh, well poor Heather. What a huge fucking sacrifice. You've got it so rough. You have to stop being a slob, and I just have to live the rest of my life without eyesight. I'm so sorry, what was I thinking, being so selfish?" The words and venomous tone in his voice were so harsh that when Heather spoke, Jason could hear tears in her voice.

"Just wear what you picked out," she said so quietly it was almost a whisper. "I'll be back in just a little bit."

"Where are you going?"

"Out! I don't want to be around you right now." Jason could hear her pulling a shirt over her head. "I'll see you in a bit."

"Sure, leave," he yelled after her. "That will solve everything." He heard the door slam shut.

He started shaving, his heart beating fast. Why couldn't he make her understand? What if she wasn't there to find his razor for him? He couldn't shave. Such a simple, mundane task could become impossible for him if she misplaced things. He knew she tried, and he did appreciate it.

But why couldn't she understand that "most of the time" wasn't good enough? And why couldn't he just be a normal fiancé that could find his own fucking razor?

****

Heather drove around the neighborhood trying to calm herself and diminish the harshness of the words he'd spewed. Her mind raced. For such a sweet, tender guy he sure knew how to dig that knife in and turn it.

In some ways, she knew that Jason was right. A small act like moving a razor ten inches from where it belonged made his life so much more difficult. And she knew that.

But she wasn't some cyborg that did everything precisely every time. Did he expect perfection? Did he expect her to live her life like a blind person, even though she could see?

Because she truly, completely changed her way of

living. Although she was getting used to it, it was often stressful. It was just too much sometimes. Always worried about putting kitchen utensils in the right drawer or leaving the TV remote in the exact spot every time without fail. Heaven forbid she move anything in the fridge. And like he said, if she screwed up, it was as if those things didn't even exist for him anymore.

If she put the remote on the end table instead of the coffee table, it was no different for him than if it vanished in thin air. He couldn't see it and didn't know where to start looking. For Heather, one quick glance around the room revealed it. For Jason, there were no quick glances, no, "Oh, it's right there." It was just…gone.

But he was perfect for her in every other way. She would gladly change her ways, do whatever it took to be his wife. But he needed so much sometimes and got so upset when she failed that she was just tired.

Would it get easier and better? Or would there always be this unending frustration between the two of them? And how on earth would a baby not compound all of this?

She felt calmer by the time she pulled back into their driveway. But she didn't have any answers, and her chest tightened with the realization that it might always be like this. Jason was blind. He required his life to be regimented, but in addition to that, he often showed intolerance to any mistakes on her part. He expected one hundred percent accuracy.

But Heather just knew she loved him so completely that she would apologize. For what, she wasn't sure. Not being perfect? Not being good enough?

When she walked into the foyer, the tension was palpable. She could feel his earlier words stinging her: "You have to stop being a slob, and I just have to live the rest of my life without eyesight."

Jason stepped into the living room from the hallway. One look at him, and her anger and hurt began to dissipate. He looked so handsome in his suit, which showed off his slender waist and broad shoulders. And his face was awash with regret.

"Sweetheart?" he asked, his voice tentative.

"Yeah, baby."

"I'm so sorry for yelling at you like that," he said quietly, almost gingerly. He walked closer to her, holding his hand out.

"I'm sorry I screw up sometimes." She took his hand and started to cry. "I know it's hard on you and I don't mean for it to be, but I'm never going to be perfect."

He pulled her close, his strong arms holding her while she shook with sobs.

"I know you're trying, I do, sweetheart." He caressed her back. "I feel like such a monster for making you cry like this. I don't mean to hurt you. I just get so frustrated. I wish…I wish I didn't need you to be so particular about everything, but I do need that. Keeping order is how I keep from going completely nuts. And I'm sorry I can't just be a regular guy for you."

"I know, baby." She started to calm in his arms. "And I want to do better. All I can do is try, okay? Is that enough for you?"

"Look at me." He put her face in his hands. "You are more than enough for me, okay? You are the woman of my dreams. In fact, you even surpass that. We'll get this worked out. I know we will. Five years from now, we'll laugh about this because in time we'll get so used to a blind guy and a sighted girl living together, it'll be second nature."

"You think so?"

"Well…don't you?" His voice and expression begged her to believe.

"I hope so." She kissed him.

He clasped his hands around the back of her neck. "I love you Heather, with all my heart. I'm sorry I upset you."

"I love you too, baby." She sighed, releasing the last of her pent-up sobs. "And you look gorgeous in this suit."

"Do I?" He smiled. "I thought you didn't like what I picked out."

"No, it's good, you look incredibly handsome. But

maybe a different tie. You've got a vibrant blue one that would accent your eyes."

He chuckled. "Do we want to accent my eyes?"

"They may not work, but they're still pretty."

****

When they arrived at the church, Jason imagined they made a striking couple. And he figured Heather was right; the blue tie probably looked sharp against the dove gray shirt and dark charcoal gray suit. He held onto Heather's arm, draped in a long sleeve off-the-shoulder dress. Before they left the house, he put his arm around her waist to kiss her and could tell that the cut clung to her small waist and the skirt flared out. She told him it was bright pink and added her black sky-high peep-toe pumps that even a blind man could tell were sexy.

"You're so tall today," he said when they walked through the parking lot. "You are Heather, right?"

"You're so funny. We're going up a dozen or so stairs—step up." When they walked through the door of the church, Heather said, "Oh, I see Christina waving at us. Looks like she saved us a seat."

They got settled, and Jason listened to the girls chat about the wedding decorations, the flowers, and programs. They talked about colors and dresses and bla bla bla... Jason tuned them out.

Instead, he listened around them, hearing the ushers asking, "Bride or Groom?" He heard the rustling of skirts and smelled the flowers hanging next to him on the pew. He couldn't identify what kind. String instruments played up ahead...he could hear a violin, maybe a cello and bass? He wasn't sure. Everyone spoke in the hushed reverent tones that Jason never heard anywhere except inside a church.

Once the ceremony began, Heather gave Jason a whispered play-by-play. When they exchanged vows, the bride and groom both got choked up, and Jason could hear Heather sniffling a bit. He grabbed some Kleenex out of his inside jacket pocket that he brought just for this occasion. Notoriously sensitive, she cried at everything—movies, books, even some commercials—and Jason was certain that weddings would be no exception. He pushed the tissues into her hand. Heather took the tissues, then elbowed him in the ribs while his smile grew broader, loving how tenderhearted she could be.

****

Music blared and appetizers tantalized from a buffet when they arrived at the reception. And much to Jason's delight, the bar was open. They hit the bar line first, got their drinks, and joined Christina and her date, Matt, at their table. Over dinner they all shared in lighthearted, casual conversation.

As dinner wound down, Jason leaned over to Heather. "So you get to see me dance tonight. See my cool white boy moves."

She grinned. "I can't wait."

After the toasts were made, the bride and groom started things off with the first dance. When they finished, the opening notes of Justin Timberlake's *Sexyback* played, and Jason smiled from ear to ear.

"Oh, sweetheart." He took Heather's hand. "I can't think of a more appropriate song for me to show off my moves."

"So you're bringing sexy back?"

"You tell me," he said with a grin, standing up. "Come on, let's dance."

"Why do I feel afraid?"

"Oh, you should be afraid. You should be very afraid." He laughed and grabbed onto her arm.

When they got to the dance floor, Heather asked, "So how do you keep from plowing down the other dancers?"

"I just kind of dance in one spot—it's all in the hips. You'll see." And with that, he let go of her and started dancing. "Just don't leave me here by myself."

"I won't, baby," she said with a smile. She started dancing too as Jason grooved to the music. A big smile spread across her face when she saw that he really could dance. She should have known that his talented moves in the bedroom would translate onto the dance floor, but it never occurred to her. He did have great hip action and really felt the music.

"Hey, Heather?" he yelled over the music.

"Yeah?"

He sang along to the chorus with a seductive, pouty look on his face.

Heather laughed and he smiled in return. "Jason, you're a good dancer!"

"I told you." He held his hand out, and when she took it, he pulled her close. *Sexyback* turned into *Angel Eyes* by the Jeff Healey band.

She put her arms around his neck and his hands intertwined, resting in the small of her back.

"Wow, those blind people sure can sing and play guitar, can't they?" he joked about Jeff Healey, the blind musician that recorded the song.

"Shhh." Heather giggled.

"Well it's true, you know," he continued in a pious voice. "They're all so gifted musically. It's like God took their sight but gave them the gift of song." Jason laughed at his own joke.

"Stop it," she whispered.

"Okay." He chuckled. "I couldn't resist making fun of all the bullshit platitudes I've heard over the years."

"You don't play any instruments, do you?"

"Nope. I'm an embarrassment to my people." They laughed together and swayed back and forth, their bodies pressed against one another. "This actually is a great song." While Jeff Healey's bluesy voice sang the chorus, Jason sang along, then put his hands on her face and kissed her with tenderness. When he was done, he rested his cheek against hers. They continued to sway to the music, cheek to cheek, until the song ended.

"I can't wait to spend forever with you baby," Heather said.

"Forever…now that sounds perfect." Jason pulled

away from her. She offered her elbow and he grabbed on, following her off the dance floor.

"Wow," Christina said when they returned to the table, "you two looked great out there. Strutting your moves and looking so romantic together."

"Thank you." Heather smiled. "Let's see you guys out there."

"Oh, I can't dance," Matt said.

"Come on," Jason urged. "Anyone can slow dance. If I can, you can."

"Maybe." Matt chuckled.

Heather put Jason's hand on his chair and they both sat down. Matt and Christina decided to go dance after all, leaving them alone.

Jason patted Heather's thigh. "You know, I was just wondering, like that song said—how was I lucky enough to win your love?"

"Oh...I don't think love is something to be won or lost. I think it's something to share. And when we met...we both just knew there was no one else we'd rather share our love with."

"You, Heather Cook, are a wise woman. And I can't marry you soon enough."

She laid her head on his chest.

Christina and Matt came walking back to the table. She smiled at them. "Now if that's not love, I don't know what is."

Chapter Seventeen

The next day, Angie's baby shower was well underway before Heather finally sat down. After helping to set up and scooping up the mounds of wrapping paper, ribbons, and bows while Angie opened her gifts (filling two trash bags), Heather was worn out. She couldn't believe the amount of gifts—it was crazy. Angie's large family consisted of three brothers, two who were married, and a host of aunts, cousins, and friends who attended as well. Angie was from Chicago, and her family had traveled to St. Louis for the shower.

They'd played some games, which no one really wanted to do, but they laughed and made it fun anyway. The activity died down while they ate cake and chatted. Since Heather didn't know anyone there except for Angie and Eve, she felt a little shy. After grabbing a plate with cake and ice cream, she found an empty seat on the couch next to one of Angie's sisters-in-law.

Heather offered a welcoming smile. "So you're Angie's sister-in-law?"

"Yes, I'm Shannon," she replied. "I'm married to her brother Todd. And how do you know Angie?"

"Oh, I'm going to be her sister-in-law too. I'm engaged to Mark's brother, Jason."

"So we're both in-laws." Shannon smiled then a concerned look clouded her face. "Wait, isn't Jason the one who's...blind?"

Don't roll your eyes, Heather, even though you really want to. "Yes, he's blind."

"Wow." Shannon nodded her head.

"Wow?"

"Well, I mean, that's a big deal. Angie says he's a fantastic guy, and I remember him at their wedding, he's really good looking. But…I just think it's admirable that you see beyond his…disability."

"He is a fantastic guy. It's no big deal—for the most part, he's just a regular guy."

"I didn't mean to…you know…I'm sorry. None of that came out right." Shannon smiled apologetically.

"It's okay, I know blindness is an uncomfortable thing for people."

"Yeah, I guess it is. But congratulations on the engagement—that's one beautiful ring."

"Thank you," Heather said, not resisting the urge to stare at it again. "So, do you have any kids?"

"One. A little girl, Ellie."

"Aw, what a cute name. I can't wait to have kids."

"It's a lot of work, but it's the best thing I've ever done." Shannon took a bite of her cake then added, "I bet it's going to be more challenging for you, what with Jason."

Heather wondered why some people thought it was okay to offer their opinions to people they'd just met. But instead of verbalizing those thoughts, she said, "I think we'll be fine. Jason's pretty resourceful."

"Well, I'm sure he is, but taking care of yourself and taking care of a baby are two entirely different things. I can't imagine changing diapers or feeding baby food or chasing after a toddler without being able to see."

Neither can I. A heaviness came over her, but she spoke the words she knew she should say, even if she wasn't so sure she believed them. "There are plenty of blind parents. They figure it out. Jason and I will figure it out." *God, I hope so.* Heather gave Shannon a look that said: *Drop it.*

"Well, I guess so." Shannon's voice was quiet. Then she smiled. "But it's good news about the genetic testing they did, isn't it?"

"I'm not sure what you're talking about."

"Oh, since Angie and Mark did IUI, they had genetic testing done. She was worried that whatever Jason has could be passed to her baby. But they found out they're okay, it doesn't pass from uncles or something."

Just then Angie came walking over, rubbing her ballooning belly. "Two of my sisters-in-law, chatting away." Angie smiled. "What are you guys talking about?"

"That genetic testing thing you did to make sure your baby won't get what Jason's got," Shannon said.

"Oh, yeah." Angie gave Shannon an exasperated look.

"Retinoschisis is hereditary?" Heather asked, suddenly concerned.

"Well, when we did genetic testing they brought up retinoschisis, because of Jason. But due to the way it's passed along, our baby is safe."

Heather's mind was reeling, and she felt sick to her stomach. Why didn't she ever think about that? It never even occurred to her that it could be genetic. Maybe Angie and Mark's children were safe from blindness, but what about Jason's?

"Is something wrong?" Angie touched Heather's arm.

"Do you know anything about how it's passed along?"

"Not specifically…but Jason knows." Heather could see the concern on Angie's face. "Has Jason never talked to you about it?"

"Umm…not really." Heather stood up. "I need to use the restroom."

"Heather, are you okay?"

"I'm fine." She dumped the rest of her cake in the trash and then headed to the bathroom. She felt clammy all over and could hear the pounding of her heart. After pulling her phone out of her purse, she went to the Internet and typed in retinoschisis. She clicked on a match from the University of Michigan Kellogg Eye Center and found what she was looking for:

If a male is affected by retinoschisis, then the disease cannot affect his sons. However, all of his daughters will inherit his X-chromosome. These women are known as carriers. They will have normal vision, but because they have inherited the X-chromosome with the non-working retinoschisis gene from their father, they are at risk for having sons and grandsons who are affected. Specifically, they have a 50% risk of having sons who are affected and a 50% risk of having daughters who are carriers, like themselves.

She let that sink in for a moment. So their children would not have retinoschisis. There was a huge measure of comfort in that. But the fact that if they had a daughter, that daughter would become a carrier for retinoschisis, disturbed Heather. They could pass Jason's condition onto their grandsons.

Heather closed down the webpage and washed her hands. She looked in the mirror at herself. She looked tired, ragged.

First, the challenge of raising children with a blind husband…and now this. Was it any less worrisome to know it wouldn't be their children, but their grandchildren who could be blind? Not really. It would just delay the guilt and tragedy. But it would still be there, just some thirty years later.

"Can I handle this?" she whispered out loud.

****

After the shower, Jason and Heather didn't talk much on the way to grab some dinner. Jason talked about his students and the wrestling season to fill the void in the car. He could tell something was wrong. When Heather did speak, she sounded unlike herself, as if putting on an act. Maybe she was just tired, Jason justified.

After they finished ordering their food at the restaurant, a lull crept up in the conversation when Jason stopped talking. They sat there in silence. Jason reached out for her hand and she took hold.

"Okay," he said. "When are you going to stop saying nothing's wrong and tell me why the hell you're acting so strange?"

She sighed.

"And don't even tell me that you're not acting strange, because you are and you know it. Did I do something wrong?"

"No, nothing like that," she said. "I learned something today that I never thought about, and we probably should have discussed."

"What's that?" Jason had never heard her voice sound that way…he wasn't sure what it was, but knew in the pit of his stomach he should be worried.

"Well…Angie's sister-in-law mentioned that Mark and Angie had genetic testing done."

"Yeah, Mark told me that."

"So, Angie mentioned her relief to hear that their kids can't get retinoschisis."

"Yes, she was worried the poor kid would end up like Uncle Jason."

"But you've never discussed that with me, about the implications for our children."

It was Jason's turn to sigh. He let go of her hand and sat back in his seat. "That's because it's not an issue. Our kids will not be blind like their dad."

"Well, I looked it up online—"

"What the hell, Heather?" he raised his voice. "Why would you look it up online? Why wouldn't you just fucking ask me?"

"Lower your voice please, people are looking at us," she whispered. "And I wanted to know because it never even occurred to me that you could pass on your disease. It said online that—"

"I know every damn thing there is to know about retinoschisis. I know that it's an X-linked pattern of inheritance. I know that if I have a daughter she will be a carrier."

"So you understand that means if we have a daughter and she has a son—that he could get it?"

"Yes," he hissed. "I understand that. A fifty-fifty shot."

"And you're okay with that?" Her voice cracked.

Jason clenched his jaw and didn't speak right away. When he did, his voice dripped with anger. "So what are you saying? Are you saying you don't want to have kids with me?"

"I'm saying we should have talked about this. You should have told me."

A sad chuckle escaped from his throat. "Oh, I'm sorry, I thought you loved me and it wouldn't make any difference."

"Well of course I love you, don't even insinuate I don't. But you know how much I want kids—"

"So do I."

"Then you have to consider the implications."

"Holy shit," he muttered, shaking his head. "Are we seriously having a conversation about what will happen *if* we have a daughter and *if* she has a son? Looking ahead like thirty years? Honestly? And you thought we should have discussed that?"

"Yes, I think we should have. Here comes the waiter with our food."

After the waiter set down the plates and walked away, Jason lit into her. "So you're upset about something that has so many variables in it, there's no way to predict the outcome. I could see if we had a fifty-fifty shot of our kid being blind, but that's not even the case with our grandchildren. Only if we have a daughter. And only if she has a son."

"But I would feel so awful if we had a blind grandson because of us—"

"Not us, *me*. It would be my fault. I would be the asshole that he could blame. You know who I have to blame? My great-great grandfather, born in 1889. Apparently I got it from him and he wasn't even blind, just somewhat impaired. But he made my great-grandmother a carrier, who passed the carrier gene to my grandma, who unknowingly passed it to my mom, who had the terrible misfortune of having a blind son."

"I never said it would be a terrible misfortune—"

"But you're thinking it! You're worried about something that took almost one hundred years to manifest itself twice in my family. So maybe someday when I'm long dead, some other boy will find out that it's because of that jackass Jason Scharp, that's who did it to him. And maybe he'll hate his life and be bitter and miserable and live off of welfare. Or maybe, just maybe, he'll live a successful, full happy life and find a partner who's happy to have children with him."

"You're not being fair—"

"I'm not being fair? Explain how I'm not being fair."

"Can't you just understand that this is not easy for me? I am in love with you and want to have a family with you, but I feel like I've been punched in the gut. I didn't know this could affect our grandchildren, and their children, and so on."

"Well, what about your sister Anna? Is her type of cancer hereditary? Maybe I don't want that in my kids' gene pool. At least retinoschisis never killed anyone."

"Stop that, stop that right now." She spoke with an intensity Jason wasn't expecting. He could hear her crying.

Jason pulled a few bills out of his wallet and threw them on the table. "Let's get out of here." He stood up. Heather brusquely took his hand and put it on her arm.

They walked through the restaurant and Jason was aware of how awkward it was to have to be attached in that way when they were both so upset with each other. Her anger radiated from the stiff posture of her arm; Jason could feel it. He was so irritated that he ever had to rely on her at all, but at the moment, it was infuriating.

He knew she felt an obligation to him, that she couldn't just stomp off. Being with him, it was an unspoken promise.

When they got outside, Heather said, "What a totally shitty thing you said to me."

"I know and I'm sorry. I just tried to make the point that there are worse things than being blind—"

"Like being dead like my sister."

"What I'm saying is there are all kinds of shit floating around in our DNA, and in the grand scheme of things, retinoschisis is not all that bad."

"Well, I don't know...because of retinoschisis you need my help to get to the car and right now I'd rather punch you in the face than help you."

Jason abruptly pulled his hand off her and stopped. "I don't need your help." He opened his cane.

"Oh, really?"

"I thought you loved me and want to help me, but hey, if I'm too much of a hassle for you then I can take care of myself. There's nothing you do for me that I can't accomplish without you."

"Why can't you ever admit that you have limitations? Why is that so bad?"

"I don't know, you tell me. You're the one that seems to think blindness would be a fate worse than death to bestow on a person. So it must be pretty fucking bad to have those kinds of limitations."

"You know what, if you're so damned independent, why don't you find your own way home?"

"Fine!"

"Goodbye!" she hollered back and started walking away from him, leaving him standing alone in the parking lot.

"Me and my fucked-up DNA will get home just fine!"

She didn't respond. He could hear her footsteps in the distance and her car door open and shut. Was she really going to leave him here? He heard her car pull out. *Screw her.*

He realized he stood somewhere in the middle of the parking lot. Because he had been holding onto her arm, he didn't pay any attention to the route they took or the direction they'd turned. Did they go straight? Did they turn? Was the restaurant in front of him or behind him? *Shit.*

He grabbed his phone, dialed Shawn for a ride, and hoped he didn't get run over before it showed up. So he made a game of twisting his cane back and forth, back and forth between his hands. He wished he had worn a warmer jacket.

A few minutes passed before he heard soft footsteps growing closer, then an older woman's voice say, "Honey, do you need help?"

"Actually, yes, if you could just help me to the front door that would be great. I'm waiting for a ride."

"How did you end up in the middle of the parking lot?"

"Long story." He attempted a smile. "May I hold onto your elbow?"

"Sure," she said, and he took hold, noticing she was very short. She led him to the door.

"Thank you so much." He smiled.

"Oh, you're welcome. I hope that long story has a happy ending."

Yeah, me too.

****

When Heather saw Shawn's car pull up in the driveway, she felt relief and anxiety all at once. She'd spent the past two hours worried about Jason as her calls and texts to him went unanswered. He was obviously punishing her by leaving her hanging. What he probably didn't know was that Shawn had sent her a text thirty minutes earlier saying: *Jason's with me. I didn't want u to worry. Will bring him home soon.* She was angry with Jason but also sad.

When he walked in, she could tell from his less-than-graceful movements that he was drunk. He put his cane in the corner and took off his shoes.

"So you're home safe," she said from the couch.

"Yes I am."

"I can smell the booze on you from here."

His mouth curled into a smirk. "Well, you kind of drove me to drink, what can I say?"

"You should have answered your phone." Heather stood up. "That was cruel to let me worry that way."

"Well, it was cruel to leave me in the parking lot."

"You said you didn't need my help—"

"But that didn't mean you should take off!"

Heather groaned. "I am so done with talking about this. I'm a bitch, then. I'm a bitch because I left you in the parking lot and because I'm trying to get my head out of the clouds and think practically about our future."

"I never said you were a bitch. You're not a bitch. I love you." His face softened.

"Well you sure didn't sound like that tonight at dinner."

"Heather, what do you expect me to say? I can't change the circumstances that bother you. I am a blind guy with compromised DNA. This is who I am. I *warned* you about this." He held his arms out. "I can't change any of it, so I guess it's take it or leave it."

"You're right on a base level, but it's not that simple, Jason, and you know it."

"Why are you making this so hard?" His arms dropped to his sides. "Let's go to bed."

"No…I'm going to sleep here on the couch tonight."

"Oh, Heather, for chrissake—"

"Stop yelling at me. I'm tired of fighting. You said some pretty harsh things to me tonight, some hurtful things, and I'm sorry if I don't feel like cozying up to you."

"Well, you weren't exactly sweet to me, either, but I still want to lie next to you."

"Just go to bed, Jason."

"Have it your way then. Good night." He walked down the hallway and slammed the door shut behind him.

Heather lay down on the couch, covered herself with a blanket and started crying. She figured that everything would seem better in the morning. Her mom always told her that. Sleep on it, and it will seem better in the morning. She sure hoped her mom was right.

****

The next morning Jason got out of bed early after a night spent tossing and turning with very little sleeping going on. He was in a daze when he showered and got dressed. The events of the previous night kept replaying in his mind, but the anger had diluted to sadness. It was quarter 'til six, and he was in the kitchen getting coffee when he heard Heather stir. Jason turned at the sound of her bare feet padding on the kitchen floor.

"Good morning," she said.

"Morning," Jason said with no enthusiasm, turning his attention back to the coffee pot. He poured some coffee in a thermal mug.

"You're ready early." Heather walked up to him and touched his shoulder.

"Yeah, well…I couldn't sleep so I thought I'd just get up."

"You look nice in that sweater."

"Thank you. It's supposed to turn colder today so I thought I would add a layer."

They faced each other, neither one speaking.

Jason wished he could gauge her expression. How much did he miss by not seeing her body language or the look in her eyes? Would it give him more of a clue as to where her thoughts were? Would he see pity, or maybe detachment? Finally he said, "I'm going to work early. You better hurry up, it's late for you."

"I know…but I could drive you today if you want."

Jason didn't respond.

"Baby, I'm smiling at you."

"Sorry, I didn't catch that. I'll just take the bus."

He felt her arms wrap around him, and he reciprocated. The smell of her hair, her perfume, her soft skin against his cheek and her hair tickling his neck…all so stimulating and yet so familiar to him. He held on tight and then whispered, "I am so scared right now," before pulling away.

"It will be okay," she said with tenderness.

"Will it?" He searched for his mug on the counter with his fingers, then picked it up, put a lid on it, and kissed Heather on the cheek. "I love you."

"I love you too."

"Then please let that be all you need. The rest will work itself out." He grabbed his phone off the charger. "I'll see you tonight."

****

Jason tried to put Heather out of his mind while he went about his day. He could tell, though, he was on

265

autopilot. Just going through the motions didn't exactly make him the best teacher. In between third and fourth periods, Shawn poked his head in to see how Jason was doing. Jason just shrugged his shoulders. He couldn't even talk about it. He told Shawn he wanted to skip wrestling practice if he could, and Shawn assured it was no problem.

Really, Jason just wanted to get home and apologize to Heather. He regretted being so defensive and cruel. But he couldn't change anything about the situation, and he knew that. He just wanted to hold her and kiss her and somehow convince her that his love was all she needed. *It will be okay. We love each other too much. This is just a little bump in the road. I bet she's missing me too.*

At the end of the day, he finished some work on his computer, rushing through it as fast as possible so he could leave and go home.

****

Heather had spent the day at school with her mind feeling like an ever-changing, morphing kaleidoscope. Thoughts of her troubles with Jason drifted in and out, emotions over-lapping and creating a confusing state of being.

She no longer had the feeling that had been getting her by the last couple of months—that their love was bigger than their troubles, that everything would work itself out. Now the pervading emotion was worry. And stress.

It had become more than she could handle. She needed to get away from it all, to make the kaleidoscope stop shifting long enough for her to see the individual pieces for what they were. Because combined together, they added up to nothing but a confusing blur.

While Jason might have been unable to see, Heather was beginning to think that she was unable to see a viable future for them together.

As she drove home, she just knew it was all too much. There was the DNA dilemma, the difficulties of raising children with him, and the relentless rigid environment they lived in. *I can't do this anymore.*

She knew what she had to do.

When she got home, she hurried inside, went to the basement and grabbed her suitcase. Back upstairs, she started putting some clothes in. She would go back to her condo. For how long? She didn't know. She didn't know what she was doing. She just knew she couldn't stay. Shoes, underwear, socks…she gathered her toiletries in the bathroom when she heard the front door open.

"Heather?" Jason yelled out. "Are you home?"

"I'm in the bedroom." She took a deep breath and dumped her pile of toiletries in the suitcase when Jason entered.

"We need to talk." He still wore his coat, and his cheeks had turned rosy from his walk in the brisk air. A bloody gash tore across his forehead.

"What happened to your forehead?"

"That damn tree again. I couldn't stop thinking about us all day."

Her voice quivering, she said quietly, "Neither could I."

"Heather? Are you crying?"

"Jason, I just can't handle this anymore. There is so much going through my head right now. I don't know what to think. It's just too much."

"It's not, sweetheart. We can work it out." He started to sit down on the bed but found the suitcase instead. A confused look came over his face. "A suitcase? You're leaving?"

Tears filled her eyes. "For now, yes. I just need some time to think."

"I don't understand how just two days ago we were on cloud nine, dancing together, talking about sharing our lives forever…and now you're leaving me?"

"Jason, it's just too much right now. I need to sort through all of this and figure out where to go from here."

"What are you talking about? We're supposed to be getting married, that's where we're going. I don't understand what you're saying." Sobs caught in his throat, and the tears started. That only made her cry harder.

"I'm not saying this is over, I don't want it to be over," she said, barely able to speak through her tears. "But I can't stay with you until I'm sure I can handle all of this. It's just a lot, Jason. Everything is so rigid, and I don't want to end up resenting you for what you can't do. I need to figure out what I can live with forever and what I'm willing to sacrifice. If we're going to get married, I don't want doubts. I want to be sure. Don't you want to know that your wife is sure when she marries you?"

"You said I could trust you. I told you this is how it always ends, but you promised me that you were okay with my limitations. You told me to take a leap of faith, and I did. How could you do this to me? How could you do this to us?"

She was sobbing, and so was he. She took him in her arms, and they cried together.

"I just have some soul-searching to do," she tried to explain. "When I told you those things, I wasn't thinking about kids or DNA or any of that. I was just thinking of you, and I love you more than I've ever loved anyone."

Jason pulled away from her. "It doesn't get any better than what we have, Heather. Do you think you can find this kind of love again? Do you think you will ever feel this strongly about anyone again? Because you won't."

A part of her knew that he was right. "I'm not saying it's over. I'm saying I need some space, I need some time to think."

"So what am I supposed to do? Just sit around and wait for you to decide my fate?"

"Baby, all I'm asking is for you to give me some time. Be patient. I can't commit to forever with this many doubts in my mind. I would love to believe in some saccharine notion that love conquers all, but we have to be realistic. I need to weigh things in my mind."

"And what is going to convince you one way or the other?"

"I don't know."

"So you're just going to walk out of here, with no plan, no time frame? How long is it going to take? A week? A month? A year?"

"Don't do that, Jason. Don't try to pin me down to something or act like I've got you on a schedule. I'm trying to save us. I'm trying to figure out what I want before I make a mistake. If I get some space, I think it will give me some perspective. I don't know. I've never done this before. I've never found the love of my life and been so conflicted about what the future could mean. But I won't come back unless I'm sure. I don't ever want to do this to you again or put myself through it either."

They were both drained, emotionally and physically. Heather walked into the bathroom, grabbed some more supplies and dumped them in the suitcase.

"So how is this going to work?" Jason's voice was quiet. "Are we going to talk? Are we going to see each other at all?"

"I can't see you, Jason. I love you. It will just confuse things more."

"Can I talk to you?"

"Maybe, I don't know. Let's just take it day by day, okay?"

Jason headed for the bedroom door and then turned around. "No, it's not okay. None of this is okay." He started crying again, his face full of anguish. "Heather, I'm sorry. I'm sorry for not being more sensitive about your concerns. I'm sorry I can't change things. I'm so sorry I can't see and just be a normal guy for you."

It was breaking her heart, watching him in so much pain. She felt like a monster. "Jason, you don't have anything to be sorry for—"

"Please don't leave me. Please don't go. We can figure this out…."

"I have to, baby. I need some distance to clear my head. Maybe you think I'm being selfish or that I'm weak…but I never dreamed of a life raising kids with a blind man. There's no doubt it will be more challenging.

And I have to figure out if I'm up to that, forever."

"Well I'm not going to stand here while you walk out on me." He walked back to her and touched her cheek. "I love you with all my heart. I know you're the one for me. I just hope you decide that I'm the one for you." They kissed tenderly, their lips moistened with tears. "Don't forget what we have together. We are better together than we are apart."

"I won't forget," she promised.

"I can't stay while you walk out that door, wondering if it will be for the last time. I'm going now." He marched out of the room, and Heather heard the front door open and then slam shut. She collapsed on the bed as sobs overtook her.

****

Mark and Angie were busy in the baby's room putting the crib together when the doorbell rang.

"I wonder who that is?" Angie asked from her spot on the floor.

"Well I don't know, but I'll get it because I bet you can't even get that pregnant body of yours up, can you?" Mark teased. He left the room and headed to the front door.

When he opened it, Jason stood there, blood on his forehead and an odd look on his face.

"Hey, brother, wasn't expecting you," Mark said. "Come on in. What happened to your head?"

As soon as Jason stepped through the door, his face contorted in sobs. Mark put his arms around him, baffled. "What's going on? What's wrong?" Mark held his brother tight while sobs wracked his body.

"She left me," was all Jason managed to get out. Mark saw Angie appear in the foyer, looking grief-stricken to see Jason in so much pain.

"What do you mean? Heather left you?" Mark couldn't even comprehend what Jason said.

Jason nodded and pulled away from Mark. "I'm sorry," he managed between sobs. "I just had to get out of there while she packed, and I didn't know where to go so I came here..."

"I'm glad you came here," Mark assured him. "What happened to your head?"

"Oh, I got whacked with a damn tree branch."

"Jason," Angie said, "why don't you sit down on the couch? Do you want something to drink?"

He nodded, taking a deep breath. "Something stiff."

They all sat down and Jason relayed the obstacles in Heather's mind that she had to decide if she could live with or not. Mark was in shock and could tell Angie was too...they knew firsthand how in love Jason and Heather were. It seemed inconceivable that they would be apart.

"So..." Jason sighed. "She said she won't come back unless she's one hundred percent sure. So if she decides she wants to be with me, there's no turning back. But I'm just afraid the problems are so big in her mind that she won't figure out a way to deal with it."

"Well, Jace, you have to stay positive," Mark urged. "Maybe having some time apart will put some perspective on everything."

"I can't lose her." Jason started crying again. "I just can't, Mark." He buried his face in his hands.

Mark looked at Angie, who shook her head.

Jason looked up. "If only I could see, none of this would be happening. Everything's perfect between us except that. If my fucking eyes worked, I would still have her."

"Yeah, it sucks, Jace, it really does. But it's just the way it is. There's no sense in stewing about it—"

"Well that's easy for you to say as you look at me with your two good God damn eyes!" Jason lashed out, yelling. "Sometimes it really pisses me off that I'm the one that got screwed with shitty genes. You don't even need glasses. You have perfect vision—you can look into your wife's eyes whenever you want. Well I've never even seen my fiancée. So I guess I shouldn't stew about that, either. And if I do have children, I'll never be able to see them. But you're right, I shouldn't stew about it."

Seeing Jason in such despair was difficult for Mark. He wanted to comfort him but worried that wasn't what Jason needed right now. Instead, Mark said, "Go ahead, then...feel sorry for yourself. Poor blind Jason. You might as well move back in with Mom and Dad with that attitude. Let Mommy take care of you—"

"Shut the fuck up!" Jason shoved Mark.

"Guys," Angie cried out. "Stop this!"

"No, Ang." Mark stood up. "Jason wants to feel sorry for himself. Let him. I'm sure self-pity and self-loathing will serve him well. Funny, though, how you could've never gotten Heather in the first place with that bullshit outlook on life. Jason the independent, happy, confident guy won her over. This guy will just put the nail in the coffin of your relationship."

Mark looked anxiously at Jason, awaiting his reaction. He didn't know what to expect...there was so much anger and pain on Jason's face he thought Jason might take a swing at him.

Finally Jason spoke with resignation. "You're right. Getting pissed about being blind won't get me anywhere."

"You taught me that, you know," Mark said gently.

"Guess I should practice what I preach, huh?" Jason allowed the slightest smile at the corners of his mouth.

"We're here for you, Jason." Angie took his hand. "Give Heather her space, and if she's truly the one for you, she'll come back. And we'll be with you while you wait or get on with your life."

"Thank you." Jason wiped his eyes.

"So you haven't eaten dinner, have you, Jace?"

"No, but I'm not hungry—"

"Oh hush, you're going to eat if you're in my house." Angie slapped his knee. "In fact, you're going to help me cook. You're the best cook here, so get off your butt and join me in the kitchen."

He stood up. "I came here, upset because my life is a wreck, and now you want a personal chef."

"That's about it." She grabbed his hand. "Let's go."

****

Cooking temporarily took the situation off Jason's mind. He knew he had the best sister-in-law in the world—Jason cherished having her in his life. After dinner, he and Mark insisted on letting her relax while they cleaned up the kitchen. When Mark left the room to finish assembling the crib, Jason put his hand on Angie's shoulder. "Thanks for that…for getting my mind off of…everything."

"Oh, it was nothing. I just wanted to take some of that pain from your face."

"Do you think…do you think I could crash here tonight?" Jason looked down. "I don't think I could handle being at home without her there. Not tonight, anyway."

"Of course you can stay." She stood up and gave him a hug. "I'll make up a bed for you on the couch." She started to pull away.

"No, wait." Jason held her as close as her pregnant belly would allow. "I just need to hold on for a little bit longer." He rested his head on her shoulder and continued to hug her. Tears came easily again, and he hated it, but couldn't help it. He held onto Angie until he composed himself. "I'm sorry, I'm so embarrassed—"

"Don't be. I'm here for a hug or a shoulder whenever you need it." Angie squeezed his hand. "That's what sisters are for."

Just then, Jason felt a small poke on his stomach. He smiled. "Did the baby just kick you?"

"No, the baby just kicked you!" She laughed.

"Can I put my hands on your belly?"

"Jason, you don't have to ask—anytime you want, just plant your hands on there."

He was gentle as he caressed her belly and got another kick in response. Jason started laughing. "That is so incredible. I think I actually felt the outline of her little foot." Jason smiled from ear to ear. "I want that someday, you know. I want that with Heather."

"I know you do. Let's hope everything works out."

The baby kicked again, and for a moment, Jason felt a bit of hope.

Chapter Eighteen

Jason's mind muddled through in a fog all the next day at school. It was as if he dared to engage himself fully in the kids, in his work, in the day, then he would be forced to believe his new reality.

Shawn stopped into Jason's classroom right after school. "So we've got practice tonight. You're coming, right?"

"Sure." Jason grabbed his bag.

"You look like shit. Did you guys work everything out last night?"

Jason chuckled. "Not exactly. She moved out."

"What?" Shawn said with disbelief.

"I don't want to talk about it."

"Wow, I didn't see that coming."

"Neither did I. Then again, I don't see much of anything, do I? Let's head to the gym for practice."

With wrestling practice well underway, Jason's mood didn't improve at all. He coached in a different way than Shawn or most any other coach, since he couldn't see the moves the kids executed. To check positions, Jason would physically touch a wrestler to see if the execution was correct. Then when two wrestlers went up against each other, he would have a student describe the action to him while they wrestled.

"What is your problem today, Miller?" Jason yelled at a kid that just couldn't get the latest maneuver he showed them. His opponent pinned him every time.

"I don't know," the kid said quietly.

"You don't know?" Jason repeated. "Well I know. You're being lazy."

"It's hard, coach."

Jason laughed. "You've got to be kidding me. It's hard?

I can do it, and I can't even see you or the mat."

"I'm trying, Coach—"

"Well, you need to try harder and you need to pay attention. That's it, Miller, I'm doing it with you. You better focus and give me one hundred and ten percent!" Jason's voice rose to a yell again. He always expected a lot from the kids, but he was known for keeping his cool and normally didn't yell. Today he clearly had no patience, though.

Jason got into position on the mat and Miller got next to him. "Go!" Jason said.

Within about five seconds, Jason flipped the kid in the air and slammed him on the mat, pinning him down.

"Ow!" Miller cried out.

"If you executed that move correctly, this wouldn't hurt."

"Coach, you're hurting me—"

"Scharp!" Shawn yelled from above, pulling Jason off the kid.

"What are you doing?" Jason hollered, shrugging Shawn off him.

"You crossed the line," Shawn whispered in his ear. "You outweigh that kid by forty pounds."

"He was complaining that it's too hard—" Jason whispered back.

"You can't hurt a student, Scharp. You need to go home."

"Shawn, don't be crazy—"

"I mean it, Jason. You are not in the right frame of mind to coach these kids. I know you're going through some shit right now, but you can't take it out on them. You could have really hurt him."

"Oh, bullshit," Jason muttered.

"Bullshit nothing." Shawn kept his voice down. "You better hope he doesn't tell his parents about this. Now go home."

"You're making me look like an ass in front of them," Jason whispered.

"No, you made yourself look like an ass. Go home,

cool off, and we'll try tomorrow if you're ready."

"Thanks a lot," Jason snapped. He started to walk away and then realized that between wrestling and Shawn pulling him away, he didn't know where he was. "Mathes?" He shook his head in frustration.

"Yeah?"

"I kind of lost my bearings. Where's the bench?" Shawn put Jason's hand on his elbow and walked him to it.

"Thanks," he said begrudgingly, embarrassed. *Fuck.*

Shawn grabbed Jason's shoulder. "Go home and relax."

"Yeah." *Go home to my lonely, empty house.*

****

When Heather got home from school that night, tears that threatened just under the surface all day sprang to her eyes. Her swollen eyes, red from crying the night before, caused people—including students—all day long to ask what was wrong. Her body and mind felt pummeled by exhaustion. She didn't sleep much the night before and was emotionally drained. She really wanted to call Jason and tell him she was coming home. She wanted to cuddle with him in bed and feel his strong arms around her. She wanted to see his gorgeous smile and kiss those lips.

But she knew that would only be a temporary fix. She couldn't go to him now.

Heather kicked off her shoes and just let them lie in the middle of the floor. She threw her jacket on the couch and dropped her purse on the table. The simple act of making a mess felt so refreshing…she hadn't done that in a while. About to sit down on the couch, a grin spread across her face, and she ran to the kitchen.

She flung open the refrigerator door and started moving around all the different things she bought yesterday at the store. Stuff from the top shelf moved to the bottom, she pulled things off the door and put them in the drawers. There was no sense of organization at all.

There! So much for everything having a place.

But instead of feeling happy with the freedom to put

things anywhere she wanted, she still felt miserable. Only now her fridge was a mess.

So she grabbed her phone and dialed Katie as she walked to the couch and sat down.

"Hey girl," Katie answered. "What's up?"

"Actually," she said, starting to sob, "I'm horrible. Do you have some time to hear me cry?"

****

The next day was equally tortuous for Jason. During the school day, the pain he felt subsided to a dull ache. He knew, though, that when he got home and made something to eat and sat down by himself, the sharp, stabbing pains would come back.

And he got whacked again by that damn tree branch on the walk home, adding a fresh gash on his forehead.

With Heather gone, his house felt vacant once more. Jason couldn't see the transformation she'd made by painting walls, hanging artwork or adding accessories throughout the house. So in his mind, everything in the house—in his life—was beige again without her. Plain and stark.

He hated the night now. He took one of Heather's shirts out of the dirty clothes basket and smelled it. It still smelled like her. Just holding it seemed to calm him. He knew it was ridiculous, but he took it to bed with him.

All through the night, he held it like a security blanket. When he woke up in the morning, though, for a brief moment he expected her to be there next to him, because when he awoke from a deep slumber induced by alcohol, the first thing that hit his consciousness was the scent of Bali Mango. Quickly, however, he remembered the shirt, and the pain filled him once again.

Jason felt like a fool, getting teary at the drop of a hat, moping around. But he couldn't help it. In the past eight months, his life became so entwined with Heather that he never even imagined life without her. When she accepted his proposal, it meant forever. He thought his life would always be that wonderful. And he couldn't even remember what he did before she came into his life.

He'd have to figure it out. Create a new life again. Only this time it wouldn't be the same, because it would be a poor substitute for the life he'd lost with her. And how long would it hurt like this? The pain was not only emotional but truly physical. Like an ache deep inside him.

The next morning when Jason woke up to pouring rain, he felt perversely pleased. Now his surroundings suited his mood. It seemed appropriate. *Let it pour. Who cares?*

But when he left his house for the bus, he wasn't so thrilled about it. He didn't like using an umbrella, because between the umbrella and his cane, he wouldn't have a free hand. So he wore a raincoat with a hood and knew from experience that he would get soaked.

He made his way down the sidewalk, hating his life at that moment. The strong winds seemed to blow the rain sideways into him. After walking for just two minutes, he had already gotten very wet. He heard Mark's ringtone coming from his phone but couldn't answer. He rounded a corner and a car speeding by splashed water all over him, leaving his left pant leg drenched.

"Are you serious?" he screamed at the car. "You've got to be fucking kidding." *Were they aiming for me? How the hell could they miss a guy swinging a long white stick?* He kept walking, anxious to make it on a bus and start to dry off.

He was aware of a car slowing down as it approached and came up beside him. He heard the window unroll.

"Jace, it's Mark. Get in the car."

Jason stopped and faced Mark's direction. "What are you doing?" Jason asked as the wind and rain pelted him.

"I'm picking you up. Get in the car—you're getting wet!"

Jason shrugged his shoulders and found the door handle and then climbed in.

"Holy shit, you're soaked."

"Yeah, it's just beautiful out, isn't it? So what are you doing here?"

"I told you, I came to pick you up."

Jason took a deep breath. "I didn't ask for your help. You know that's one of the reasons Heather left me—because she's worried I need too much help."

"Calm down," Mark said, exasperated. "It's like a damn monsoon out there, okay? No one should be out in this, and you don't even have an umbrella. So I thought I'd swing by and grab you, that's all."

"I don't mean to be ungrateful, but I was just fine."

"So do you want to get out then?" Mark challenged.

Jason grinned. "Not really."

"I didn't think so."

"Thanks, Mark." Jason chuckled. "It was miserable out there. And then some piece of shit splashed water from his car all over me."

"Yeah, I can see that. Why don't you ever just call me or Mom on days like this and ask for a ride?"

"Because I could have just taken a cab, but I'm used to walking."

"Cabs get expensive. I'm free." Mark looked over at Jason. "You're never going to call and ask me for a ride to work, are you?"

"Unlikely. But thanks for picking me up." They didn't talk for a minute, and Jason was momentarily distracted by the mournful song the wipers created on the windshield.

The car came to a stop at a light and Mark put his hand on Jason's shoulder. Mark didn't say the words, but Jason knew Mark was there for him—and he always would be.

****

That first week without Heather was hard for Jason. He didn't want to hear "I told you so" from his mom, so he lied and said he had a wrestling event that Friday night so he wouldn't have to go to the family dinner. Mark promised he wouldn't say anything about his little brother's life falling apart.

Then one week bled into two, and he couldn't lie anymore. He made up a lame excuse to ditch the Friday dinner again, but he couldn't hide the truth forever. Besides, his pantry and fridge looked pretty bare, so he needed her to take him to the grocery store.

He hated that his mom had been right about Heather, when he was so sure she was different from the others he'd dated. When his doorbell rang that Saturday morning, he took a deep breath and opened it.

"Good morning, my sweet boy," his mother said with cheer. She walked in and gave him a quick hug.

"Morning, Mom. I'm not quite done with my list, sorry."

"That's okay. I smell coffee—can I get myself a cup while you finish up?"

"I'll get it. Two sugars, right?"

"Yes, sweetie, thank you." She followed him in the kitchen. "You know, your house looks so much better since Heather decorated. The difference is amazing—she did a great job. And I was so excited to be grocery shopping with my boy again that I forgot to ask why Heather couldn't take you today."

Even though he wouldn't be able to see the look on her face, Jason couldn't bear facing his mom when he broke the news. He was at the coffee pot, his back to her when he said, "She left me, Mom."

"What?" The shock in her voice matched the despair he felt.

"She moved out."

"I…I don't understand. What happened?"

He held out a mug of steaming coffee. "I guess it had been building up for a while, she felt overwhelmed. She needs some time to figure out if she wants to spend the rest of her life married to a blind guy."

"Oh, sweetheart, I'm so sorry." She set down her coffee and embraced him.

He willingly gave in to the hug, recognizing how good it felt to be held. "You were right all along, Mom. No woman with two good eyes would ever want to be with me. I was stupid to believe it could happen." He was trying so hard not to cry. Not to his mom. Then he'd be like that scared blind boy again and might as well pack up and move back home.

"No, you were right to believe. And I was wrong, I really was." Her words shocked him.

"But you weren't wrong—she's gone. I thought she was my forever, but my bullshit drove her away. I might as well plan on being alone or start trolling for women at National Federation of the Blind meetings."

"Now, Jason, listen to me." Her voice sounded stern, and she pulled away from him. "I was wrong about Heather. She does love you—anyone that saw you two together could see that. You said she needs some time...I'm sure she'll decide she does want to marry you. I honestly think she'll be back."

He couldn't believe she wasn't saying I told you so. Her words left Jason surprised and grateful. "I'm not so sure, Mom."

"Just stay positive." She patted him on the back. "Don't give up. Now go finish that grocery list, and we'll get you out of the house. It's a nice day out. The sun is shining. Maybe we could go for a walk after the store."

"Maybe." He kissed her on the cheek. "Thanks, Mom."

****

With Heather gone, Jason felt like his life had turned into some kind of old-school country song where the guy loses everything and is left with nothing but the stool at the bar where he drinks away his misery. No doubt about it, Jason certainly tried to drink away the pain. It just wasn't working.

Instead, it provided an endless series of morning-after hangovers that were becoming redundant. Whether he went out with Mark or Shawn or one of his other buddies—he made a habit of drinking way too much. It dulled the pain, but not much and not for long.

Heather had been gone for almost three weeks, and he'd had no contact with her. Jason was up late grading papers, listening to the radio. He nursed his fourth beer and the Lady Antebellum song *Need You Now* came on the radio. He'd heard it hundreds of times before but never really paid attention to it. Tonight it struck him and fit his mood exactly.

The chorus soared and he said out loud, "Well I am a little drunk, and God knows I need you, Heather."

He picked up his phone, his heart racing when Heather's phone rang on the other end. He checked his watch: eleven-fifty.

"Hello?" she answered, sounding groggy. "Jason, is that you?"

"Yes," he said quietly, his eyes welling up at the sound of her voice. "I'm sorry to call you so late—"

"That's okay. Is something wrong?" She sounded a little more alert.

"No, nothing...just...everything." It was all he could do to keep from crying full out; he didn't want her to hear him.

"I know," she whispered.

"It's been almost three weeks since I heard your voice and I just want to talk with you. How are you?" he asked.

"I'm...I don't know. I'm miserable, really."

"So have you been thinking about us?"

"Every day." Tears were obvious in her voice.

"Are you going to let me know if you decide it's over or just leave me hanging?"

"Jason, I would never do that to you. I'll let you know when I figure this out."

"Well, are you any closer to the answers?" His voice begged.

"Oh...I don't know. I just miss you so much, that's all I can focus on."

"Well shouldn't that tell you something?" He started crying then—he could no longer hide it.

"All it tells me is what I've known all along, that I love you more than I've ever loved anyone. But it doesn't tell me what our future holds."

"Everybody's future is uncertain. We're no different."

"We are different."

"No, *I'm* different," he said with resignation.

"Baby…you're my everything. I just have to make sure I can handle this before we move forward."

"I know, I know, I hear what you're saying. This is just so fucking hard. I think I'm a damn alcoholic now or something…."

"You need to take care of yourself. I'm so sorry…." She was obviously crying herself.

"I'm sorry, I shouldn't have called. I didn't mean to make this harder for us."

"No, I'm glad you called. I miss you so much, and your voice is soothing to me."

"Yeah, me too." He took a deep breath. "I guess I'll go now. Please figure this out soon, I'm dying here."

Chapter Nineteen

The next night, Heather was half-heartedly watching an American Pickers marathon when her doorbell rang. She put her eye to the peephole and stepped back in surprise.

Opening the door, she said, "Uh, hi, Mark." She was embarrassed that she had no makeup on, her hair was in a ponytail and she was pretty sure there were bags under her eyes. "Is something wrong with Jason?"

"Well, not really," Mark said. "But can I come in? I'd like to talk."

"Oh…I don't know…my place is pretty trashed…"

"Heather, I don't care what your place looks like. I just want to have a conversation with you."

"Okay." She gestured him inside.

When he walked into the great room from the foyer, Heather wished she could hide. Shoes littered the floor, dishes lay piled up in the sink and on the counters, and clumps of discarded clothes cluttered various pieces of furniture.

"I'm sorry. I've been kind of rebelling I guess."

"Hell, somebody with perfect eyesight could get hurt in here," he said with a chuckle.

"I know, I know. And it's not like it makes me feel any better. Just symbolic, I guess." She shoved some clothes and papers aside on the couch. "Please have a seat. Can I get you something to drink? Soda? Beer?"

"No, I'm fine." They sat down, side by side, and Mark sighed. "Heather, I know you need this time away from Jason to figure things out. I don't fully understand, although Jason seems to. But do you have any idea what you're doing to him?"

Tears welled in her eyes. "Probably about the same thing that I'm doing to myself. I mean, look around you.

Does this look like the home of a happy person? I spend all of my time either crying, or sleeping, or talking about Jason, or just listening to music trying to make sense of it all."

"Well, Heather, that's the thing. This doesn't make sense. You two love each other, and you're both miserable apart. What good can possibly come of this?"

Heather took a deep breath. "Mark, let's be honest for a minute. You used to live with Jason. Didn't it get a little exhausting sometimes, always making sure you placed everything in the same spot in the fridge, every time? And always remembering to pick up your shoes off the floor and just...everything?"

"Well, actually, I was probably kind of hard for Jason to live with. I caused a lot of stumbles for him, and my parents always bitched at me for not putting things where they belong."

"See? Now, I'm not saying it's horrible or anything, because it's not. And I'm getting used to it. But there's just never a break, you know? It's constant. And when I screw up, he jumps all over me. I get why. I can't imagine what a pain it is to have someone else's carelessness mean that you can't find something or have to ask for help. I would hate that, so I know why he does too. But it doesn't make it any easier when I'm getting yelled at because I set the razor down ten inches from where it belongs."

"I'm sorry, Heather, I didn't know it was like that."

"If it was just that, it would be a no-brainer. I can put up with that all day long if it means I get to spend my life with Jason. But let's bring a baby in the mix. So now I'm sleep deprived and adjusting to motherhood...and I still have to put everything in its exact spot and keep everything perfectly clean. And what if Jason can never help with a late night feeding or a diaper change? So it's me, every single night, all alone, without even the luxury of kicking my shoes off when I climb into bed. Then the baby's crawling and playing with toys, and I'm solely responsible for keeping everything clean for the baby and Jason. What if I miss a toy, and he trips and falls? How will Jason watch our child when it can't talk yet?"

Mark took a deep breath. "Heather, I don't know. But I do know that we'll be your family. You won't be alone. If you need some help because Jason can't, then we're here for you. Mom and Dad would be happy to come over and pitch in, and so can Angie and I."

"That's so sweet, and I appreciate it, but I don't know how realistic that is." She leaned back. "You never know. It might not be that bad. Jason is a smart, innovative guy. He just might be more hands-on than most dads."

"I actually think he will."

Heather buried her face in her hands. "But it's just a lot to think about because we don't know. Even he says he doesn't know. And then there's his DNA...we could have grandsons that are blind." She looked up at Mark. "I'm not sure I can make that decision to condemn an innocent child to that—to *this*."

"Would you be any happier right now if Jason had never been born?"

"Of course not. But you can't say his life has been easy."

"No." Mark looked down. "I've spent most of my life looking out for Jason, helping him when he needs it. But I don't know how to help him now. Is there anything I can do to help you come to a decision?"

"I have to do this on my own."

"Well, please hurry. You're breaking my brother's heart, and I don't know how long I can stand to watch."

****

Jason's life and memory was so intertwined with touch. He knew the feel of his favorite spatula's handle, the contours of the shampoo bottle in his hands, the exact grain of the fabric on his couch and the difference between his blue polo and orange polo by the texture of the material.

It was the same way with his memories of Heather. The specific way her fingers felt interlaced with his was forever etched in his tactile memory. The curve of her hips when he put his hands around her waist; the soft, full pressure of her lips against his cheek; the smooth, round bump of the small mole near the crook of her right arm; the firm muscles in her thigh when he put his hand on her leg. He knew all these things intimately; they formed his mental picture of Heather. Just as some would long to see an old lover, his fingers and arms ached to feel her again. They felt empty, purposeless without her.

He was, in a word, lost.

Jason was conscious of this ache when he walked home from the bus stop. With each passing day, the temperature dropped. The sounds and smells of summer on his walks were replaced with the crackling of leaves under his feet and the crunch of his cane scraping them across the pavement. Somewhere in the distance, he could smell burning leaves. There weren't as many children playing outside, although he could hear a basketball being dribbled somewhere down the street. He figured it was getting darker out earlier, although he didn't know when. Was it dark out yet?

A distinct crinkling sound, all too familiar to Jason, made him stop. He picked up his cane and sure enough, a plastic grocery bag had ensnared itself around the stick. An annoying and frequent occurrence. He pulled it off and heard five-year-old Kennedy yelling from her yard, two houses away.

"Jason! Jason!"

"Hello… Is that Frank?" he teased, sticking the bag in his pocket to throw away at home. He started walking again.

"No, it's Kennedy." She giggled. That joke never grew old.

"Oh, Kennedy, hello!" He stopped in front of her yard and instantly felt her arms hugging his legs.

He tousled her hair. "I think you're getting taller, kiddo."

"I think so too. I'll be six next month. Then I'll be really tall."

"So how's my favorite girl?"

"Good. Did Heather come home yet?"

Bam! Just like that, a dagger to his heart. They had invited Kennedy to be their flower girl, and if there was no wedding, he knew she understood that meant no gig for her.

"No, sweetie, not yet." He wondered if he should just say *No, she's not coming back.*

"Well, I've been praying every night that she'll come back. And I'm praying for God to make a miracle so you could see. Then Heather would come back."

Well, there you go, Jason thought grimly. *I just need my vision miraculously restored. Problem solved.*

He knelt down to her level. "My eyes are never going to work. They're just filling up space in my eye sockets. And if Heather comes back, it will be because she loves me enough to put up with a guy who can't see."

"But it looks like you're looking at me sometimes." She squeezed his cheeks.

"Right now, does it look like I'm looking at you?"

"Yes."

"Well, I don't see a thing." He turned when he heard Tina open her front door.

"Hi, Jason," she hollered.

"Mommy, why are you waving to him?" Kennedy laughed. "He can't see you."

Jason laughed too. "Hello, Tina! And no, I didn't see you wave, but I appreciate the sentiment."

"Well, then you can't see me blushing, either," she said. "Do you want to have dinner with us tonight?"

"Oh no, but thanks. I'm just going to make myself a sandwich or something and get to grading some papers."

"Are you sure? You could eat and run, we wouldn't mind."

How can I say that I want nothing more than to wallow alone in the pain of my failing love life? "I'll take a rain check, if that's okay."

"Anytime, Jason."

"Can I play with your cane for a minute?" Kennedy asked.

"Well, only for a minute, I'm getting cold out here." Jason held out the stick for her.

She grabbed it. "Show me how."

"Okay." He bent over and held her hand with the cane in it. "Keep your elbow next to your side and move your hand like this." With the cane just barely above the sidewalk, he moved it back and forth with his wrist, tapping right, left, right, left. He let go and off she went.

"Kennedy, keep your eyes open," he said in his stern teacher's voice, "or you could get hurt. I mean it, okay?"

"Okay." Her voice trailed away in the wind.

Jason crossed his arms and stood awkwardly in the middle of the sidewalk. He didn't like the feeling of standing in the middle of nowhere. He always thought anchors were nice—a table, a wall, a chair or cane. Holding onto an object was proof that something existed beyond him; it tethered him to a world that he couldn't see. Without that, it was an odd sensation to be in a sea of nothingness.

"Kennedy," Tina yelled out. "That's enough, come back."

Jason heard the cane tapping back to him, along with Kennedy's giggles.

"That was fun. I like the way you see."

"Glad I entertain you, Kennedy." He smiled.

"Here's your cane," she said.

He figured she was probably holding it out to him, but since the mythical "here" meant nothing to him, he put his hand out. "Can you please hand it to me?"

"Yep."

He felt the rubber handle in the palm of his hand and took it. "I'm going inside now. Good night, kiddo. Good night, Tina."

"Good night, Jason," Tina responded. "Thank you for being patient with her curiosity."

"Beats the heck out of people staring and not asking

questions. Good night." He waved. "Wave back to me, would you?"

Tina laughed. "Okay, I am."

"Smell you later!" Kennedy piped up.

"Smell you later." Jason continued down the sidewalk to his house.

Later that night after grading papers, Jason flipped through the TV channels to find something of interest. He sipped on a beer, though he was conscious to limit his intake to one drink tonight. He worried if he didn't slow down he'd be caning his way into AA meetings.

Mark's ringtone played from his phone. He checked his watch as he answered—ten after eleven.

"Hey, Mark—why are you calling me so late?"

"It's time, Jace. I'm gonna be a dad!"

Jason put down his beer and sat up straight. "No shit?"

"No shit! Angie's water broke, and the doctor told us to head to the hospital."

"Oh, wow," Jason whispered. "This is crazy."

Mark and Angie headed to the hospital, while Jason's parents were en route to pick him up on their way.

****

"What's the matter with you, Jason?" his dad asked.

Jason buried his face in his hands. "I am soooo freaking bored." He checked his watch…eight-twenty-one in the morning. "I mean, I know labor takes a long time, but we've been here for like nine hours."

"Your brother took fifteen to come out." His mom patted Jason's hand. "You only took about five hours."

"That's because Mark's always been a pain," Jason said with a smile. "Seriously, I am dying here. The TV is tuned to that damn home improvement show, which is obviously lost on me. I finished my book. Listened to three different podcasts, called my boss to tell him I would be out today, emailed the sub with instructions, and have browsed every imaginable website of interest. Do you see any Braille magazines around here?"

"Come on, Jace." John patted Jason on the shoulder.

"Let's get some fresh air."

"You bet." Jason threw on his jacket, opened his cane and grabbed the elbow his dad offered.

The sterile, medicinal smell of the hospital was so pungent that Jason felt relief the minute they stepped outside. In spite of the cold, there was no wind, so it felt crisp outside without being biting. He heard birds chirping and the rustle of dried leaves around him. He smelled pine. "Where are we, Dad?"

"In a little garden area. So can you believe your brother is going to be a dad?"

"No, not really. And you're going to be a grandpa, whether you like the sound of that or not."

They shared a laugh. "And you an uncle, Jace. I can't wait to see you holding that baby. You've always been so good with kids."

"Yeah, I guess so." Jason shrugged.

"Which makes me think of you having your own someday. What's the latest with Heather?" The mere mention of her name brought pain to Jason's face.

"Nothing new, Dad. I've talked to her once since she left, a few days ago."

"And?"

"She's still trying to figure out what she wants." Jason stopped, so John did too. "Dad, was it hard on you and Mom when I lived with you? I mean, having to keep it so regimented and organized and everything?"

"Well…I don't know if hard is the right word. It was just constant vigilance. If you were walking around, it meant we always looked out for potential accidents waiting to happen. Telling you the dishwasher door was open before you ran into it, or there's a glass of soda on the counter before you knock it off, or the dog's right behind you—don't back up. And when Mark lived there, he was such a slob if we didn't stay on top of him, there would be shoes in the middle of the floor or cups and dishes lying all over the place." He patted Jason on the shoulder. "We still do those things. I'm always on the lookout."

"I guess you guys are so good at doing that, it's seamless—I don't even notice. I never realized how much help I get without even asking."

"But like I said, Jace, it's not hard. It's just what has to be done. We love you, it's no big deal."

"But would you have married Mom if she needed all that help?"

"Oh, son…that's an impossible question to answer."

"Why?"

"Because she's not blind. It's a very big hypothetical question."

"You wouldn't have." Jason sighed.

"You know, Jason, you're probably right. Maybe I wouldn't have back then. Whoever you end up with is going to be a special selfless person, signing up for more than the average wife."

"Do you think there's anything I can do to make it easier for her?"

"I don't know…sometimes you get a little nasty when something's moved and you can't find it or you run into something or whatever. If you want to make things easier, maybe you could be a little more forgiving."

Jason sighed. "Yeah, I know what you mean. I need to work on that. I didn't realize until lately how much Heather's been doing to accommodate me. It's just so frustrating because when I live by myself, it's easy. Nobody moves stuff around, I always know where things are, I never run into a half-open door."

"Well, do you want to live alone forever?"

"No. I want Heather back where she belongs."

"So maybe you need to put up with some inconveniences to share your life with someone. And I hope you get what you're looking for, Jace. I really do."

"But you just admitted you wouldn't have married Mom if she was blind."

"Well, I'm not Heather."

They grabbed some doughnuts and bagels from the cafeteria, along with coffee, and headed back to the waiting room. Jason had just settled into his seat when the doors outside the waiting room burst open.

"I'm a dad!" Mark yelled, rushing to his family. They all shared hugs and congratulations. "She weighs seven pounds two ounces, and she's twenty-one inches long. She's got a lot of hair and…and she's just perfect!"

"What's her name?" John asked.

"Jacie Michelle Scharp." Mark slapped Jason on the back. "We named her after you, little brother. Jacie is the closest girl's name we could find to Jason."

"Really?" Jason asked, a huge smile spreading across his face.

"Really."

Jason heard the smile in Mark's voice loud and clear. Overwhelmed, he grabbed Mark in a hug. "Wow, thank you. Congratulations!"

"So do you guys want to come back and see her?"

"Oh, you bet we do," Eve said.

Mark put Jason's hand on his elbow and they took off down the hall. "Here's the foot of the bed," Mark said.

Jason reached out and found it, hearing his parents fuss and aww over the baby while Angie and Mark chimed in. Standing there, Jason had difficulty comprehending his brand new niece in the room, with no confirmation of her. He couldn't smell her—only cleaning chemicals and antiseptic. Jacie didn't seem to be making any sounds that he could hear. He didn't even know where she was—in his mom's arms? Angie's? He felt a bit disconnected from the whole thing while he listened to their chatter.

"Hey, Jason," Angie said from the bed, with exhaustion in her voice but also a smile. "Why don't you come up here? Walk to the right and follow the bed." He did, bumping into a stand on wheels of some sort. "It's okay, that's just a monitor for when the baby was still inside. You can push it a little farther over if you need more room. Come here." She took his hand and he leaned against the bed.

"You sound tired, Ang." He squeezed her hand.

"Well, I'm tired but also exhilarated. Do you want to see Jacie?"

A timid smile crept on his face. "I don't want to bother her by pawing all over her."

"It will be fine. Eve—can I have the baby? I want to introduce her to Uncle Jason."

"Of course."

"Here, Jason," Angie said, "she's all swaddled up so I'll un-wrap her for a minute so you can check her out."

"Hold your hands out Jason," Mark said. "I've got some Germ-X."

Jason obliged and rubbed until it dissipated.

"Okay, she's ready for you," Angie said warmly. "She's on my lap."

"I don't want to poke her—can you put my hand on her?" He held his hand out.

"She's right here." Angie placed his fingers on Jacie's stomach.

Jason put his other hand there too, and broke out into a huge grin when he felt her scrawny, downy-soft legs. Then he moved on to her feet. He fought to hold back the tears that threatened his eyes as he got the first glimpse of his niece. "She's impossibly tiny."

"Yeah, she really is," Mark agreed, smiling.

Jason felt her little belly and then her chin, her petal-soft lips and button nose. He was careful around her eyes, which were closed.

His tears brimmed, overflowed, and trickled down his cheeks. "Her head is itty-bitty." He laughed through the tears. "My God, she's so precious. Who does she look like?"

She started fussing a bit, amazing Jason with her unfamiliar sounds.

"I think she looks like Angie," Mark said.

"I think so too," Angie agreed. "I'm going to wrap her back up."

Jason moved his hands away, although he hated to. "Well, it's a damn good thing she doesn't look like you,

Mark," Jason joked, "because from what I remember, you would not make an attractive girl."

"Jason, she's all bundled back up—do you want to hold her?" Angie asked.

"Are you sure you're comfortable with that? I understand if you're not."

"Oh, please." Angie pushed the baby toward him and touched his arm. "Hold your arms out."

He followed her lead and soon held a tight bundle in his arms that felt a lot like a hot water bottle. Mark helped settle her in the crook of his left arm.

With his right hand, Jason touched her cheek. "Hi, Jacie," he said in a singsong voice. "I'm your Uncle Jason."

"She just opened her eyes," Eve said.

"Are you looking at me?" Jason asked. "I guess you don't see much better than me right now, little Jacie."

"She can probably make out your face," Angie said, "but not in much detail. They're extremely nearsighted and can't see all colors yet."

"Well, you'll be seeing perfectly in no time and then you'll show me all kinds of things." He felt her nose again and found her tiny ears. He could hear someone snapping pictures. "I'll apologize in advance for all the poking and prodding you're going to get from me. But I'll make it up to you. I'm going to spoil you with gifts so I'll be your favorite uncle. And I'll show you how to shoot a basketball, 'cause your daddy is no good at that."

"Hey!" Mark protested.

"And you'll get lots of hugs and kisses from me too." Jason inhaled her delicious baby scent. He felt her head. "She's got a fair amount of hair, doesn't she?"

"Yeah, she sure does," Angie said.

"What color is it?"

"Actually, kind of light brown like yours."

"Hey girl, we match." Jason smiled. He heard the camera going again. "Who's taking all the pictures?"

"Your father," John boomed.

"Do you want one of me facing the camera?"

"Yeah, smile at me."

Jason looked at what he hoped was the camera and smiled. "Hey, Mark, can you take one with your phone and text it to me?"

"Sure." Mark pulled his phone out of his pocket. "Look over this way at me. Got it."

Jacie started fussing a bit.

"Okay, Uncle Jason is done. I don't do cries. Somebody please take her." He felt her being taken from his arms, but by whom, he didn't know. "You guys, I'm in love. She's perfect."

"Thank you." Mark squeezed his brother's shoulder.

Jason's phone beeped with a new text.

"Is there a chair in here?" he asked.

Mark showed Jason to a chair and he checked his phone. It was the picture from Mark. Jason titled it: Jacie, 1-hr-old with her uncle.

"So is this a good picture?" He held up the phone to anyone that would look. Eve walked over.

"Oh yes," she said. "Shows off your great smile and my adorable granddaughter."

"Okay, thanks." Jason sent the photo to Heather in a text. He knew exactly what he was doing. Sure, he wanted her to know that Jacie was born—he didn't want her to miss out on a big Scharp family event. But he also knew how much she loved babies, and he was holding one in the picture. Maybe it would warm her heart. He'd use any angle he could at this point.

Within just a few minutes, Heather's ringtone lit up his phone. He stood up right away, opened his cane, and answered the phone.

"Hello." He caned his way across the room and eventually found the doorway. He stepped out into the hall for some privacy. But was there anyone nearby? He hoped not.

"Hi, it's me," she said.

"Hey."

"I got your text. Oh my gosh—she's beautiful!"

"That's what I hear." He smiled. "She's so tiny, Heather. So delicate."

"That's a great picture of you too."

"Thanks."

"It's great to see your smile," she added.

"It's great to hear your voice. Really great." He didn't know what to say or how to act, so he didn't hold back.

"Be sure to tell Mark and Angie I said congratulations."

"I will. I just thought you'd want to know—"

"Oh, I'm so glad you sent me the picture. I wish I could be there with you."

"Yeah, me too. Hey, Heather?"

"Yeah?"

"I've been thinking about things. A lot. And...and I don't think I realized how much you do for me. How much work it is to live with me. Always keeping an eye out to make sure I don't get hurt or break something, or moving things out of my way before I even encounter them...just everything. It must seem pretty relentless to you."

"Sometimes it does."

"Well, I'm sorry I was so hard on you. I promise if you come back, I'm going to work on cutting you some slack. This time apart is giving me time to reflect too, and I don't think I've been appreciative enough of all that you do to accommodate me."

"Well, when you love someone Jason, you just do what you have to do."

"But being with me requires more than most people. So thank you, and I'm sorry I was too selfish to see that before."

"Thank you, baby." They were both quiet for a moment.

"I also thought we could have a room just for you at the house. It would be off-limits to me. You could throw shoes on the floor, clutter up a desk, do whatever you want in there. It would be your blindness-free room. Your own personal haven."

Heather laughed. It warmed him to his very soul.

"Sweetheart, I just want you home with me. What can I say to get you home?"

She didn't answer.

"Heather?"

"I don't know."

Jason slid his phone back in his pocket with a sigh and heard Angie's hospital room door open.

"You okay?" Mark asked.

"Yeah. I'm going for a walk. What room number is this?"

"Four thirty-three. There's Braille on the room sign to the left of the door, about shoulder height."

"Thanks." He started walking down the hall and then stopped and turned back around. "Mark, are you still there?"

"Yeah, I'm still here."

"I'm sorry you have to always help me like you just did, telling me where the room number is and lugging me around on your arm all the time and helping me find chairs and…everything."

"Jason, what are you talking about? Why would you be sorry for that?"

"I'm just beginning to realize fully how much my blindness affects everyone around me. I'm sorry it's that way, but thank you for always helping me."

Then he turned and continued down the hall.

"Where are you going?"

He stopped. "I don't know. I just need to get away for a bit. Actually, there's a bus stop here…I think I'm going to head home."

"I'll drive you home…."

"I can take the bus."

"I have to run by the house and grab a few things for Angie, anyway. I'll drop you off on the way."

****

Mark started up the car, and Jason grinned to himself when the Kiss song *Do You Love Me?* came blaring from the speakers. It reminded him of when they were kids and pretended to be Kiss in concert, using tennis rackets in lieu of guitars. Jason always thought he rocked a mean air guitar.

Mark turned down the music as the car started moving. "How did the conversation with Heather go?"

"She still won't make a decision. I guess that means that *is* her decision."

"Give her time."

"I know there are things I can change to make life easier for her. I need to chill out. I can be…difficult. I'm starting to realize that."

Mark chuckled. "Is that what the whole thank you business with me was about today?"

"Well, yeah." Jason faced Mark. "I take all of you for granted, all you do for me. I've just been thinking about a lot of stuff lately. I act like I'm so independent and can do everything on my own, but that's not entirely true. I have all of you guys to help fill in the gaps. But it's hard for me to admit I need help, you know? So that's why I said thanks."

"Well, just so you know, it doesn't need to be said. You know how proud we all are of you, and you've always been appreciative, never demanding anything. I wouldn't have named my daughter after you if you were a selfish prick." They shared a laugh together, like they had a million times before. "So why is it so hard for you to admit when you need help? Sometimes it's like pulling teeth with you."

"I guess…I guess because it makes me feel dependent and weak." Jason swallowed. "Nobody wants to feel that way."

"Jace, you're anything but weak. You're the strongest person I know—"

"I don't think that."

"Then you're selling yourself short. You're a very strong person. And did you ever think of this? Maybe being strong doesn't mean you don't need help—maybe it means being able to admit your limitations. You just might be at your strongest when you can ask for help."

Jason didn't respond right away. "No, I never did think of that. I always thought asking for help was admitting defeat."

"Not at all. There's strength in accepting that you have limitations. Everybody needs help sometimes, Jace."

"Well, I seem to need a lot more help than the average person."

"Because the average person can see their hand in front of their face. Cut yourself some slack, seriously."

"Yeah, I guess so." Jason slapped Mark's thigh. "You're getting pretty deep and profound today, eh?"

Mark laughed. "It's the lack of sleep. I get more meaningful when I'm in a daze. We're almost to your place—oh, shit!"

"What?" Adrenaline rushed through Jason at the sound of panic in Mark's voice.

The word was barely out of his mouth when Jason heard the screech of tires, the surge of the car's engine and the sickening thud of metal hitting metal. He felt the car shoot sideways and Mark's body slammed into him as he was shoved into the door.

Suddenly, everything was still and Jason was aware of glass covering him. He felt wetness on his head and face. Blood?

"Mark?" No answer. "Mark!"

Mark moaned and then whispered, "Jace..."

"Are you okay?" More moaning. "Mark, what's going on? Are you okay?" Jason reached over and felt his brother, his hands now wet with what he knew must be blood.

"It's bad," Mark managed to say.

"I'm calling 911." Jason struggled to get his phone out of his pocket. He quickly dialed.

"911, what's your emergency?" asked a woman on the other end.

"We've been in a car accident. I think it's really bad."

"Where are you?"

"Mark, where are we?" He mumbled something in response. "Mark, can you tell me where we are? Ma'am, I don't know where we're at."

"Can you see any street signs?"

"No, I'm blind. I can't see anything."

"What?"

"I'm blind," Jason yelled in a complete panic. "I don't know where we're at, or what's going on…I need help. My brother's hurt."

"Okay sir, I'm picking up your location from your cell phone…I've located you and I'm sending help right now. It should only be a minute or two. Do you want me to stay on the line with you?"

"No, I need to check on my brother. Thank you."

He hung up and heard a man outside the car say, "Are you okay?"

"I am, but I don't think my brother is."

"Oh, fuck."

"What?" Jason asked.

"Oh man, look at him—"

"I can't, I'm blind, I can't look at him. What's wrong?"

"Oh…"

"What?" Jason screamed.

"It's not good, man, he's in really bad shape. Let me help you get out of there—"

"No, I'm staying with my brother. Mark? Mark?"

"Jace…" Mark moaned softly.

"Help is on the way." Jason was crying, his face a mess of blood and tears. He found Mark's hand and held on tight. "Mark, hang on…it's gonna be okay…" Jason heard sirens in the distance. "See, they're almost here…Mark?" Jason was aware that his brother had stopped responding. "Mark, hang on. Don't leave me, dammit! I need you. Mark!"

The sirens were deafening and then cut off. Jason heard doors opening and slamming shut, and felt someone open his door. "Are you the police?"

"No, I'm a paramedic."

"I'm fine, just help my brother!"

"They've got your brother," the paramedic said as

Jason felt Mark's hand slip out of his own. He heard someone say "unresponsive, pupils are dilated."

"Is he gonna be okay?"

"We're going to do all we can. Now let me get a look at you—"

"I want to ride with him to the hospital."

"What's your name?"

"Jason. I need to stay with Mark—"

"Jason, my name is Troy. Dispatch said someone at the scene is blind. Are you blind?"

"Yes. Take me to Mark—"

"Jason, listen to me. I need to take care of you—you've been in a very serious accident. The best thing for you to do right now is let me take care of you while they work on your brother."

"He needs me. Mark!" Jason yelled.

"Jason, Jason. I need you to stay calm. Do you want me to check on Mark?"

"Yes." He knew he sounded hysterical; he felt hysterical. There were so many sounds, so much happening...he felt overwhelmed and terrified.

"Don't move. You're covered in glass. I'll be right back." He heard Troy walk away, the sound of glass crunching under his shoes. Jason heard the murmurs of a gathering crowd and heard a man say "fatality on the scene."

Troy's footsteps returned and Jason asked, "Did the driver in the other car die? I heard someone say there's a fatality."

"No, Jason, she's fine. Let's get you taken care of."

Jason didn't say another word. He didn't dare. They put a neck brace on him before strapping him on a backboard and lifting him into the ambulance. In a daze, he rattled off his parents' phone number when asked. Troy climbed in with him and slammed the doors shut.

"Are we going to Mercy?" Jason asked when they sped off, sirens going.

"Yeah, we'll be there in just a few minutes."

"We just came from there." Jason felt like someone else was talking, not him. Like he was listening to the TV.

"Were you visiting someone?"

"Mark just became a dad. They had their baby this morning. He was taking me home." Jason grabbed Troy's arm. "Is he…?"

"Jason, I'm sorry. They did everything they could."

Jason wouldn't allow Troy's words to sink in. He knew if he kept talking, he wouldn't have to. "But he was taking me home. I was going to take the bus, but he offered—"

"It was an accident, Jason. The girl was texting—"

"He wouldn't have been there except for me…he said we were almost to my house." No matter how hard Jason tried to block it, the truth came crashing through. He started sobbing uncontrollably.

"Jason, it wasn't your fault—"

"He was taking me home…." He continued to wail, his anguished cries blending with the blaring sirens while the ambulance sped through the streets.

Chapter Twenty

The funeral was sheer pain for Jason. Raw, gut-wrenching pain. At first, at the hospital right after the accident, none of it seemed real. He heard his mother's screams when she arrived at the ER and was told the news about Mark. It was a couple of hours later when they released Jason after two-dozen stitches on his face, a cast on his arm and plenty of pain meds.

It was all a scrambled, jumbled mess of memories in his mind. Maybe from the drugs, or the grief, or just shock. He remembered crying with Angie, hugging her across the cold steel rails of her hospital bed. Desperate apologies whispered. Guilt so overpowering he could barely breathe. Angie's reassuring voice, tear-filled, telling him it wasn't his fault. Hospital smells everywhere. Jacie crying, everyone crying. The sound of the crash replaying over and over in his mind. Mark's labored, ragged breathing sounds rattling in Jason's brain, wanting to settle as a dream but firmly planted as reality. Blood, the smell of blood followed him everywhere. Two showers later, it was still inside his nose. Eventually sleep...where? Maybe he was at his parents' house. Nothing made sense.

By the time of the funeral three days later, the fogginess had gone, and Jason was acutely aware of what was happening. But still none of it made sense.

Heather was with him, holding his hand, never letting go unless she sensed—how, he didn't know—that he needed to walk outside alone, get away from everyone. Which happened a lot. He kept feeling out of breath. Like he was slowly, slowly drowning. Fresh air seemed to help. Never enough though.

When he'd called Heather the morning after, it was early. Just after five o'clock. He woke up, startled, everything rushing back at once. Troy's calm voice, the squish of Mark's blood on his hands, blaring sirens...he leaned over the side of the futon he was lying in at his parents' house and grabbed the trashcan. He threw up violently, as if his body was trying to rid him of all the pain. When he was finished, he lay back and found his phone in his back pocket and called Heather.

She sounded asleep when she answered the phone. "Hello?"

He couldn't get any words out, just a moan.

"Jason? Jason, are you all right?"

"No..." He couldn't say the words. They wouldn't form.

"What's wrong?"

"Mark," was all that escaped and the sobs began.

"Mark? Did something happen to Mark?"

"There was a...car accident..."

"Oh my God! Is he okay?"

Jason didn't respond.

"Jason, is he okay?"

"He died."

"Oh..." Heather's own crying began. "I'm so sorry, baby. Oh my God. I'm coming over."

"I'm...I'm at my parents'...."

"Give me twenty minutes."

"Hurry," he whispered before he hung up the phone.

She'd pretty much been by his side since then. They went with his parents to the funeral home to make the arrangements. That night she stayed with him, holding him while he slept, fitfully—crying out in his sleep for Mark.

At the funeral, she walked him to the podium where he struggled to maintain his composure when he talked about his brother. He talked about growing up together, their laughter, about Mark always being there for him. It was then the tears began running down his bruised and bandaged face, and he came to the realization that Mark would never be there for him again. He couldn't finish, and Heather led him back to his pew. When he joined the other pallbearers to carry his brother's body to the hearse, she was there for him when he was done, to take his hand and guide him to the car.

For three days, they didn't speak much. She was just physically there for him. That was what he needed. Her hand in his, her body to hold when he felt like he was sinking. But despite her presence at his side, he knew she wasn't really back.

But she showed up and didn't leave him when he couldn't stand on his own.

The day after the funeral was a Saturday. Jason woke up with no purpose. No work, nowhere he had to be. Go see Angie and Jacie? Or would she just resent his presence? Go to his parents' house?

While he lay in bed, trying to convince himself that he really should climb out, he heard sounds coming from his kitchen. "Heather? Is that you?"

"Yeah, it's me. I'll be right there."

He sat up in bed and heard her bare feet padding down the wood floors in the hallway.

"I brought you some breakfast."

"I'm not hungry." He shook his head.

"You have to eat, Jason. I think all you had yesterday was half a piece of chicken."

"I don't have an appetite."

"You're going to get sick—"

"I can't eat. Besides, you can't cook." It wasn't said with a smile or as a joke. It was a condemnation.

"Well, maybe not, but I can heat up frozen waffles and slice strawberries."

"I'm sorry, that was rude of me to say." He ran his fingers across the ridged surface of the cast on his left arm.

"That's okay." She put the tray of food down on the dresser and sat next to him. "Will you at least eat a strawberry or two?"

"Ugh…" He sighed. "No, I can't. I'm sorry, thanks for going to the trouble, but the thought of food is just so unappealing."

"You need to eat…" She bit into a strawberry.

"It's my fault, you know," he whispered, closing his eyes.

"What's your fault?"

"Mark."

"How was it your fault?"

He took a deep breath. "He was taking me home. I was going to take the bus, but he insisted he'd do it. If it weren't for his helpless fucking brother, he'd still be here. Jacie would have a dad and Angie would have a husband." His voice was calm and firm.

Heather took his hand in hers; his still-swollen fingers were sore, but she was gentle. "The only person at fault was that woman who ran a red light while texting."

"I hope that was one hell of a text." His laugh sounded bitter, with a coldness ringing through. He faced Heather. "I know nothing's changed between us, I know you're just here to help. So thank you. I don't think I could have made it through the last few days without you."

"You would have done the same for me."

"Yeah." Jason caressed her hand. "I would have." He climbed out of bed. "But you might as well go now, before I get used to you being around again. I can only handle so much right now, you know? So please leave…you've been incredible, so strong for me…but I'm in love with you, Heather. I can't have you with me and depend on you when you're not really mine."

"But I don't want you to be alone right now—"

"Every minute you're with me just messes with my emotions. Being alone is safer."

"Are you going to be okay?"

"I don't know, Heather…I'll have to be, won't I? I certainly don't want you with me just out of pity or obligation."

"I'm with you right now because I love you—"

"But I don't want you to be with me unless you're going to stay. Forever." Jason leaned against the wall and quietly asked, "Can you promise me that?"

"No…not yet. I'm still sorting things out in my mind. So I think I understand where you're coming from. But you can call me if you need me—"

"I know that. And thank you." He sighed, crossing his arms.

****

Heather looked at him, noticing a hardness, a detachment she hadn't seen before. She hardly recognized him. His empty eyes seemed to capture his state of mind. Jagged lines with cuts and stitches were scattered about his face. Since she'd showed up at his parents' house three days before, never once had she seen him smile.

She climbed off the bed and put her arms around him. At first she was the only one participating in the hug, but soon his arms wrapped around her and held her tight. They stayed that way, silent, for a few minutes. Their breathing found a shared rhythm. Eventually, Heather reached up to kiss him and saw tears pouring down his face. For Mark? For them?

They kissed gently, softly. The desire between them was ignited, and their kisses grew more feverish. It had been too long since Heather had been wrapped in his arms, and now in nothing but his boxers, the firm muscles of his chest up against her…she felt the familiar passion that he always stirred in her. Suddenly, Jason pulled away. Without a word, he walked to the bathroom, and when he came back in, his face had hardened again.

"I love you with all my heart, Heather. Well, what's left of it, anyway. But I can't do this with you. I'm fucked up beyond belief right now, and if I make love to you it will torture me the whole time we're apart. Please leave."

Heather swallowed. "I do love you, but I'm sorry I'm not ready yet…." There had been so many apologies from both of them lately. Hers hung in the air until she broke the oppressive silence with, "I'll go grab my things."

****

Jason made a point to listen to her leave him this time, felt like he had to. Her firm steps fading into the living room, the door opening and gingerly closing shut behind her. The hum of the engine when she started her car, and the sound of it fading while she drove away.

He walked in the living room, to the foyer, to lock the door. She had left it cracked open, just a bit. He held onto the handle for a minute before he pushed the door shut and turned the deadbolt. It took all his strength to make his way back to the bedroom. He climbed into bed, Heather's smell lingering everywhere, and stayed there until Monday morning.

****

On the spur of the moment on the way home from work, Heather decided to get her hair colored. Maybe some highlights of auburn? Something, she needed something. A pick-me-up.

After spending those days with Jason for the funeral, she was more despondent and confused than ever. There was no doubt in her mind that she loved him, and the attraction was undeniable.

But leaving Jason the day after the funeral was almost harder for her than the first time she'd left. He was in so much pain and wasn't himself at all. Heather felt like she was leaving him when he needed her most. She wanted to stay, but he was absolutely right. The longer she stayed, the easier it would be to fall right back into what they'd had.

Heather didn't want to settle for a life she hadn't chosen. She wanted to decide that she could live with his disability, forever. That she was willing to sacrifice certain things to be with him.

And she just couldn't get there in her head. She didn't know why. A part of her was afraid she was more callous and coldhearted than she had ever imagined herself to be. But she didn't think she was; it felt more like she was struggling with all the dreams she'd created.

All her life, she had dreams of raising a family someday…but none of those dreams had ever included a husband who couldn't drive their kids to soccer or watch them in a dance recital. There would be no dad building a tree house in the backyard or teaching the kids to ride their bikes.

They were selfish dreams, she knew. But committing to Jason meant giving up on some dreams she'd cherished for years.

Could she make new dreams, though?

She could picture Jason with their future children, holding their hands while going on a walk. Or teaching them to swing a bat or throw a basketball through the hoop. She knew he would be hands-on, no doubt in her mind.

But she also imagined months of diaper changing on her own, sleep-deprived and exhausted. Toys left out, accidents just waiting to happen all over the place. What if she couldn't keep up? What if she moved the high chair too far away from the wall and he ran into it? What if he was watching the toddler and the child fell and got hurt, but he couldn't see what was wrong?

Heather was so tired of the "what ifs"...they invaded her every thought. But the thought of walking away from the best relationship she'd ever had, well, that scared her too. He felt like the one.

But after leaving him the last time, she sensed that maybe she'd already lost him. Maybe her decision, whatever it was, would be too late.

She sat in the hair salon's waiting room, flipping through magazines for color inspiration, when a child in a wheelchair was brought in. Heather looked at the little girl, probably around eight years old, and smiled. Her hair was cut so short, so boyish, that she was fairly certain it was growing back from chemo. The girl smiled back, and Heather's heart ached with the memory of Anna.

Her thoughts drifted to that time, when she felt so scared about what was happening to her little sister, and so alone. Her parents were there physically, yes, but emotionally they were vacant. Worrying and caring for Anna sucked every drop of emotion from them. There was nothing left for Heather—she felt invisible.

Heather felt a sudden anxiousness, as she looked at the little girl again. Being with Jason was making her feel invisible again sometimes. He couldn't see her…her parents hadn't seen her…could it happen all over again? Maybe she was afraid she would lose too much of herself in his blindness. That her life would become so accommodating to his she wouldn't recognize herself anymore. Heather hadn't even noticed who was pushing the girl's wheelchair…she had only noticed the girl.

Would she become that invisible person next to the guy with the white cane? If he couldn't see her, would no one notice her anymore?

She had to get out of there. She tossed the magazine back on the table in front of her, and in a panic, said to the woman at the front desk, "I can't do this—I need to leave. I'm sorry."

She turned to walk out the door and the woman said, "Honey, it's just hair color. Don't worry about it."

But it wasn't about hair color at all. Heather left the salon and once in her car, the tears let loose.

****

Jason carried with him such a heavy load of guilt that he didn't know how to approach Angie. He felt like it was his fault that she was now a single mother, a widow. But he hoped maybe she needed him now as much as he needed her. They were family, like brother and sister. He needed her to help him grieve and to help him get through it, and he wanted to be there for her, too. So he decided to show up with the only peace offering he could come up with: dinner.

He cooked some of his famous vegetable noodle soup that he knew was her favorite. Keeping a little bit at home for himself, he loaded up the rest in Tupperware containers, threw it in a big bag and called a cab.

He felt some dread when he paid the cab driver and began to climb out of the car. He thought for a moment about telling the driver to just take him back home, but he took a deep breath and shut the car door. His cane sounded unusually loud to him while he made his way up the driveway, then the walkway, and to the front door. Before he could even knock, the door opened.

"Jason," Angie exclaimed, "what a surprise!"

"Hi," he said quietly, surprised by her enthusiasm.

"Well get inside, it's cold out there."

He walked in, the familiar smells of Angie and Mark's home greeting him when he entered. But new was the strong aroma of baby powder. "Where's Jacie?"

"She's right here in my arm," she said, smiling. "Say hi to Uncle Jason."

Jason put the bag of food down and propped his cane in the corner. It was where he always kept it at their house, but somehow now that act seemed too familiar. He felt like he was a stranger now, an enemy of sorts. It was his fault Mark was gone. He had lost the right to be welcomed here. So why was Angie being so nice to him?

"You look tired, Jace. But then, I look about the same. Take off your coat. I'll hang it up. I wish you would have called, I could have thrown something together for dinner—"

"Oh, I brought you dinner." Jason almost forgot about the bag at his feet. He picked it up. "Vegetable noodle soup. I thought you'd be tired and maybe could use a warm meal—"

"Oh my God, that sounds perfect right now. Thank you so much." She kissed him on the cheek. "Let's go heat this up so we can eat." She headed to the kitchen, and he followed.

"I don't need to stay…I don't want to impose…."

"Jason, I haven't even seen you since…since the funeral. You haven't returned my calls, either. I was getting worried about you. Please stay, keep me company. I miss you."

Jason stood awkwardly in the middle of the kitchen and then found the counter and leaned against it. He bit his lip and then spoke in a quiet tone. "I didn't think you'd want me around."

"Why on earth not?"

He didn't say anything, just turned his face down to the floor.

"Jason, what's going on? I already lost one Scharp man I loved with all my heart. I can't stand the thought of losing another."

"Because it's my fault—"

"What's your fault? What are you talking about?"

"The accident. If I didn't need a ride, he would never have been at that intersection."

Angie firmly put both hands on his face and turned his head in her direction. "Listen to me. This was not your fault. I told you that at the hospital. No one is blaming you but you. It was a random act. Someone's carelessness caused it—not you. Do you hear me?" She was almost yelling when she moved her hands from his face. "Do not do this to yourself, and don't pull away from me, please. I couldn't bear losing you, too. I need you more than ever now, Jason. You are Mark's brother. You were his best friend. I love you, and I need you to get through this."

"But we were almost to my house, turning into my subdivision—"

"Stop it!" She started crying. "Let it go. You lost your brother that day. That's painful enough. Don't beat yourself up, pretending that it was because of you that it happened. It wasn't."

"I'm just so angry that my worthless fucking eyes made me lose him!" He yelled, banging his fist on the counter. Jacie started crying from the living room.

"But they didn't," she said, her voice quiet. "No one else sees it that way. Or do you want me to blame you? Do you want me to hate you? Would that make you feel better?"

"God, no," he whispered, shaking his head. "I just feel like I don't deserve you anymore—"

"We're family, Jason. I love you. There is nothing more that Mark would have wanted than to have us stay close and for you to help me raise our daughter."

Jason reached his hand out to her, and she took it. Angie pulled him close, and they wrapped their arms around each other and both sobbed. They held on tight, their bodies shaking from their crying. Soon Jacie's cries from the living room became more demanding, and Angie pulled away.

"I need to get her. It's time for a feeding." She wiped her eyes. "Will you please stay?"

"Definitely." A hint of a smile appeared on his face.

"Do you want to feed her? I'm breastfeeding, but I've got breast milk in the fridge too, so you can bottle feed if you want."

"Well, you're definitely not going to see me breastfeed." He chuckled and followed her footsteps into the living room.

She picked up Jacie, and he could tell Angie was rocking back and forth as she spoke in soothing tones that calmed the baby. "You don't have to feed her, Jason, I just thought you might want to."

"Sure," he said, intrigued but a little apprehensive.

"I'm going to go warm the bottle—can you do me a favor?"

"Yeah, what?"

"Go in my bedroom and grab the Boppy off the bed. It's at the top, by the pillows."

"Um, Ang?"

"Yeah?"

"What the hell is a Boppy?"

She giggled. "It's a pillow that helps prop up your arms while you feed her. It's shaped like the letter C. Why didn't you know that?"

"Gee, I don't know, must not be a single twenty-something guy thing. I'll go get it." He walked down the hallway, into the bedroom and quickly found the Boppy. While he was grabbing it off the bed, a scent wafted toward him that stopped him in his tracks.

Mark. It smelled like Mark. His cologne, or deodorant or whatever...there it was. So familiar. He missed it. He missed Mark.

"Do you need help?" Angie hollered from the kitchen.

"No, I got it," he managed to respond, though his heart was racing. He sat down on the bed for a minute, not sure where the smell was coming from, but not ready to leave it. Somehow the scent brought Mark a little bit closer to him, like a sighted person gazing at a picture. Brought back memories, emotions. It was a connection to Mark.

"What's wrong?" Angie stood at the doorway.

"Oh, I'm sorry, here's the Boppy." He stood up with the pillow in his hand.

"Are you okay?"

"It's…it's just that I can smell him in here."

Angie put her hand on his shoulder. "So you can smell it too, huh?"

"Yeah," he said with a smile and then sighed. "It's kind of nice. Like catching a glimpse of him. Makes me feel closer to him."

"Me too. I don't want to wash the sheets. Sometimes I sniff his cologne bottle."

"Why don't you just look at pictures?"

"Now you should know better than anyone that seeing someone is only a small part of a person's physicality."

"Yeah, I know that. I just thought pictures would mean more to most people."

"Pictures are great, don't get me wrong. But his voice, his smell, the feel of him…I miss it all." She attempted a smile. "Or maybe I've just been hanging around you too much."

"Maybe." He grinned. "So where am I gonna feed my little niece?"

****

The next day, Jason arrived at school with a little less weight on his shoulders. Spending time with Angie and Jacie and letting go of some of the guilt were steps toward healing. When he approached his classroom, his cane struck a box. He reached over and found two boxes in front of his door. After unlocking the door, he carried the boxes inside, wondering what was in them and if he should open them up.

Jason walked down the hall two doors to Shawn's room. His door was shut, so Jason knocked. "Mathes, you in there?"

No response. He checked his watch; Shawn was usually there by now.

"Jason?" Elizabeth James called out from across the hall.

"Good morning, Elizabeth." Since their scuffle, they had done their best to avoid each other, but to her credit, she'd actually been saying hello to him when she saw him.

"Do you need something? Is there something I can help you with?"

Jason was surprised that she sounded sincere. Her voice sounded softer, somehow, than what he was accustomed to from her. "Oh, uh, thanks. No, it's no big deal. It can wait until later." He turned to head back to his room.

"I don't mind helping, really." She stepped out of her classroom and closer to Jason. "You know, I haven't had a chance to express my sympathy about your brother. I'm sorry for your loss. I lost my sister last summer, and I know how devastating that can be."

Jason was taken aback by the sudden kindness from such an unlikely source. And the mention of Mark stopped him in his tracks. "Yes, it is. Thank you."

"Were you two very close?"

He could only nod.

"Jason, I know we've had our differences, but I'd be happy to help you since Mr. Mathes isn't in yet."

He was about to say "no thanks" when he changed his mind. She was extending an olive branch; he shouldn't leave her hanging. "Well, sure, I appreciate the offer."

"What can I help you with?"

"There are a couple of boxes in my room, and I want to make sure they're addressed to me before I tear them open. Plus half the time, after it's opened, I still can't figure out what's inside."

"Well, let's go see what you've got." She followed him toward his room.

When they got there, Elizabeth verified they were addressed to him. She opened them up to find some artwork he'd ordered for his bulletin boards with timelines of World War I and World War II. The other box was a Braille calendar he ordered for the upcoming New Year.

"Thank you," Jason said, feeling awkward at getting help from Elizabeth, of all people.

"I don't mind at all," she said. "You know, I'd like to apologize for my behavior in the past. After our little fallout, I did some serious thinking. You're right—I was biased against you from the start. I think because the thought of trying to teach students without being able to see them terrifies me, I assumed it couldn't be done. But I was wrong."

Jason couldn't believe what he was hearing. "Well, I appreciate that. Very much."

"It's just...I've never known anyone that was blind, and here you were, this young, funny, charismatic guy...and I felt threatened. And I just didn't want to believe that you could do as good a job as me."

"I'm sorry for what I said about you being out of touch—"

"No, you're right. And it's not necessarily because I'm older. It's because I'm burned out. I've been doing this for thirty-nine years. I think I stopped paying attention to the kids or trying to understand them. I'm going to retire in two years, and I'm making a real effort to engage myself more with the students in these final years. I know you make an impact on your students...I think I still can too."

"I'm sure you can." Jason smiled.

"And I am truly sorry about your brother and the injuries you sustained from that accident. It looks pretty painful."

"No, I'm not in pain—I imagine it looks pretty bad though. There goes my modeling career, huh?"

Elizabeth chuckled. "Well, hopefully it will heal nicely."

"The plastic surgeon said the scars shouldn't be too noticeable." His fingers traced a heavily stitched cut on his cheek. "Well, thanks for helping me, Elizabeth."

"You're welcome, Jason."

She left his room and he smiled to himself, shaking his head as he started reading an email.

"Checking to make sure you're not bloodied," Shawn said, poking his head in the classroom. "I just saw Elizabeth leave your room."

Jason chuckled. "No, Mathes, it's all good. She actually offered to help me with getting some boxes open and see what was in them."

"It wasn't any of your Braille porn, was it? That could have been embarrassing." Shawn laughed at his own joke.

"No way, I have all of that sent to my home address." They both laughed. "Actually, she was really kind. Even apologized for underestimating me."

"Wow, did hell freeze over?"

"Must have. Now let me get back to my email. I have an important one about male-enhancing drugs I need to check out."

****

Over the next couple of weeks, Jason became a frequent visitor to Angie's. It seemed to help them both—they were each a connection with Mark. Sometimes it was just the three of them, or sometimes one of her friends or family were there too, or his parents. Either way, the baby was a great distraction for a lot of grieving people.

And Jason was falling fast for Jacie. He could hold her for hours, just listening to her breathing, her warm body resting against him. The feel of her tummy rising and falling, the impossibly silky feeling of her skin, and her downy-soft hair. When he was with Jacie, it was a reminder Mark would always live on in her. She was a part of Mark, and so was Jason. He wanted to make sure that Jacie grew up knowing all about her dad—how funny, and selfless,

319

and warm he was.

Jason was also learning a little about caring for a baby. He fed her and seemed to have a special talent for getting her to burp. "It's all in the technique," he liked to tease Angie. He'd even changed her clothes a couple of times and knew the tricks to get her to sleep and then put her in the crib without waking her up.

He knew more than ever that he wanted to be a dad.

Which led to the other source of the funk that he now lived in. Heather. Or lack of Heather.

Between the absences of Mark and Heather, he was left with the sensation of walking around with a gaping hole in his chest. Visiting Jacie and Angie helped to fill a small portion of the vast Grand Canyon-like gashes in his heart. And while moments of bliss with Jacie were gradually easing the pain…it was still always there.

Heather now sent him a text every few days, checking in on him. He was brief in his responses. What he wanted to type was *Come back, my life doesn't make sense without you* or *I want you so badly, please just come home*. But he didn't. He didn't want to pressure her. So when she asked how he was, he'd lie and respond with *Fine* or *Better*. He knew she wanted more from him, but he wasn't going to give it. If she wanted more, she'd have to come back.

He and Angie had both learned that happiness could be fleeting, and life could be tragically cut short. Her happily-ever-after abruptly ended, just when their relationship was shifting from being a couple to being a family. He thought about what they once had and knew that he deserved that, too.

He was starting to think he didn't want to keep his life on hold for much longer. Heather had moved out more than two months ago.

Life was short. If she didn't want to spend forever with him, surely there was someone else out there that would. Wasn't there? He hoped so. And if not, he'd create a full life on his own. Maybe Mark was right, maybe he *was* strong. Living through all this pain was making him even stronger.

But he thought Heather was the one. His happily-ever-after.

With all his heart, he wanted her to be.

Chapter Twenty-One

Heather knew she was testing the magnitude of her friendship with Katie. There were only so many nights crying on the phone, so many days lying listlessly on her couch, and so many times that a friend can be asked for advice before they feel smothered and the need to bolt. Heather knew that.

And yet here she was again, getting ready to whine on the phone to Katie on a Sunday morning, spent like so many Sunday mornings over the last few weeks—alone. Heather dialed Katie and wondered if this would be the day that Katie stopped taking her calls.

"Hello my jolly friend," Katie quipped when she answered the phone. Heather could hear the baby babbling in the background.

"Oh, shut up. I haven't even started whining yet."

"But you said 'yet.' So we know it's coming."

"Maybe not, you never know."

"Oh, Heather, how long has it been now?"

"Nine weeks tomorrow."

"God, it seems like a year." Katie laughed. "No, I'm kidding. I'm all out of advice, sister. I've never been in your shoes, and I'm just tired of seeing you so sad."

"Me too," Heather sighed. "I'm sorry I'm such a Debbie Downer lately."

"Well, you listened to me whine about swollen ankles, heartburn and endless urination for nine months. Payback's a bitch."

"I just need to get my life figured out so I can move on. To whatever that is."

"I agree. But what's going to make that happen?"

"Hell if I know. I want my damn a-ha moment. Oprah has them all the time. Why can't I?"

"Because you're not a gabillionaire and you're busy paying the bills instead of being enlightened all the time. I could be enlightened on a daily basis with that kind of bank."

"True." Heather laughed. "So what are you doing today?"

"Nothing on the agenda. Hang on a sec." Heather could tell Katie covered the mouthpiece for a minute. "Okay, my wonderful husband has just agreed to watch the baby while you and I go out for lunch today. How does that sound?"

"Really? We haven't had any grown-up girl time in a while."

"I know. It's hectic when you're a mom. But let's get you out of the house, get some lunch, and maybe take you shopping. Lunch is my treat, and you can pick the place."

"I'm so excited! Okay...I'll have to think of a good spot."

"Well get to thinking, and I'll pick you up at noon."

"Perfect. Thank you so much, Katie."

"You're welcome. Put on a happy face today, okay? This is the day you're going to snap out of your Jason pool of despair."

"I'll do my best," Heather said with a sigh. "But then you had to go and say his name."

"Well, it's not like he's the bad guy."

"No, that's the problem. He's the perfect guy. With the biggest piece of baggage I've ever seen."

"Well he can't even see it, Heather—at least you can."

"True." She looked at the sparkling ring on her finger. "See you at noon."

****

Jason was glad he met up with his friend Mike, who always made him laugh. They played on the beep baseball team together, and when Mike called him to grab a burger, Jason decided it beat moping around at home on a Sunday. Plus, he felt a measure of comfort, at least every now and then, to be with someone who understood the unique experiences of wandering through life in the dark. It made them more conspicuous than normal, two men with white canes traveling as a pair—the poor patrons probably felt like they were being invaded by the sightless.

Jason figured they turned heads (and not in a good way) when they left the restaurant. He walked behind Mike, caning his way between a row of booths and a row of tables. He got closer to the door and caught a whiff of a familiar smell.

Black Amethyst.

Could it be her? Jason stopped when the scent grew stronger and faced the booth to his right. No one spoke...probably wondering why the crazy blind man stopped in front of their table. *Of course it's not her,* he reasoned and continued on. *Lots of other women probably wear that same fragrance.* But the way it mingled with the woman's own scents...

Give it up, Scharp. You're hallucinating now. And you apparently don't even hallucinate with vision anymore. Just smell.

****

"Oh my God," Katie whispered while she watched Jason walking out. "Heather, why didn't you say something to him?"

"I...I don't know," she stammered. "I haven't seen him since the day after the funeral, and I certainly wasn't expecting to see him at lunch. I panicked, you know how you hide from someone you don't want to see you?"

"Yeah, but he stopped right next to you."

"He knows what I smell like. He said my scent is distinct."

"He loves you so much he knows your smell? And you just sat there and didn't say a word?" Katie shook her head, looking right at Heather.

"I'm horrible. I can't believe I did that. I've got to go catch up with him. I'll be back." Heather bolted out of the restaurant.

She saw Jason walking about a block down the street, so she took off in his direction.

"Jason!" she hollered.

He paused.

"Jason Scharp!"

He turned around.

"It's me, it's Heather."

He smiled and started heading toward her. The minute she saw his smile, she felt a fullness inside that had been missing for weeks.

"Hi, baby," she said when he was close enough not to yell. She realized when she shivered that in her haste, she left her jacket behind.

"I thought that was you inside." Jason smiled as he approached. "Are you sitting near the door?"

"Yeah…I didn't see you, but Katie's with me and she caught you going out the door." She couldn't possibly admit that she hid from him in plain view.

Jason caught up with her, and without even thinking, she threw her arms around him. They held each other tight for much longer than a normal hug. Heather forgot how strong and inviting his arms were. Eventually, she pulled away.

"Well, this is a great surprise." Jason held her hand.

"Yeah, it sure is," Heather said, soaking him in. He looked even cuter in person than she remembered. He wore the pea coat he had when they first started dating nine months earlier. With cargo pants and loafers and wearing his trademark smile, he looked adorable. The last time she saw him he was covered in stitches, but they were gone now. The wounds were still visible, but beginning to heal.

"You switched back to Black Amethyst, eh?"

"Yeah, it's my fall and winter scent you know."

"It reminds me of when we first met." He touched her cheek with so much tenderness she thought she would melt. The electricity that always existed between them still radiated. "Are you shivering?"

"Yeah, I—"

"You're not wearing a coat!" He felt her shoulder.

"I ran out to catch you and forgot to grab it."

Jason folded his cane, shoved it in the pocket of his cargo pants, and took off his coat. "Here." He put it around her. He wore the blue polo that brought out the intensity of his eyes. The cast on his arm was visible now. "Is that better?"

"Yes it is. But now you're going to freeze."

"No, I'm fine." She noticed the bags under his eyes that weren't normally there. He looked thinner, too.

"So how are you?" she asked.

His face hardened a bit. "Getting by. What about you?"

"Well...okay, kind of miserable. I miss you."

"Sweetheart...you're the one controlling this whole thing. If you miss me, you can just come home." His face looked so earnest, so pleading.

"I don't think it's that simple—"

"But it is." Jason looked angry now. "Heather, this is me. I can't change that. These don't work." He pointed to his eyes. "Being with me may never be easy, but the choice *is* simple. You either love me enough or you don't."

She didn't say anything as tears streamed down her cheeks. He was quiet as he said, "I don't want to waste my days waiting for you to decide if you want to be with me. I know what I want—I want you, forever. But I'm going to have to move on. I gave you my best shot. I've promised I will ease up on you and not be so unforgiving. But I'm gonna need help sometimes. That's just the way it is. And I don't want you to ever regret choosing me."

"I really do love you—"

"I know that." He spoke with no malice, only tenderness. "So just decide if you love me enough." He grabbed her hand. "Why don't I take you back inside so you can finish your lunch with Katie?"

When they reached the door, she took off his coat and handed it to him. He slipped it on. "I love you, Heather, but I'm done waiting around. You need to figure out what you want." His voice betrayed him with a quiver of emotion. "Goodbye."

He turned around and headed back down the street. She watched him for a minute before heading in the restaurant.

Katie looked expectantly at the door when Heather walked inside.

"So?" Katie asked.

Heather sat down, her cheeks tear-stained. "I have to make a decision. I'm losing him." Heather looked down at the plate of food in front of her. "Oh God, Katie, it felt so good, so right in his arms. I mean, when I'm with him, all the crazy bullshit cluttering my mind just goes away. The only time my life makes sense is when we're together. I mean, I worry about losing myself in him, in his blindness. But when I'm with him, it's like...the rest of my world is in black and white, and he's the most vibrant of colors."

"Well, maybe that's your answer then. Maybe you need to stop listening to the doubts in your mind, and go with what you do know." Katie locked eyes with her. "You know I had reservations about Jason from the start. I was concerned that you would be taking on a lot with him. But I have to tell you...I've never seen you happier, more fulfilled, or more comfortable with anyone. And we've been friends forever. I've seen you with just about every boyfriend you've ever had. Jason's different. Jason seems like he's just...yours. You know?"

Heather nodded and tears flowed again. She grabbed a napkin and used it as a tissue.

"So when you were out there with him," Katie continued, "I just thought to myself, you've been such a miserable mess without him. You seem like you're missing a part of your body. What could be worse than that? Certainly a rough year or two with a baby couldn't be worse. 'Cause it seems to me like you're pretty much living in hell right now."

"Which would be worse, huh?" Heather repeated, deep in thought. She pushed her plate away. "What would I do without you, Katie?"

"You'd be even more of a mess," she said with a

chuckle. "Are you going to be okay?"

Heather looked at the concern in her friend's eyes. "I don't know. I've got to make up my mind."

****

Heather stayed up all night. Pacing, thinking, pouring through pictures of her life with Jason and trying to find an answer. At almost four in the morning, perhaps from exhaustion, things started to seem clear to her for the first time in a long time. Two things kept going through her mind.

The first was Katie's observation. What would be worse—feeling the loss of Jason forever or facing some challenges with him? And the other thing playing over again and again in her mind were Jason's words: "The choice *is* simple. *You either love me enough or you don't.*"

****

Jason didn't sleep well Sunday night and woke up thinking of Heather.

He was even more unsure after seeing her. A part of him thought that if she saw him, it would remind her of what they had. One touch, and she'd know she needed to be with him. But that didn't happen.

And he wondered if she was just keeping him hanging on? Was she unwilling to commit but afraid to officially dump a blind guy? Was there pity in her eyes?

Or did she want him as much as he wanted her? When he held her hand, he felt the engagement ring still on her finger. That must mean something. She wasn't ready to let go. Or was that just being hopeful?

Worst of all, he worried that by a cruel twist of fate, the blindness that drove her away was also preventing him from seeing a look on her face that showed it was already over.

While he got dressed for work, he could hear rain beating on the roof and the wind howling. He wondered how bad it was. He flicked on the TV and heard the weatherman say, "It's an absolute downpour out there for most of the viewing area. There's a chance we might see some hail, and the gusty winds are making it seem like a hurricane in the Midwest. Visibility is significantly reduced, so drive slowly and be cautious on your morning commute."

"Shit," he muttered, walking to the patio door and opening it. The rain blew into the house with a blast of wind, so he quickly shut the door.

He remembered all the mornings Mark would call to offer a ride, and how he hated to take him up on it. Then he recounted that last conversation with Mark, one he went back to a lot. "Maybe being strong doesn't mean you don't need help—maybe it means being able to admit your limitations. You just might be at your strongest when you can ask for help."

He'd already accepted help from Elizabeth James and that turned out to be a good thing. "Okay, Mark, let's see what I think when I try it your way," he said out loud. He grabbed his phone out of his pocket and dialed Shawn.

"What's up, Scharp? Are you out in this monsoon?"

"No, not yet," he said with a chuckle, suddenly feeling self-conscious. "Actually, I was hoping to avoid Mother Nature's wrath on the walk to the bus stop. Any chance I could bum a ride with you?"

"Sure, no problem. You're right on the way. I just left the house—can you be ready in ten minutes?"

"You bet. Are you sure it's no problem?"

"Well, you'll have to buy me a beer the next time we're out, but it's no problem." Shawn laughed.

"I can do that. See you in ten."

"Later."

Jason hung up, smiling to himself. That wasn't so bad after all. In fact, he did feel stronger. Instead of feeling ashamed for asking, he felt empowered. Like he was taking charge of his life by admitting he needed some help. Only a dumb ass would walk in a torrential downpour and ferocious winds if they didn't have to.

"Thanks, Mark," he said, pouring coffee in a mug.

****

He went to work, feeling a new sense of strength, of acceptance. A little more at peace. But he still felt numb and sad when it came to Heather…it was another long day in a long month. He honestly didn't know how much longer he could hold out hope.

Something in him had changed since Mark died. He wasn't content to sit around and wait for life to happen to him anymore—he had to take charge of his life. This morning's call to Shawn for a ride to avoid the rain was a step in the right direction. If Heather wasn't sure about him, maybe the time had come to move on and let her go.

Those thoughts still tortured him when he walked home from the bus stop after work, down the street to his house. The rain had passed through and left a cold, bitter wind behind it. He kept his left hand in his pocket to protect from the harsh winds and brisk air, but his right hand grew cold as it moved his cane back and forth.

"Hi, Jason." Heather's voice startled him, from what sounded like his porch.

He stopped for a moment, shocked. "Heather. Hi. Are you stalking me? This is two days in a row you've hollered at me while I'm walking down the street."

Heather laughed and his smile grew larger. "So what if I am? Is that a bad thing?"

Jason headed up the driveway. "I don't know…you tell me." His heart pounded wildly in his chest. Why was she here? When he approached the porch, his cane struck something other than the concrete. He reached out and felt a suitcase.

"I'm sitting here on the steps," Heather said.

He folded up his cane and sat down next to her.

"What's with the suitcase?" he asked, almost not wanting the answer. Was she coming home? Or collecting more of her things?

"Yesterday you said it was simple. Either I love you enough or I don't." Her voice quivered with tears.

Jason felt an overwhelming urge to comfort her, regardless of her next words. He put his arm around her.

"And…?"

"I love you enough." He could hear the smile in her wavering voice, and when he put his hands on her cheeks, they were wet with tears.

He kissed her…a kiss that was passionate and joyous and long overdue.

"Are you sure?" he asked, almost afraid to hear the answer. His heart had taken a beating over the past weeks, and he wasn't sure he could believe things might be looking up. "I mean, I promise I will lay off on being so rigid and difficult. But I'm still going to be a pain in the ass—nothing's changed there."

She giggled, and he smiled at the joyous sound.

"I'm sure, baby. I finally figured out that all my worries pale in comparison to the thought of spending my life without you. I know I can handle anything we come up against…anything except being apart."

For a guy that had spent the past fifteen years using his ears to see the world, he was certain he'd never heard a more beautiful sound than the words she'd just spoken. They held tight to each other. He felt exhausted but also elated—like they'd finally found each other after a long, lonely journey.

Heather was home. And that was more than enough.

THE END

To my readers:

I hope you enjoyed reading *Love in Sight*. This is my second published book, but in some ways, one of the first I ever wrote. A very different version of this story started when I was only twelve years old, when I wrote my first full-length novel. Over the next thirty years, the story changed quite a bit!

I did a vast amount of research to capture the essence of what it is like to live with a visual impairment. I hope I am somewhere close to the mark. Jason's story isn't unique to someone who is blind. It is a story of acceptance—of one's self and what we're willing to sacrifice to share our life with someone else. I think we can all relate to that.

What I ultimately write about is love. Whether it's between lovers, family, or friends, I think that's what life is all about. To share love, experience it—lose ourselves in the vulnerability and magic that love can bring.

In my first released novel, *'Til St. Patrick's Day*, Jason makes a cameo appearance. You can get your copy now, as either an e-book or paperback from your favorite online book retailer. And if you enjoy *'Til St. Patrick's Day*, you'll be happy to know there are two sequels, scheduled for a 2015 release.

You can keep up with all my latest releases, appearances (either in person or cyberspace) and ramblings by checking my **website** or following me on **Facebook** or **Twitter**. Feel free to contact me—I love to connect with my readers!

Thank you for reading *Love in Sight*!

Holly Gilliatt
St. Louis, Missouri
August 2013

PRAISE FOR *'TIL ST. PATRICK'S DAY*
BY HOLLY GILLIATT

"If you like a good love story, then this should be on your 'to read' list. Gilliatt creates characters who you connect with…."

~BestChickLit.com

"…The main theme of this novel was friendship, but it's followed very closely by love. …To anyone who likes to read stories about these themes, you HAVE to read this book. It's fantastic."

~ Pink Fluffy Hearts, 5 Hearts

"With the author's ease of putting words on paper, the story flows through your mind, connecting on a deep emotional level. You will find yourself hoping, gasping, shedding a tear or two and smiling with happiness as the story unfolds."

~Literati Book Reviews, 4 Stars

MANY THANKS TO...

Angie Linan—for being my Katie. Writing a great best friend is a piece of cake when you've got the real deal on speed dial. I always wanted a sister, so God gave me you. I love you.

Kara Mathes and Leigh Cook for being two of the most funny, giving, loving people on the planet. And for the record...you guys are worth a whole jumbo size can of Shaper Plus hairspray.

My mom, LouAnn Schnider, for being my tireless first reader. You are an amazing sounding board and a life raft of encouragement in a sea of doubt. Simply put, I couldn't do it without you.

My dad, Richard Schnider, for always believing in me. I miss you and wish you could have seen this. I've taken your advice so I'm trying not to make a fool of myself. Really I am.

Kathy Kelley, Annie Anderson, Troy and Kelly Schnider, Dianne Clark and Kara Mathes—for braving early drafts to offer your two cents. Cindy Douglas and Susan Canada for query help. Sherry Rosenberger for the gift of beautiful pictures and a lasting friendship. Brandy Warthman for your technical EMT expertise.

Christie Ashabranner for your encouragement and friendship. You've given me so much when I needed it most. You're all heart and I'm lucky to call you my friend. Anything for you.

Turquoise Morning Press for seeing something in Jason's story and to Judy Alter, for carving it into a better one with less mushy stuff. And to my fellow authors at TMP (especially Margaret Ethridge, Karen Booth and Renee Vincent)—thanks for the advice, encouragement and laughter.

Ryan Knighton for emails with your insights into writing (pun intended). I began your memoir as research but have read it again and again for pure entertainment. You are a master wordsmith.

Dr. Karuna Murray, Dr. Andrea Wang-Gillam, Danielle Crites and the whole gang at Siteman Cancer Center in West County for doing all you can to kick cancer's butt. Keep it up—I've got a lot of words left in me. I'm nowhere near done yet.

Troy Schnider for your support and advice. I can't believe we've somehow managed not to kill each other. I love you, big brother. And I'll check on your order for dippin' noodles.

Tressa, Emily and Nate for making my biggest dream come true—being a mom. You are the best thing in my whole world. I love you so much it sometimes hurts. Now will you please get along?

Jay for knowing absolutely everything about me and still loving me. I've loved you for half my life and hope that somehow I'll get to grow old with you. I've got my fingers crossed, Bobaloo.

ABOUT HOLLY GILLIATT

When she's not busy daydreaming of someday spending her life writing from a cozy house in the woods, Holly Gilliatt has a hectic life in the suburbs as a wife and mom to three glorious—and crazy—kids. Working full-time selling packaging supplies and equipment in St. Louis, Missouri pays the bills (most months). A hopeless romantic and music addict, she finds time to pursue her passion for writing by avoiding housework. Her biggest ambition is to someday be caught up with the laundry.

If you enjoyed Holly Gilliatt's *Love in Sight,*
please consider telling others and writing a review.

You might also enjoy these women's fiction authors
published by Turquoise Morning Press

Margaret Ethridge, author of *Commitment*
Karen Booth, author of *Bring Me Back*
Karen Stivali, author of *Meant to Be*

Turquoise Morning Press
Dip your toes into a good book!
www.turquoisemorningpress.com

8858823R00203

Made in the USA
San Bernardino, CA
24 February 2014